DELTA BELLES

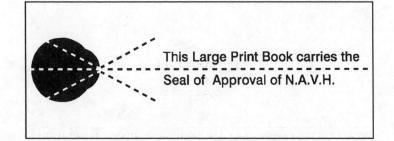

This Large Print Book carries the
Seal of Approval of N.A.V.H.

DELTA BELLES

PENELOPE J. STOKES

THORNDIKE PRESS
An imprint of Thomson Gale, a part of The Thomson Corporation

THOMSON
★ ™
GALE

Detroit • New York • San Francisco • New Haven, Conn. • Waterville, Maine • London

THOMSON
GALE

Thorndike Press® Large Print Clean Reads.

The text of this Large Print edition is unabridged.

Other aspects of the book may vary from the original edition.

Set in 16 pt. Plantin.

LIBRARY OF CONGRESS CATALOGING-IN-PUBLICATION DATA

Stokes, Penelope J.
    Delta Belles / by Penelope J. Stokes.
        p. cm.
    ISBN-13: 978-0-7862-9396-4 (hardcover : alk. paper)
    ISBN-10: 0-7862-9396-9 (hardcover : alk. paper) 1. Female friendship —
Fiction. 2. Women college students — Fiction. 3. Class reunions — Fiction.
4. Widows — Fiction. 5. Lesbians — Fiction. 6. Large type books.
7. Coming out (Sexual orientation) — Fiction. I. Title.
PS3569.T6219D45 2007
813'.54—dc22

                                                                    2006039153

Published in 2007 by arrangement with Doubleday,
a division of Random House, Inc.

Printed in the United States of America on permanent paper
10 9 8 7 6 5 4 3 2 1

To the memory of Frances and Sue,
mentors who inspired me,
believed in me,
challenged me,
and tuned me to hear the singing in the
stars.

Your spirit lives on
and will never be forgotten.

Music, when soft voices die,
Vibrates in the memory . . .

— PERCY BYSSHE SHELLEY, 1821

PART 1
INVITATION

The sweetest word
upon the tongue
is
"Come."

Come back to where
you once belonged,
back to those who
knew you,
loved you,
believed the best of you.

Row, if your ship has sailed;
Swim, if all your bridges have been burned;
Fly, if the chasm seems too wide or deep —
But come.

ONE:
DELTA ALONE

DECATUR, GEORGIA
SEPTEMBER 1994

"Rankin!"

Delta Ballou sat bolt upright in bed, shaking and sweating, the familiar sickening panic washing over her. Something had roused her — a noise. She inhaled deeply, trying to regulate her breathing, trying to shush the pounding of her heart.

Delta might not be alone in the world, but still she felt it — every day, every waking moment. Especially every night, before sleep overtook her, lying there in the dark with his side of the bed cold and untouched. She always stayed up too late these days, dragging herself reluctantly to a few hours of fitful sleep, only to awaken groggy the next morning and discover that it hadn't been a terrible nightmare, after all. That her husband really was dead. That she was, at the age of

11

forty-seven, a widow.

She had been annoyed with Rankin the morning of his death, exasperated over some real or imagined slight — she couldn't remember now what it was. Something minor, no doubt, something utterly unimportant in the cosmic scheme of things. But at the time it had seemed sufficient cause to snub him, to refuse to kiss him properly as he went out the door.

As usual, he had not taken offense at her irritability. Instead he gave a benign laugh, kissed her cheek as she turned away, and told her he loved her. His civility only exacerbated her peevish mood, and she had railed at him for ten full minutes after he was gone.

Strange how the qualities that distinguished her husband as a minister were the very things that aggravated the hell out of her. He was so . . . *good*. Generous, understanding, compassionate in the face of anger and opposition. Gracious amid stress, poised to listen to anyone who needed him.

Delta, on the other hand, "did not bear fools gladly."

Or at all, her husband jokingly amended.

It was true. When she and Rankin had met and fallen in love, she had shared his passion for peace and justice, had taken his hand and sung "We Shall Overcome" with a soul-deep conviction that change was just beyond the horizon. But he had a serenity about him that she had never managed to achieve, a patience with human shortcomings and failures.

By all accounts, Rankin Ballou had been an extraordinary man. In both his work and his life he blended spirituality with social conscience, weathering criticism over his stands on equal rights and fair housing and a multitude of other injustices. His persuasiveness and passion made a difference in people's lives. He spoke the truth. He protected the weak. He lived by what he believed, died by it.

Died with God's name on his lips. The very thought of it infuriated her. . . .

"Delta?" Cassie's voice came to her, low and anxious, through the bedroom door. "I heard you yell. Are you all right?"

Delta looked at the clock. It was ten till seven. The sun had barely risen, and beyond the slatted blinds she could see the faint rose-hued wash of dawn.

She pushed the flame of anger down, banked it against the back wall of her chest. She held still, not breathing, hoping her sister would go away. She hadn't wanted to leave the parsonage she had occupied for almost twenty years and finally made her own. Hadn't wanted to crowd her belongings into her little sister's garage and live in this travesty of a guest room, decorated in blood red and mildew green as if designed by one of Satan's more flamboyant henchmen. But she hadn't any choice. Other people's lives went on, even if hers had stopped. Her daughter, Sugar, had gone off to college. The new pastor had arrived, moved his family in, and begun the process of trying to fill Rankin's shoes.

"It's only temporary, Delta," Cassie had said. "Until you're ready to find a place of your own." And Delta had thought, *You're damned right it's temporary.*

That had been five months ago. Five months of fitting herself into the busy lives of her younger sister and her brother-in-law, Russell, and her six-year-old niece, her namesake Deborah, whom Russ called Mouse.

"Delta, I'm coming in."

The door opened a crack, and Cassie's head appeared at an angle, as if detached from her body. She edged into the room, followed by Mouse in footed flannel pajamas and the golden retriever Grand-Nanny, two generations removed from the original

Nanny, who had belonged to Delta and Rankin when Sugar was just a baby. Mouse crawled onto the bed and snuggled up next to Delta. The dog jumped up and laid her chin across Delta's feet.

With the warm little body crowded up against her side, Delta's anguish and rage flared up again. She thought of Sugar, now eighteen and beginning a life of her own. Rankin would never experience the joy of seeing his girl become a woman, get married. He would never hold his grandchildren, would never —

He knows, a faint voice inside her whispered. *He sees.*

Delta shoved the assurance away. The promise of heaven, of another life, gave her no comfort. Time healed nothing. God's presence was an illusion. She wanted Rankin back. Here. Now.

"We're going out to breakfast, Aunt Delt," Mouse said, butting her head against Delta's shoulder. "And to the Disney Store. You come too."

Delta regarded the child, who had Russell's olive skin and brownish hair, but Cassie's narrow chin and startling blue eyes. Objectively speaking, her nickname fit her perfectly, but Delta wasn't about to admit that to Russ. "I don't know," she hedged,

15

then tweaked Mouse's nose. "Don't you have to go to school? Doesn't your mom have to go to work?"

Mouse giggled. "It's *Saturday,* Aunt Delt."

"Ah," Delta said. "I forgot."

Cassie ran a hand through her short-cropped blonde hair, sighed, and fixed Delta with a come-on-snap-out-of-it look. "Come with us, Delta. It'll be fun. We'll do some shopping, maybe catch a matinee. You know —" She grinned at her daughter. "Girls' day out. Just the three of us."

"I don't know," Delta repeated.

"Suit yourself. It'll be an hour or so before we leave, in case you change your mind. Russell's got a golf date. There's chicken salad for lunch if you want it." She glanced at her watch and motioned to Mouse. "Let's go, honey."

Mouse gave Delta a pleading look and slid off the bed.

The door shut behind them, and Delta looked down to see her hands gripping the blanket as if daring someone to drag her out of bed and back into life.

Delta sat at the small desk in the guest room and sorted through the mail Cassie had brought to her. There wasn't much. Junk mail — ads, unsolicited catalogs, mostly.

For a moment she fingered the large bulky envelope from Publishers Clearing House. *You may have already won ten million dollars.*

Delta snorted. What could she possibly do with ten million dollars, besides pay half of it to a government she didn't trust and set up a college fund for grandchildren who hadn't yet been born? What did normal people do? Take an around-the-world cruise? Buy a gas-guzzling SUV? Accumulate stocks, houses, boats, diamonds?

None of that appealed to her knee-jerk sense of justice. It was hard to break a habit ingrained by twenty-five years of standing up against power systems that encouraged personal greed and oppressed the little people. Hard to forget that it was all woven of one fabric — big business, racism, sexism, poverty, warmongering. From the early days in college, when she and her friends had sung at voter registration rallies, she had gone on to marry a man of deep social conscience and embraced other issues — fair housing, food banks, help for the homeless, environmental concerns, human rights, women's rights, domestic abuse.

Rankin called it "walking the way of Jesus."

Theoretically, it sounded good, noble, the right thing to do. But did the outcome have to be so damnably predictable?

She sighed, ran a hand through her hair, and kept on sorting. There was a newsletter from the Human Rights Campaign and a renewal notice from the ACLU, both in Rankin's name and forwarded from the parsonage. She really ought to notify them of Rankin's death and the change of address, but every time she thought about him, she felt the phantom pain of the severed limb, nerves hanging loose from the joint so that the least current of moving air brought fresh excruciation. Every time she wrote *deceased* next to his name, a little more of her own soul died.

She was forty-seven years old. What was she supposed to do now? Start over? Become the merry widow, begin dating, kick up her heels? She had her master's degree, of course, and most of the coursework toward her Ph.D. She had taught some lit classes off and on over the years. But most of her energy and attention had been taken up with the church.

She hadn't resented it, not then. Not consciously. But she sure as hell resented it now.

"God," she groaned into the empty, silent house.

Not a prayer. Not a supplication. She wanted nothing to do with God, with the church, with the expectations of sacrificial

18

living. She had sacrificed enough, thank you very much. She was done.

One final piece of mail caught her eye. A manila envelope on the bottom of the stack, addressed to *Delta Fox Ballou* in a loopy, flourishing handwriting. It had been sent to the parsonage and forwarded on.

She considered the logo in the upper left hand corner: a large scrolling *W,* with *Mississippi College for Women* superimposed across the middle, and below, in smaller print, *Alumnae Office.*

Probably a plea for money, Delta thought. She received mailings from the college every six months or so and a thick four-color newsletter once a year. As always, it would go in the trash largely unread, but she pried up the flap nevertheless and took out the sheaf of papers inside.

Twenty-Fifth Anniversary Homecoming, the header of the first page read. *Class of 1969.* Delta let out a short laugh, which even to her own ears sounded mirthless and empty, the rustle of a sudden wind over dead leaves. She was about to toss the whole thing on the junk mail pile when a handwritten note at the bottom of the page arrested her attention.

Please come, the note said in that same loopy style. *Please say yes.*

Delta sat back in her chair and scrutinized the cover page more carefully.

Dear Delta,

Our twenty-fifth reunion is coming up soon, and even though we haven't seen each other in ages, I can't seem to get you out of my mind. I'm on the Alumnae Board this year, and part of my job is to contact people about the reunion and anniversary banquet.

I remember our time at the W and how the Delta Belles made those years so special. Surely you recall those wonderful concerts, how everyone loved the group and the music and the . . . well, the life *those songs represented.*

And so I am writing with a request. I think it would be wonderful to get the Delta Belles back together to play for the anniversary banquet. It wouldn't have to be anything elaborate or formal. A few familiar tunes, just for old times' sake.

Enclosed you'll find plans for the weekend, which is scheduled for the third weekend in October. Hope to see you there.

There was an address somewhere in Tennessee, two phone numbers. And then the handwritten postscript. *Please come. Please say yes.* The letter was signed *Tabitha Austin Black.*

"Well, I'll be darned," Delta muttered. "Tabby."

Tabitha Austin's face swam up from the depths and hovered before her like a relentless ghost. By now she was probably dumpy and showing her age like everybody else, but Delta's memory insisted on the younger version. In her mind's eye, Tabby was still fresh and beautiful, with long lustrous red hair and that ubiquitous effervescent smile.

Yes, she remembered Tabby. She remembered the Delta Belles. But it didn't matter. The answer was unequivocally no. The Delta Belles were dead. Exhuming them was completely out of the question.

She fingered the edge of the letter and formulated a polite but resolute response to Tabby in her mind: *It was sweet of you to ask, but I couldn't possibly . . .*

With the internal refusal came a wave of relief, a lifting of tension Delta hadn't even known was there. That was settled. She'd send a letter this afternoon and be done with it. She pushed the reunion information and Tabby's letter off to one side of the desk and stared out the window.

But despite her best intentions, the ghosts rose up to haunt her. . . .

TWO:
HARVEST FEST

October came shyly to Mississippi, a virgin bride to the wedding bed, clad in golden silks and rustling sky-blue satin. One tree on front campus, however, had no patience for a slow and sinuous fall. There, near the tall iron fence that surrounded the college, a hundred-year-old ginkgo spread its massive branches overhead and shook its amber, fan-shaped leaves in a seductive dance, a teasing preview of the annual shedding ritual.

Chinese legend held that the ginkgo dropped all its leaves in a single autumn night, baring itself to the onslaught of winter with a bold striptease. According to the accompanying college lore, any girl who stood under the tree by moonlight and caught a ginkgo leaf in flight would find the love of her life before the ancient tree reclaimed its

22

modesty and reclothed itself in spring.

Delta had little tolerance for legends and lore and voodoo spells contrived to trap a man. If she had been looking for a husband, she would have gone to Emory and hooked up with a med student who had both money and prospects. She wanted an education, and for that purpose, Mississippi College for Women was the best the South had to offer.

Still, the college lived and breathed such traditions. The Kissing Rock at the front gate had been worn smooth by the oblations of generations of students — virtuous young women who kept their lips primly closed and their tongues to themselves when saying good night to a gentleman caller but were eager enough to press their open mouths against the top of a mossy old boulder. It struck Delta as ironic that otherwise intelligent women could be so terrified of remaining "spinsters." But intelligent or not, when the ginkgo began discarding its leaves, every student in every dormitory was expected to drop whatever she was doing and bolt to the tree.

It was a glorious Saturday afternoon. On her way back to the dorm from the library, Delta ambled toward front campus and gazed up at the ginkgo tree. The leaves had gone from green to pale yellow. It wouldn't be long until shedding day, and even though she secretly ridiculed the legend and didn't give a second thought to meeting Mr. Right, any tradition that allowed for a midnight bonfire and the chance to be out after hours was just fine with her.

This afternoon the wide shaded space under the tree was crowded with folding tables and chairs. A cardboard poster thumbtacked to the tree trunk read:

MCW HARVEST FEST,
OCTOBER 29–30, 1965

The girl sitting behind one of the tables looked vaguely familiar to Delta. She tossed her hair — long and red and lustrous, as if it too had undergone an autumnal metamorphosis. The crown of her head shone copper in the dappled sunlight. "Hey," she said. "Want to sign up?"

"Hey," Delta responded automatically. She looked down at the clipboard the girl held out. "Sign up for what?"

The redhead pointed to another poster, this one affixed to the front of the table with wide strips of masking tape. "The Harvest Fest Talent Extravaganza. It's a W tradition, the last weekend of October. Today's the final day to register."

"This is like a big Halloween bash, right?"

The girl tilted her head. "We don't do Halloween at the W. It's *Harvest Fest*."

Delta gazed down the line at the signs attached to other tables:

DECORATIONS. REFRESHMENTS. HARVEST FAIR. FLAG FOOTBALL.

"Flag football? At a women's college?"

"Oh, yes." The redhead nodded enthusiastically. "Friday night is the talent show. Saturday night there's a street dance. During the day on Saturday there are all kinds of games — three-legged races, that kind of thing. The sophomores put on a fair with contests and prizes, and the athletic department sponsors junior-senior flag football. Mostly for the P.E. majors, though. It can get pretty rough." She peered up at Delta. "You're a freshman?"

Delta nodded.

"Me too." She held out a hand. "I'm Tabitha Austin, from Jackson. Tabby, to my friends."

Tabby, Delta thought. Perfect. The girl almost purred.

She knew of Tabitha Austin, of course, although they'd never met. Everyone had heard about Tabby — wealthy, smart, and immensely popular, she was already involved in a dozen campus organizations and was a shoo-in for freshman class president. The golden child. The perfect W girl.

"And you are?"

Delta realized she was staring and gave herself a little shake. "Deborah Fox, from Stone Mountain, Georgia. People call me Delta."

"You live in Castlebury Hall, right?" Tabby said with a laugh. "I heard what some of your cronies did to you last weekend. Wish I had seen it."

"It wasn't a pretty sight."

"A friend of mine told me they lathered up your sheets pretty well. Used two cans of shaving cream."

Delta nodded. "I had been up until one in the morning, down in the common room writing a paper, and I was exhausted. Believe me, when I slid into bed and felt that stuff all over my sheets, I was not amused." She chuckled. "I made them clean it all up, but not before we'd had a shaving cream fight and made so much noise the house mother came up and gave us five reps each."

"Five reprimands? For a shaving cream fight?"

"Not for the fight. For waking her up at that hour." Delta grinned. "My revenge is coming. Don't know what I'm going to do just yet, but I'll think of something. We'll probably all get campused."

Tabby smiled broadly. "Sounds like you've had quite a welcome to the W."

"Yeah." Delta shifted from one leg to another. "So, if you're a freshman, how come you know so much about what's going on?"

"Third generation. My mother and my grandmother are both alumnae. Also two aunts, three cousins, and my older sister." Tabby leaned across the table. "Getting involved — that's the key to making your college years memorable," she said, putting a hand to her heart. "The W is rich in heritage and tradition —"

Tabby's well-rehearsed tribute was interrupted by the appearance of an upperclassman who bent over the table and scrutinized the list for the Talent Extravaganza. "Where's the football sign-up?"

"Down at the end."

"Great." She straightened up and smiled. "Don't miss the game. We're going to kick some senior butt this year."

Delta watched as the woman made her way down the line.

"So, do you want to sign up for an act in the talent show?" Tabby repeated. "It's going to be loads of fun. Last chance."

Delta started to refuse, and then an idea dropped into her head. A perfectly brilliant, evil idea.

"You bet I do," she said. "Let me have that clipboard."

"You did *what?*" Rae Dawn DuChamp sat cross-legged on the bed with a thick American history book open on her lap.

"You heard me." Delta looked across the room with satisfaction. Lined up on the bed were the girls she already thought of as her best friends, the three coconspirators in the shaving cream incident: Rae Dawn, dark-eyed and olive-skinned, with her low sexy voice and exotic New Orleans ways; and the small towheaded Cantrell twins from North Carolina, Lauren and Lacy.

"You signed the three of us up for the Harvest Fest talent show?" Lauren said.

"Without our knowledge or permission?" Lacy's voice cracked like an adolescent boy's, screeching to a panicked crescendo on the final word.

Delta nodded vehemently. "Yes, I did."

"Forget it," Lacy said. "We'll go back on Monday and take our names off the list."

"Too late. Today was the last day to sign up. By Monday the list will be at the printer's. If you renege now, everybody will know you chickened out."

"But we have no talent!"

"Speak for yourself," said Rae Dawn in her low, husky voice. "I've been playing piano since I was twelve years old."

Lauren turned to Rae Dawn. "You play the piano? I thought you were an elementary ed major. Why didn't you —"

"It doesn't matter," Lacy protested, talking over her sister as if she'd been doing it all her life — which she probably had. "We'll make fools of ourselves!"

"Exactly." Delta grinned. It was a wickedly ingenious idea, to put them up onstage with guitars and straight blonde wigs, looking like clones of Mary Travers. They would bring the house down simply because they were so *bad*. "And in case you're curious, you're billed as the Delta Belles All-Girl Folk Band. Call it payback, for the Burma-Shave incident."

For a minute no one moved. Then Rae Dawn responded. "I think it sounds like a hoot," she said. "Let's go for it."

They all stared at her as if she'd lost her mind, but no one objected. Not even Lacy.

"On one condition," Rae Dawn continued. She pointed a long brown finger in Delta's direction. "The Delta Belles will be a *quartet,* not a trio. If we're going to make idiots of ourselves in front of the whole school, you're going to be onstage too."

"Oh, no —" Delta began, but any misgivings she might have expressed were drowned out by the laughter of the others and by the pillow that sailed across the room into her face.

"All right," Delta said the next evening as the four of them waited for the doors of the dining hall to open for supper. "I've been thinking about this, and we need a plan."

The crowd around them jostled and pushed, edging them nearer to the entry. Meals at the college were all home-cooked and served family-style in an elegant antebellum hall, with work-study students as servers. The logic, Delta thought, was to teach them to behave as proper young ladies — chandeliers overhead, napkins in laps, elbows off the table, quiet conversation with the table monitors serving from the left, removing from the right (or vice versa — she could never quite remember). But the result proved far different from the intent. When the dinner whistle blew and the doors opened, there was a wild stampede for tables, pigs to the trough. The servers were so eager to get their jobs done and get out of the kitchen that they'd take your plate out from under your nose if you didn't hold onto it with one hand for the duration of the meal.

Sunday suppers tended to be sparsely attended, so there wasn't the usual crush tonight. Sunday dinner, at twelve thirty after church got out, was another matter altogether. It was an elaborate affair. By college mandate, all the students dressed up — skirts, heels, and hose — whether they had attended services or not. There were white tablecloths and linen napkins and lots of visitors, and the tables were decked with fried chicken and homemade yeast rolls and four or five kinds of vegetables. Where most college students faced the Freshman Ten — those inevitable ten pounds that appeared like magic during their first semester away from home — W girls had to contend with the Freshman Twenty. Or Thirty.

The six o'clock whistle blew, and the crowd moved forward as the doors opened. Delta led them toward a table on the left side of the hall, behind one of the high Corinthian columns.

"Good," she said when everyone was settled and grace had been sung. "We've got the table to ourselves. Now, about my plan —"

Delta was interrupted twice more as their server arrived, first bringing iced tea and then setting steaming bowls of vegetables and platters of cornbread and sliced ham in the middle of the table.

"Your plan for what?" Rae Dawn asked as she helped herself to fried okra and collard greens and passed the bowls on.

"For the Delta Belles, of course. For our act."

Lacy scowled. "Since when did this become an *act*?" she asked, spearing a chunk of ham and sandwiching it inside a triangular wedge of cornbread. "It was just a joke, right?"

"Well, it kind of started out as a joke," Delta said. "But since you're determined to make me do it too, we're going to do it right."

Lauren raised her eyebrows. "If you've got a plan, Delta, let's hear it."

"Can I leave?" Lacy asked irritably, rising from her seat.

Lauren glared at her. "Sit down." Lacy sat. "All right, out with it. What's your problem?"

Lacy shrugged. "I don't know. I just don't like the idea of . . . of being laughed at."

"Who's laughing at you?" Rae Dawn motioned toward Lauren to pass her the butter.

"Well, nobody . . . yet," Lacy hedged. "But if we do this talent show thing, we're going to be the laughingstock of the whole school."

"And why is that?" Delta asked calmly.

"Because when she was in kindergarten," Lauren volunteered, "she was asked to sing in a Thanksgiving pageant, forgot the words, then peed in her pants and had to be carried dripping offstage."

Lacy shot her twin a venomous look. "Will you shut up? You don't have to tell everything you know."

Delta leaned forward, grinning. "Is that true, Lace? You peed in your pants onstage?"

"I was five years old," Lacy said between gritted teeth.

"Yeah," Lauren jibed. "But you never set foot on a stage again, did you? Come on, admit it. You don't want to do this talent show because you can still feel that warm pee running down your leg —"

"For God's sake, can you quit talking about pee?" Rae Dawn snapped. "I'm trying to eat here." She lifted her fork and sniffed at the collards.

"I don't want to do this talent show *because we've got no talent!*" Lacy slammed a fist against the table, rattling the ice in her glass. "I devoutly wish we'd never even thought of that shaving cream." She looked around at the others. "Don't you get it? She's out for revenge, just to make us look like fools. And now you're all acting as if this is some great career opportunity. As if — as if we're not going to be booed off the stage and totally humiliated."

Delta sat with her chin in her hand, waiting for Lacy's tirade to wind down.

"Okay," she said when Lacy fell silent. "First of all, this is a college talent show, not the Met. Second, there are going to be lots of stupid acts designed simply to make the audience laugh."

Lacy glared at her darkly.

"And third, we are *not* going to be one of those acts."

Lauren picked a corner off her cornbread, shredded it to bits between her fingers, and smiled slyly. "Lacy's teaching herself to play the guitar."

Lacy exploded. "Lauren, what kind of sister are you? Why'd you tell them? Whose side are you on, anyway?"

"We're all on the same side," Delta said as Lauren gave Lacy a shut-up-and-listen look. She turned to Rae Dawn. "You play the piano, right?"

"Right."

"So you know music." Delta smiled triumphantly. "Lacy can play the guitar, and you can teach us — chords, harmonies, stuff like that."

34

"In less than three weeks?" Rae Dawn shook her head.

"Haven't you seen *The Sound of Music*?" Delta rushed on. "You know: 'Do, a deer, a fe-male deer; Re, a drop of golden sun.' It's easy. If Julie Andrews could teach seven kids in three minutes, you can teach us in three weeks."

"I don't know, Delta."

"Come on, Rae. It'll be fun. A challenge."

"Hold it!" Lacy was boiling now; Delta could see the fury building in her eyes. "No one's bothered to ask, but I am *not* going to play the guitar in front of a thousand people. I'm just starting to learn; I only know a few chords. I —"

"Folk music only *uses* a few chords, Lacy. It's simple." Rae Dawn chewed her lower lip. "Let's see. We could do 'Blowin' in the Wind' — that's easy, and everybody knows it. And then for an encore —"

"Encore?" Lacy jerked an arm convulsively, and the remains of her cornbread sandwich shot off her plate onto the center of the table. Lauren smiled sweetly, retrieved the cornbread, and set it back on her sister's plate.

"We'll have to practice a lot." Rae Dawn went on, ignoring Lacy's outburst. "I'll track down some sheet music and book a rehearsal room in the music department. I use their pianos all the time." She pulled an appointment book out of her bag and jotted down a note to herself. "All in favor of Delta's idea?" she said.

Three hands went up. Lacy sat frowning with her arms crossed and her elbow in the butter dish.

"Then it's settled. Rae Dawn, let us know when we start practice."

"Isn't *anyone* listening to me?" Lacy demanded.

"Oh, lighten up, Lace," Lauren said. "We're all in this, and you're going to have fun, whether you like it or not."

THREE:
OLD FRIENDS

DECATUR, GEORGIA
SEPTEMBER 1994

Delta had fully intended to craft a polite response, send her regrets, and inform Tabitha Austin that she would not be attending the reunion. Or at the very least promise to think about it and then call back and tell her no.

It was a ploy she had often used as a pastor's wife, when someone wanted to volunteer her for a job she didn't want to do. Most of the time she didn't need to think about it — or, in religious terms, *pray* about it — but inexorable personalities could, on occasion, be mollified by this semblance of consideration.

Delta, however, made the mistake of telling her sister about Tabby's invitation.

"Well, you should do it, of course," Cassie said with a determined nod. "It sounds like a great idea, getting the old group together. I remember how much fun you all had. And you haven't seen them in ages. Go visit them, Delta. Go for it."

"Visit them?" Delta balked. "Don't you mean call them? Write to them?"

Cassie sat down on the bed next to Delta. "If you really want to reconnect with these friends of yours, you need to do it in person."

"You're assuming this is a good idea, reuniting the Delta Belles." Delta shook her head. "I don't know, Cass. It sounds like a lot of effort. Makes me feel overwhelmed just thinking about it."

"What else do you have to do? Since Rankin's death you've been holed up here like some sort of hermit. Remind me again where they are."

"Lauren and Lacy are in Durham and Hillsborough. Rae Dawn's in New Orleans."

"Give me their addresses. I'll get online and plan a route for you." Cassie got to her feet. "You can pack. Clean clothes are in the basket in the laundry room."

"What, you mean go *now*? I can't just drop everything and go off on a road trip."

Cassie sat down again. "Drop what, Sis? Exactly what is it you're going to miss so desperately if you take a few days to go visit your friends? Besides, you need some time away."

An icy chill crept into Delta's gut, an inner paralysis that came all too frequently since Rankin's death. "I can't do this."

Cassie tilted her head and looked intently at Delta. "Well, then, call them at least. Ask them if they're going to the reunion. Spend a little time catching up with them. You can manage that, can't you?"

"I suppose," Delta said reluctantly.

That evening after dinner, Delta sat in her room with her address book in one hand and the telephone in the other, battling with a nagging suspicion that she had been hood-winked by her little sister.

Cassie hadn't believed for a minute that Delta would jump up and go visit her old friends at such short notice. But given the choice between a road trip and a telephone call —

Delta exhaled a sigh and flipped through the address book. Lauren lived in Durham, North Carolina, and her sister Lacy in Hills-borough, only a few miles apart. The last time she had seen them had been five or six years ago, when she and Rankin had driven from Asheville to Raleigh for a church con-ference, and the dinner they had shared had seemed strained and uncomfortable. Afterward, Rankin had questioned her about the twins.

"What's going on with those two?" he asked. "I thought they had a pretty good relationship in college."

"They did. I mean, they had the typical sibling rivalries and picked at each other sometimes, but mostly it was all in fun. We laughed a lot." Delta shrugged. "Something happened during our last year, though. Lacy had been dating this guy named Trip Jenkins, and then later on, after graduation, we found out he had married Lauren."

"Ouch," Rankin said. "That's got to hurt."

"I'm sure it did. But Lacy and Lauren were far too close to let that get in the way of their relationship."

Now, thinking about the twins, Delta wondered. That night at dinner, they had all skated around the issue as if on wafer-thin ice. Lacy had become a high school history teacher and seemed to love her work, but she had never married. Lauren had raised a son — a handsome boy if the pictures were any indication. He would be grown now, in his twenties. Lauren might even be a grandmother by now.

Delta turned forward a few pages from the *C*'s to the *D*'s and found Rae Dawn

DuChamp's number. New Orleans, on Dauphine Street in the Quarter.

Only once since graduation had Delta managed to get together with Rae Dawn. Three years into their marriage Rankin had accepted a call to a new church in Asheville, and during a two-week hiatus between pastoral duties, they had taken a few days to drive down to the Big Easy.

She remembered Rae Dawn just as she had been in college — dark and exotic-looking, with a deep smoky voice and a musical laugh. Delta and Rankin had sat in the club and listened to Rae sing, and at the memory a bittersweet longing rose up in Delta. She hadn't realized until this moment how much she missed Rae Dawn and how much her friendship had meant.

Over the years they had written only sporadically — Christmas cards, mostly, a hasty note now and then. Much as Delta hated to admit it, Cassie was right. It would do her good to talk to her old friends again.

She picked up the receiver and dialed Rae Dawn's number. It rang six times before anyone picked up.

"Maison Dauphine," a male voice answered.

"Oh —" Delta stammered. "I may have the wrong number. I was trying to reach Rae

41

Dawn DuChamp."

The man on the other end hesitated, and Delta heard noises in the background — a vacuum cleaner running, she thought, and the clinking of glassware. "Uh — yes," he said at last, "this is the correct number. But I'm afraid she isn't available at the moment. May I take a message?"

Delta paused, thinking. "I suppose so, if you don't mind. Do you have a pen?"

"Yep," the man said. "Whenever you're ready."

"Please tell her that Delta Ballou called. Delta *Fox* Ballou."

"B-a-l-l-o-u? As in *Cat Ballou*?"

"That's right. Area code 404 —" She gave him Cassie's number. "Tell her I'm in Atlanta. Decatur, actually. Emory University area."

"Atlanta," he repeated.

"Right. Do you know when she might be available?"

She heard a mumbling, as if he had put his hand over the mouthpiece and was consulting with someone else.

"I'm not sure, but I'll give her the message and have her get back to you."

"Okay, thanks," Delta said, and, with a sense of disappointment that left her unaccountably bereft, she hung up the phone.

FOUR:
BOURBON STREET DREAMS

Rae Dawn took the cocktail napkin from Nate the bartender and leaned her elbows on the shiny mahogany surface of Maison Dauphine's bar. Behind Nate she could see her own reflection in the lighted mirror, and she stared forlornly at the image.

"Who is she?" Nate asked, gazing down at the name and number on the paper napkin.

"An old friend," Rae said. "From college. My best friend, to be more precise."

"And you didn't want to talk to her?"

Rae Dawn shook her head. "I don't want to talk to anyone right now." She gave him a narrow glance, and he raised both hands in surrender.

"Okay, I get the message." He retrieved a clean towel from under the bar and began polishing glasses.

"Could you get me a Diet Coke, please?" Rae asked.

"Coming right up." Nate filled a glass with

ice, poured the soft drink with a flourish, and set it in front of her.

"Thanks." Rae looked at him, the familiar boyish face, the blond curly hair, the soft downy beard he had been growing for two months now. Nate had been with her for years at Maison Dauphine — not just an employee, but a friend. A good friend. He didn't deserve to be on the receiving end of her depression. "Sorry I snapped your head off."

Nate grinned and twisted his head first to the right, then the left. "Still attached. No problem." His blue eyes softened as he gazed at her. "I understand."

"You're a good man, Nate," she said as she moved off toward a table near the front windows.

"Yes, I am," he called to her retreating back. "And don't you forget it."

Rae Dawn installed herself at the corner table, sipped at her Diet Coke, and fingered the cocktail napkin. Nate *didn't* understand. It wasn't that Rae didn't want to talk to Delta; she simply couldn't bring herself to do it at the moment. Like everything else in her life, even a simple telephone call felt completely insurmountable to her. She would have to make conversation. She would have to explain.

Besides, she'd lay odds on the fact that Delta was calling about the twenty-fifth anniversary bash, to ask if she was interested in coming. She'd probably gotten an identical letter from Tabitha Austin, suggesting a reunion show of the Delta Belles.

Rae would have to call her back, of course. But not now.

Nate appeared at her elbow and put a bowl of fresh popcorn on the table, then silently slipped back to the bar. Rae Dawn stared out the window at tourists passing by on the sidewalk, at old Mrs. Beaulieu upstairs across the street, shaking her rugs over the wrought iron railing of her balcony. Her husband had died last year, and Mrs. B had grown frailer and thinner every day since his death, until now she looked like a naked baby bird with parchment-thin skin and clawlike hands. Rae Dawn wondered how much longer the old dear would last, having to climb those stairs to her apartment.

Rae ate a handful of popcorn and sipped at her drink, crumpling Delta's telephone number into a ball in her fist. So many losses. And yet so many gifts, too, as Mrs. B would undoubtedly remind her. *You only feel the pain if you've felt the love.*

She smoothed out the napkin and stared at Delta's name, scrawled in blue ballpoint in

Nate's distinctive handwriting.

Even the name took her back. Back to the autumn of her freshman year. Back to the place where her life — where the gifts — had truly begun.

FRESHMAN YEAR
AUTUMN 1965

Most of the rehearsal rooms in the music building were dark and quiet this early in the morning, but the front doors were unlocked. Rae Dawn slipped inside and stood in the echoing marble foyer. At a distance she heard a *click-click* of footsteps, the creak of a door, the hollow *thunk* of a lock being turned, and then the faint, haunting sounds of scales from a clarinet.

She leaned against one of the massive columns in the entryway and closed her eyes. Music — any kind of music — carried her to a different place, a better place than where she'd come from. A clean, green, sun-lit place caressed by fresh breezes and the scent of hidden blooms.

Music, for Rae Dawn, generated a kind of homesickness of the soul, a bittersweet longing, a faint hope on the horizon.

Not that she'd ever had much hope. Not

until two months ago, when she came to college, anyway.

The clarinetist had segued from scales into some bluesy, improvisational runs — easy on the ear, hard on the heart. An old Louis Armstrong tune: *Do you know what it means to miss New Orleans. . . .*

The song reminded Rae Dawn of home, and she felt tears prick behind her closed eyelids.

Home. She always claimed the Big Easy as home, and maybe it was, at least on some mystical, soul-deep level. New Orleans reached out to her, with its French flavors and its sensuous, gutsy music. Every good thing that filled her senses, every creative impulse that nurtured her spirit, had been birthed between Canal and Esplanade on the cobbled streets of the Vieux Carre. The soulful piano tunes that lingered like smoke on the air above Bourbon Street. The gray stone towers of St. Louis Cathedral and the bright, optimistic artists' canvases that lined the wrought-iron fence around Jackson Square. The rich crispy smell of fried oyster po'boys from Acme Oyster House on Iberville. The scent of strong chicory-laced coffee and fresh warm beignets at Café Du Monde.

The truth was, Rae Dawn had always

wished New Orleans was her home. Not Picayune, Mississippi, thirty miles northeast of the magic. Not a broken-down Airstream trailer at the dead end of a rutted, sandy track that bordered a tributary of the Pearl River called Hobo Creek.

At thirteen, she had made her first solitary journey to New Orleans, accepting a ride from a gregarious trucker who never questioned — at least out loud — her far-fetched story about going to visit her estranged birth mother. After that one trip, she was hooked. Every school holiday and most weekends she managed to hitch a ride or scrounge up money for the bus. Anything to get back to the place where she belonged. She never questioned the risks, never felt in danger. The Quarter was a womb, not a threat. It fed and nurtured her, birthed her into a life marked by music and beauty and hope. As long as she roamed those familiar streets, she could forget all about her real life and become the person she was destined to be. The dirty brown water of Hobo Creek might run in her blood, but the heart that pumped it was pure New Orleans.

And then, every time, came the moment of leaving. . . .

It was like dying over and over again. Forever, it seemed, she had been trying to flee

Picayune permanently, to escape the Airstream and her father's drunken rages and her mother's deadening inertia. She dreamed about making New Orleans her real home, living there, being part of its blood and breath, adding her harmony to the music in the air. But she had no money, no education, no skills.

Thus, when the grant offer from MCW came — not the piano scholarship she longed for, but a "resident need subsidy," what Rae Dawn called "the poverty package" — she took it and was grateful.

It wasn't New Orleans, but it wasn't Picayune, either. . . .

The front doors opened with a creak and a bang, startling Rae Dawn out of her reverie. She jumped and turned to see Dr. Manfred Gottlieb, head of the Music Department, standing backlit by the morning sun.

"Guten Morgen," he said with a little bow. The professor was tall and thin. His wild graying hair stood up at all angles, and he reminded Rae Dawn of pictures she had seen of Albert Einstein. He was dressed in a starched white shirt and a worn brown tweed cardigan with suede patches on the elbows. His eyes were a soft gray-blue, and his smile revealed a dimple in his right cheek. He looked very old, but other things besides

the passing of years could age a person.

Against her will, Rae Dawn's eyes jerked toward his forearm, where the sleeve of his sweater covered any evidence. Rumor had it that twenty years ago Gottlieb had been liberated from a Nazi death camp — Dachau, Buchenwald, Rae Dawn couldn't remember the details. She had seen the professor in the halls and around campus, but mostly at a distance, never close up. She wasn't quite certain what she expected of a survivor of a concentration camp — an expression of blank emptiness, perhaps, or else an unquenchable fury. But Manfred Gottlieb's face, now gazing into hers, held only kindness, interest, and a tinge of mild amusement.

"You are one of my students?" he asked in a quiet voice, his head tilted to one side.

"I — ah, no," Rae said. "I'm just — just coming in to use one of the pianos."

"I see. Unfortunately, there are no pianos out here in the hallway."

"N-no," she stammered. "I know. I was . . . thinking."

He wiggled his eyebrows at her — a high arch, up and then down again. "Thinking, this is a good thing. People should engage in it more often, I suspect."

Rae Dawn chuckled. "You're probably

right. Except that what I was doing was more like daydreaming. Woolgathering."

"Ah. And yet such wool can keep the heart warm on a cold winter night, no?"

It was a lovely thought — and indeed, Rae Dawn's dreams of New Orleans did have a warming effect when life seemed cold and barren. She smiled at him. "I'd better go practice."

He inclined his head. "And I have lessons to prepare."

She moved off down the hall, but Gottlieb spoke again. "Pardon me. Your name?"

"DuChamp," she said, turning to face him once again. "Rae Dawn DuChamp." She uttered the name in the French way, although her father and his father and all the Picayune DuChamps before them pronounced it *champ,* like the winner of a boxing match or a racehorse itching to run.

"A pleasure to meet you, Miss DuChamp," Gottlieb said, and turned toward his office.

When he was gone, Rae Dawn made her way down the dim-lit corridor and into one of the practice rooms. The space was barely large enough for a baby grand and a bench, but the ceiling was fifteen feet high, and a frosted glass window diffused the morning sun and cast a cheerful yellow glow across the walls.

The sunlight on her back warmed her as she sat down and flexed her fingers — warmed her almost as much as Manfred Gottlieb's respectful words and gracious smile. Only one person in Rae Dawn's life had ever affirmed her desire to become a musician — Teresa Cheever, a seventh-grade teacher who had discovered her pounding away at the ancient, battered, out-of-tune Everett upright in the school auditorium. Rae had a gift, Mrs. Cheever said, a gift that ought to be developed. Whatever she heard, she could instantly reproduce from memory. But she had no understanding. No foundation.

Until Mrs. Cheever came along, Rae had no idea how to read the mysterious runes of a music score — she simply played by ear, by instinct. Like a starving refugee, she devoured everything the teacher put in front of her — fingering techniques, form, dynamics, music theory. She learned to read with unbelievable speed and accuracy, and soon experimented with composing music. By the time she entered high school, she had begun work on her own sonata.

The DuChamp family had no piano, of course. The only instrument Rae Dawn ever got her hands on was the school's old

Everett, and she had to wait until late afternoon, when everyone was gone, to get in any practice time at all. But whenever she sat at the keyboard, everything else disappeared — the trailer, the fear, the abuse, the stench of whiskey that hung about her father, the haunted expression in her mother's eyes.

Over the years other teachers had written her off simply because she was poor and the only child of the town's most notorious drunk. Her mother never had an encouraging word to say about life in general or her daughter in particular; she spent the bulk of her days sitting at the small built-in kitchen table in the Airstream, chain-smoking and tracing patterns in the Formica with a blunt fingernail. And Daddy — when he was there, which wasn't often — entertained himself either by yelling at the two of them or by parking himself in a rusted metal lawn chair and firing shotgun pellets into the eroded bank of Hobo Creek.

No one cared much about a ragged, introverted child caught in a web of crushing poverty and neglect. No one except Teresa Cheever.

Mrs. Cheever had saved her. Mrs. Cheever and the music.

The woman taught Rae Dawn everything she knew, encouraged her, believed in her.

But in the end, she readily admitted that Rae Dawn's genius far outstripped her own abilities as a tutor. Rae needed another mentor, someone with advanced education and abilities.

Given her background and financial situation, however, Rae knew that wasn't likely to happen. She was on her own, and had to make do with what she knew.

She ran some scales to limber up her touch, then began to re-create the tune the clarinetist had put into her mind. The music transported her, and she moved easily through three or four familiar pieces — torch songs, mostly, from Billie Holiday, Lena Horne, Sarah Vaughan. She played by ear, by heart, feeling the riffs in her soul.

Rae Dawn loved all kinds of music, but mostly she loved jazz. Loved the freedom of it, the way she could experiment with it to make it her own. Just for fun, she had re-invented some of Bach's inventions, taken classical pieces and fiddled with them to bring them into the twentieth century. And now, as the music took her over, she simply let herself go and began to pour out her soul into music of her own creation.

At last, when she had played herself far away from Picayune and the Airstream trailer and Hobo Creek, back into the embrace of the French Quarter, Rae Dawn stopped for a moment and rifled through her bag. She had found some rudimentary melody sheets and chord charts for the folk songs the newly formed Delta Belles would be singing at the talent show. Not exactly her kind of music, nor an auspicious beginning to a career in performance, but it would be a chance to find out how well she could do in front of a large crowd.

Within five minutes, she was bored out of her skull and wondering why she'd ever agreed to such an insane idea. Folk music, the way most people played it, was infuriatingly simple. Three or four chords, always in major keys like G or C. Rae Dawn experimented a little with the accompaniment for "Blowin' in the Wind" and came up with a version that was recognizable but infused with her own particular style.

She jotted down a few chord changes and made notations for an improvisational bridge between the second and third verses. No reason a song like this should be insipid and predictable, even if eighty percent of people under the age of forty could play it passably well on the guitar.

Another thirty minutes passed, and by the time the warning whistle blew for nine o'clock classes, Rae Dawn was confident that she would be able to give the Delta Belles some good options for their debut at the Talent Extravaganza.

She felt oddly satisfied. This was what she'd always dreamed of doing — not simply playing for herself and Mrs. Cheever in an empty school auditorium, but performing before an audience, drawing them into the world she had created, making the music her own.

A light knock sounded on the door. Rae Dawn stowed her music in her bag and prepared to clear out to allow someone else into the practice room. But when she opened the door, she found a weathered face and a shock of gray hair.

"Dr. — Dr. Gottlieb!" she stammered. "Were you — have you — how long have you been out here?"

"Long enough," he said. "Do you happen to be free at four o'clock this afternoon?"

"I — ah, yes," she said, scrambling to think of her schedule. "I have practice with my friends at four thirty. For the talent show."

"Then meet me in my office at four, if you please," he said. "I believe there are some things we should discuss."

And without another word, he turned on his heel and moved noiselessly back down the hallway, as if gliding on a song.

■■■■

At four o'clock, Rae Dawn stood outside Manfred Gottlieb's office door. Her stomach squirmed, and her brain spun out imaginary scenarios, most of which centered around being banned from the practice rooms, told that she had no right to think of herself as a musician.

She raised a tentative hand and rapped lightly. Through the frosted glass window, she could see a shadowy form rise and move toward her.

The door swung open. "Miss DuChamp, come in please," Dr. Gottlieb said, giving a slight bow and a wave of his hand. "Punctuality is one of your virtues, I see."

Rae Dawn looked at him. The starched white shirt was limp and a little rumpled, and his tie was slightly askew. The tweed cardigan he had worn earlier that morning now draped casually across the back of his desk chair. He seemed more approachable, somehow. More human.

She entered the office — a spacious room with high ceilings, scarred wood floors, and an ornate chair rail that ran the perimeter of the walls. Or rather, it would have been spacious, had it not been cluttered with books and papers on every available surface.

The professor's desk sat squarely in the center of the office, flanked by overflowing bookcases and tall filing cabinets. In an alcove to one side stood an ancient baby grand piano, finished in mahogany and piled with stacks of staff paper and spiral-bound music scores.

Dr. Gottlieb scooped an armload of books from a battered leather chair in front of his desk and nodded for her to sit. He dumped the pile on the corner of his desk, where it teetered precariously. Rae Dawn kept a wary eye on the heavy volumes, expecting them to fall at any moment. Dr. Gottlieb, completely unconcerned, went behind the desk and sank into his office chair.

"Now, Miss DuChamp," he said, tenting his long fingers together, "let us have a talk about your career."

"My career," she repeated stupidly.

"Precisely." He ignored the obvious — that she sounded like an ill-trained parrot — and continued. "This morning you informed me that you are not a music major, is that correct?"

Rae Dawn nodded. "Yes, sir."

"And why is that?"

"Excuse me?"

"Why are you not a music major?"

"Well, I . . . I guess because —" She

shrugged and lifted her hands in surrender.

"Because some foolish, ignorant pragmatist in your past — some so-called teacher, perhaps, or a parent — informed you that music is not a viable option for making money and fulfilling the American Dream? That smart people position themselves to have a regular paycheck coming in, a house in the suburbs, a white picket fence, a color television set?"

He paused and ran his hands through his hair, making it stand up even more wildly. "Forgive my bluntness, Miss DuChamp. My own life experience has led me to value that which nurtures the soul above all else. Beauty, art, poetry, music . . ."

At the words *life experience,* Rae Dawn's mind jerked to images of emaciated bodies from the concentration camps, and she shuddered. She barely heard his next words: "For me, of course, music is the primary passion. And from what I heard this morning, for you as well."

She stared at him. "You think I have *talent?*"

Dr. Gottlieb raised an eyebrow. "You are, shall we say, unfinished. Rough, like unsculpted marble. But talent? Yes. A fire in the belly. A hunger in the spirit. I hear these things. I see them in your eyes." He leaned forward. "This is your first year in college?"

"Yes, sir. I'm a freshman."

"And yet you say, quite decisively, that you are not a music major."

"Yes."

"So you have settled on something else, even so early in your education?" He tugged at one ear. "May I ask what you have determined to be your life direction?"

Rae Dawn ducked her head. "Elementary education."

He cleared his throat. "Because there are jobs available to you when you graduate."

It was not a question, and Rae Dawn did not answer. She kept her eyes fixed on the unsteady pile of books on the corner of Gottlieb's desk. Something in her gut told her that everything in her life was about to tumble.

All she had ever wanted to do was live in New Orleans and make music. But growing up in an Airstream trailer on the banks of Hobo Creek had skewed her values. Teaching might not make her rich, but it wouldn't keep her poor either. As much as she loved music, it was — as Dr. Gottlieb himself had admitted — a calling that destined her to financial instability.

He was still gazing at her from under his bushy white eyebrows.

"I could —" she began hesitantly, avoiding his gaze. "I could *teach* music."

"You could." He nodded. "Bringing music to children is a noble profession. But not for you." He leaned back in his chair and closed his eyes, as if considering a monumental decision. "I will train you, if you would be willing."

Rae Dawn blinked, and for a moment her heart soared. "*Willing?* Of course I would be willing." Then she came back to herself. Lessons cost money, money her scholarship did not provide. The momentary flame of hope guttered and died, and the dream went out of her on a sigh. "I can't, Dr. Gottlieb. I wish I could, but I can't."

"And why not?"

Memories flashed across her mind — all the times she had come home to find that once again Daddy had blown the welfare check on liquor and shotgun shells. The week after Christmas in third grade, when Julie McKenzie identified Rae Dawn's new red wool coat as a castoff her mother had given to the Goodwill. The winter they had lived on nothing but sweet potatoes stored in an ammo box under the trailer and a few tough, stringy rabbits her father shot in the woods near the creek.

But she wasn't about to tell Gottlieb any of

this. She had escaped. She was barely getting by on her stipend, but she still had her pride.

"Pride nourishes the ego but does not feed the soul." He said the words softly, as if he'd read her mind.

Rae Dawn looked up and, to her dismay, a tear slid down her cheek. The professor did not turn away, but continued to gaze at her, his blue-gray eyes shining.

"Your family is poor?"

He uttered the word boldly and without apology, and it pierced her like a blade. The sharp edge of poverty was usually tempered by euphemism: families had *financial challenges* or just needed time *to get on their feet*. No one used real words like *destitute* or *indigent* or *impoverished*.

Dr. Gottlieb's honesty broke loose something inside Rae Dawn. She swiped the tear away with one hand and stared him down. "Yes," she said fiercely. "We're poor. Dirt poor. My father is an alcoholic. My mother's useless. I grew up wearing clothes other people had thrown away. I'm in college now only because I received a resident need stipend."

Admitting the truth brought an unexpected sense of liberation. She exhaled a pent-up breath and ventured a tentative smile.

He crossed his arms and smiled back. "Yes.

The poverty package."

Rae Dawn felt laughter welling up inside her. "Dr. Gottlieb, I have never met anyone quite like you. You make me feel . . . I don't know. Accepted."

He unbuttoned his cuff, rolled up his sleeve, and held his arm out toward her. The inside of his forearm bore a hazy, bluish tattoo, a string of numbers. "How old do you think I am?" he asked.

She hesitated, not wanting to offend him. On appearance alone, she would have guessed seventy, perhaps more. But his spirit seemed younger than that, and his step lighter. Besides, he wouldn't likely be teaching if he were that old.

"Sixty?" she offered.

"You are kind," he responded with a smile. He rolled his sleeve down and rebuttoned the cuff. "I will be fifty-two in January."

Rae Dawn tried not to let the shock register on her face, but she felt a hot flush creep up her neck.

"I was not yet thirty when the Nazis came," he went on. "We lived in Berlin, and my family was well off — wealthy, by many people's standards. My father was an art dealer, and my mother a pianist and composer. On the train to Auschwitz, I worried most about what would become of our beautiful piano, and my father's art collection." He shrugged. "But when the ovens began to belch out smoke and people were being murdered, twenty thousand or more a day, material things no longer mattered."

His eyes took on a faraway look, as if calling up memories Rae Dawn didn't even want to imagine. "I do not often talk about those terrible days," he said. "But I felt it imperative that you should understand. I have known abundance, and I have known deprivation. There is no shame in either." A slight tremor went through him, and he shook his head. "What matters is life. What matters is holding fast to the dreams and values that fill your heart, even when others try to rip them away from you. What matters is hope."

Rae Dawn had no answer for this, and so she kept silent.

"You are a musician," Dr. Gottlieb went on. "It is in your soul. To deny it would be death to your spirit and would rob the world of beauty we so desperately need. And so I repeat my offer: I will teach you, if you are willing."

This time Rae Dawn understood. He was offering to teach her for free.

He rose from his chair. "Come by tomorrow, and we will set a schedule for your lessons."

"Thank you so much," she said as she walked with him to the door. "I don't know how to express my gratitude — for your offer, for your faith in me. For everything."

He held the office door open for her and reached to shake her hand. "I am grateful too. For the opportunity to hear and create music. For the honor of teaching a student such as yourself. For the grace and the joy of being alive."

Rae Dawn left Dr. Gottlieb's office and walked down the hall into the echoing foyer of the music building. She felt as if she had just stepped out of a dream — or into one. For the second time in her life, someone believed in her. Someone who could teach her, mentor her. Someone who could help her find her voice, the music of her soul.

She would not tell anyone, of course, what Gottlieb had revealed of his horrific past. It was his story to tell, if and when he chose to share it. But she knew, or thought she knew, why he had opened those painful memories to her. It was a link between them, a connection. He understood suffering and poverty and did not bow to shame.

She would learn much from him, this man who had survived such terrors and still found hope and wonder in the world.

FIVE:
THE TWIN FACTOR

HILLSBOROUGH, NORTH CAROLINA
SEPTEMBER 1994

Lacy Cantrell stood in the center of her living room, looked around, and sighed. Having a spotless house was a great feeling; actually *doing* the cleaning was a royal pain in the butt.

Still, fall was upon her. School had already started, and she hadn't yet finished her spring cleaning. Yesterday she had discovered a bit of old tinsel from last year's Christmas tree in Hormel's litter box. Where he'd found it she had no idea, but she was pretty sure that sparkly things in the cat's poop couldn't be healthy.

"You could help, you big lazy lug," she said.

The cat, an enormous cinnamon-colored brindle with a snow-white belly, lay sprawled across the sofa taking her in with his inscrutable green gaze. He twitched his tail but made no reply.

Lacy laughed and sat down beside him. When she began rubbing his ears, he responded with a rumbling purr and closed his eyes in ecstasy. He had come to her as a kitten three years ago — simply showed up on her doorstep one Saturday morning when she was cooking sausage, and demanded to be let in. She complied, and as soon as her back was turned he filched her breakfast off the kitchen table and wolfed it down, then dragged the empty sausage wrapper out of the trash can and wore it on his head like a hat. Clearly, the beast had chosen his own name.

Despite his penchant for stealing food, however — a habit Lacy had never been able to break — Hormel turned out to be a most loving and noble animal. Fastidiously clean, he never made messes except when she inadvertently left the lid off the kitchen garbage, and his loyalty and affection rivaled that of the most devoted dog. He followed her everywhere, waited in the window when it was time for her to come home from school, slept at the foot of her bed, and gave unerringly accurate advice about the character of her friends. Hormel was wise beyond his years. If he didn't like you, you didn't stand a chance.

Lacy gave the cat a kiss on the top of his furry head and went back to the onerous job of cleaning the hardwood floors and washing the baseboards. As she worked, her mind drifted to yesterday's mail, which still lay on the coffee table. To the invitation to her college reunion. To the answering machine message from Delta Ballou. And to the past — inexorably, to the past.

Everyone had gathered in Practice Room C for the first rehearsal of the Delta Belles — everyone except Lauren, who was always late. "All right, Lacy," Rae Dawn said, "come over here and let's tune your guitar." She plunked out an E, and Lacy fiddled with the tuner peg until the first string more or less approximated the sound of the piano. "Up, up," Rae Dawn said. "That's it."

They continued tuning until Rae Dawn seemed satisfied. "Okay, now." She pointed at the sheet music. "We're going to start with 'Blowin' in the Wind.' Here are your chords, up here above the staff. It's pretty simple — just C, F, and G."

Lacy strummed the guitar and hummed under her breath as Rae Dawn played slowly through the accompaniment. "Now, when we get to here" — she pointed — "I'll play an interlude on the piano before we go into the next verse."

She ran through the segue. By this time Delta had come to stand next to the piano. "That sounds great, Rae," she said.

"I worked on it a little bit earlier this morning," Rae Dawn said. "You think the interlude's all right? I can tweak it some more."

"You *wrote* that?"

"Yeah, well, it's kind of instinctive. This song is so familiar to everybody, always sung the same way. I just wanted to give it a little something extra."

Delta put a hand on Rae Dawn's shoulder. "Well, there goes *my* plan."

Rae Dawn turned around. "What plan?"

"The plan to have you all get up onstage and make fools of yourselves. This is going to be good. Really good."

"Don't get your hopes up," Lacy said gloomily. "You haven't heard me sing yet."

Fifteen minutes into the rehearsal, Lauren finally did show up. Perhaps it was the dramatist in her. She did love to make an entrance. All their lives, Lauren had been upstaging Lacy, grabbing the spotlight for herself — walking first, talking in sentences while Lacy still struggled with "Mama" and "Daddy" and "no." Lauren was the one who garnered most of the attention, sometimes angelic and adorable, sometimes petulant and demanding, in opposition to Lacy's steady, compliant, docile nature.

Now Lauren's late arrival interrupted what might have been a pretty good first run-through.

Lacy rolled her eyes and bit her tongue to keep from saying something rude, but clearly Lauren got the unspoken message, because she shot a glare at her twin and said, "Don't start with me, Lacy. I'm late because I was *doing something for all of us.*"

She held up an enormous bag so full it bulged at the seams.

"Right," Lacy said, not even trying to curb her sarcasm. "Shopping. For the group."

Lauren propped the bag on the seat of an empty chair. "That's exactly what I was doing." She dug around and came up with something that looked suspiciously like a rug made from dead ferrets. "Here."

She tossed it toward Delta, who shrank back and let it fall to the floor. "Jeez, Lauren," Delta said, poking it with her toe. "What is that thing?"

"It's a vest." She pulled three more out of the sack, in various fur patterns, and passed them around. "I've been thinking about wardrobe," she said. "We want to be folky, right? I thought we could wear black pants and black turtlenecks and these vests."

"I don't want to wear this," Rae Dawn protested. "Dead animals creep me out."

"They're fake fur," Lauren said, as if this answered all their objections. "And then I found *these* —"With a flourish she extracted something yellowish and stringy from the bag. "Ta-da!"

"Wigs?" Delta began to laugh.

Lauren shrugged. "Well, we ought to be blonde, right?"

"We're *already* blonde," Lacy said.

"Of course you and I are blonde," Lauren shot back. "But we don't have long hair. Rae Dawn's a brunette, and Delta's hair is blonde, but not light enough."

"Light enough for what?"

"For the Mary Travers look, of course." Lauren gazed around as if expecting applause.

"*You* be Mary," Lacy said, eyeing the wig with distaste. "I'd rather wear a beard and be Peter. Rae Dawn's tall and thin; she can be Paul."

Delta chuckled. "What about me?"

"Matthew, Mark, Luke, or John," Lacy suggested. "Take your pick."

Everybody laughed. Lauren was clearly not happy about being upstaged by her twin

71

sister. She stuffed the wig back into the bag. "Fine."

"Ah, come on, Lauren," Delta said, sidling over to her. "We're just kidding. Where'd you get all this stuff, anyway?"

"At the thrift store downtown. The vests cost five bucks apiece. The wigs were only two." She put on a wig and one of the vests and modeled for them.

Amid general laughter and hoots of approval, a thought occurred to Lacy, an idea that infuriated her. Where had her sister come up with money to buy these costumes? Since she had spent every cent of her monthly allowance on new loafers, Lacy suspected Lauren had probably embezzled the funds from the stash Lacy kept hidden in the dorm room.

"Lauren," she began in a threatening tone, "where'd you get the money?"

Her twin turned, and the identical face took on a guilty expression all too familiar to Lacy. "I, uh —"

"You stole my allowance to buy this crap, didn't you?"

"Well, I — I sort of *borrowed* it."

Delta intervened. "Hold on, let's not have a war here." She put a restraining hand on Lacy's shoulder. "She was just trying to help out, Lace."

Lacy narrowed her eyes, shooting Lauren an I'll-get-you-for-this look, but said nothing.

"I think we can all pitch in to pay for the wigs and vests," Delta went on in a calming voice. "You'll get your money back, Lacy."

"That's not the point —"

"The point is," Rae said in a determined voice, "whatever we wear, we've still got to *sing*. Can we get back to rehearsal, please?" She heaved an exaggerated sigh. "If we don't get this right, *I'll* be the one peeing onstage."

As the memories came, Lacy found herself fighting back tears. Despite herself, she missed the camaraderie of those days, missed her old college friends, missed her sister most of all.

Growing up, she had longed for an identity of her own. Being a twin could be complicated. Lacy recalled how captivated she had been in Psych 101 when the professor first introduced her to Maslow's hierarchy of human need. She had latched onto the concept, clung to it like a drowning woman to a life raft. *Self-actualization.* That was what she wanted. To be not someone else's mirror image, but her own person, a unique, fully self-actualized human being. . . .

An image from their teenage years rose in

73

her mind, what Lacy thought of as *the burger ritual*. It happened every time: Lacy would remove the pickles from her cheeseburger, setting aside each slice one by one, and one by one Lauren would pick them up and eat them. It was the same with salads; Lacy took the tomatoes off Lauren's greens and gave her all the croutons. They never asked, never discussed it; they did it automatically, in fluid movements as if a single person just happened to inhabit two bodies.

Lacy cringed at the thought. That was the way most people perceived twins, after all. Because they shared the same DNA, the same physical appearance and stature and coloring, folks assumed that they shared a mind too, and a personality. Teachers and friends, sometimes even family members, were forever mixing them up, and although occasionally in junior high and high school they had used that confusion to advantage, Lacy had always loathed the idea of being mistaken for her sister.

She wasn't quite sure why. Lauren was more outgoing, better at sports, and generally more popular. Lacy, the studious, serious one, was included in her sister's circle of friends, but always as an afterthought, a tagalong. All her life Lacy had longed for one thing, her single wish every time she blew out candles on their shared birthday cake: *She wanted to be different.* Even before she was old enough to articulate it, she wanted it so badly that she took drastic measures to distinguish herself from her twin. Like cutting all her hair down to the scalp during Christmas break of second grade.

Now they were grown, and Lacy realized — at least theoretically — that she no longer had to compete with Lauren in order to be a self-actualized individual.

Unfortunately self-actualization had its downside too. The bond had been stretched beyond its limits, the connection severed. At forty-six, Lacy Cantrell was her own person.

But her emancipation had cost more than she bargained for.

SIX:
THE OTHER SISTER

DURHAM, NORTH CAROLINA
SEPTEMBER 1994

Water poured down the eaves and ran in gushing streams out the gutters into the backyard. From the screened porch that overlooked the lawn, Lauren could barely hear the chiming of the mantel clock underneath the steady thrumming of the rain.

Midnight.

The air was chilly and damp, and she shivered, pulling her robe more closely around her shoulders. She ought to be in bed, but she couldn't sleep. For an hour she had tossed restlessly before deciding to get up again. Now she sipped at a steaming mug of tea and read Tabby Austin's letter for the third time.

Neither the letter nor the invitation to the reunion had affected Lauren as much as Delta's voice mail message. She had sounded depressed, empty, her voice flat and emotionless. Delta hadn't pressured Lauren to agree to Tabby's wild notion of getting the Belles back together again — in fact, Lauren had gotten the impression that Delta didn't really want to do it either. Nevertheless, the very idea of reuniting their old singing group brought up a wave of nostalgia and longing in her, a yearning that would not let her go.

And despite her attempts to push the realization away, she knew that her wakeful restlessness wasn't only about the group, but about her sister.

Lacy. Her mirror image, her second self. Her womb-mate.

She could hardly believe how far they had drifted since college, when they stood onstage and sang together, laughed together, lived together. How much they had lost over the years.

One of those old folk songs surfaced in Lauren's mind — Peter, Paul, and Mary's version of a childhood ditty: *Rain, rain, go away, come again some other day.* . . .

But the storm did not diminish. Mist seeped through the screens and gathered on her cheeks, and on the rhythm of the pounding rain, the music took her back.

Backstage at Coltrane Auditorium was pure

bedlam. Half the students, it seemed, had cooked up some kind of act for the Talent Extravaganza, and the other half were out in the audience, stomping their feet and yelling for the show to begin.

Lynn Stanton, leader of a group called the Pillowcase People, had her crew all dressed and ready to go on. The group wore pillowcases pulled down to their knees, painted with enormous faces so that the girls all looked as if they were giant heads with little stick legs and no arms at all. Presumably they had eye slits somewhere near the top, but evidently they couldn't see a thing, because they kept thrashing into people and tripping over equipment.

Lauren caught a glimpse of Tabitha Austin dashing around with a clipboard, making sure all the acts knew what to do. Tabby glanced over and waved and then, looking frazzled and dazed, went to break up an altercation between a ballet dancer and one of the pillowcases who had just stomped on her toe.

"Come on," Rae Dawn said, gripping Lauren under the elbow. "Let's go back here and collect ourselves."

Lauren followed Rae to a dim back corner near the emergency exit, where Lacy was doing a last-minute tuning. She and Delta were wearing the outrageous straight blonde wigs Lauren had bought, but by majority vote they had dispensed with the ferret vests and were all clad in black pants and black turtlenecks.

"All right," Rae said as she tucked her dark hair up under the wig, "are we ready?"

For a moment no one spoke. Then, as if on cue, everyone turned and looked at Lacy, who seemed very pale and was breathing more heavily than usual.

"What?" she demanded. "Yeah, I'm okay. What are we singing again?"

An expression of horror rippled through the group. Lauren was about to say something when Lacy poked her in the ribs and started to laugh. "Just kidding."

"Don't *do* that!" Lauren said. "We're all nervous enough as it is." She folded her arms and regarded her sister. "Did you go to the bathroom?"

"Let's focus, all right?" Rae Dawn interrupted. "We start with 'Blowin' in the Wind.' Do you want to go ahead and do 'If I Had a Hammer,' or wait to see if they want an encore?"

"I think we should wait," Delta said. "I'll check with Tabby and let her know we've got a second song if she wants us to do it, and if there's time."

"Okay then. Delta will give us the sign if we're going to do the second one."

"Of course we'll end up doing it," Delta said. "They're going to love us."

"Ha!" Lacy jibed. "And you started out thinking this would be a big joke."

"It *will* be a joke if we don't get onstage," Rae said. She pointed to the wings, where Tabby was frantically motioning to them and holding up two fingers. "We've got two minutes. Let's go."

For just an instant, when they first stepped out onto the stage, Lauren thought that *she,* not Lacy, might be the one to pee in her pants tonight. The auditorium was packed all the way up to the balcony. Halfway across the platform, she froze in her tracks. Her feet had turned to stone, and her knees were about to give way. She looked out into the audience, and faces swam before her eyes, an enormous sea of them, undulating like a wave.

When the audience caught sight of the long blonde wigs, they began to laugh and point and applaud. Lights glared, and from somewhere above her emanated an earsplitting squeal, feedback from one of the microphones.

Then out of the darkness a calming hand

touched her shoulder, and Rae Dawn's low voice spoke into her ear. "Relax. It'll be fun. If you get nervous, just look around at me."

Miraculously, Lauren was able to move again. She followed Rae to center stage and took her place at the mike farthest from the piano. Lacy moved in opposite her, while Delta claimed the remaining microphone, closest to Rae Dawn. Rae nodded, and Lacy jumped in on the second bar of the introduction.

It was amazing. The microphones, the speakers, the acoustics in the auditorium swelled their voices. After three weeks of practice in the rehearsal rooms, Lauren knew they had the notes and the blend right. But she had never in her life imagined this . . . this *sound*. This enormous, confident, harmonious *sound*.

Everyone else seemed surprised too. Delta and Lacy wore dazed, stunned expressions, and at one point during Rae Dawn's segue, Lauren turned around and mouthed, *Is this us?* And they all laughed, right out loud, because it was so much *fun*.

Then, almost before she realized what had happened, Lauren heard it: a surging noise, the sound of wooden auditorium seats clattering. The crowd was on its feet, applauding, cheering, whistling. Rae Dawn stood up at the piano, and the rest of them stepped from behind the mikes, waving and nodding. Tabby, shrouded in the near dark of stage right, stepped forward, gave them a thumbs-up, and made a rolling motion with her hand.

"She wants the encore!" Delta hissed over the noise of the crowd. Rae sat down again, adjusted her mike, flexed her fingers, and launched into "If I Had a Hammer."

This time no one in the auditorium bothered sitting down. They clapped and swayed and nodded their heads in time to the music. Lacy pounded away at the guitar, and Lauren could barely sing because her grin kept getting in the way. The music sailed and swirled around and through her — Rae Dawn's gorgeous deep alto, Delta's clear lead.

As the song lifted and soared, Lauren's heart lifted with it. By the time they came to the last verse, she was flying.

The words echoed in the hall: *Justice. Freedom. Love.* The crowd roared its approval.

Lauren grabbed her sister's hand, took a bow, and grinned. "Damn," she said as the applause washed over them, "that was *fun!*" And perhaps for the first time in her life, Lauren Cantrell felt herself totally set free.

■ ■ ■ ■

If only I could know that freedom again, Lauren thought as the rain continued to pour from the dark sky.

But she was forty-six years old. It was too late to change. Too many years had gone by, too much pain. Too much water had passed under the bridge.

Or perhaps the bridge had been washed out altogether.

PART 2
THE GOLDEN YEARS

Like amber leaves upon a branch,
the hopeful gilded dreams of youth
shimmer in the sunlight,
tempting, out of reach,
yet never out of mind.

Ah, we were true believers then,
convinced our dreams
were weightless
and would
never
fall.

SEVEN:
AT THE GOOSE

For generations the college grill had been known as the Gray Goose, a reference to certain ceramic figurines that had decorated the tables back in the early 1900s, long before the current café had been so much as a glimmer in an architect's eye. Here and there a few goose remnants remained, such as the goose-shaped clock on the wall and an enclosed patio with the outline of a goose stamped in the paving stones.

At a wrought-iron table on the outdoor terrace, Delta Fox pushed aside her textbooks — English lit, *Crafting the Short Story, Intro to Social Work*. Last year had been core courses mostly. Now, as a sophomore, she was finally getting into subjects that really interested her. Especially literature and creative writing.

At last the heat of September had spent itself and given way to cooler weather and glorious autumn colors. This was Delta's favorite season, the time of year that always stirred a restless energy in her. A leatherbound journal — a gift from Cassie last Christmas — lay on top of her books, and she picked it up and flipped through it. Only a month and a half into creative writing, and already the journal was crammed with notes — descriptions of characters, snatches of dialogue, titles, fragments of ideas. Even an opening scene for the short story that was due in two weeks. Delta had no delusions of becoming a writer, but she was thoroughly enjoying the process. Creative writing was her favorite class.

She closed the journal and settled herself in the afternoon sunshine to read through her mail. The process took a while, since people kept coming to the back windows of the grill, knocking and waving to get her attention. She waved back but did not invite any of them to join her.

Delta took a sip of iced tea. The first letter, thinner and rather crumpled looking, was from her longtime boyfriend, Ben Rutledge, in Atlanta. An architectural engineering student at Georgia Tech, Ben wasn't much of a writer, and his letter would undoubtedly be short and to the point, a hastily scribbled note, a memo: *When are you coming home? Or, Everything's fine here. I miss you. Will call Friday at 7:30.*

The second letter, postmarked Stone Mountain, Georgia — a thick, heavy, legal-size envelope with extra postage — was addressed in her mother's handwriting, old-fashioned and flowy. From the heft of it, it probably included pictures drawn by her six-year-old sister Cassie, who worshiped Delta.

Delta's father called her *Daddy's Little Afterthought.*

She laid her mother's letter aside and opened Ben's. As Delta had expected, it was one page, printed neatly in the angular, precise hand of a future architect.

Hey, cute thing —

Had dinner with your folks on Sunday. Your dad took me out to the park to see the progress on the Big Rock. He appears to think it's a matter of Southern pride to follow every move of the torch, and can't seem to remember I'm a Yankee at heart.

Classes are going well. My Architectural Design prof, Dr. Butts, says he thinks I have a lot of promise. More potential than if my name was "Butts," that's for sure.

89

Will call on Friday eve, usual time. Try to come home for a weekend soon, OK?

Love,
Ben

Delta reread the letter and smiled. Ben was right: Delta's father still had trouble realizing that Ben wasn't really a southern boy. He had moved with his parents from Vermont to Atlanta during junior high, and by then his liberal northern turn of mind was already firmly entrenched. It was one reason among many that Delta adored him. He was different, and unafraid. He didn't own a single firearm, didn't drive a pickup truck, didn't fall in line and salute the Confederate flag like most of the boys she had grown up with. He kept his own unshakable opinions. And yet he indulged Daddy in his fascination with the Stone Mountain carving.

Since 1928 the six-hundred-foot granite dome that gave the town its name had sat untouched, its unfinished carving a mute testimony to the faded glory of the old South. A year ago work had finally resumed on the project, an enormous bas-relief of that Holy Trinity of the Confederacy — Robert E. Lee, Stonewall Jackson, and Jefferson Davis. Delta's father was ecstatic.

To anyone who would stand still long enough to listen, he rhapsodized about the magnificence of the sculpture, prophesying that one day the Stone Mountain park would be a world-class attraction, drawing people from all over the world. He went out to the park at least once a week, rain or shine, to check on the progress, as if he were personally responsible for the completion of the sculpture. And whenever Ben was around, Daddy would drag him out there to oversee the work as well.

Neither Ben nor Delta could understand the obsession. Stone Mountain was a nice little town with a picturesque main street and a laid-back atmosphere that contrasted sharply with the tension and haste of Atlanta proper. But, as Ben often pointed out, the mountain itself wasn't a mountain at all — just a huge slab of granite sticking up out of nowhere, with none of the charm or peacefulness of the Green Mountains of Vermont or the Blue Ridge Mountains three hours north of Atlanta. Besides that, the sculpture, though massive, wasn't exactly Mount Rushmore. Thus, while everyone around them oohed and aahed over the carving and its historical significance, Delta and Ben privately shook their heads in amazement and dismay.

This was the 1960s, for God's sake. The War Between the States had been over for a century, and in case nobody in Georgia had noticed, the South had *lost*. Atlanta, once burned to rubble, had in the past hundred years risen from its ashes to become a thriving, diverse, cosmopolitan city. Last summer President Johnson signed the Civil Rights Act into law. The future was Coke and Delta Airlines and Martin Luther King, not *Gone With the Wind* and the KKK and Lester Maddox.

Delta did not, of course, voice these opinions aloud. Her parents, though good people and not overtly racist, seemed apprehensive and confused by the changes that were rapidly coming to the deep South. They had difficulty moving beyond their nostalgia for the simpler, more placid days gone by, and the knowledge that their eldest daughter supported such a revolution would have troubled them even more.

Delta sighed, set aside Ben's letter, and opened the one from her mother.

Dear DeeDee . . .

Delta cringed. She despised this nickname her mother had imposed on her before she had the vocabulary to protest. It brought up memories of scratchy pink crinolines and uncomfortable black patent shoes, and the hideous perm she had endured when she was six and about to enter first grade. Daddy was the one who had first called her Delta.

She pushed her irritation aside and read on:

Dear DeeDee,

Hope all is going well with you there at college. We are all right. Cassie is (as we knew she would be) far beyond any of her little friends in first grade. While they're learning to sing the alphabet and can barely manage "See Jane run," she sits in a corner and reads everything she can get her hands on. I swear she goes through about a dozen books a week.

I worry for her. She doesn't seem to be adjusting well to being with the other children. The teacher says she's bossy sometimes, and other times withdrawn. I wonder if we ought to let skip ahead, except that she's so small. People see her and think she's four years old, and then she opens her mouth and sounds like she's thirty. Last week she complained about having to participate in a reading circle. "The stories are just so juvenile," she said.

"I wouldn't mind school so much if it wasn't so infernally boring.*"*

Where does she get this stuff?

Anyway, I've included some pictures she drew for you and a story she wrote. She still thinks she ought to be at college with you, and occasionally I suspect she might be right.

Daddy says to tell you that the carving is coming along nicely. They're using something called thermo-torches to slice away the stone. Your father made friends with Roy Faulkner, who's the new chief carver, and Roy took him up on the mountain to show him how the torches work.

Ben came for dinner on Sunday. He's so nice and intelligent and considerate, even if he does have some strange ideas for a southern boy. And he's really sweet on you. I think you could do worse than marrying an architect.

Write soon and come home when you can. We all miss you.

Much love,
Mama, Daddy, & Cassie

All three names were signed in Mama's handwriting. After the two pages of Mama's letter came three heavy sheets torn from a sketchbook. Cassie's crayon drawings showed a good deal of artistic promise, Delta thought. First a landscape scene of a brown and white horse running through a meadow, with a giant rock in the background. Then a rendering of Stone Mountain's main street, again with the granite slab hovering overhead. And finally — a tribute to Daddy, no doubt — a close-up rendering of the monument itself, with a half-carved head dominating the foreground.

Delta wondered what a psychiatrist would make of these drawings. She could just see Sigmund Freud scratching his beard: *Ja, but what is the psychic oppression symbolized by the colossal boulder hanging over her head?*

The last few pages had been ripped from a first-grader's writing tablet, wide double lines with a dotted line in the middle. In a careful, childish hand, Cassie had filled these sheets with a story that made Delta laugh — the tale of a young and beautiful princess, captive in a high tower on a massive stone outcropping. But when the handsome prince climbs up to the tower window to rescue her, he finds his true love surrounded by tall stacks of books. The princess refuses to leave with him because she hasn't yet finished the one she is currently reading.

It was the last sentence that cracked Delta up: *"Go away and learn your alphabet,"* the

Princess told him. "And don't come back until you've got something interesting to say."

"What's so funny?"

Delta looked up, startled, to see a flash of wispy light brown hair backlit by the sun. She hadn't heard anyone come out onto the terrace. It was Dr. Suzanne Hart, her creative writing professor, holding a white ceramic mug in one hand and several books in the other.

"Am I interrupting?"

Delta stood up abruptly. "No, it's fine. Let me clear some space." She moved the letters to one side to give Dr. Hart room on the table for her books.

"Do you want something? Coffee?"

Delta had already resumed her seat, and now she found herself craning her neck to look at Dr. Hart. The woman was in her forties, perhaps, but seemed younger. She had a round, girlish face with just a hint of crow's feet. Delta knew from experience that those hazel eyes could go steely and stern in class, but at the moment they seemed open and welcoming. Dr. Hart was smiling, anticipating an answer to her question. Suddenly Delta realized the incongruity of the scene — herself seated, her professor standing there like a waitress poised to take her order.

She jumped to her feet. "Yes, coffee would

be great. But I can —"

"Stay put," Dr. Hart said amiably. "I'll get it. You want cream or sugar?"

Delta sank awkwardly back into her chair. "Saccharine, if they've got it. No cream. Ah, thanks."

"You want me to take that in?" She pointed at the plastic glass that held the remains of Delta's watery iced tea.

"That'd be great."

Dr. Hart took the glass and her own coffee cup and returned in a moment with two steaming mugs, several paper napkins, a spoon, and a small bottle of liquid sweetener. "It's getting a little chilly out here."

"It's autumn, all right." Delta shook a couple of drops of the sweetener into her cup, stirred it, and glanced at her watch.

"Do you have to be somewhere?" Dr. Hart asked as she settled herself across the table from Delta.

"Not until four thirty. I have a rehearsal. For the — uh, for the Delta Belles." Delta felt herself flush. "It's kind of a singing group, informal, really. Folk music. We got started as an act for the Harvest Fest last year, and it just snowballed from there. Now we're being asked to sing other places, and —" She sputtered to a stop. How embarrassing was this, to be talking with a professor about a stupid talent show?

Dr. Hart grinned. "I remember. You were the highlight of the show. You and Lynn Stanton's Pillowcase People, that is. From the sublime to the ridiculous, I suppose. Lynn's act is so dumb it's funny. Your group is really good."

Delta gaped at her. "Thanks."

"So, what were you laughing at when I came up?" the professor asked. "It seemed pretty hilarious, whatever it was."

"My little sister Cassie," Delta said. "She sent me drawings and a story she wrote." She showed Dr. Hart the pictures, then gave her a brief synopsis of the princess's tale and read her the last line.

"Sounds like you're not the only one in the family with creative talent. How old did you say she is?"

"Six. Just started first grade — which is, in her words, *infernally boring.*"

"She sounds smart."

"Maybe too smart for her own good. She learned to read before she was four."

Dr. Hart sipped at her coffee and looked at Cassie's pictures again. "She's six, and you're — what, nineteen? That's quite an age difference. How is that for you, being a big sister?"

Delta grinned and ducked her head. "I

have to admit, at first I wasn't thrilled about it. I was thirteen when she came along, and accustomed to being an only child. Besides, when you're thirteen, you pretty much feel different all the time — you know, out of step with the rest of the world, uncomfortable in your own skin."

Dr. Hart raised an eyebrow. "I can't imagine. You're attractive and intelligent — and, unless I miss my guess, popular."

"Think newborn colt, all legs and eyes, then add braces, and you'll get the picture. I was a test model for some alien species."

The professor smiled. "I suppose we all feel that way in adolescence."

"Then, as if your typical teenage angst weren't enough, add a new baby sister to the mix. I felt as if I were walking around wearing a sign that said, 'My parents still have sex,' and believe me, that's the last thing a thirteen-year-old wants to advertise."

Dr. Hart laughed. "But clearly you dealt with it and have a good relationship with her."

"Yes, I do — now," Delta said. "As a teenager I complained about babysitting for free, but for the most part I liked being a big sister. I grew up. And now I can't imagine life without her." She took another sip of coffee, shook in two more drops of sweetener, and chanced a surreptitious glance at the professor. "Did you mean that, about me having creative talent?"

"Relax, Delta," Dr. Hart said. "This isn't an inquisition, it's a coffee break. And yes, I did mean it. You're doing very well in my class. Creative writing is about creative thinking, and I like the way you think."

"Really?"

"Really. In fact, that's why I stopped by today. Frankie and I would like to have a talk with you."

"Frankie?"

"Frances Bowen. She teaches Shakespeare and Renaissance Poetry, among other things. She's —" Hart paused for a moment. "My housemate."

"I haven't met her yet."

"Trust me, you will. You'll either love her or hate her, but however you feel about her, you'll learn a lot in her classes." The professor chuckled. "Compared to her, I'm a pushover."

"Ah," Delta faltered, not knowing quite what to say, "I'll look forward to it."

"Anyway," Dr. Hart went on, "Frankie and I have been talking about you, and we believe you'd make a good English major. Have you declared a major yet?"

"Actually, I haven't. But I've thought

about English," Delta said, a little less intimidated. "Lit was always my favorite class in high school, and I do like to write."

"Great. Come to dinner Wednesday, and we'll talk."

"Dinner? At your house?" Delta fought it but couldn't keep the panicked tone out of her voice.

Dr. Hart gathered up her books. "Right."

"Wednesday," Delta repeated.

"Six o'clock. I'll give you directions. It's walking distance from campus."

"All right," Delta said. "Thanks for the invitation."

Dr. Hart drained the last of her coffee and stood up. "It's not the lion's den, you know." She gave a little laugh. "Well, to be perfectly honest Frankie *does* roar a little, I'll admit, but she rarely bites. And she's one hell of a cook. You won't be sorry you came."

EIGHT:
FLINT AND STEEL

Delta stood on the tree-lined street in the gathering dusk and pulled her jacket more closely around her. A few tired leaves let go in a gust of wind and swirled around her feet.

She checked the address Dr. Hart had given her. This was it: a cozy-looking brick Arts and Crafts cottage that sat back from the street with an enormous maple tree arching overhead. The maple hadn't shed yet, and its crimson leaves caught the last glow of sunset and blazed in fiery radiance against the purple sky. Above the maple, one star winked on — Venus, she thought, low in the southwest.

Nervously Delta checked her watch. Five-fifty-seven. Was she dressed all right? She had chosen bell-bottom jeans and a sweater — casual, but not too scruffy. She didn't want to look like an unwashed hippie or a disrespectful teenager.

102

Okay, she thought, *no more stalling.* Exhaling heavily, she opened the gate, latched it behind her, and went to ring the bell.

Immediately all hell broke loose. From behind the closed door Delta heard a wild scrabbling sound, deranged barking, a crash, a curse. At last the door opened on a harried-looking Dr. Hart clutching the collars of two enormous poodles — one black, one white.

"Sit," she commanded.

Delta looked frantically around for something to sit on.

"Not *you,*" Hart amended. "You come in. I hope to God you like dogs."

The poodles had stopped barking and, much to Delta's amazement, were perched on their haunches gazing eagerly at her, their tongues lolling. She had never seen a standard poodle up close before and had always derided the miniature variety as pampered little furballs. These were *real* dogs, muscular and alert, surveying her with intelligent, perceptive eyes.

"Sure, I love dogs," she said, stepping across the threshold and extending a hand for the animals to sniff.

"Meet Bilbo and Frodo, then," the professor said. "Frodo's the black one."

"Hello, boys." Delta got down on one knee

103

and petted each of them in turn.

"Beasts," Dr. Hart muttered. "Well, come on back to the kitchen. Frankie's cooking. Hope you like Chinese."

Only once had Delta seen her writing professor outside the classroom, and now she looked small and unimposing in faded jeans and a navy pullover sweater, with her hair tied up in a ponytail.

Dr. Bowen, hovering over a wok in the kitchen, was also clad in blue jeans, and wore a denim work shirt. Delta hadn't had her for a class yet, but the woman had a reputation for being an excellent professor, hard as nails and extremely demanding. Up close, she reminded Delta a little of Hawthorne's Great Stone Face, with intense, deep-set eyes divided by a permanent frown line, uncompromising features, and short, thick, salt-and-pepper hair.

"Frankie, this is Delta Fox," Dr. Hart said.

She looked up and smiled briefly. "Frances Bowen," she said, wiping a hand on her jeans and extending it in Delta's direction. "We're having egg rolls and crab Rangoon and Cantonese chicken with mushrooms. Oh, and there's sweet and sour soup on the stove." She turned to the dogs, who had come to stand on either side of her. "No begging," she said in a quiet but authoritative voice.

"Out of the kitchen and into your beds."

The two poodles gazed up at her with an utterly crestfallen expression, then went to the breakfast room and lay down on two enormous pillows situated under the windows.

"They're very obedient," Delta said.

"Discipline is a gift to intelligent minds," Bowen said. She arched an eyebrow in Delta's direction. "Remember that when you get into my class."

Dr. Hart had been right. Dr. Bowen was, in Hart's words, "one hell of a cook." Dinner was exquisite, especially the crab Rangoon, which turned out to be delicate, crispy wonton shells filled with cream cheese and crab. Delta had never used chopsticks before, and it took her a while to get the hang of it, but once she mastered the technique, she found the Cantonese chicken to be equally good.

Even more interesting than the dinner, however, was the discussion around the table. Dr. Hart mentioned the Delta Belles and folk music, and from there the conversation segued to protest rallies and civil rights and the state of the nation. It took Frankie Bowen all of ten minutes to get wound up and going strong.

"Anyone who's not outraged," she said,

"isn't paying attention. It's 1966, for God's sake. The Civil Rights Act and the Voting Rights Act have both been passed, but how many black students do we have here at the W? Two? Three? How many high schools in this state are still segregated? How many people are hindered from registering to vote, or required to take literacy tests or pay poll taxes? We might as well be living in *1866,* for all the difference it's made."

"Frankie —" Dr. Hart said, reaching a hand in her direction.

"Don't shush me," Dr. Bowen said, glaring at her. "Somebody needs to speak the truth. King said, 'Injustice anywhere is a threat to justice everywhere.' If we don't stand up for other people's rights, it'll be *our* rights that are taken away next."

Dr. Hart listened patiently until Dr. Bowen's rant wound down and then said, "Well, that was, ah, *impassioned.*"

Dr. Bowen turned and gave a little nod. "Thank you. I'm glad you enjoyed it."

Delta suppressed a chuckle. Dr. Bowen might have a reputation for being forged of steel, but Delta liked her. Most professors lived in the academic netherworld, not bothering with anything that did not relate directly to their areas of expertise. Dr. Bowen was intelligent and articulate and passionate about issues that went well beyond the range of Renaissance literature. She was real. Her friendship with Suzanne Hart was real. Clearly they cared about each other, but they challenged each other too. Like flint on steel, sparks flew and fire was born.

Now that fire rose up inside her, a compelling voice, and for the first time she had a name to put to it: a sense of calling. It felt like driving on a country road with all the windows down, like standing at the ocean at sunrise.

Like leaving home and coming home all at the same time.

NINE:
RAE DAWN'S REVELATION

SOPHOMORE YEAR
SPRING 1967

Alone in her dorm room, Rae Dawn sat staring at her philosophy textbook. She had read the page in front of her three times already, and not a single word of it had registered.

She sank back in her desk chair and looked out over front campus, dappled in light and shadow as moonlight shone through the trees. Across the quad, porch lamps illuminated the wide veranda of the music building. Two students sat on the top step, talking and laughing, and over their voices she could hear the sounds of a piano drifting on the night air. A rectangle of yellow light pooled on the grass outside Manfred Gottlieb's office window.

Philosophy didn't concern her in the least. Oh, she would study it dutifully and would no doubt do well in the class — she had always compensated for her background by being a good student, and those habits were hard to break. But philosophy was a requirement for the education program, and the idea of teaching had fled to the farthest recesses of her mind.

She was now an officially declared music major. She was being taught by Manfred Gottlieb. Nothing else mattered.

She gazed down at the golden rectangle of the professor's window and felt a glow rising up in her, as if the light were a fire that warmed her through to the core. A complicated counterpoint echoed inside her head — a score the professor himself had recently composed and had played for her in his office after her lesson yesterday. A piece of such immense power and emotion that it seemed to swirl within her very soul, filling her like helium, inspiring her and lifting her beyond herself. She couldn't get it out of her mind.

Nor could she rid herself of the nagging voice that told her she had been untruthful with her friends.

Every time she left a lesson with Dr. Gottlieb, Rae Dawn was flying, exultant, empowered as if nothing could touch her. But whenever she thought about her deception, she felt twisted, wrung out, and hung to dry.

With Lauren and Lacy — even with Delta, her closest friend — Rae had kept her secrets. No one except Gottlieb knew about her background, about her parents or the Airstream or growing up on Hobo Creek. Not even about the nature of her scholarship. They all thought she was from New Orleans. They teased her about being exotic and mysterious, and she played along, content to keep them in the dark. On holidays, when she had no choice but to go back to Picayune, she returned to school as soon as possible and spoke to no one about her family.

But she couldn't keep up the charade forever. She couldn't share with them her excitement about Gottlieb's lessons or her change of major or her hope for the future unless they knew the rest. And besides, she was weary of the facade.

She had determined to do it at dinner tonight. But then Tabitha Austin appeared at their table, and Rae Dawn clammed up. She wasn't about to confess all with Tabby hanging on every word.

Rae sighed and raked her hands through her hair. People like Tabby inevitably set her nerves on edge. Rich, beautiful, popular people who seemed utterly convinced that the world owed them everything.

Delta Fox was popular, of course. And pretty. And if not rich, at least well off enough not to have to worry about things like tuition and clothes and books. But Delta was different. She wasn't caught up in herself. She was . . . *real*. Authentic.

That was the word Dr. Gottlieb had used today when they were discussing principles of creativity. "For a composition to live," he said, "it must be *authentic*. It must rise from the very depths of the soul. It may emanate from agony or joy, from struggle or victory. At its best, it comes from all of these, reflecting the breadth and depth of human experience. But whatever else it is, it must be transparent, vulnerable, holding nothing back." He had looked into her eyes with his cloud-blue gaze. "If the composer hides in darkness, the light will not shine through the music."

Now Rae Dawn looked again at the light streaming from the professor's window and made her decision. She snapped the philosophy book shut, slipped on her loafers, and went out into the night.

"May I come in?" Rae asked when Dr. Gottlieb answered her knock.

He stood aside. "By all means."

"I'm sorry to come so late. I saw your office light on, and —"

Gottlieb shrugged. "The hour is of no consequence. I am a night bird."

Rae Dawn smiled. "Night *owl*."

"Ah." The professor gave a little self-deprecating laugh. "I would think that after twenty years my English would be better. But your idioms escape me at times."

Rae entered the office and seated herself in the leather chair across from his desk. "I've been thinking about what you said. About authenticity. Transparency."

He nodded and motioned for her to continue.

Despite her earlier determination, a shudder of nervous tension ran through her. "This isn't really about music, Professor," she said apologetically. "I probably shouldn't be taking up your time."

"I am here for you no matter what you wish to speak about," Dr. Gottlieb said. "Surely we are more than professor and student by now." He laid a hand on his chest. "For my part, I think of you as the daughter I never had. The child of my heart." He smiled. "Besides, for a musician, everything is about music. Life is music. Music is life."

At his words, a radiant warmth shot through Rae Dawn's veins. He was so kind, so accepting. So . . . fatherly. She'd never had a father — not a real one, anyway, and with a shock of recognition she realized that she had grown to think of him that way too.

"All right. Well, you see, I haven't told my friends the truth about myself. About Picayune. About my family and background. I've been rationalizing it, telling myself it doesn't matter. But then you said what you did about hiding in darkness and not letting the light shine through the music —"

Dr. Gottlieb twined his fingers together and inclined his head. "And . . . ?"

"And I need to tell them, don't I? I need to be honest. I can't be authentic in my music if I'm not authentic about myself. Otherwise I'm just blowing smoke out my —" She stopped abruptly and felt heat rise into her face.

"Smoke out your ass?" he finished with just the hint of a smile. "That is the correct phrase, yes?"

"Yes."

"I must admit I do not understand that one very well. I have never personally seen this smoke from the buttocks, and believe it to be a physical impossibility. But then there are many things I have not yet experienced."

Rae Dawn laughed, and her tension dissipated a little. "Anyway, I want to tell them the truth. I really do. But —"

"But you are afraid of how they might respond," the professor finished.

She nodded.

"You fear they might not wish to be your friends any longer if they knew the secrets you have been hiding from them?"

"I don't know," Rae said miserably. "I can't really believe they'd reject me because of my background. But they might not be too happy that I've kept it from them for so long."

"And yet —" He made a rolling motion with his hand.

"And yet I have no real choice."

The professor raised an eyebrow. "We always have choices, child. As long as we live, we choose. You can choose to be honest or not. They can choose to accept you or not. You are responsible not for their reactions, but for your own integrity." He tilted his head. "Besides, how do we ever know that we are fully loved unless we are fully known?"

Rae had intended to return to the dorm, gather her nerve, and then go down to Delta's room to talk. But while she was still pacing, trying to formulate the right words, the door opened and Delta came in.

"Hey," she said, plopping down on Rae

Dawn's bed. "This is such a great space. I'm jealous." She looked around. "Where's your roommate?"

"Gone." Rae shrugged. "She transferred to Rowan Hall to room with a friend, and the Student Affairs office never got around to assigning anyone else. I lucked out."

"I can't imagine why anyone would move out of Castlebury into Rowan," Delta said. "Those dorms on back campus are like rabbit warrens. Small rooms, with high little windows and concrete block walls. Reminds me of jail."

"Like you've ever been in jail." Rae Dawn forced a laugh. "I prefer being on front campus too. It's so peaceful. We may not have private baths or elevators, and sometimes going up three flights of stairs is a pain, but it's a fair trade-off."

Delta wandered over and peered out the window. "I love these tower rooms. Nice view. You've even got a balcony up here." She pointed to a small glass-paneled door angled across a corner of the room.

"Yeah, but I have to keep the door closed. A small colony of bats has taken up residence in the eaves."

Delta shuddered and moved away from the corner.

The superficial talk dissipated like fog, and

115

an uncomfortable silence settled over the room. Delta continued to pace.

"Okay, what's up?" Rae Dawn said at last.

Delta looked at her. "That's exactly what I was about to ask you. You've been acting strange lately."

"Strange?"

"I'm your best friend — at least I think I am. But lately I don't feel as if I know what's going on with you. And you were really rude to Tabby Austin at dinner tonight."

"Rude? How was I rude? I was very restrained, if you ask me. Didn't say a word to her."

"Exactly. You ignored her completely, as if she wasn't even there. It's not like you, Rae Dawn. Something's bothering you."

Rae let out a sigh. This wasn't going the way she had planned, not at all. "Yeah," she said, "something *is* bothering me. But I'm not about to spill my guts in front of Miss Priss."

"What do you have against her? She's a perfectly nice girl."

"Right. She's perfect." Rae Dawn flexed her shoulders and twisted her neck, trying to release the tension. "Want to know the truth? It's *because* she's so perfect. She makes me feel — I don't know. Different. Inferior."

The word was out before Rae could call it back. She felt a tingling chill creep up her spine.

"Inferior?" Delta repeated. "How could you possibly feel inferior? You're smart, you're talented —"

"I've *always* felt inferior," Rae Dawn said, cutting her off. "And it's not a figment of my imagination, Delta. You don't know what it was like, growing up the way I did. You have no idea."

Delta leaned forward, and when she spoke her voice was quiet, entreating. "So tell me."

The compassion, the openness in her voice took Rae Dawn by surprise. No wonder Delta was so popular, so welcome anywhere she went. It wasn't because of her looks or her personality. It was because she cared.

Tears stung Rae's eyes, and she swallowed against the rising emotion. Then the floodgates opened. She propped her elbows on her knees and looked directly into Delta's eyes. "When I was a little girl —" She paused.

"In New Orleans," Delta supplied.

"No, not in New Orleans." Rae Dawn sighed. "New Orleans is a fantasy, a dream wish. I was born and raised thirty miles northeast, outside of Picayune, Mississippi."

"But you told us —"

117

"I made it up, all that stuff about New Orleans. I mean, the places I told you about are real enough. I spent a lot of time there as a teenager. But I never lived there, even though I desperately wanted to. To live *anywhere*, actually, other than Picayune." She took in a ragged breath and went on, describing the broken-down trailer, the experience of living on Hobo Creek, her father's drunken rages, her mother's apathy.

"So anytime I could hitch a ride, I'd escape to New Orleans. I'd hang around the Quarter, listen to the music. Sometimes tourists would take pity on me and give me a little money. All I dreamed of was being able to live in New Orleans and play the piano. And then out of the blue I got a scholarship to come here." She paused. "A resident need stipend."

Delta looked puzzled.

"It's a grant for state residents who have no way of paying for college otherwise," Rae Dawn explained. "Reserved for the most desperately poor." She shook her head. "And I almost didn't get that, because I had a hell of a time just convincing my parents to sign the application papers. They didn't think I needed to go to college. I suppose they expected me to work at Winnie's Washeteria and take care of them for the rest of my life."

The memory of the trailer, and her parents, and the moldy, fishy smell of Hobo Creek caused Rae Dawn to cringe. "I'd had enough of being teased and taunted, of being yelled at or rejected — or worse, invisible. I got on a Greyhound and left it all behind, and once I've graduated I'm never going back there. Never."

"You were laughed at because you were poor?"

"Because I was poor and dirty. Because I wore clothes from the Goodwill. Because my daddy was a drunk and my mama was a zombie. You name it."

"And the worst offenders," Delta ventured, "were little clones of Tabitha Austin. Rich, pretty, privileged."

A stab of remorse caused Rae Dawn to flinch. "I guess so."

Delta smiled. "Or little clones of me."

"Not you," Rae protested. "You're not like that. You're different. You understand. You care."

"But how would you know I cared if you didn't give me a chance?"

Rae Dawn looked up. Delta was gazing at her, and there was no hint of condemnation in her expression. Just a softness that spoke of empathy and affection.

"What makes me different from Tabby?" she asked.

"Well . . . I *know* you."

"Right." Delta nodded. "So let us know *you*. Tell us what's going on in your life."

"As a matter of fact, there's a good deal going on," Rae said. "But I should tell Lauren and Lacy too."

On the way downstairs to round up the twins, Delta considered the implications of Rae Dawn's revelation. She couldn't even imagine what it was like to be that poor, to grow up ashamed of your own parents, to hate going home.

Delta had never considered her parents rich, by any stretch of the imagination. Solidly middle class, with a split-level house, two cars in the driveway, and two children, the Foxes represented the consummate small-town family.

Mama seemed bored once in a while, now that Delta was looking at her family from the outside, with a dispassionate eye. Occasionally Daddy was grouchy if business was in a slump. But nobody got drunk or yelled or cursed, and everybody always had clean clothes and plenty to eat and lots of books and a television to watch Ed Sullivan.

Delta had never known deprivation or

hunger or isolation. Never been teased or bullied. There had never been a question of whether she could or would go to college, or whether there would be money enough for tuition. If she lived to be a hundred, she would never truly understand the kind of upbringing and family life Rae Dawn had endured.

She paused outside the twins' open door and then entered without knocking. Lauren sat at the desk painting her fingernails a violent, ghoulish shade of red, and Lacy sprawled across one of the beds practicing her guitar.

Both of them looked up.

"Hey," Lauren said. Lacy waved and went back to strumming.

"Can the two of you come upstairs for a minute?"

"Give me a sec," Lauren said. "I'm almost done." She held up a hand. "Like it?"

"Ah, sure." Delta winked at Lacy. "It's kind of the color of vampire blood."

Lauren blew on her fingernails and capped the polish, then stood up. "Exactly the look I was going for. Lady Dracula."

Rae Dawn tried to suppress the writhing in her stomach as she sat facing Delta and the twins lined up sideways on her bed, shoulder to shoulder. The image of a firing squad came to mind, but she pushed it aside. She'd already told Delta the bad part, which had turned out not to be so bad after all. But now she had to repeat everything for Lauren and Lacy, and the stiff formality of the situation made her even more anxious.

She blew out a breath. "Okay, here's the deal," she said. "I, ah —" She paused. This hadn't been quite so difficult in the context of the conversation about Tabitha Austin. But just to blurt it out, cold turkey, while Lauren and Lacy sat there eyeing her with curious expressions . . . well, she hadn't the faintest idea how to get started.

"Do you want me to summarize our earlier conversation?" Delta offered.

A surge of gratitude flowed over Rae Dawn. "Please. If you don't mind."

"All right." Delta adjusted her position on the bed so she could make eye contact with the twins. "It's like this — we all thought Rae was from New Orleans, but she isn't. She's from Picayune, Mississippi, and she grew up really poor, and she's here on a need scholarship, and she didn't want to tell us about it because she was ashamed." She said all of this very quickly, then turned back toward Rae.

Stunned, Rae Dawn gaped at Delta. She

hadn't been prepared for such a blunt, trun-
cated narrative of her past. And yet it seemed
easier, somehow, to hear it in such a matter-
of-fact tone, without any drama.

"What, you're embarrassed about your
family?" Lauren asked.

"Yes." Rae Dawn nodded. "My father is an
alcoholic. A drunk. My mother pretty much
checked out of life years ago, except she still
keeps on breathing. I was raised in a broken-
down trailer and never knew where my next
meal was coming from. It was —" She
paused. "Bad."

"And you were self-conscious about telling
us?"

"Yes. No." Rae frowned. "Not self-
conscious. Mortified. Humiliated."

"What a load of rubbish," Lauren said.
"For God's sake, girl, we don't give a damn
about your family."

"Well, yes, we do," Lacy broke in. "We give
a damn about how it has affected you and
hurt you. But it doesn't matter where you
came from. It matters who you are."

Relief rolled over Rae Dawn, a cleansing,
healing wave. She began to tell them the
whole story, even parts Delta hadn't heard.
Her visceral response to music, the longing
to play and write and be somebody. Her love
of New Orleans, details of her furtive visits

as a teenager, her fantasies about being part of the music scene in the Quarter. Her ultimate escape from Picayune via the scholarship offered to her. The way she had resigned herself to becoming a teacher instead of a musician because it gave her security, a means of supporting herself.

And then, finally, she came to the best part. The miracle. She told them about Manfred Gottlieb listening outside the practice room and asking her to come to his office.

"I don't know how he knew about me," Rae Dawn said, "but it was like he had an inside track on my life. He *understood*."

She judiciously omitted the part about *why* he understood. She wouldn't feed the rumors about him or betray his confidence.

"Anyway," Rae Dawn concluded, "he's been giving me lessons. Teaching me — for *free*." She beamed at them. "He believes I have real talent, both as a professional musician and as a composer. And he's helping me."

Hoots and whistles and applause filled the little tower room as Rae Dawn's friends celebrated with her. They hugged her and laughed and talked over one another. At last a serious-looking brunette stomped down the hall and stood in the doorway staring at them until they all shut up.

"Sorry," Rae said, glancing at the clock on her bedside table. "I didn't know it was so late." It was after eleven, and ten o'clock was the start of quiet time in the dorm. They were lucky the house mother hadn't heard them.

"Never mind about that," the girl said. "I'm just passing the word. There's a moon tonight, and the ginkgo is shedding!"

With a whoop and a holler, the four of them trooped down the stairs and out into a beautiful October night. Someone had built a bonfire in the fire pit on front campus. "Dean of Students has brought s'mores!" a tall upperclassman informed them as she dashed by on her way to the tree.

Together they ambled over to the ginkgo tree and watched as the yellow, fan-shaped leaves cascaded down in lazy spirals. All around them, girls were jostling and jumping to grab a leaf before it touched the ground.

"Catch it!" Lauren called to Lacy. "You'll find the love of your life before next spring!"

"Do you believe this stuff?" Delta asked Rae.

Rae Dawn shrugged and held up both hands in an attitude of surrender. A single ginkgo leaf drifted into her palm and lay there quivering like a golden butterfly.

"Not really," she said. "But I'll keep it anyway."

Delta snatched a falling leaf from the air and stuffed it into the pocket of her pajama top. "Come on, everybody," she said as she grabbed each of the twins by an arm. "Let's go get some s'mores before they're all gone."

Out of the corner of her eye, Rae caught a glimpse of burnished copper illuminated by the moonlight. She turned. Tabitha Austin was standing under the ginkgo alone, with a single leaf caught in her hair.

Gently Rae Dawn pulled it out and handed it to her. "This is yours, I believe." She hesitated. "Why don't you come on over and have s'mores with us?"

After a moment's indecision, Tabby nodded. "All right," she said in a tentative voice. "I — ah, I've been meaning to tell you. I really enjoy your music — with the Delta Belles and all. You're so gifted — on the piano, I mean. And your voice. You could be a star."

"Thanks." Rae Dawn smiled, and she felt something warm and accepting break open inside her. For the first time in her life, she didn't feel ashamed to be standing next to the likes of Tabitha Austin.

TEN:
THE PROMISE OF THE GINKGO TREE

SENIOR YEAR
FEBRUARY 1969

In the empty parking lot behind the maintenance building, Lacy sat in the back seat of a 1964 Chevy Corvair convertible making out with Trip Jenkins. The top was up, but a weak spot in the roof dripped rain onto her neck, and her shoulder blade pressed painfully into the edge of the seat.

She struggled to a more comfortable position and pulled away slightly. The windows were fogging up. A raindrop slithered down her spine, causing her to shiver.

"What's wrong?" Trip asked. He shifted his long legs, but there wasn't enough room, and his knees knocked hard into the back of the driver's seat. "Ow." He grinned and raked a hand through his already disheveled hair. "Not the best venue for getting hot and heavy, I guess."

"It's all right. I have to go soon anyway." Lacy peered at her watch. "Dinner's in fifteen minutes."

Trip heaved himself up a little and retucked his shirt while Lacy regarded him. The ginkgo tree had taken its own sweet time, but it had finally come through. This was the love of her life, the man of her dreams. She was certain of it, even though they'd only been dating for six weeks.

He was a senior at State, twenty-five miles due west of the W. Drop-dead gorgeous and smart to boot. A pre-law student who bore a striking resemblance to Richard Chamberlain, with his lean muscled body, ash blond hair, and boyish smile.

And except for a fluke, a twist of fate or magic or miracle, Lacy never would have met him.

"Lacy, you've *got* to go," Lauren said. "I've borrowed Delta's car, but she wouldn't let me take it unless I promised you'd come too, in case I had a little too much to drink. Steve's expecting me. We haven't seen each other since last year."

"Last year was two weeks ago," Lacy said.

"A technicality." Lauren let out an exaggerated sigh. "We went out on December 18, and then he went to his parents' for Christmas and we went home to Hillsborough and I haven't seen him since."

"You talk on the phone every damn day."

"It's not the same, and you know it." Lauren hesitated. "Well, maybe you don't know it, but —"

Thus, with much wheedling and begging, Lauren dragged an unwilling Lacy over to State to attend a fraternity New Year's party where she was meeting her current boyfriend, Steve Treadwell. The moment they crossed the threshold into the frat house Lauren predictably disappeared, leaving Lacy to fend for herself.

The noise in the house was deafening. From some unseen stereo, the Beatles were belting out "Back in the USSR." Couples were dancing, spilling beer, making out; the crowd was so dense you could barely walk across a room without getting caught up in the surge of bodies. Lacy accepted a beer in a plastic cup from a guy in a maroon football jersey and found an overstuffed armchair in a corner. For twenty minutes she sat there, watching the action and feeling desperately out of place and furious at her twin. She was just about to go track down Lauren, get Delta's keys, and leave her sister to find her own way home when someone sidled up to her and perched on the arm of her chair.

"Hey," he said. "I'm Trip Jenkins, and I'd like to know how such an adorable girl can look so thoroughly miserable." He took her hand, led her to a quiet room off the back of the frat house, and shut the door. It was a library of sorts, with books lining the walls, comfortable sofas and chairs, and gas logs burning in the fireplace.

Trip was the perfect gentleman. For the next three hours, while his frat brothers were groping their dates in various dark alcoves of the house, the two of them talked, ate junk food, and drank about a gallon of Coke.

Trip, amazingly enough, was not involved with anyone else, nor was he a sociopath or a mama's boy. He had, as it turned out, been dating a girl who had graduated early and gone on to Harvard Law, but they had broken up three months before.

"The long-distance thing was just too difficult," he admitted. "I've been accepted to Ole Miss, Duke, and Emory, so whatever law school I end up at, we'd still be separated. We finally realized that it wasn't going to work. It was a mutual decision." He grinned sheepishly. "Besides, I'm not so sure it's a good idea to have two lawyers in the house. Makes for a lot of arguments."

"Well then, I'd better leave now," Lacy said. "I'm in pre-law too."

He flushed a bright pink. "I'm sorry. I didn't mean —"

"Just kidding. I'm actually a secondary ed major. History and social science. I just started my practice teaching." She winked at him, and he grinned back.

Lacy had dated a number of boys during her years at the W — mostly guys Lauren lined up for her, double dates, a lot of first dates that didn't go anywhere. But always, when Lauren was around, Lacy felt like an also-ran, a second choice. When the two of them double dated, she could see her own date's eyes drifting toward Lauren, who perpetually held the center of attention. Finally Lacy quit going out with Lauren and her boyfriends altogether, and turned her concentration to her studies.

And now here she was, in a frat house of all places, having a wonderful conversation with a man who didn't even know her twin sister existed.

"Listen," he said finally, "it's after midnight, and I really don't want to end this, but I have a study group early tomorrow morning."

"On Saturday?"

"Yeah." He shrugged. "Can we go out sometime — on a real date, I mean?"

"Of course," Lacy said immediately, then

cursed herself as he looked away. Now she had done it. She had sounded too eager, and guys hated that.

He chewed on his lower lip for a minute, then gazed directly into her eyes. "I don't want to sound too eager or anything, but I also don't want to play games. I like you, Lacy — a lot. I want to see you again. So just tell me and put me out of my misery, okay? How long do I need to wait before I call you?"

"Have you got a pen?"

"Let me look." He dug in his pocket and came up with one.

"Give me your hand."

He extended his left hand, and she wrote the dorm telephone number across his palm. "Call me before you wash this off," she said. "If you wait more than two days, I'll know your personal hygiene isn't up to par, and we'll be history before we ever get started."

He put an arm around her and walked her into the living room, where the party was beginning to wind down. "Do you need me to take you home?"

"No, I came with —" She paused. "I've got a ride. Let's just say good night here, all right?"

He leaned down and kissed her — a kiss much more chaste than Lacy would have liked, but very gentle and sweet. "Tomorrow. We'll talk tomorrow."

"Where'd you go?" Trip said, running a finger lightly across the nape of her neck.

"Oh, sorry." Lacy smiled. "I was just thinking about the first time we met."

"That horrible fraternity party." Trip grimaced. "To tell you the truth, I can't stand living in the frat house. If it weren't for my dad, I'd never have pledged at all."

"The party was pretty awful," she agreed. "But it turned out just fine for me."

"For both of us." He leaned forward. "Anything you regret about that night?"

"Well, maybe one thing."

Trip's eyebrows arched up into his hairline. "What's that?"

"The kiss."

"I shouldn't have kissed you?"

"No." She chuckled. "It was the *way* you kissed me. So . . . restrained."

"I was *trying* to be considerate. We'd only just met."

"Yes, but I was already crazy about you. I wanted you to kiss me and never stop. I went home worried that you might not be any good at it, and kissing is *very* important to me."

He gathered her into his arms and kissed

her again. Rain drummed on the cloth roof of the Corvair in time with the pounding in her veins.

"I guess we've got that kissing thing taken care of," he whispered.

"I guess."

"So," he said, leaning closer, "when do you think we might —" He paused. "You know."

Lacy's stomach began to writhe. This wasn't the first time he had asked. She loved him, she really did, and there was no question that she was physically attracted to him. But the idea of sex — not just petting, but going all the way — was foreign territory for her, and a little scary. What if she didn't like it — or worse, if he didn't like doing it with *her*? What if she got pregnant? What if, afterward, he didn't want her any more?

Overhead, a shrill whistle sounded, an eardrum-splitting noise, given that they were sitting directly under it.

"What the hell is that?" Trip yelled over the shriek.

"The warning whistle for dinner," Lacy said when the racket had subsided. "Five minutes till they close the doors." She grinned at him. "It doesn't sound that loud from elsewhere on campus."

He opened the door, pushed the seat forward, and moved to the front behind the wheel. "I'll drive you up there."

Lacy climbed over into the front seat as well. Two minutes later she kissed him good-bye, ducked out of the car, and ran through the rain into the dining hall.

"Where have you been?" Lauren demanded before Lacy even had a chance to sit down. "You're all wet."

"Yeah, well, it's raining outside, isn't it?" Lacy ran her fingers through her dripping hair, removed her raincoat, and slung it across the back of the chair.

"So, where *have* you been?" Lauren repeated.

"What Lauren means," Delta interpreted, "is that we tried to find you and were a little worried about you."

Lacy began to laugh. "What Lauren *means,*" she corrected, "is that she's pissed off at me for *not informing her of my every move.*" She finished the sentence in a hiss, through gritted teeth, and shot a mocking scowl at her twin.

"Actually, we were *all* wondering, when you didn't show up for practice this afternoon," said Rae Dawn. "We were going to work on a couple of new songs for the senior banquet, remember? Simon and Garfunkel's 'Sound of Silence' and 'Flowers Never Bend

135

with the Rainfall.' "

Lacy slapped a palm to her forehead. "Damn! I forgot. I'm sorry, I really am." She looked around the table. "What else have I forgotten? We don't have a gig this weekend, do we?"

"No." Delta shook her head. "There's an antiwar protest at the courthouse on Saturday afternoon, and I'm going, but we're not scheduled to sing or anything."

"That's a relief," Lacy said. "I don't usually lose track of things like that. I guess my mind is somewhere else."

Lauren leaned in and gave her sister a rakish look. "Don't think we don't know where your mind *is* these days," she said. "Button your blouse, Lace; you look like a tramp."

Lacy's stomach lurched, and her fingers went instinctively to the front of her blouse. All the buttons were firmly in place.

"Gotcha!" Lauren gloated. "Now, are you going to tell us about this secret love of yours?"

"Details, please," Delta added. "You've been keeping him under wraps for over a month. All we know about him is his name and the fact that he's a senior at State."

"And *handsome*," Lauren added. "He's in Steve's fraternity, but even I haven't met him yet."

"Well . . ." Lacy thought about it for a minute. She had her reasons for keeping quiet about Trip, and yet maintaining her privacy had its drawbacks. It had been hard not to tell them; she was in love, and she wanted to shout it from the roof of the administration building. She wanted them to be happy with her, to share her joy. And as much as she hated to admit it, she wanted their approval.

"All right," she said at last. "As you know, his name is Trip Jenkins, and —"

"What kind of a weird name is that? Trip?" Delta asked.

Lacy raised an eyebrow. "No stranger than *Delta,* I'd say. Especially when you live in Stone Mountain." Everybody laughed. "His real name is Thomas — Thomas Edward Jenkins III. He was named after his father and grandfather, but three Toms in a family was pretty hard to negotiate. Thus, Trip."

"Oh, like in *triple,*" Delta said.

"Exactly. He's a senior at State — an honor student, I might add — and he'll be going to law school in the fall."

"Where's he going?"

Lacy shrugged. "He's been accepted at Ole Miss, Duke, and Emory. Personally, I'm hoping for Duke."

"Is Duke close to home?" Rae Dawn

asked. "I don't know North Carolina geography very well."

"Hillsborough to Durham? It's practically in our backyard," Lauren answered. "Ten or twelve miles, maybe." She narrowed her eyes at Lacy. "You're thinking marriage, aren't you?"

Lacy felt herself flush. "Well, he hasn't asked me yet, if that's what you mean. But yes, I think it's getting pretty serious."

Rae Dawn looked skeptical. "How long have you been dating this guy? A month?"

"Almost two months," Lacy said. "Well . . . six and a half weeks. But you know, don't you? When it's right, you just . . . *know*." Rae opened her mouth to protest, but Lacy rushed on. "That doesn't mean we'd get married right away. I could live at home for a while, try to get a teaching job while he starts law school."

"Aren't you getting a little ahead of yourself?" Delta asked. "It's customary to get engaged before you get married."

"And to introduce your intended to your *family*," Lauren chimed in.

"And to your *friends*," Rae Dawn added.

"All right, already!" Lacy laughed. "I suppose you're right. It is time you met him. And just for the record, Lauren, I'll invite him to come to North Carolina during spring break."

"Great," Lauren said. "Maybe I'll ask Steve to come too. Now, when do we get to meet the wonder boy?"

"How about Sunday dinner?" Lacy narrowed her eyes and looked around the table. "That way you'll already be dressed up so I won't have to make excuses for you."

They all seemed to think this was a good idea, and Lacy went back to her catalog of all Trip's wonderful features. She was gushing, she knew, but she couldn't seem to help herself. Once the floodgate had been lifted, everything she was holding inside rushed to get out. It was pure glory, telling them about the man she loved, having her feelings for him confirmed over and over again in her heart.

One little tooth of nagging doubt chiseled away at her gut, but she couldn't identify it, nor could she make it go away. One small torque of uncertainty, a nervous flutter in her stomach.

Ridiculous. He *was* the right one; she was sure of it. Trip loved her, and she loved him. They were perfect for each other. And nothing — *nothing* — could ever change that.

ELEVEN:
THE GREEN-EYED
MONSTER

After dinner Lacy had run off through the pouring rain to meet with her student teacher group in the library, and for once Lauren was glad to have the room to herself. Delta was crunching a deadline on one of Dr. Bowen's innumerable lit papers, and Rae Dawn, as usual, was practicing in the music building. A couple of girls from the other end of the floor had invited her to come down to their room and study with them, but Lauren had made an excuse about a project due the next morning.

There was no project. Lauren and her fellow elementary ed students were scheduled to be at the local kindergarten tomorrow, and she didn't exactly have to prepare to do ABCs and teeth-brushing. She simply did not want to be with people tonight. She spread a towel across the top of the door — the W's dorm symbol for "Do Not Disturb" — and shut herself in.

Normally Lauren would do almost anything to avoid being alone. From the cradle she had been with Lace, with her family, with dozens of other friends. Since puberty she had been surrounded by boys who clamored for her attention. Always there had been laughter and joking and endless activity, a manic white noise that kept her from having to think too much.

But tonight she *needed* to think. Needed to figure out the source of this burning in her gut, this heavy weight that lay over her like a shroud.

Lauren had little experience with self-examination, and she hardly knew where to start. She knew only that the feeling had begun over dinner, as her twin sister had talked — finally — about Trip Jenkins, about the newfound wonder of their love.

The cynic in her was tempted to blow off her sister's joy as so much naïveté. Lacy had always been an innocent. She had never been in an intimate relationship, didn't have a clue what love was about. Lauren could have told her a thing or two about men, about how they used that four-letter word to lure a girl on until they succeeded in coercing her into acting on the three-letter word that consumed their every waking moment.

Not that Lauren didn't like sex. She had

lost her virginity on prom night her senior year in high school, with a bony basketball star named Phil Putnam. He had been an inefficient, groping, selfish lover — most high school boys were, she supposed — and she clearly recalled the sensation of revulsion and disbelief when she caught her first glimpse of his penis. The experience had been . . . well, not exactly electrifying. But once that ship had sailed, there was no turning back.

After Phil, Lauren had known a succession of boys, even a few who might be counted as men — not hundreds, of course, but several. Enough to realize that for the male of the species, sex was the end goal of all things romantic.

The pattern rarely varied: a few walks in the park, a few dinners, a few movies, all of which inevitably led to a dark car in some isolated make-out spot, where kissing and petting led to panting arousal and eventually to an uncomfortable, half-clothed coupling in a back seat littered with hamburger wrappers and beer cans. And afterward, when the dinners and movies and long walks had vanished into the mist, the guy became either possessive or indifferent, leaving nothing but the sex as common ground between them.

A few of Lauren's boyfriends had been

more skilled than Phil Putnam and had managed, even in less than ideal surroundings, to awaken her to her own pleasures. But she had discovered that pleasure itself could be disturbing when her mind and heart did not follow where her body was going. On one or two occasions, she could actually recall looking down to see some oaf sucking on her breast, fumbling to get his hand between her legs, while she reacted with little more than mild surprise. She was, for all intents and purposes, somewhere else — planning a midterm project or making a list of Christmas presents she needed to buy.

Her current steady, Steve Treadwell, was by far the best of them, the most attentive, the nicest, the least demanding. But even with Steve, Lauren had never felt for a man what her virginal sister obviously felt for Trip Jenkins.

Lacy actually *knew* Trip, it seemed. Knew how he thought and felt about things like politics and religion and the state of the world. Understood his passions and dreams, why he wanted to become a lawyer, what he hoped to accomplish with his life. According to Lacy, they talked. They cared about each other. Their relationship was based on more, much more, than the convergence of body parts.

And Lauren was jealous.

When the word darted into her mind unbidden, she tried first to ignore it and then to bat it away. But it kept swooping back, a bold blue jay harassing a prowling cat. Vaguely she recalled something from sophomore lit, some Shakespeare play, she thought, where a character referred to jealousy as a big green monster.

Never in her life had Lauren been jealous of Lacy. Why should she? For twenty-one years Lauren had been the one in the spotlight, garnering all the attention. Lauren was the one who had the boyfriends, the popularity, the good looks —

Her mental processes squealed to a halt. Wait a minute. How could she possibly believe she was prettier than Lacy, when they were twins? These days Lacy kept her hair short, but other than the haircut, the two of them were virtually identical: same facial features, same eyes, lips, teeth. Even the same figure, down to the half-inch.

And yet, Lauren realized, she had *always* felt that way; she had just never admitted it to herself. All these years she had felt superior to Lacy — had *needed* to feel superior.

Now she was on the outside looking in. Lacy had Trip, and she had . . . Steve. Lacy had love and passion and joy and excitement, while Lauren had —

Sex.

Good sex, sometimes. But nothing to build a future on.

The bitter taste of bile rose up in her throat. She went and leaned against the window, where raindrops pelted like rubber bullets across the frozen glass.

A shiver overtook her. But even as she stood there trembling, Lauren could not deny the truth: The chill came not from the February storm, but from an icy emptiness deep in her own soul.

TWELVE:
SOMETHING MORE THAN MUSIC

Rae Dawn sat slumped over the piano in Rehearsal Room A, shivering from the rain that had soaked her on the way to the Music Hall. For the past hour she had been playing frenetically, trying to escape the writhing in her stomach, the throbbing in her head. But it was no good.

All during dinner, while Lacy had been extolling the virtues of her new love, Rae Dawn had managed to keep a cheerful face plastered on, had even forced herself to ask a few questions and pretend to be happy for Lacy.

And Rae *was* happy for her. Truly she was, deep down.

She was just not happy for herself.

None of it made any sense, these conflicting feelings that assaulted her. She had what she wanted, didn't she? She had a wonderful mentor in Dr. Gottlieb. She had prospects and possibilities for after graduation. The professor even had a contact in New Orleans, someone who owned a jazz club and might be willing to give her a chance. She was passionate about her music, loved what she was doing. Why then did she have this insane, unpredictable response to Lacy's good news?

Immediately after dinner, she had sequestered herself in the rehearsal room, as she always did when she was upset or confused or had something she needed to figure out. Music soothed her soul, set her mind free, enabled her to get to the deepest, most hidden emotions of her heart.

But this time, what came to the surface when she played only served to intensify her agony. Every tender ballad, every hot jazz riff, every plaintive love song reminded her of the adoration in Lacy's voice when she talked about Trip, the light in her face, the fire in her eyes. The sensations crashed in upon her, a clashing dissonance, a cacophony of desire and self-contempt.

She played until her fingers grew numb, trying to outrun the emotions. But she hadn't succeeded. The feelings followed her, terrified her, a rabid dog snarling at her heels.

She was jealous. Jealous of Lacy Cantrell.

She had known jealousy before, of course. As a child she had envied those around her whose lives were easy. Kids who had relatively normal parents, a decent home, enough to eat, new clothes rather than hand-me-downs. She had felt the gut-twisting burn, had understood, when she had finally read *Othello,* why Iago called jealousy "the green-eyed monster which doth mock the meat it feeds on."

But she had never been jealous of a *friend.* Never envied the good fortune of someone she had grown to love. And certainly never thought herself capable of being jealous because Lacy had finally, deservedly, fallen in love.

It simply wasn't possible.

After all she had endured growing up — her father's liquor-induced rages, her mother's gaping emptiness — the last thing in the world she wanted was to marry some man and risk living out the rest of her days as a stranger to herself, ripped to pieces by the shards of her own shattered dreams.

She had her music. She had a future.

But suddenly, unexpectedly, it wasn't enough.

The truth overwhelmed her, and she sat rooted to the piano bench, sobbing, her tears dripping onto the keys. How long she stayed that way, she did not know, but at last her weeping subsided, and her mind began to drift.

She thought of Delta's major professors, Dr. Bowen and Dr. Hart. She had spent a bit of time with them now and then, when the Delta Belles had sung for voter registration rallies and civil rights protests. She had even been invited for dinner at their house a time or two.

They had never done anything inappropriate in her presence, had barely even touched. But nevertheless, Rae Dawn saw it. The love between them. The commitment. The *connection*. A connection that, because of society's prejudices, had been and would continue to be unspoken, unacknowledged.

The injustice of it sliced through her like a hot knife.

For a long time, she had been dimly aware of a truth lurking deep beneath the surface of her consciousness. A dragon, a subterranean beast waiting for the moment it would strike. But she had kept it leashed, suppressed it, escaped it through her music. Now the dragon reared its head again, and she could feel it stirring within her.

Yes, she was jealous. But not because she wanted what Lacy had. She was jealous because Lacy had the freedom to speak it, to let the world know how she felt and what she hoped for.

Rae Dawn's desire was different, and yet the same. She wanted to be a professional musician, certainly, but she wanted more than that too.

A life, a love. A house and two dogs and a leisurely late breakfast of waffles and scrambled eggs on a Saturday morning. A piano in the bay window and someone to listen when she played.

The awareness writhed within her, a truth she could never declare the way Lacy Cantrell had declared her love for Trip Jenkins.

Because that *someone,* in her imagination, was not a husband but a partner.

Not a man but a woman.

Thirteen:
Springtime in
Stone Mountain

Spring Break
March 1969

Delta stepped out of the car and stretched. At the end of the driveway, twin forsythia bushes draped their yellow skirts across the lawn. Up next to the house, azaleas stooped under a load of blossoms — pale pink, magenta, and snowy white. Fragrant blue and yellow hyacinths lined the sidewalk. On a single breath she inhaled the scent of new grass and pine trees and daffodils.

It was spring. She was home.

She barely had time to exhale, however, before the front door slammed open and a small towheaded missile launched through the door and rocketed toward her.

"Delta! Delta! You're *here!* You're finally here!"

Cassie gave a flying leap and hurtled into her arms, knocking her back on her heels.

Delta staggered, recovered herself, dropped her purse. Then, laughing, she embraced her little sister, swung her around, and set her back on the ground.

"You're getting so big!" she marveled, though it wasn't really true. Cassie had always been compact and petite, and although she had grown a little, she was still very small. Over her sister's bony shoulder she caught a glimpse of her mother and father standing on the front stoop. Mama had a handkerchief in one hand and was pulling distractedly at one frayed corner. Daddy's eyes looked empty and tired. In that unguarded moment, Delta saw something she knew instinctively she wasn't meant to see. But she couldn't quite articulate what it was.

Then her mother was bustling down the steps, pasting on a smile. "Well, come on in, DeeDee," she said while Cassie danced in wild circles around her sister. "Cassie, where are your shoes?"

Cassie shrugged. "Look, Delta, I can do a cartwheel." She flung herself onto the grass, all elbows and knees, flipped over, and landed on her skinny little butt.

"That's enough, Cassie," Mama said, a bit more sternly this time. "Get inside and put on your shoes — it's not summer *yet*. Delta can watch you perform later."

Reluctantly, Cassie obeyed. Delta followed her father as he went to the car and extracted her suitcase from the trunk.

"Car running all right?"

Delta smiled. It was such a dad thing to say. "Yes, Daddy. It's running just fine. I love it."

"Can't beat a Ford. I'll change the oil and rotate the tires while you're here. Maybe do a tune-up, too." He stroked the rear fender. "Needs washing."

He had bought the used car for her the summer between her sophomore and junior years — a silver '63 Falcon convertible with a black top and matching leather interior. The leather got hot in the summer, but otherwise the little car was a great ride. Daddy claimed to have purchased it in self-defense, so he wouldn't have to make the trip to and from the college every spring and fall. But Delta knew better. He had fallen in love with the Falcon and wouldn't dare buy it for himself.

He was still standing there, holding her suitcase in one hand and fondling the fender with the other.

"Want to take it for a spin, Daddy?"

He shook his head but didn't smile the way Delta had expected him to. "Your mama would kill me. Let's go inside. Maybe later

153

the two of us can take a drive out to the park to see the carving. There's something I need to talk to you about."

Delta frowned. "Is something wrong, Daddy? Mama's not sick, is she? She looks a little — I don't know. Worn out. Worried."

"Later," he said. Then he hefted her suitcase and headed toward the house.

Dinner that first evening home turned out to be a boisterous, chaotic affair with no time for real conversation. Mama had cooked all of Delta's favorite foods — pot roast with potatoes and carrots, creamed baby peas, and, for dessert, a homemade buttermilk pound cake with sliced strawberries.

She had also invited Ben Rutledge, who was on spring break as well but had stayed in Atlanta once he found out Delta was coming home. Besides, Ben never turned down an opportunity to feast on Mama's cooking. According to the bits and pieces of conversation that swirled around the table, it appeared he came to dinner at least once a week.

Since the moment she had arrived, Delta had known something wasn't quite right. Now her antennae were up, and she began to see things that as a child growing up in this house she had never noticed. The way her parents didn't really talk, or even look at one another, but used Cassie — and even Ben — as a kind of buffer between them. Her mind cast back to the pre-Cassie years, when it was just the three of them in the house. Mama cooked and cleaned and did whatever else mothers did. Daddy got up every morning and went to work, came home and watched the news, ate dinner and fell asleep in front of the television. Mama knitted. Beyond that, they had few other interests, and none in common.

Had they been doing this all their lives, passing back and forth like two flashlight beams in a darkened room, and she had never noticed?

"Tell my daughter about the progress on Lee's horse, Ben," Daddy said. "She thinks I'm totally obsessed —"

"Have some more potatoes," Mama said. "I know you like them. Why, last time you were here —"

"Ben and Delta, sit-tin' in a tree, k-i-s-s—"

"Cassie! None of that!" Mama reprimanded. "You'll embarrass your sister."

Cassie's bright eyes darted from Delta to Ben and back again. "Ben, what are you going to do when you get out of college?" she asked with a teasing note in her voice.

155

Ben leaned across the table and tousled her hair. "You know perfectly well what I'm going to do, Squirt," he said. "We've talked about this a hundred times. I'm studying to be an architect. I'll design houses, maybe, or skyscrapers or bridges."

Cassie pounced. "So when you and Delta get *married,* you'll build her a house and you'll live together and spend all your time hugging and kissing and —"

"Cassandra Elizabeth Fox!" Mama snapped. "Unless you want to be sent to your room right this very minute —"

The little girl drew herself up and gazed placidly at her mother. "All right, Mama, if you're determined to stand in the way of my education. . . ."

Ben let out a howl of laughter. "How old are you, Cass? Thirty?"

"Eight and three-quarters," she said. "But I'm very advanced for my age."

Everyone was too full for dessert right away, so after dinner Delta and Ben went out onto the covered patio and sat in the porch swing that hung suspended from the beams. Now and then Delta could see Cassie peering out at them through the blinds.

Ben put an arm around her and pushed his foot against the paving stones to get the

156

swing moving. "They all expect it, you know."

Delta leaned against him and looked across the back yard at the rising moon. "Expect what?"

"For us to get married, of course. Cassie's just repeating what she's heard."

"Cassie," Delta said, "makes things up just fine without anyone's help."

Ben chuckled. "Quite true."

Delta gazed into his eyes. He was so sweet, and she was so content in his presence. Ben Rutledge was like an old pair of jeans that had been washed a thousand times. A perfect fit. Familiar, soft, and comfortable.

The metaphor continued to spin out in her mind. Preshrunk. Faded. Predictable.

Her mind shifted to Lacy Cantrell's romance with Trip Jenkins. She recalled with vivid clarity the spark in Lacy's eyes when she finally broke her silence and told them about Trip. The passion. The anticipation. The goose-bump, fire-in-the-veins, mice-in-the-stomach thrill that Delta knew she would never, ever have with Ben.

Still, he was a good man. Solid. Reliable. Already part of the family. As Mama had pointed out, she could do a lot worse.

On Wednesday, five days into spring break,

Delta was out in the backyard, playing Wiffle ball with Cassie. Delta was getting pretty adept at making the perforated plastic ball curve and dip, which frustrated Cassie to no end. The kid was accustomed to doing things right, and a strike rather than a home run was simply not acceptable.

Finally she threw down the bat in exasperation, ran to the patio, and flung herself into the swing. Delta followed, sweaty and breathless.

"That was fun." She pulled the rubber band out of her hair and rearranged her ponytail.

"For you, maybe." Cassie crossed her arms and scowled in the direction of the back fence.

"Ah, c'mon, don't be a spoilsport. It *was* fun. Admit it."

Delta poked at her ribs and began to tickle her. "Okay, I give," Cassie said at last. She leaned against her sister and heaved an exaggerated sigh. "I just hate to lose."

"Lose?" Delta repeated. "There's no winning or losing in Wiffle ball. Hell, it's not the world series."

Cassie's eyes grew wide. "You *swore*."

"Oh. Yeah, well, I apologize. I guess shouldn't have said *hell* in front of you."

"I don't care about that," Cassie said with

158

an impatient shake of her head. "Can you teach me to do it?"

"Teach you to swear?" Delta laughed. "Honey, it's not something you have to be taught. You just pick it up. *When you're older.*"

"Other kids at school do it, and they're my age."

Delta regarded her sister, taking in the disheveled blonde hair, the round blue eyes, the heart-shaped little face, already tanned though spring had just begun. At five, Cassie had possessed the appearance of a three-year-old and the vocabulary of a high school junior. Now, at almost nine, she looked to be six or seven at most, and although she was the smartest kid in her class, she undoubtedly got teased at school for being so diminutive. It probably didn't help any that she had skipped third grade.

"Listen," Delta said, pulling Cassie onto her lap and putting her arms around her, "you don't have to swear to be accepted. You don't have to pretend to be tough. You're intelligent and gifted and beautiful. Just be yourself."

Cassie picked at a loose thread on the hem of her shorts. "I'm not beautiful. *You're* beautiful."

Delta suppressed a smile, noting that her

little sister did not challenge the notion that she was intelligent or gifted. "When I was your age, or maybe a tad older, I had a mouthful of metal and pimples and knobby knees."

"Did not!" Cassie objected, but she seemed heartened by this bit of news.

"Did so. Go look at Mama's photograph albums. I was hideous."

The child squirmed her bony butt in Delta's lap until she was sitting more or less upright. "Like the ugly duckling growing into a swan," she mused. "Okay, maybe I do have a chance. The genetic combinations seemed to work pretty well in your case."

Delta gazed at her. "What do you know about genetic combinations?"

"I know plenty," Cassie declared. "I've been reading all about it. Genes are carried in the DNA, and the combination of genes from your mother and father determine what you'll look like, talents and abilities you'll have, maybe even personality. Did you know that it's impossible for two blue-eyed parents to have a brown-eyed child? Blue is recessive — that's Mama, she's got two blue chromosomes. Daddy has brown eyes, which is dominant, but he must have a blue chromosome, because I came out with blue eyes instead of brown, like yours. Do

you realize there's a one in four chance

She went on that way, talking at abou hundred facts per minute, until so synapse in her brain jolted her onto a diff ent track.

"So, are you and Ben going to get ma ried?"

"Shit," Delta muttered.

Cassie perked up. "Ooh, that's a good one. I should write it down."

"Forget I said it. Listen, Cassie, whatever you might have overheard, Ben and I have been friends since junior high. *Friends*. That's all, at least for now. Maybe he's the right one, and maybe he's not. I don't even know if I want to marry *anyone*. Maybe I —" Delta stopped short. Cassie was biting her lower lip, and her wide eyes glittered with unshed tears. "What's the matter, Cass?"

"How do you know for sure?" she said in a gritty whisper. "How do you *know* who's the right one? The one who will stay forever?"

Delta narrowed her eyes. "What's this about?"

The tears welled up and brimmed over. "You'd better ask Mama and Daddy," she said. "I'm not supposed to tell."

But Delta didn't have a chance to ask. That evening her father didn't come home from

work — a meeting, Mama said, although the exact nature of the appointment remained undisclosed. The three of them ate a silent meal of leftover fried chicken at the kitchen table, and her mother's distracted, snappish mood precluded conversation.

At eleven Delta was reading in her bedroom at the front of the house when her father's car drove up. She heard footsteps on the porch, the creak of the front door opening, the squeaking protest of the loose floorboard on the stairs. Then the rasp of their bedroom door closing, and voices.

If Daddy had intended to be quiet so as not to wake Mama, he evidently had not been successful. Delta could hear her mother's muffled voice through the wall, although she couldn't make out the words. The groan of the bedsprings followed by two dull thuds — Daddy sitting down to take off his shoes, Delta guessed. Muted steps down the hall, a toilet flushing, water running. Then the shutting of the door again, and more conversation.

Most of what they said Delta couldn't make out. The words were garbled, hushed, although a time or two a voice would be raised, and she caught snatches of sentences — something about *your own daughters in the house* and *not my decision*. Mama's

voice, when Delta could hear it, sounded angry, and Daddy's simply weary and resigned. Within a few minutes she heard the click of a lamp being turned off, then silence.

On Thursday morning Delta awoke at quarter to nine, stumbled sleepily down to the kitchen in her pajamas and slippers, and found both her parents sitting at the table drinking coffee. The instant she saw them, she was wide awake with a churning of acid in her stomach. Her father, punctual as a Swiss watch, invariably left for the insurance office at eight thirty, and her mother always cooked breakfast for him before he went. But this morning there was no sign of breakfast anywhere — not even toast, or those little white powdered doughnuts Daddy liked.

"What's wrong?" Delta said. "Did somebody die? Where's Cass?" She dropped into a chair.

"Cassie's at school." Mama set a mug of coffee in front of her and pushed the sugar bowl in her direction. "Your father has something he needs to talk to you about." She resumed her seat and stirred her coffee so manically that Delta was sure the cup would shatter.

She looked at her father. He had his head down and was busy turning a spoon over and over in his hands.

"Your mother and I have decided —" he began

"No," Mama interrupted, a tone of warning in her voice.

"All right." He sighed and ran a hand through his thinning hair. "I don't know how to say this that will make it sound any better."

"Just say it," Mama snapped. "Tell the truth, for once in your life."

He took off his thick glasses and rubbed the bridge of his nose, pressing a thumb and forefinger into the oval indentations where the glasses sat. "I'm in love with another woman," he blurted out. "And I've asked your mother for a divorce."

Time pitched and shuddered backward, ground to a halt, then began to move forward again, in slow motion. On a screen in the back of her mind, images flashed across Delta's consciousness. Her father in his chair. Her mother at the stove or at the sink or sitting in the rocker knitting. The boredom in Mama's eyes. Daddy's bald spot, spreading wider every year.

Then, without warning, another image presented itself — a picture of Daddy with his arm around a woman who was not her mother, his head thrown back, laughing as he had not laughed in all the years she had known him.

She should have had a hundred questions, a thousand. But only one pushed its way to the forefront of her mind: *Why hadn't this happened sooner?* Twenty-five years they had been married, and suddenly Delta realized that most of those years had been unhappy for both of them. Caught in the quicksand of familiarity, they had gone on slogging in place, hardly aware that they were sinking until Daddy had caught hold of a branch Mama couldn't reach.

As the awareness overtook her, one of Dr. Bowen's favorite aphorisms came to Delta's mind: *A rut is a grave with the ends kicked out.*

Mama was crying quietly now, leaning her whole body away from Daddy, refusing to meet his eyes. Just briefly, Delta wondered what she had to cry about. Surely she was relieved. Surely a sense of liberation was mixed in there with the anger and betrayal and, quite possibly, shame.

"What will you do?" she asked, the question addressed to nobody in particular.

"Your mother will stay here in Stone Mountain," Daddy said. "The house is paid for, and I'll take care of basic expenses. I've sold the agency to my partner. Caroline and

I will move into Atlanta and start over. I'll be close enough to see Cassie, and far enough away to —" He paused. "This is a small town. There's no sense putting your mother through any more embarrassment than necessary."

Delta stared at him. "Caroline? Caroline Lawler, your secretary?"

Her father nodded.

Delta let this pass without comment. She doubted it was necessary to point out the stereotype — a middle-aged man falling in love with a secretary fifteen years his junior. She supposed the red sports car would come next.

But despite this cynical turn of mind, Delta knew in her heart that it wasn't just a midlife crisis. It was a moment of truth two decades in the making.

After her father's revelation, all Delta wanted was to get away. Instead she waited around all day Thursday, holed up in her room trying to avoid her parents. When Cassie finally got home from school Delta sat with her through the difficult and emotional conversation, took her out for pizza, cuddled with her until she finally went to sleep. On Friday she packed her bags and left Stone Mountain shortly after noon.

166

Now Delta gripped the wheel and aimed her car due west, out of Atlanta and across the state line into Alabama.

Cassie would be all right, Delta thought. The girl had amazing inner resources, a grit and determination no one would guess from looking at her. She was a fighter. A survivor.

Her mind drifted toward her parents. Twenty-five years. A quarter of a century. All those days and nights without any real connection.

"My parents are getting a divorce," Delta said aloud, trying to make herself connect with some emotion, some grief — something. But all she could feel about their breakup was a sense of inevitability. How, she wondered, had two people so ill suited for each other ever gotten married in the first place?

Delta tried to remember the wedding photos her mother kept in a small, yellowed album in a box under the bed. April 1944. V-E Day was still a year away, but her father had stayed home, classified 4-F because of his abysmal eyesight. Mama stood thin and pale in a tea-length dress with a matching pillbox hat, Daddy in a shiny-looking suit with a rose in his lapel. They had both been smiling at the camera, she recalled. Had they been madly in love at the beginning? Had they met at the altar and said their vows with absolute certainty that their relationship would last forever, that their life together was and would continue to be perfect, exactly as they had envisioned it?

And what *was* the perfect relationship, anyway?

Another image crept into her mind, superimposed upon the picture of her parents. An image of herself and Ben. A weight pressed down on her chest.

This wasn't what she wanted for her life. Of course she wanted security and safety and steadiness. But she also wanted fireworks and candlelight and insanity, challenge and intensity and growth.

Delta focused on the mental reflection of his lean, familiar face. A pang of regret shot through her.

She wouldn't marry Ben Rutledge. Not now, probably not ever. When she got married, if she ever did, what she wanted was a relationship that engaged all of her — heart, soul, mind, and body. Not an inevitability but a choice. A partnership. A love that would never grow stale or boring.

And God help her, she'd rather be single her whole life long than to settle for anything less.

FOURTEEN:
JUDAS

HILLSBOROUGH, NORTH CAROLINA
MARCH 1969

Spring break had been pure agony for Lauren. All week she had stood to one side while Lacy and Trip reveled in the attention that washed over them like a fountain. Mother fawned over him, feeding him, laughing at his jokes. Dad welcomed him home like the Prodigal, the long-lost son, and barbecued the fatted calf — or the ribs, at least — to celebrate his coming.

Steve Treadwell had not made the trip. Lauren had fabricated a reason, some reading he had to catch up on — an excuse that caused Trip to raise his eyebrows in skepticism. The truth was, Lauren didn't *want* Steve with her. Two days before they were scheduled to leave for North Carolina she had ended their relationship, telling him in vague ramblings and nonspecific clichés that she was sorry but it just wasn't going to work out between them.

If she were honest with herself — a practice woefully unsuited to Lauren's temperament — she would have to admit that poor Steve suffered terribly by comparison. He was a nice enough guy, she supposed. Easy on the eyes, and a hell of a lot more considerate than most of the boys she had dated, slept with, and then rejected. He liked her, certainly, and she had no problem with being physically attracted to him.

But once she saw Lacy and Trip together, her spirits plummeted. Every time she looked at Steve, she was forcibly reminded of what she'd never have with him. What she'd never have, she feared, with anyone.

Precisely what it was, this connection that Lacy and Trip had between them, Lauren was not certain. But she was determined to find out, even if her heart broke in the process.

Her chance came on Thursday, two days before they planned to leave to go back to school. Mother had determined to take her girls shopping, and although the M word had not been spoken a single time during the entire week, Lauren sensed that the clothes-buying spree was for Lacy's benefit, a kind of pre-engagement trousseau, a celebration of the celebration to come.

Trip had decided that, instead of following the women around and carrying their packages, he would take a drive over to Duke and scope out the college. Sometime during the early part of the week, the decision had been made that he would attend law school there. Duke University, like the W, was on spring break this week, but he hoped he'd at least be able to get a tour and meet the dean.

"You know," Lauren said casually as she walked with her mother and sister out to the driveway, "I think I'll pass on the shopping trip."

Both mouths gaped open. Never once in anyone's memory had Lauren missed the opportunity to model clothes for an entire store full of admirers.

"Trip's not familiar with Duke's campus," she hurried on. "I thought maybe I'd ride over there with him and show him around. We haven't had any time to get to know each other." She caught Lacy's frown and averted her eyes quickly. "If it's all right with you, Lace. He *is* likely to be my brother-in-law, after all." She gave her sister a wide, innocent smile.

Before Lacy could respond, Mother jumped in. "Why, I think that's very considerate, Lauren. Don't you, honey?" She

171

peered at Lacy, whose face had hardened into an inscrutable mask. "We'll bring you a surprise." She ushered Lacy into the car, slid in behind the wheel, and waved as they headed off.

It was a sunny spring day, and at Lauren's insistence, Trip put the top down on the Corvair. Her long hair swirled around her face as they drove. The front bucket seat, she noted, was much more comfortable than the cramped rear where she had ridden all the way from Mississippi, and she stretched her legs and leaned back with a sigh.

Trip almost ran off the road staring at her.

"Whoops!" She leaned forward and guided the car back onto the pavement, grinning at him. "Strange, isn't it?"

"What's strange?" His face had turned a brilliant pink, as if he'd been out on the beach all day.

"Dating a twin. You wouldn't be the first guy who felt it."

His eyes veered back to her. "Lacy didn't tell me. I didn't know it until that day I came to Sunday dinner."

Lauren nodded. "Sometimes she prefers to keep me out of the picture."

"It's eerie," he said. "It's like I'm looking at Lacy, and yet it's not Lacy. Except for the hair, you're exactly alike."

She gave a low purring laugh. "Well, not . . . *exactly*." She winked at him, and he blushed again.

The Duke campus was a magical place in springtime — or any time of year, for that matter. A few students loitered about here and there, but for the most part Lauren and Trip had the place to themselves. Once they had driven around for a bit, Trip decided not to bother touring the law school. Instead, like children playing hooky, they walked around the grounds and lounged on the grass, talking under the shadow of the imposing brick and stone buildings.

He told her about how he met Lacy and how they had hit it off immediately, about his enthusiasm for the law, about his passion for Van Gogh and his love of the blues. He laughed a lot and seemed to grow comfortable with Lauren, but didn't ask her much about her own life and plans for the future. After a while Lauren began to feel as if she were standing in for her sister, as if he were talking to Lacy by proxy.

Trip was clearly mesmerized by the beauty of the campus — the expanses of green lawn and blossoming trees, the gargoyles that leered down at them from rooftops, the magnificent gothic chapel with its central tower rising two hundred feet into the sky. At last they entered the Duke Gardens, which lay spread out as the centerpiece of campus, fifty acres of emerald velvet adorned with ponds and fountains, shaded walks and sun-drenched bridges, blooming things in a hundred hues of sapphire, topaz, ruby, and amethyst.

Midweek, in the middle of the day, in the middle of spring break, the gardens were nearly deserted. They walked and gazed and said little to one another, stopping as if by mutual consent to toss pennies from a bridge and make a secret wish. "I've seen Ole Miss," Trip said at last, "and I've seen Emory, both of which are nice enough. But if I had ever seen this campus, I can't imagine I would have applied anywhere else."

He turned to face her, and the pure dazed joy in his expression made Lauren's heart lurch. In that instant, she knew — if she had ever doubted — why Lacy loved him, and why Lauren herself would never be able to settle for the likes of Steve Treadwell.

They walked some more; she stumbled; he took her hand to steady her and somehow never let go. Lauren wondered if his mind had lost track of which twin he was with — it had happened before. But at this moment she didn't care. She didn't care about any-

174

thing except the sensation of her hand in his, the soft blue lake of his eyes.

"Let's go sit awhile," she suggested, and led him off the path into a dappled grove. Here the springy ground was soft and cool, with dogwood blooms fluttering like tiny fairy wings overhead. A secluded spot, invisible to anyone who might be walking in the gardens.

Trip dropped down onto the moss-covered bank, lay back, and closed his eyes. Above them birds sang and a breeze stirred the branches. The hush was hypnotic, restful, a lullaby. Within a minute or two his breath grew even and shallow, and he slept.

Lauren's gaze roved over him. He had a swimmer's body, muscled but not bulky, sculpted features with blondish hair swept back from the temples. A wide, untroubled brow, and tiny indentations on either side of his mouth, the hint of dimples around his smile. A man in wakefulness, a boy at rest.

He stirred in his sleep. She reached out a finger and stroked the side of his cheek, lightly touching the smooth skin above the line where he shaved. He gave a little moan of pleasure.

Carefully, so as not to wake him, she stretched out next to him, laid her head into the crook of his out-flung arm, and nestled against him. Her fingers continued to trace the contours of his face, down his jaw line, across his chin. She wet a forefinger on the underside of her own lip and ran it gently, the barest kiss of a touch, across his mouth.

She heard the little intake of breath, saw his tongue come out and run across his lower lip. A lightning flash shot through her. She had to touch him — *had* to. She eased his shirttail out of his jeans and moved a hand lightly up his chest, feeling his nipples harden under the caress.

Lauren was on fire now, pulsing with desire. He felt it too, even in the hazy world of sleep. She could see his arousal, and it inflamed her all the more.

His eyes snapped open, wide and darkly dilated. "What are you doing?"

"Giving you what Lacy can't — or won't." She gazed at him. "Don't tell me you don't want it."

He bit his lip but said nothing.

"I know my prude of a sister," she went on. "She's given you this —" She kissed him, fluttering her tongue inside his parted lips. "And maybe even this —" She took his hand and slid it inside her blouse. "But never this —" She guided his hand down between her thighs and pressed her legs together.

Trip let out a groan. "I can't do this."

"You can," she countered, her voice husky with emotion. "You want to." She pushed closer to him. "My sister is in love with the notion of being in love," she whispered. "She has no idea what it's all about. But I know. I can give you what you want."

She shifted a leg over him, felt him stiffen, felt her own craving ignite even further. He was still murmuring "No, no," as he arched toward her. His mouth closed over hers, his tongue probing, his hands reaching for her. Locked in his arms now, she rolled over onto her back, bringing him with her.

His hand went inside her blouse, inside her bra, around her breast. He writhed against her, as if desperate to get closer, closer. Her body responded to his movements, the sensuous dance of passion driving them on, propelling them toward the point of no return.

"God, no," he breathed as his hands touched bare flesh. He pulled her nearer, caressing her, impelling her hunger with lips and fingers and tongue. A fumbled moment with zippers and underwear, and then —

She'd had sex before, plenty of times. But it had never been like this. This joyous ache, this exquisite pain, this soaring, this flying . . .

A dazzling light, a pounding crescendo like

nothing she had ever known. Her breath caught in her throat, and she let it out in a burst. "Ah!"

Trip's eyes snapped open. "Yes!" he cried, then shuddered and collapsed in Lauren's arms.

If Lauren had thought watching Trip and Lacy together made her jealous before, it was nothing compared to the way she felt now. The last two days of break she could barely stand to see them together. Trip turned out to be the consummate actor, smiling and laughing and pretending everything was normal, but casting side-long glances at Lauren every chance he got.

Lustful glances, or regretful ones? Lauren hadn't been sure until Friday, when they were packing Trip's car. They had decided to leave a day early and break up the long drive with an overnight stop at a motel along the way. Lauren was already entertaining fantasies of sneaking out of her and Lacy's room and into Trip's.

Alone in the garage, he had pressed her up against the side of the car and kissed her, one eye on the garage door and one hand sliding down inside her shorts.

"We'll have to be careful," he warned, his

deft fingers stroking her. "Lacy can never know."

How they would manage to keep such a thing hidden, Lauren had no idea. But at the time, distracted by his caress, she had merely nodded.

Shortly after they got on the road, it began to rain — a dull gray drizzle that suited Lauren's mood perfectly. Lacy sat in the front seat, fawning over Trip, laughing at his jokes, holding his hand on top of the gearshift.

Trip Jenkins was everything Lauren had always longed for, everything her other boyfriends were not. And even while she burned with resentment toward Lacy, she clutched the precious secret to her breast. *She* was the one Trip wanted. The one he had made love to. She had won.

All during the drive, she replayed it in her mind. The way his eyelashes lay in dark feathers across his cheeks. The way his lips and tongue moved against hers. The sensation of his hands on her flesh, his weight pressing down upon her, the tenderness, the virility. The explosion of intensity and power at the moment of climax.

The feelings rushed into her on a warm wind, remembered passion giving way to fresh fire. She ought to feel remorse, Lauren thought. She'd had sex with her sister's boyfriend and was planning to do it again at the first opportunity. But all she could think of was Trip. The way he looked at her, the way he touched her.

She drew her knees up to her chest and huddled uncomfortably in the back seat as the leak in the convertible's roof dripped water on her head. But even the thrumming of the rain could not stem the tide of her desire.

FIFTEEN:
FACING THE DRAGON

Rae Dawn lay across the bed in her dorm room and stared at the tree outside her window. The spring green leaves stirred on a breath, cutting the light into lace and spreading it in moving patterns across her pillow.

She had not even considered leaving the college for spring break. The mere idea of returning to Picayune, even for a day or two, was unthinkable. Everything she owned was here, everything she was. Delta and Lacy and Lauren were her family. And Dr. Gottlieb, of course. This was home.

Rae missed her friends and would be glad for their return, but she had needed this week alone, this time to think.

Since that cataclysmic moment, that flash of jealousy over Lacy and Trip and the insight that followed, her entire world had changed. She had — finally — admitted the truth to herself, and there was no going back.

All her life Rae Dawn had assumed she felt different, an outsider, because her family was poor, because she wore hand-me-down clothes, because her father was a notorious drunk. But that had been only part of the reason. There was more.

Far more.

The hard lessons of childhood experience had taught her not to get too close to people, not to allow herself too much hope. She had never dated much, never been particularly interested in boys. She had watched from the sidelines as girls her age underwent the sea change of puberty and became obsessed with the idea of love and sex and (eventually) marriage. They talked about it constantly — not to Rae, certainly, but to each other. In the hallway and at lunch and in the locker rooms as they dressed for gym. Who had kissed whom. How far this girl or that one was willing to go — first base, second base, all the way. The baseball metaphor always seemed a bit odd to Rae Dawn, and it took her a long time to figure out what the bases represented. But every time she overheard such conversations, she felt a nervous flitting in her stomach, that you-don't-fit feeling that had become so familiar to her.

One experience stood out in Rae's mind, a

long-ago memory now marked in her mind with a flapping red flag. She had been in junior high — eighth grade, she thought, fourteen or so. Everyone was in the dressing room after P.E., and a girl named Maria Curtis, an extroverted life-of-the-party type, was holding center stage. "Look, everybody!" she called. "I'm preg-nant!"

Minimally dressed in bra and panties and half slip, Maria had pulled the elastic of her slip up over her breasts and thrust out her belly so that she looked as if she were wearing a maternity dress.

Rae stared at her, curious. All the other girls were crowding around, imitating her, chattering like squirrels about how they all couldn't wait to be in love, to be married, have babies. About what they would do with — or to — the boys who were smart enough to choose them. As far as Rae was concerned, they might as well have been speaking Swahili. She couldn't identify with a word they were saying.

Then Maria's best friend, Kate Killian, stepped into the little drama, adopting the part of a man. She swaggered up to Maria and put an arm around her. "Oh, baby," Kate said in a low, growling voice, "you make me so hot." With that, Kate yanked Maria into a mimicry of a passionate embrace, ground her pelvis lustfully into Maria's, and kissed her full on the lips.

In that moment the world stopped dead. Everyone else was laughing, clapping, cheering the performance. Rae Dawn stood rooted to the spot, breathless. Something warm and fizzy moved through her veins, spreading into her chest and down into her crotch, and she gave an involuntary gasp. The sight of two girls kissing, even in mocking play, roused a response in her that had never been awakened by all the constant talk of boys and body parts and fumbling experimental sex.

She should have known, Rae thought. Should have realized. All her childhood crushes had been on women teachers, all her adolescent longings centered around having a girlfriend. A best friend, she had rationalized at the time. But now she knew better. Not just a best friend. A *girlfriend*.

How many nights during those teenage years had she lain on the sofa bed in the cramped living room of the Airstream, listening to make sure her parents were asleep, sinking into a half dream with her hand under her nightgown, fondling herself until she thought she'd go mad with a desire she didn't understand? How many times had she dreamed of someone falling in love with her, taking her away from Picayune and Hobo Creek and the perpetual depression that was her life? And when the fantasies came — those romantic scenarios of being swept away, kissed, touched, made love to, adored — the person who aroused her and loved her, who took her hand and led her into their new life was . . . a woman.

Rae had known nothing about lesbian sex back then, not even enough to fantasize about. To tell the truth, she didn't understand much more as a senior in college. Now that she was exploring the past more objectively, she did admit to occasional attractions, but the self-protection she had learned so well in her early years had served to keep her from pursuing any of them.

This was an aspect of sexuality that no one ever talked about, except in obscene jokes punctuated by nasty words like *fag* and *dyke*. And if she *had* talked about it, she supposed that most people — even her best friends — would likely tell her that since she'd never acted on those feelings, she couldn't possibly be . . . that way.

But as little as she comprehended about the matter, Rae Dawn was certain of one thing: It wasn't exclusively about sex, any more than being straight was only about who you slept with. It was about connection, about love and romance and attraction and how you felt on the inside. It was about being yourself and being accepted for who you were.

Rae had never known true acceptance until she had come to college, and her friendships with Lacy and Lauren and Delta — especially Delta — had made life worth living for the first time. She had to tell them, had to be honest with them. Yet she worried how they might take it. This wasn't just a confession that she was poor and hadn't really grown up in New Orleans. Would she lose the only friends she had ever known? Would they be concerned that she might be attracted to one of them, an attraction that could not be reciprocated?

She sighed and sat up on the bed. Well, she'd just have to deal with that when it came. In the meantime, she knew — or thought she knew — two people who could help her work this out.

Frankie Bowen and Suzanne Hart.

"To tell the truth," Dr. Bowen said when Rae Dawn had finished telling her story, "we wondered when you might be coming to see us." She grinned over at Dr. Hart, who was throwing a tennis ball for Bilbo and Frodo.

Rae gazed out over the lawn as Frodo came loping back to the patio carrying a ball lopsidedly in his mouth. Against the far wall a pink dogwood tree bloomed, and beds of irises and daffodils blossomed purple and yellow in a sunny bed in the corner. It was a peaceful place. A safe place.

"You knew?" she asked. "How? I wasn't even sure, until recently."

Dr. Hart shrugged, took the slobbery ball, and tossed it into the yard again. "We get a sense about these things," she said. "But we would never have asked. It's not our place to pry. Still, it might help you to know that you're not the first student who has come to us with a similar tale."

Rae Dawn took a sip of her iced tea and reached down to pet Bilbo, who had abandoned the game and now sat next to her with his curly muzzle propped on her knee. "I don't know quite what to do with all this," she admitted. "I haven't met anyone. I'm not in love."

"But you'd like to be." Dr. Hart reached over and squeezed Dr. Bowen's hand, and they both smiled.

"Well, sure." Rae Dawn felt herself blush. "But people never talk about this stuff. How am I supposed to find the right person? Nobody wears a sign."

Dr. Bowen chuckled. "Some do. But knowing you, I doubt if you'd hit it off with any of them."

"There are places more open and accepting," Dr. Hart interjected. "California, New York." She pointed a finger in Rae Dawn's direction. "New Orleans. You're going back to New Orleans after graduation?"

"Yes. At least I'm going to try."

"Good place, New Orleans. We have a couple of friends down there who might be able to introduce you around."

"That would be great." Rae fell silent for a minute. "What's it like, being . . ." She paused. "Being a lesbian couple?"

Lesbian. Rae Dawn was pretty sure it was the first time she had ever said the word aloud, and it felt good. Rebellious. Liberating. Just hearing the word roll off her own tongue gave her the sensation of stepping out of a dank, moldy basement into sunlight and fresh air.

"It's absolutely wonderful, when you've found the right person," Dr. Bowen said. "But it can also be hard to live with the rejection and condemnation. Critics talk about the moral issues — you know, that it's a choice against nature and against God. Absurd. This *is* nature. No one would choose to be part of a maligned and censured minority."

"Still," Dr. Hart added, "once you *have* found the right person, you wouldn't go back even if you could." She shrugged. "Sometimes it's just frustrating, feeling as if you have to live a secret, to hide the most important relationship in your life in order to keep your job or protect your safety."

"I don't know how the two of you do it," Rae said. "I mean, you've been together how long? Ten years?"

Dr. Bowen rolled her eyes. "Fifteen. Suze was twenty-five and a first-year instructor when we met. I was thirty-six, an associate professor." She chuckled. "I robbed the cradle, I suppose."

Dr. Hart laughed. "Or I robbed the grave."

"And you've never been able to name your relationship publicly."

Dr. Hart shook her head. "As long as we're not obvious about it, everything's fine. People know, but they don't want to *know,* if you get my drift. Frankie and I just go about our business, and folks perceive us as two old spinster teachers sharing our living expenses."

"God, that must be hard."

"In some ways it is," Dr. Bowen agreed.

"But we have supportive people in our lives. And we try to be careful. It would only take one phone call to bring the whole house of cards crashing in on us."

SIXTEEN:
WOMAN ON THE WIND

The morning after her conversation with Dr. Bowen and Dr. Hart, Rae Dawn awoke to a chilling fear that she had made a terrible mistake. Three times she picked up the telephone to call them, to beg them not to tell anyone what she had said, to convince them — or herself — that it couldn't possibly be true.

After all, she'd never had any kind of sexual relationship with another woman. Delta Fox was her best friend, the person Rae loved most in the world, and she wasn't physically attracted to Delta. Not much, anyway.

Besides, you couldn't be a lesbian unless you had actually *done* something, could you? She'd never even kissed a girl.

For hours — alone in her dorm, walking across campus, working on her senior composition in the rehearsal room — she carried on the internal debate. How could she deny what she felt? But how could it be true when she had never acted on those feelings? This argument, she now realized, had been going on inside her for years. All her life, or at least since puberty, she had been trying to figure it out. Trying to ignore it. Trying to learn to live with the anxiety that bubbled like molten lava in the subterranean crevices of her heart.

And yet in a deeper place beyond her fear, the reality was there, inside her. Even the word *lesbian* conjured up images in Rae Dawn's mind of soft, willing body parts — small attentive breasts and warm liquid caresses, the electrifying newness of skin on skin, the curve of a thigh, the arch of a back . . .

And the liberation — no, the *resurrection* — that had come when she had finally said, "Yes. This is who I am."

She could suppress the feelings, dismiss the longings. She could live celibate for the rest of her life, stay safe, never let anyone get close enough to be a danger. But she could not deny the fresh air that had rushed into her lungs in that instant, the sun that had blazed down upon her light-starved soul. The tomb had cracked opened and could not be sealed again.

"This is who I am," she repeated to herself. "Come hell or high water, whatever the cost, this is who I am."

Much to Rae Dawn's surprise and pleasure, Delta arrived back at school just before dinner on Friday evening. The dining hall was practically empty, and the two of them sat at a table alone while Delta told Rae what had happened with her parents.

"I am so sorry," Rae said. "Divorce is awful, no matter what the circumstances. But believe me, I can understand when you say you wonder why your parents ever got married in the first place. My folks are the same way, only I doubt they will ever split. They're too stuck in their ways. They'll just go on tormenting one another until one of them dies."

"It's weird," Delta said. "I don't feel any of the things I'm supposed to feel. I just keep thinking that maybe now Daddy will be happy and maybe Mama can find a way to recover her dreams again."

"What dreams are those?" Rae asked.

Delta shrugged. "I have no idea."

"And how's your little sister taking it? She's pretty young to have to deal with this."

"Cassie will be fine," Delta said in a voice that sounded to Rae like wishful thinking. "She's smart, and she's tough. She'll adjust."

She exhaled heavily. "So, what have you been doing with yourself this week? Working on your senior composition, I suppose."

Rae hesitated. She had planned to wait until she had a better grip on things herself, but suddenly she wanted to tell Delta everything. She was hopeful that Delta, given her love for her two major professors, would be supportive and accepting. But no matter what the outcome, Rae wanted to pour it all out in a rush and get it over with, like pulling an abscessed tooth. Her stomach twitched and heaved with the risk of telling, and yet she felt a fluttering of anticipation too.

Rae's mind had drifted. Delta was frowning at her.

"Are you going to answer my question?" Delta said. "I asked about your senior composition."

"Oh." Rae Dawn dragged her attention back to the present. "It's going very well; I think Gottlieb will be pleased. I've decided to call it 'Woman on the Wind.'"

"That's a fabulous title. I can't wait to hear it."

"I'm still tweaking it, but I'll play it for you later, if you like," Rae said.

They were done with dinner. Rae Dawn pushed her plate back and steeled herself to launch into her disclosure. But she never got a single word out.

Delta jumped up from the table and jerked her by the hand. "What's wrong with right now?" she said. "Come on, Rae. I want to hear your masterpiece."

The music building was deserted, so they took one of the larger practice rooms. Delta perched on a stool while Rae Dawn settled herself at the piano. She couldn't decide if she was disappointed or relieved to have been given a reprieve from the confessional.

She shifted on the bench and fiddled with the score. "As I said, it still needs some revision."

Delta rolled her eyes. "Always the perfectionist. Just let me hear it, please."

Rae Dawn began to play, a minor-key, bluesy piece reminiscent of the old slave songs. Soulful enough to make you weep, the melody wound around them like a living vine, a tether forged of tears and heartbreak. Something within the music strained against its bonds, seeking release. And then, just as the agony became unbearable, there was a breath — a flash of light, a flutter of wings, a wind high in the trees. Like new life erupting from the womb, the notes burst forth into glorious movement, streaking skyward, plummeting toward earth again, soaring on the currents of the song.

The music was ecstasy, indeed, mounting up from earthbound bondage to climb the currents of the wind. Rae Dawn played on, her head thrown back and her eyes closed as the harmony rose toward a climax of the soul so deep and powerful that it ended, for both pianist and listener, with a breathless tremor.

The final notes drifted into silence. Rae Dawn sat at the keyboard for a moment, then opened her eyes.

Delta's face was streaked with the silver tracks of tears. Her mouth hung slightly open, and she had both hands clenched in her lap. Neither of them spoke.

Then Delta seemed to come awake. "Wow," she said.

Rae Dawn put her hands to her cheeks and could feel the heat emanating from her skin. Unaccountably, she felt exposed, embarrassed, as if she had been glimpsed naked.

"That was amazing," Delta went on. "It was —" She hesitated. "Pure poetry. It reminds me of Hopkins's poem 'The Windhover' — the bird darting and falling, rising and swinging." She closed her eyes and tried to call up the poem from her memory: "His riding/ Of the rolling level underneath him steady air, and striding/ High there, how he rung upon the rein of a wimpling wing/ In his ecstasy!"

Rae smiled and ducked her head. "Coming from you, that's high praise."

"It was incredible, Rae. I've never heard any piece of music that moved me so profoundly." Delta leaned forward. "I want you to talk to me about how it happened. What goes on inside your soul that enables you to write something like that?"

Rae Dawn gathered up the music and sat for a moment, her hands absently caressing the score. This was her invitation, her open door. She wouldn't get a better chance than this. "Let's go to the Goose and get some coffee," she said. "I'll try to explain — about the music, and about a lot of other things."

They walked in silence. It was a glorious evening, the stillness broken only by invisible birds twittering in the rustling trees overhead. The Goose was uninhabited except for Mary Jo, the wiry, blank-faced woman who worked behind the counter. She filled their order — two cups of coffee and two slices of coconut custard pie — and then went back to reading her paperback novel.

They settled themselves in a corner booth near the glass wall that looked out onto the patio. Rae Dawn, facing the window, could see her own reflection in the glass as clearly as if she were looking into a mirror. She lowered her eyes and busied herself with the pie.

Delta took a sip of coffee. "So tell me," she said, "where does genius like that come from?"

"Genius?" Rae Dawn shook her head. "I wouldn't call it genius."

"I would." Delta smiled. "You're going to say I don't know much about music, and that's true, but I know plenty about poetry. 'Woman on the Wind' is a poem, the kind of poem that evokes deep and significant images in the listener. Don't be modest, Rae. It's genius. It's artistry. It's a gift."

Rae took a bite of her pie and pushed the plate back from the edge of the table. It was delicious, but her stomach swarmed with fluttering wings. Maybe she could finish it later, afterward.

"What images?" she asked Delta, trying to buy time while her mind scrambled for some semblance of order. She had thought she was prepared for this, but now that the moment was upon her, her brain had gone to mush. "What images does the music evoke in you?"

Delta bit on the tines of her fork while she considered her answer. "Well, in the beginning, the minor-key part, I felt weighed down, trapped. In chains, perhaps, but less like forged metal chains than natural chains, if you know what I mean. Like heavy vines growing and wrapping around my limbs. I felt as if gravity had increased, pulling me downward toward the earth."

Rae nodded. "Go on."

"And then something — I don't quite know what it was — broke free. The sun came out. The air was fresh and clean, the way it is after a rainstorm. And I began to fly. Not just released from gravity, but soaring, dancing in the air, chasing the clouds and darting toward the heavens. It was liberating, powerful. It was —" she paused. " 'Woman on the Wind.' "

Rae Dawn smiled. This was exactly the response she had hoped for, exactly the reaction she had experienced when writing the music — and when coming to grips with the truth about herself. "What about the ending?"

"Whew," Delta said. "I can still feel it. It was like —" She shook her head. "This is going to sound strange, I know, because I'm not religious and I don't usually talk about God stuff. But it was like being present at the moment of creation. Like making love to God and the universe."

Rae felt tears sting at her eyes. "Thank you."

"No, I should be the one thanking *you,*" Delta said. She tapped her fork rhythmically on the table top. "I'm fascinated with the imaginative process, with what goes on in an artist's mind and heart during a moment of creativity. Is it just instinct, or can you articulate where it came from?"

"I can try." Rae Dawn had the sensation of standing on a cliff edge, the precipice of now or never. "You know my background, know what my childhood was like," she began. "I always felt different, ostracized."

"Because of your parents and your living situation. Because you didn't fit." Delta nodded. "That experience is reflected in the minor-key section at the beginning, feeling trapped and held down."

"Yes. But it has to do with more, much more, than just growing up poor and isolated. It has to do with —" Rae Dawn felt her resolve weakening. "Well, it's a little hard to explain."

Delta leaned forward, her expression intense. "Something happened to you during spring break, Rae. A change. A transformation. I see it in your eyes. I felt it in your music. Trust me to understand. Tell me."

"All right." Rae Dawn took a deep breath,

peered over the ledge, and leaped. She told Delta about the dark flame of jealousy that had overcome her concerning Lacy's relationship with Trip, about that visceral memory from junior high when Kate Killian kissed Maria Curtis, about her conversation with Frankie Bowen and Suzanne Hart and her self-examination during spring break.

"I suppose I've known subconsciously since eighth grade or so," she finished, "although I couldn't admit it, not even to myself. Maybe I felt I was different enough already and didn't have the courage to add anything else to the mix. But I can't deny it any longer. I have to accept myself, even if other people don't accept me."

"And when you finally did name it and accept it," Delta said, "you experienced a miraculous burst of wonder and freedom and lightness and joy, all of which poured out into your score — that soaring, leaping dance of passion and intimacy."

The tightly wound spring inside Rae's chest let go, and a flood of love and gratitude flowed into her. "You understand," she whispered.

"Well —" Delta shrugged. "I can't really comprehend what it means, since I have never experienced those particular feelings. But I think I do understand about breaking free, about taking the risk to be true to yourself no matter what the cost."

"I — I wasn't sure you would," Rae said quietly. "The first time we heard the rumors about Bowen and Hart, back during our freshman year, I got the impression you weren't quite certain what you thought about the idea."

"I'm an English major, for God's sake," Delta shot back with a mocking scowl. "I spend most of my time with those two, and I'm neither stupid nor naive. Besides, I think we've *all* grown up since then." She tilted her head. "Well, maybe not Lauren, but the rest of us, anyway."

Their laughter drew the attention of Mary Jo, who left her post behind the counter and brought them a refill of coffee. "You two okay?" she said, narrowing her eyes at them as if she were certain they'd been drinking. "Black coffee, that's the ticket. Lots of it."

She moved away, muttering to herself. When they had finally regained their composure, Delta pushed Rae Dawn's plate back across the table. "Eat your pie," she said. "Everything's going to be fine."

SEVENTEEN:
THE OUTING

But everything wasn't fine. On Saturday afternoon, all hell broke loose.

By the time Rae Dawn got to the quad in front of the administration building, it was packed with people, many of them carrying signs and yelling. She made her way across the grass, scanning faces as she ran. At last she spotted Delta near the front of the building. She threaded her way through the press of bodies until she reached her, flushed and panting.

"What's going on?" she shouted above the clamor.

Delta turned. She looked haggard and worn, and her eyes held an expression bordering on panic. "It's Bowen and Hart," she said. "Apparently someone called the academic dean and complained about them. The Board of Trustees is having a special meeting right now, to decide whether to fire them or not."

"Fire them?" Rae repeated. "For what?"

"For being gay, I guess," Delta said. Her eyes were red-rimmed with tears. "They're the best teachers this college has ever had."

The bottom dropped out of Rae Dawn's stomach. "Shit," she muttered. "They can't get fired."

"No? Look around."

Rae Dawn looked. The quad seemed to be divided straight down the middle by an invisible barrier about ten yards across. On the opposite side of the fountain stood a group of people, mostly adults, holding up hand-lettered posters.

PARENTS AGAINST IMMORALITY

one of the signs read. And another,

GOD HATES DIKES AND FAGOTS

"Jeez," Delta breathed. "You'd think they'd learn to spell, anyway."

Despite herself, Rae let out a chuckle. "Thanks, Delta. I needed that." She peered into the crowd. "Who are these people, any-way?"

"I don't know," Delta said. "Some are townspeople, I think. Most of them are parents — I recognize a few of them. Over there on the right, the tall woman with auburn hair and the man in the Ole Miss jacket? Those are the Austins."

"Tabitha's parents?"

"Yep."

"I should have known. Tabby looks just like her mother."

Nearby a group of students milled about, carrying counterprotest signs that read

LIBERTY AND JUSTICE FOR ALL

Some of the faculty were there as well, looking nervous and angry.

"Seems like the professors have a good many supporters, though," Rae said.

"Yeah, but the other guys are louder."

"How did this all come about? Bowen and Hart never did anything to hurt anyone. Who on earth would call the administration?"

Delta sighed. "I don't know."

"I do." The voice came from behind them, and both Delta and Rae turned. It was Tabby Austin, looking even more miserable than Rae felt. "It was all a mistake," she said. "A huge, awful, terrible mistake."

Rae took Tabby's elbow and steered her to the edge of the crowd where the noise wasn't so deafening. "Who told?"

"I did."

"What?" Rae, still holding Tabby's arm, gripped harder and shook her a little.

"Like I said, it was a mistake," Tabby wailed. "Somebody — I don't know who — called my dad. He's given a ton of money to the college over the years, and there are a lot of alumnae in our family —"

"Yeah, we know all that," Rae snapped. "Five generations or something, dating back to the Civil War. Get on with it."

"Apparently a rumor was going around, some student who had told her parents she was a lesbian. She said she had talked with a couple of professors who helped her come to an acceptance of herself. Everybody got all riled up, like they had recruited her or something, and then my father said he was determined to find out who they were and put a stop to it, and that he had the clout to do it. I said I didn't know why it had to be such a big hairy deal, when they were just nice, normal people —"

"You didn't."

"Well, yeah. I never dreamed it would come to this —"

"So what happened then?"

"My parents made me tell them —" Tabby choked and began to sob. "And then my father called the dean and the president, and —"

"And here we are." Rae Dawn rolled her eyes. "I swear, Tabby, if Bowen and Hart are fired, I will have your head on a plate. Count on it."

Rae had vanished with Tabby, but Delta hadn't moved. She stood on the front edge of the crowd, her eyes scanning the opposition. In the center of the quad between the two groups stood a fountain, a square marble base with a bronze likeness of a woman, reaching upward toward the heavens. Water fell around her like tears, and on the ledge of the base were inscribed words from Tennyson's poem "Ulysses": *'Tis not too late to seek a newer world . . . To strive, to seek, to find, and not to yield.*

A newer world. Delta sighed. If memory served, Tennyson published "Ulysses" in the 1840s. Evidently the new birth was a long time coming. She felt the labor pains in her own soul every time the Delta Belles sang, every time she faced down racists at voter registrations, every time she read a hateful picket sign. Where was the hope for a newer world when malice still reared its head at anyone who was deemed different?

The crowd across the way had resumed its

chant: *"Fire the queers, fire the queers."*

"They won't be fired," a voice at her elbow said. "They've got tenure."

She turned to look. Beside her stood a man in blue jeans and a brown suede shirt — not tall, but well built and modestly attractive. He seemed vaguely familiar to Delta, but she couldn't place where she had seen him. He had shaggy brown hair and a beard, and his eyes, also brown, brimmed with confidence and an expression she could only define as joy. A hippie. A flower child. He grinned at her. "You're Delta Fox, aren't you?"

"Yes, but I —" She hesitated. "Have we met?"

He extended a hand. "Rankin Ballou. Our paths have crossed. I've heard your group sing on several occasions."

Awareness flared in Delta's mind, a light bulb coming on. "Right. You've been at a couple of the voting rallies."

"And the antiwar demonstrations, and the civil rights sit-in over at the courthouse. I'm surprised we haven't been formally introduced before now."

She regarded him with interest. His gaze was warm and entreating, and she felt immediately drawn to him. He was older than she — late twenties, thirty, perhaps — but wore no wedding ring . . .

Delta jerked herself back to reality. She was here to support her major professors, for pity's sake, not to get a date. Besides, she had just broken up with Ben Rutledge and vowed not to get involved with anyone else, at least for a long, long time.

"How do you know they won't get fired? Tenure can be overturned."

"True. But the chairman of the trustees is a — let's just say a close acquaintance of mine. He says the charges won't stick. There's no evidence of any wrongdoing, any inappropriate behavior or undue influence on students, and although I suppose they could be dismissed for moral turpitude, a handful of distraught parents won't be enough to turn the tide."

"Looks like more than a handful to me." Her eyes drifted to the crowd across the way.

Rankin smiled again. "Hatred always seems to shout louder than love," he said. "But love will win in the end."

It was an odd thing to say. "Do you really believe that?"

"I do," he answered. "And so do you, deep down. I've seen you in action. You're far too passionate about justice and truth not to have hope."

Delta felt herself at a distinct disadvantage. He seemed to know her so well, seemed to look right down into the depths of her heart. Her first instinct was to be obstinate, to tell him he didn't know what the hell he was talking about. But he was right about the hope, and even though Delta had a stubborn streak, she recognized the truth when she heard it.

"I hear you'll be hanging around after graduation," he said, "starting your master's program. How would you feel about having dinner with me next week, getting to know each other better?"

As soon as the words were out of his mouth, Delta realized she had been praying he'd ask. Well, maybe not praying, exactly, but wishing. Wanting.

"Sure," she said casually, as if it didn't matter one way or the other. "Why not?"

It was a minor deception, downplaying her enthusiasm, but in the face of his openness it felt like betrayal. "I'd like that very much," she amended.

"Good. I'll call you."

"Don't you need my number?" Delta asked.

"I've got it," he said. "But I should give you mine in case you need to get in touch." He fished in his pocket and handed her a small card. "And now, if you'll excuse me, I have something I need to do."

Delta watched him move toward the front of the crowd, then glanced down at the business card.

FIRST COMMUNITY CHURCH
REV. RANKIN BALLOU, PASTOR

"Holy shit," Delta muttered. "I've got a date with a *preacher*."

But he was like no preacher she had ever heard. He mounted the steps of the administration building two at a time, and when he turned back toward the quad, a rippling murmur ran through the crowd. The shouting and jeering died, and on both sides of the invisible barrier, all eyes turned toward him.

"Some among us," Rankin began, "would have us believe that God hates those who are different from the majority. That people who do not live the way we live or love the way we love are an abomination." His voice rang with confidence and authority across the green, and his eyes rested on the group to his right with an expression not of hatred or contempt, but of compassion. "We are afraid, and in our fear we strike out at those who threaten the beliefs we hold dear.

"Fear expresses itself in words and deeds of hatred," he continued. "Ugly, embittered

211

words like *dyke* and *faggot*." He lifted his eyes. "*Dyke,* by the way, is spelled with a *y,* and *faggot* with two *g*'s." A titter began to thread its way through the crowd. "Just for future reference," he said. "You might want to correct your sign before the next protest."

The laughter increased, and whoever was carrying the poster in question put it down. Rankin's gaze swung around toward the left, and he caught Delta's eye and gave a solemn nod.

"I am sometimes ashamed of being a Christian," he went on, "because of what Christians have done to the name. I am sometimes ashamed of being a minister because of how ministers have abused their power. I am sometimes ashamed of claiming the Bible as my sacred text because of how it has been misused to hurt millions of people.

"But it remains my sacred text," Rankin declared, "because the voices of hatred and hostility do not tell the story of who God is."

The crowd had fallen silent now, mesmerized. No one moved or spoke. Delta felt a presence at her side and turned to see Rae Dawn standing next to her, with Tabby Austin in tow.

■ ■ ■ ■

Rae, still furious with Tabby, pushed in beside Delta. She refused to stand next to the traitor who, in her utter stupidity, had shot her mouth off and caused this commotion in the first place. But it didn't take long for Rae to forget her irritation. Peace emanated from the man who was speaking, a peace that had to do with his inner spirit as well as his words.

"Who is this guy?" she murmured to Delta.

"His name is Rankin Ballou, and he's the minister at" — she glanced down at the card she was holding — "First Community Church."

"Jeez," Rae breathed. "I've never heard of a preacher who would stand up for gay folks. That's the kind of church I might actually want to go to."

"I've seen him around at protests and rallies," Delta whispered. "He's very involved in social causes. But I never met him until today."

Rankin Ballou was speaking again, his words gaining momentum, rolling over his listeners like the waters of righteousness.

"God's voice," he said, "is not the voice of violence and malice. God's voice is the voice of love.

"The voice of love is heard in the words of

Martin Luther King, Jr., who declared, 'Injustice anywhere is a threat to justice everywhere.'

"The voice of love is heard in the words of a Holocaust survivor, who wrote, 'Thou shalt not be a victim. Thou shalt not be a perpetrator. Above all, thou shalt not be a bystander.'

"And the voice of love is heard in the words of Jesus of Nazareth, who proclaimed, 'Let the one who is without sin cast the first stone.' "

The silence deepened. "Jesus was not a bystander. Not only did he speak with the voice of love, he lived by the law of love. He ate with sinners, drew outcasts into his circle of friends, embraced those whom society called unclean. He touched. He healed. He forgave. In the end he died for it, but while he lived, he lived the best example of the love of God the world has ever seen. An example not of hatred and exclusion, but of acceptance and affirmation."

Rankin's eyes roamed over the assembled multitude. "Who will cast the first stone?" He looked into the eyes of one person, and then the next. "Who among us is so pure of heart and so perfect in love as to dare to judge another? Who among us is so righteous as to condemn another's love, when

God's own name is Love? Who will cast the first stone?"

His voice had grown quiet now, but the crowd had no difficulty hearing him. "Who will cast the first stone?" he repeated.

A murmur ran through the knot of those gathered on the opposite side of the green. Some of them were shaking their heads, and a few threw angry glances in the minister's direction. But many were shifting, walking away. The knot unraveled, and Rankin Ballou stood there in silence, unflinching, as most of them returned to their cars and drove away.

Rae Dawn watched as the protesters on the other side of the quad dispersed. A breath of hope blew into her soul. Hope for Frankie Bowen and Suzanne Hart. Hope for herself. Hope for the future.

And then she saw him. In the back of the crowd, almost hidden at this angle by the tall bronze fountain. A thin, wiry figure with a shock of unruly white hair.

"How could you?" Rae Dawn demanded. "How could you advocate the dismissal of two of your own colleagues? How could you betray them like that? How could you stand there on the side of bigotry and injustice? You, of all people!"

Dr. Gottlieb sank down into his leather office chair and ran his hands over his face. "Why me, of all people?" he asked in a weary voice.

"Because you were *there*. You survived. You saw it firsthand, the result of blind hatred and inequality."

"This is not the same."

Rae towered over him, and he seemed to shrink. "Tell me why it is not the same. Why is it evil for Jews to be persecuted and ostracized and murdered, but it is not evil to do the same to any other group?"

Gottlieb managed a wan smile. It seemed a monumental effort. "You are like a daughter to me, Rae Dawn. God's gift to an old man's heart. When I look at you, when I hear your music, hear your laugh, I can almost believe you have been given to me as a gift, a reparation for those years behind the barbed-wire fences. I would willingly throw my body between you and the Nazis' rifles, between you and the gas and the ovens. But you are young. Young and innocent and impressionable. Do not be angry with me. You do not understand the ways of the world."

"I understand a hell of a lot more than you give me credit for," she snapped.

"Perhaps. Perhaps not. Trust me, this issue

of homosexuality — it is different."

"You haven't answered my question. *Why* is it different?"

A momentary fire blazed in his eyes, and his jaw clenched. "Because I could not *choose* no longer to be a Jew."

The words, clipped and precise, beat a staccato rhythm against her eardrums. She wanted to respect him, to love him. But the implications of his position burned like acid in her gut. "And they could choose not to be gay?"

He stood suddenly, slamming his hands down flat on the top of his desk. "I saw them there, in the camps, those pink triangles!" he shouted. "They defied the laws of God and human nature, and they were punished. They *chose* their fate!"

"So it's their fault that they died?" She held his eyes and would not look away. "Or is it God's fault?"

All the fire went out of him and he sagged into his chair like a deflated balloon. "They chose," he repeated stubbornly.

"They did not choose," she whispered.

"And how are you so certain, daughter of my heart?" he said in a cracked and shaky voice.

Rae Dawn leaned on the edge of the desk and gazed down at him. Her answer would hurt and confuse him, but she spoke the truth anyway.

"Because *I* would have worn a pink triangle," she said, "and *I* did not choose."

PART 3
LOSING TOUCH

Frozen, captured in the dark,
we take an arbitrary step,
squint our eyes and strain our ears
but cannot see or hear
what lies beyond,
shrouded by fog and shadows.

And so we stumble forward,
oblivious to how one small diversion
veers us toward a different path,
or how one voice
can lure us to our doom
or to our calling.

EIGHTEEN:
WOMAN ON THE WIRE

Upstairs, in the spacious apartment on Dauphine Street, the memory returned to Rae Dawn in such vivid clarity and detail that it might have been a movie reel spinning out inside her head. That day in his office, when they had argued, had been the last time she had seen Manfred Gottlieb alive — really alive, anyway.

They had both gone through the motions until graduation, speaking with caution and restraint when they had to speak, keeping silent and avoiding one another when they didn't. Rae had completed the final revisions of "Woman on the Wind" and played it at her senior recital to a rousing ovation. She had sat through the mind-numbing commencement speeches, received her diploma and the music department's coveted composition award, played one last concert with the Delta Belles at the graduation banquet — events that should have been highlights, and yet her recollections of them were grainy and faded. In those final weeks between her confrontation with Gottlieb and her departure from the college, Rae had apparently been on autopilot.

Still, Gottlieb had been true to his word. He had contacted an old friend from New Orleans, the owner of a small club called Maison Dauphine. The man hired Rae Dawn, sight unseen, on the strength of Gottlieb's word alone.

"Manny said I wouldn't be sorry for doing this," Chase Coulter said the first time Rae met him. "Don't make a liar out of him."

"Manny?" Rae almost laughed, then caught herself. She had never heard anyone refer to Gottlieb with a nickname, and the idea that he'd be friends with a man like Chase Coulter was almost beyond belief. Chase was a beefy, red-faced tough guy who looked more like a bouncer than an owner. Rae suspected he probably still did double duty during Mardi Gras and on weekends. "How did you two meet?"

Chase ducked his head. "My unit, we were the guys who went in to liberate the camps in Germany," he said in a low, choked voice.

"Jesus, what a mess. Bodies piled up everywhere. People caged like rats." He cleared his throat. "Anyway, Manny was there, all skin and bones and looking like he was a hundred years old, but alive. Once we secured the camp, we took the survivors into the officers' quarters to get them some food. There was a piano in there. Everyone else was chowing down, but Manny, he went over to the piano and started to play. In a daze, almost. Like he had been starving for music."

"Yes," Rae said. "That's exactly how he'd put it, I bet."

"I liked him," Chase went on. "Gave him my address and told him to look me up after the war. When he came to the States, well —" He shrugged. "You go through something like that, you become friends for life."

That had been more than twenty years ago, and never once had Rae Dawn given Chase Coulter reason to regret his decision to hire her. From backup pianist, she had gradually moved up to headliner, with her photograph posted out front on Dauphine Street. Word spread, and customers had flocked in droves to hear her sultry, smoky renditions of the old blues and jazz pieces, love songs, torch songs. Eventually she had begun to work her own compositions into the act, attracting the attention of talent agents and music publishers. Contracts followed, and gold albums, and concert tours. Rae Dawn had become the new Billie Holiday, and everybody adored her.

Still, she never forgot her beginnings. Wherever she went, her heart drew her back. Back to New Orleans. Back to Maison Dauphine, to Nate the bartender, to Chuck Coulter, Chase's son, who now managed the place since his father's death, to the fans who jostled in the street trying to get in. Back to the place she called home.

Rae crossed the wide living room of her apartment to the old mahogany baby grand that sat in the front window. She sat down at the keyboard and played a few runs, only to be interrupted by a voice drifting in the open window.

"Helloooo?"

Rae went to the wrought-iron balcony that faced the street and looked out. On the other side, Mrs. Beaulieu stood at her own balcony, waving a shaking hand. "Hellooo," she called again. "I'm so glad you're home, Rae."

"Do you need something, Mrs. B?" Rae shouted back. "Is everything all right?"

"Oh no, dear, I'm fine. Just fine. I was just wondering. . . ."

Here it comes, Rae thought. Mrs. B was a grand old lady, and Rae loved her company. But since her husband's death, she had been seeking Rae out more and more. Of course she was lonely. Of course she needed someone to talk to. But —

Rae was about to make up an excuse to get herself off the hook when Mrs. Beaulieu spoke again. "I was just sitting here thinking," she said, "and then I heard you at the piano. Would you — could you," she stammered, running a claw through her thin white hair. "Would you mind very much playing that song for me? The one I like so much? It was our song, Robert's and mine. . . ."

She drifted away again, back into her apartment, and Rae Dawn could see her through the open window as she sank into her chair and began to rock.

Rae knew without question what song Mrs. B wanted to hear. The song she had refused to play since —

She sighed. What difference did it make now? It was just a song. A favor for a sweet, sad, grieving old lady.

Rae barely got through the first line of "Come Rain or Come Shine" before her voice cracked. The tears came. And with the tears the memories she desperately wanted to suppress, memories dragged to the surface by Delta's telephone call. Memories of a certain December, nearly five years after she had first come to sing at Maison Dauphine. . . .

CHRISTMAS 1973

Rae Dawn aimed her eight-year-old Honda into the December darkness and sped toward Picayune, a reluctant missile launched northward against her will. The night was black and chilled, the waning quarter moon already set over the Crescent City, but now that she was outside the range of the city's pink glow, she could make out a spangle of stars overhead. Just north of Bayou Sauvage, she crossed the eastern tip of Lake Pontchartrain. To her left, on the surface of the dark lake, she could see the distant dance of glimmering lights — not stars, but artificial lights, human lights. And on the shore, reflected in the placid waters, a Christmas tree strung with red and green and gold.

On the radio, Bing Crosby was crooning "I'll Be Home for Christmas." With a grunt of disgust Rae Dawn snapped it off and was plunged immediately into a claustrophobic silence, broken only by the Doppler whine of the occasional car whizzing by and the thud of her tires on expansion cracks in the pavement.

Rae hated Christmas. She ought to love it, given the increase in business for Maison Dauphine and the resulting increase in her own meager revenues. New Orleans was a favorite holiday destination, and from Thanksgiving to New Year's the Quarter was alive with twinkling lights and festive music, concerts and plays and laughter and costumed carolers in the streets. Not to mention money — the *ching* of the cash registers, the tips pressed down, shaken together, and running over in the large brandy snifter on top of her piano.

But Christmas also meant that she got endless requests for those sappy Christmas songs, the ones about love and family and how wonderful it is to be home again. Never mind that most of the folks who asked for these tunes weren't home at all, but rather drowning their loneliness in a French Quarter bar, waxing nostalgic about Christmas past and inventing memories out of pure imagination.

Never in her life had Rae Dawn experienced the kind of Christmas portrayed in the songs or depicted on Christmas cards. Even as a child — *especially* as a child — she had not known the tantalizing excitement of an interminable Christmas Eve waiting for Santa Claus, or the thrill of colorfully wrapped presents under a glittering tree, or the warmth of friends and family gathered around a table groaning with the weight of the Christmas feast.

No, Christmas at Hobo Creek had been nothing like the photos in the advertisements. No tree, no stocking, no presents — unless you counted the new underwear from the Dollar Store or a secondhand coat or sweater from Goodwill. Once, years ago, Rae Dawn had taken it upon herself to try to make the Airstream a little more festive. She had found a couple of strings of old multicolored Christmas lights in the dumpster and, by switching bulbs, had gotten one string to work. The flame-shaped bulbs looped across the front of the trailer did make the place a bit more cheerful, until her father came home drunk and used the lights for target practice.

After that, Rae gave up on Christmas entirely.

Besides, what kind of Christmas would she have even if she had the desire to celebrate? She lived alone, played at the club every night. Karen and Charlene, who owned the tiny apartment she had rented for the past five years, were kind to her and always invited her when they threw a party, but most of the time she politely declined. Spare time, what little there was of it, she gave to writing music.

Rae had never deliberately determined not to have a social life. Sometimes she wished she could meet someone and fall in love, have a real home and a family — that old dream she cherished back in college. But real life got in the way. Taking the stage at Maison Dauphine from ten till two six nights a week tended to eliminate the possibility of dating. And without a partner, a lover, or even close friends to share it with, the holiday season had little meaning beyond the opportunity to work harder and make a few extra bucks.

Her drive to Picayune tonight, certainly, had nothing to do with celebrating the season. A nurse had called from the hospital shortly before midnight, just as Rae was about to begin her second set. Her mother had suffered a heart attack, a bad one, and had been taken to the emergency room. She was stabilized for the time being, but there was no assurance she would make it.

Rae's emotions as she sped along the deserted road vacillated between sorrow and relief. Sorrow for her mother, that her life had been so empty, so totally bereft of love or friendship or any sort of meaning or purpose. And relief for herself, that once Mama was gone she could finally and forever leave Picayune behind her.

Daddy had died two years ago — wrapped his pickup truck around a telephone pole and never felt a thing. At the funeral Mama had barely spoken to her daughter, and not once did she turn to her for comfort or consolation. Rae had dutifully made the requisite arrangements, stood beside her mother at the graveside, and then, confronted with her own uselessness, had quickly gone away again. Mama had stayed put in the Airstream on the banks of Hobo Creek.

Rae hadn't set foot in Picayune since the day they put Daddy in the ground. But she could imagine how things had been since her father's death. Her mother still sitting at the table in the kitchen, smoking and staring into space and tracing patterns in the Formica with a broken fingernail. She could envision the place disintegrating around Mama, the trailer covered with kudzu and gradually being absorbed into the wildness.

A stab of regret shot through her. What a rotten daughter she had been, thinking only of her own needs, the compulsion to extricate herself from the past and its oppressive memories. She had gone straight to New Orleans after graduation, without giving more than a passing thought to Picayune or Hobo Creek or the Airstream that hunkered on its red clay banks. She had made it. She had escaped.

But now, picturing Mama alone in the Airstream, Rae wondered: How was her life that different from her mother's? She sang her songs, wrote her music, played three sets a night, and went home to an empty apartment at two o'clock in the morning. What had she accomplished, really? She had realized her dream, only to discover that a dream fulfilled, when there is no one to share it, can be every bit as empty as no dream at all.

The blinding white lights of the hospital emergency room loomed up before her. Rae dashed in through the sliding doors, dazed and disoriented by the brightness after the dark womb of the car.

This was a small-town hospital, and at this hour the place was nearly deserted. One old man with a grizzled beard dozed in a chair in the corner. Behind a high counter two nurses in green scrubs talked in quiet voices, their heads bent over a patient's chart.

"Lorna DuChamp," Rae Dawn demanded, raising her voice to get the nurses' attention. "Where is she?"

One of the nurses came over to the counter and checked a list. "DuChamp. Yes. She was brought in a couple of hours ago. Room 104, down the hall to the left."

Rae took off down the corridor, rounded the corner, and stopped short. The door bearing the number 104 stood ajar, and from within she could hear ominous sounds — beeps and clicks and a kind of wheezing noise.

She pushed the door open and went inside.

Mama lay motionless on the bed, covered with a pale green sheet and connected by a maze of tubes and wires to an array of monitors. On one side of the bed stood a young woman in a white lab coat — about her own age or a little older, Rae guessed. She had short reddish brown hair and tanned freckled skin, and her eyes, when she lifted her head to look at Rae, were an arresting shade somewhere between hazel and light brown, and very kind.

"You must be Rae Dawn," the woman said, leaving the bedside to come to her. "I'm Noel Ridley, your mother's doctor. We spoke on the phone."

Rae couldn't quit staring at her. The hair,

the complexion, the eyes, all combined to give her the look of a young lioness, fiercely protective but with no hint of violence or aggression.

"*Y-you* called?" she stammered. "I thought — I thought it was a nurse."

"An easy mistake to make," the doctor said. She refrained, Rae Dawn noticed, from commenting on the stereotype that assumed a woman to be a nurse rather than a doctor. "I wanted to do it myself," she said simply. "We're all so fond of Lorna."

Rae frowned. "You *know* my mother?"

"Well, yes, of course." Dr. Ridley nodded. "Picayune is a small town. Everyone knows her. She has many friends here."

Rae opened her mouth to respond but could think of nothing to say, so she shut it again. "How is she?" she asked at last.

Dr. Ridley shook her head. "Not good, I'm afraid. It was a massive heart attack, and although we thought at first she might pull through it, she took a downhill turn about twenty minutes ago. Apparently she threw a clot. She's in a coma. The respirator is keeping her alive, but —"

"But she won't come out of it."

"No. I'm sorry."

Rae Dawn exhaled a deep, ragged breath, and felt the warm weight of the doctor's hand on her arm.

"Things are pretty quiet around here at the moment," she said. "Why don't we go down to the cafeteria and get some coffee and talk?"

"All right." Rae cast a glance at her mother. "Give me just a minute."

"Take your time. I'll meet you there." She smiled. "Left at the nurses' station, then all the way down the hall at the end."

When the doctor was gone, Rae went to the bedside and took her mother's hand. Her skin, rough and reddened, was cool to the touch — not cold as death, but not warm with life either. It seemed to Rae Dawn that Mama was hovering someplace between the two worlds, waiting for release, and it was clear she couldn't come back to this one even if she wanted to.

Rae gazed down at her mother's face. Years of stress and misery and despair had ravaged her, cutting deep lines into her cheeks and brow. And yet now, here, in this waiting place, her skin had smoothed so that the wrinkles appeared as tiny hairline scars instead. She looked . . . peaceful. Almost pretty. The way she might have looked had her life taken a different direction.

Rae Dawn brushed an errant hair back from her forehead and again that knife-edge of remorse sliced into her. "I'm sorry, Mama," she whispered. "Sorry for everything."

She couldn't remember the last time she had kissed her mother, but Rae kissed her now, her lips lingering on the soft cheek, a single tear running down to salt the kiss. "I'll be back soon," she promised. "And then this will all be over."

Rae Dawn found Dr. Ridley in the cafeteria at a corner table next to the window. She took the seat opposite and focused her eyes on the doctor's graceful, freckled fingers as they wrapped themselves around a white ceramic mug of steaming coffee.

"It's regular," the doctor said, pointing at the carafe that sat on the table between them. "When I'm on nights I prefer the caffeine. If you want decaf, it's available."

"This is fine." Rae poured herself a cup and took a sip. It was strong but not bitter, and tasted faintly of the chicory blend she had become accustomed to in New Orleans. "Tell me about my mother."

The lioness lifted her eyes and held Rae Dawn's gaze. "The patient, or the woman?"

Rae bit her lip. "Dr. Ridley, I can only imagine what you think of me. I haven't been a very good daughter."

"Noel," she corrected. "Please, call me Noel. It's funny, I know — especially at Christmastime. I keep hearing my name on the radio." She drained her cup and pushed it to the center of the table. "Your mother," she said, "was very proud of you."

"Excuse me, but how do you know her?" Rae interrupted. "She's lived in this town for years and never, to my knowledge, had a single friend. She spent her life —" She stopped. No. The way they had lived — the crushing poverty, the isolation, her father's drunken rages — none of it was this doctor's business, however kind and compassionate she seemed.

"She spent her life in that dismal trailer?" Noel Ridley finished the sentence, then nodded. "Yes, I know all about it. About your father too. About the way you grew up."

"How . . . ?"

"Lorna told me," she said simply.

Rae felt heat rising into her face, and she put her hands to her cheeks.

"There's no need to be embarrassed," the doctor said. "I'm very clear on your family's situation, Rae Dawn. How you were raised. What your father was like. How your mother buried herself out there, purely out of shame."

"So what changed?"

Noel shrugged. "Your father died. And your mother came alive. You didn't know, I suppose, that she volunteered here at the hospital. That she spent Tuesday afternoons reading to children in the library. That she went to church."

"Church?"

"Yes, she was very faithful. Our paths crossed there too. As I said, she was very proud of you. Talked about you all the time — what a gifted musician you are. How you write your own music and have built a career for yourself at the club — Maison Dauphine, isn't it? How do you think I found you?"

Rae shook her head. "I didn't —"

"Listen," the doctor said. "In situations like this, when a parent dies without the chance to say good-bye, the emotion it most often brings up in survivors is anger. Self-recrimination. I knew your mother fairly well, and I feel I know you too. Don't beat yourself up, Rae Dawn. Your mother understood why you had to separate yourself from this place. She was proud of you. Proud of who you are. Proud you got away."

Rae heard the words but didn't quite believe them. "How can you be so sure?"

"Because she told me. Her only regret for you was that you hadn't yet found love. She said she always hoped you'd meet the woman of your dreams and —"

"Hold on," Rae interrupted. "Did you say the *woman* of my dreams?"

"Yes, that's exactly what I said."

"But she didn't —"

"She *did* know. We talked about it." Noel chuckled. "In fact, she thought the two of us might be a good match."

Shocked to the core by the revelation of her mother's uncanny insight, Rae Dawn almost missed this last sentence. "Excuse me?"

"She wanted to introduce us," Noel repeated. "Unfortunately, she never had the opportunity — until now." She stood up and extended a hand in Rae Dawn's direction. "If you're ready, I think it's time to go and say good-bye."

It was a little after three A.M. when Lorna DuChamp slipped quietly from this life to the next. She never woke. Rae stood holding her hand while Noel shut down the respirator and removed the tubes.

"Thank you, Mama," she whispered. "Thank you for setting me free. I'm glad you found your own sort of freedom in the end."

And then she was gone with nothing, not even a breath, to mark her passage to the other side. Just a gradual cooling of the flesh, a softening of the lines of her face.

At the end Noel came and stood beside Rae Dawn with one arm around her shoulders. The warmth of her nearness felt right, somehow — familiar and alive and comforting.

"We need to take the body," she said in a quiet voice.

Rae nodded. Her mother's organs would be harvested — heart, liver, and kidneys — to give life to nameless others waiting for transplants. What remained would be cremated. It was Rae's decision, and she made it without hesitation. She would not have her mother buried alongside the man who had made her life a living hell.

"That's it, I guess." Rae Dawn sighed when the orderlies had left with the body.

"What will you do now?" Noel asked.

"Go back to New Orleans, I suppose." Rae shrugged. "I suppose I do need to go out to the trailer, but I really don't ever want to see the place again."

"My shift ended at two. I'll go with you if you like."

"You've done enough already. This is not a doctor's duty."

"I didn't offer as a doctor."

Rae Dawn looked into the tawny eyes and found them filled with a strange luminosity, burning like liquid gold. She felt quite suddenly as if she could drown in those eyes, as if they were drawing her home. And then, just as quickly, she realized what vulnerability her own gaze must be revealing, and she tried to break the link.

But Noel did not look away. "Let's go," she said softly.

The track leading from the main road to the trailer was black as midnight, overgrown and muddy. The headlights of Noel's car revealed deep ruts in the earth, fresh grooves made by some heavy vehicle. The ambulance, Rae Dawn supposed.

The closer they got, the more violently her stomach churned. Her hands were trembling, and she clenched them in her lap. All the old memories flooded over her — the hungry, miserable days, the terrifying nights punctuated by her father's rampaging drunkenness and the deafening crack of his shotgun. The resigned emptiness of her mother's face.

Everything looked so much smaller than it did in recollections from her childhood. The rusted Airstream, illuminated in the headlights, tilted oddly to one side, crouched in its nest of kudzu like some strange and frightened forest creature, its curved haunches riddled with buckshot. Behind and to the right, the shadow of a dilapidated shed, barely larger than an outhouse, leaned precariously toward the bank of Hobo Creek. The air was permeated with the stench of decay — rotted wood, leaves gone to mulch, stagnant water. Rae Dawn's interior atmosphere, too, smelled of deterioration, despair, and shame.

"It's all right," Noel's low voice murmured behind her.

The door to the trailer stood half open, and on shaking legs Rae climbed the rusted metal stairs, stepped inside, and turned on the lights. Here, too, the world she remembered had shrunk. The cramped living room where she slept, the meager kitchen with its scarred Formica table, the narrow passageway that led to a tiny bath and a single bedroom barely wide enough to lie down in. Something scuttled along a baseboard.

A wave of nausea gripped her, and for an instant she was sure she was going to retch. She reached for the edge of the table and felt Noel's strong warm hand supporting her instead. "It's all right," she repeated. "Take it easy."

Rae Dawn sank onto one of the vinyl kitchen chairs and took several deep breaths.

"You okay?" Noel asked.

Rae nodded. "I just — I can't believe —"
She squeezed her eyes shut and slammed a
fist down on the table. "How could my father do this to us? He was supposed to love
us, to protect us —"

"Get it out," Noel urged. "All the anger, all
the pain. Don't let it poison you any longer."

The penetrating compassion in her voice,
the innate understanding, nearly undid Rae
Dawn altogether. She began to cry — deep,
racking sobs. She put her shaking hands up
to her face. "I've got to pull myself together."

"No, you don't," Noel countered. "Not on
my account. Your mother told me everything, Rae. I know how bad it was."

"I hated him," Rae said. The admission felt
strangely liberating, cleansing, like the first
good breath she had taken since she set foot
in the trailer again. "I *hated* him! I *still* hate
him." All the rage she had suppressed
throughout her childhood came
roaring back. She stood up, tipping the chair
over with the force of her movement, and
with two steps she was standing in the living
room. "This place! This terrible, filthy, shitty
place!" She careened through the confined
rooms, tearing down the ragged curtains,
kicking over a chair, pounding her fist into
the lumpy sofa cushions. "He sucked all the
life out of everything he touched. My

mother, me. That's where I slept," she said, pointing toward the sagging, mildewed couch. "I didn't have a room of my own, dammit, didn't even have a space of my own. Even if we were poor, we didn't have to live like this. He had a pension; there was a little money coming in. But every last dime went to liquor. I can still smell it — his precious whiskey, his stinking vomit in the rug."

She lifted her head, caught her reflection in the dirty glass window, and turned, suddenly shamed by her outburst. "I ought to forgive him, I suppose."

"There's a time for forgiveness," Noel said in a firm, quiet voice. "But right now, at this moment, what do *you* want, Rae Dawn? What do *you* need?"

Rae wheeled around. In that instant, as she looked into Noel Ridley's eyes, she saw what she had been looking for all her life. A kindred spirit. Someone who, even though she hadn't lived it, instinctively understood.

"Matches," she said. "I need matches. I want to burn this hellhole to the ground!"

Noel pointed toward the stove. On the back ledge sat a large box of wooden kitchen matches, the kind Mama used to light the propane burners.

"Take the car up to the road," Rae Dawn said. "I'll be there in a minute."

■ ■ ■ ■

Above them, over the dark country road, a million stars gleamed against the blackness. Rae stood on the gravel, shoulder to shoulder with Noel Ridley, and watched as her childhood home went up in flames.

At first it was just a glimmer of yellow light in the living room window, as if someone had lit a lamp to welcome in a stranger. Then the sofa caught, soaked as it was with old kerosene from the shed, and the fire worked its way through the kitchen to the mattress on the bedroom floor.

Now the whole place was ablaze, a bonfire at a pep rally, a giant Yule log roaring in the grate. Yellow and orange flames leaped and danced, candle-shaped, like hands clasped in prayer. The ceiling gave way and fell in. Sparks flew skyward, mingling their gold with the silver stars overhead.

It was, for Rae Dawn, a moment of complete release. As the fire raged and spread, engulfing the Airstream in a matter of seconds, some chrysalis in her own soul cracked open. All the years of suppressed fury and shame rose and left her, propelled toward heaven on the rising flames.

Music threaded through her mind, a score she had written for her final performance project in college. The minor-key oppression of a burdened soul. The turn, the movement upward, the change to a lifting, soaring flight. "Woman on the Wind," she had called it, but until this instant she had not fathomed all its varied meanings. What new life would rise from the ashes she did not know, only that her spirit, at last, was free.

Rae Dawn's eyes never left the trailer, but she felt the doctor's hand reach for hers and drew strength from its warmth.

"Now *that,*" Noel said softly, "is what I call a Christmas celebration."

NINETEEN:
COME RAIN OR COME SHINE

Maison Dauphine, jammed to the rafters, seemed to close in on Rae Dawn as she took the stage for her second set of the evening. Friday nights the club was always packed, but when the audience consisted mostly of regulars she knew by sight if not by name, the place didn't feel so claustrophobic. On this Friday before Mardi Gras, however, with a wild and rowdy mob of out-of-town revelers, she found her nerves on edge.

The lights came up, diffused by a haze of blue smoke. At the bar, a group of guys in LSU jerseys, clearly drunk, were causing some commotion. Rae glanced to the edge of the stage, where Arlen Crocker, Chase's army buddy and head of Maison Dauphine's security, stood with his arms crossed over his massive chest. She caught his eye and nodded in the direction of the troublemakers.

Mardi Gras might well be called the biggest bash on earth, but it was also the most dangerous time to be in New Orleans. Large quantities of alcohol did not mix well with thousands of anonymous partygoers shedding their inhibitions in the streets. Bar fights were common, and a broken beer bottle served as well as a shiv for a murder weapon.

Arlen moved toward the bar and positioned himself close to the college boys. The crowd quieted a little, and Rae Dawn launched into an arrangement of "Come Rain or Come Shine."

"Hey, baby!" one of the boys yelled. "Take it off, why don't you? Come on, show us some tits!"

Rae kept on singing. This was the downside of the career she loved so much. The regulars at Maison Dauphine showed respect. They listened when she sang and filled her tip jar when she remembered their favorite tunes. Even the habitual drunks fell into a stupor quietly, without interrupting the show.

The LSU boys were wound-up, ugly drunks. Over the music and the low buzz of conversation, they shouted obscenities and made lewd suggestions about their own personal endowments and what they could do to make Rae Dawn happy.

She chuckled to herself. These dogs were definitely barking up the wrong tree.

"Tits!" the leader of the pack yelled again, and his cohorts took up the chant: "Tits! Tits! Tits!"

Then it happened. The alpha dog lunged off his bar stool and made for the stage, evidently intent on helping Rae Dawn undress. He shoved several other patrons aside, spilling drinks. Someone threw a punch, and all hell broke loose.

Arlen was on top of the situation and jerked the college boy into a choke hold long before he reached the stage. But his intervention, though effective, came just a little too late. By the time he and his other bouncers had corralled the troublemakers and shown them the door, the floor was covered with shattered glass and blood was flowing. One man had been hit in the head with a bottle and clearly needed stitches.

"Stand aside; I'm a doctor," came an authoritative voice from the shadows.

The crowd parted like the Red Sea before Moses' staff, and out of the darkness stepped a diminutive woman with red-blonde hair and the tawny eyes of a lioness.

Noel Ridley knelt before the injured man, examined his wound, and staunched the bleeding with a bar towel. "You're going to be all right," she assured him, "but you need to get that cut sewn up. Did anyone call an ambulance?"

The bartender nodded, and as if on cue, flashing lights appeared outside the doorway of the club. Two paramedics came in and took the guy away to have his head stitched. Cops hustled the college boys into a couple of squad cars and carted them off to the drunk tank.

The rest of the crowd, much subdued, went back to their beer while the bartender began sweeping up the broken glass.

Rae, however, did not return to her piano. She stood on the edge of the low stage and watched, entranced, as Noel got to her feet and turned in her direction.

Suddenly Maison Dauphine didn't seem claustrophobic at all. For Rae Dawn, there was no one in the club but Noel. The woman had an aura about her, an unearthly gilded brightness. As if in slow motion she turned and smiled, radiating that light in Rae's direction.

This, Rae Dawn thought, *is it.*

To be perfectly honest, she wasn't at all sure what "it" was, only that Noel's presence

— in the room, in her life — changed everything.

Since New Year's, Noel had been coming to New Orleans almost every week on her days off. They had taken in a few of the quieter clubs, listening to other singers, but mostly they sat in Café Du Monde drinking coffee and eating beignets, strolled among the artists in Jackson Square, bought po'boys, picnicked along the river.

They talked about Rae Dawn's music and Noel's medicine. Healing was not a job, Noel said, it was a calling. It was art and poetry, prayer and worship, heart and soul. It was the place where she felt most connected to God and herself and the universe.

The strands of their conversations coiled and twisted inside Rae Dawn, a haunting motif, diverse notes weaving together into impossibly beautiful harmonies. The differences between them were every bit as lovely as the similarities, an ethereal inner melody that caught her heart and held her fast.

Noel came, and she went. Her coming brought a measure of peace and well-being unlike anything Rae had ever known; her going left that golden glow behind like a benediction. Expectation lit Rae Dawn's days as she waited, and when Noel departed no emptiness remained in her wake, only a contented fulfillment and a sharpened sense of glad surprise.

But Rae Dawn had not known that Noel was coming tonight, and her unexpected appearance sent a palpable flash of longing through her veins. With her eyes fixed on Noel's, she stepped back to the mike. "I'm going to take a break and regroup after our little melee. But don't worry, I'll be back."

"How about finishing the song, at least?" someone suggested.

Rae Dawn's brain had turned to mush. She couldn't for the life of her think what song she had been singing when the fight broke out. Then it came to her, and with a self-deprecating smile she sat down at the piano. "Just this one," she agreed. "And more later."

Noel sank down into a chair in front of the stage. Her amber eyes shone, illuminated from within. Rae Dawn couldn't have looked away even if she had tried.

Rae began to sing. The words flowed through her veins, reborn, newly alive, words about a love that was high as a mountain, deep as a river. A love like no other. A love that would last forever. How many times had she sung this song? Hundreds? Thousands, even?

And yet she had never sung it at all until

this moment, this night.

Backstage, in the ten-by-ten closet that had been made over into Rae Dawn's dressing room, the two of them clung together as if they'd never let go.

"What *happened* out there?" Noel said, searching Rae's eyes.

"I don't know." Rae Dawn shook her head. "When I saw you, sort of materializing out of the darkness, it was like a vision. A dream. Like all the pieces fell into place."

Noel collapsed into the single chair that nearly filled one side of the room and pulled Rae Dawn down onto the padded arm. "I have to be back tomorrow, but I needed to come. Needed to talk to you. It's all right, then, my just showing up like this?"

"All right?" Rae began to laugh. "What do you mean, 'all right'? It's *wonderful*."

A look of relief passed over Noel's face. "That's good to hear. Because —" She hesitated. "What would you think about me taking a job here?"

Rae Dawn stared at her. "What are you talking about?"

"An old friend of mine from med school is opening a practice. A twenty-four-hour clinic for low-income families. He's invited me to join him."

"In New Orleans?"

"Yes." Noel nodded. "But our patients will mostly be single mothers and their kids. I won't be making much."

"So what?" Rae said. "You'll be here, and that's what counts."

Noel's expression changed — subtly, but Rae Dawn saw it. "There's one other thing we have to talk about."

Rae slid off the arm of the chair and sat on the rug at Noel's feet. "Okay, shoot."

"I want us to be together."

Rae Dawn frowned. "We *are* together."

"No, I mean, *really* together." Noel ran a hand over her face. "I don't know how to say this. There's no language for it. We can't be, well, married. Not technically. Not officially. But that's what I want. A commitment. For life."

Rae stared at her as this bit of information sank in. For a minute she said nothing. Then the humor of the situation overcame her. "Damn, honey, if that's a proposal you really need to work on it. Sounds more like a criminal conviction than a romance."

Tears welled up in Noel's eyes and she looked away.

"Whoa!" Rae said. "Hold on. I was just kidding. I didn't mean to hurt your feelings." She reached up and pulled Noel out of the chair and into her arms. "There is nothing I want more," she whispered, "than to be with you forever. I want you with me — here, now, all the time. We fit. We complement each other. Like melody and harmony." Rae kissed her on the eyelids and tasted the salty tears on her tongue. "When I saw you come into the club tonight, I thought, 'This is it.' I wasn't quite sure what that meant, but now I know."

She glanced down at her wristwatch. "It's time for my last set. Come listen to me sing."

Noel got to her feet. "If you sing anything else the way you did 'Come Rain or Come Shine,' I'm going to have difficulty restraining myself." She arched her eyebrows. "You *were* singing it to me, weren't you?"

"What do you think?" Rae finished touching up her makeup and held out a hand. "Let's go."

"Wait," Noel said. "I forgot to tell you something."

Rae opened the door to the stage, and the noise nearly knocked them over. She had to shout to be heard. "What did you forget to say?"

In that instant the house lights went down and the noise in the club subsided. "I'm in love with you!" Noel yelled into the sudden quiet.

In the darkness someone let out a piercing whistle.

"I'm in love with you too," Rae Dawn whispered, and kissed her.

With Billie Holiday playing on the stereo, Rae Dawn moved swiftly around the apartment, clearing out drawers and closets, purging, filling black plastic garbage bags with things she didn't really need and shouldn't have kept all these years. House-cleaning wasn't her favorite activity by a long shot, but today she worked with a fervor born of love.

They had talked until dawn and then, after two hours of sleep, Noel had left to return to Picayune. But everything was decided. It would take her some time — several weeks, probably — to tie up loose ends and get moved. Still, Rae Dawn was determined to be ready. Eventually, once Noel got settled in her new practice, they would look for a larger place together, maybe even a small house. But in the meantime, they would share this apartment.

She swept the dust bunnies out from under the bed, then straightened up and regarded the bedroom with a critical eye. The apartment, though quite sufficient for one, seemed to draw in and constrict upon itself when she considered how it might work for two. The closets were inadequate, the kitchen outdated, the bathroom barely large enough to turn around in without putting one foot in the tub. But the living room was light and spacious and would easily accommodate Noel's furniture, which was far superior to the hodgepodge of secondhand stuff Rae Dawn had collected over the years.

She wished, just briefly, that they could afford the apartment over Maison Dauphine. It was an expansive place, with two bedrooms, a terrace that extended over the back garden, and a wrought-iron balcony that faced toward the river and offered a view of the spires of St. Louis Cathedral two blocks away. Unfortunately, it was far out of their league. Noel's new practice wouldn't bring in a great deal of money, and Rae had long ago resigned herself to the reality of what kind of income a musician made. It was a nice dream, but that's all it would ever be.

Still, it didn't matter. They would be together.

Together. The very word caused Rae's heart to swoop and soar. Never in her life had she felt this way, as if the world itself rejoiced. Never had she known that anything other than music could bring this sense of wholeness, of well-being.

For years she had sung the love songs that had propelled her career forward, had watched the way couples in the audience held hands and gazed into one another's eyes when she sang. Somehow she had infused into those songs a passion and desire that came from a well of longing deep within her. But now for the first time she realized that the images in those songs were not mere metaphors. Skies really *were* bluer, stars closer, the moon brighter. All creation moved together in a windswept dance of celebration. Life really *did* begin when you fell in love.

At last Rae Dawn understood. She had awakened from a dream to find that the dream had come true. The dream of loving and being loved. The dream of Noel Ridley.

TWENTY:
ECSTASY AND AGONY

NEW ORLEANS
FEBRUARY 1979

"Are you planning to sleep all day?"

Rae Dawn opened her eyes to see Noel standing over her with a tray. She struggled to a sitting position, and Noel placed the tray on her lap. Waffles and scrambled eggs, steaming strong coffee, fresh orange juice.

"Good morning," Rae mumbled.

"Never mind morning," Noel said with a laugh. "It's almost afternoon, and I don't want to waste our entire anniversary." She sat on the edge of the bed and leaned forward expectantly.

Rae put a hand to her mouth. "Trust me, you don't want to kiss me until I've brushed my teeth." She shifted the tray, pulled on a robe, and dashed to the bathroom. When she returned, Noel had arranged the pillows against the headboard and settled the breakfast tray between them.

"So, what would you like to do with our day?" Noel forked up a slice of waffle.

"I'd like to *celebrate*." Rae sipped at her coffee and smiled. "Dance in the streets and throw confetti in Jackson Park."

"I know exactly how you feel." Noel grinned. "Five years. The best five years of my life."

At noon the following Monday Rae Dawn sat in Chase Coulter's office with the door closed. She stared at him, not believing what she was hearing.

"You expect me to do *what?*" she demanded.

Chase's jaw flinched convulsively beneath the flesh of his cheek. "I'm sorry, Rae. I'd be the first to argue that you should be able to live however you want. But you've got to consider your career."

Rae frowned. "What are you talking about?"

"I'm talking about you, Rae, and your doctor girlfriend."

"My life with Noel is nobody's business, Chase. Besides, this is New Orleans, not Podunk, Iowa."

Chase slammed a palm down on the desk. "You have to listen to me, Rae Dawn. Why

259

do you think people line up every night to get in here?" He gritted his teeth and pointed at the door. "Because of *you*. Because of your music. Love songs, torch songs, jazz, blues. Look at you. You're steamy, you're sexy. You're gorgeous and mysterious and fascinating."

"No, I'm not. I'm just — me."

"Well, *just you* is what they're buying. The men want you and the women want to *be* you. And if word gets out about you and Noel —" Chase shook his head. "Nobody's going to come hear you sing if they know you're belting out love songs to another woman."

"So you're saying that I'm public property and don't have the right to be in love? That I'm supposed to hide my relationship with Noel?"

"I'm saying you can't bring your private life into the public eye, especially when it would ruin your career — and mine, if you get my drift."

Rae could hardly believe this. Chase Coulter *knew* Noel, for pity's sake. He liked her, thought she was cute and funny and smart. And now he was talking about her as if she were some kind of one-night stand, a minor employee in an all-girl escort service.

She tried to reason with him. "Chase, what's changed? Noel has been living with me for five years now. She moved here to be with me, took a new job for me. She has an established practice, and —"

"I know," he interrupted. "She's a saint. She's Mother Teresa. But she talks too much."

Rae frowned. "What do you mean?"

Chase sighed. "This guy came in yesterday afternoon looking for a job. Said he had been to the clinic and his doctor had told him that her partner was the headliner here and we were advertising for another bartender."

"So what?"

"So if your girlfriend is talking that freely about the two of you —"

Rae Dawn shook her head. "Chase, this is ridiculous. The Quarter is a very diverse and accepting place. This is my life —"

"And it's my club. Besides, we're not just talking about the Quarter. We're talking about the *country,* Rae. Middle America. White-bread heterosexuals. Two talent agents and a scout for Arista Records are coming to hear you on Friday night. You're going national, and I'd bet my ass you're going to be big. This is your chance. I suggest you think long and hard about whether you really want a future as a singer."

■ ■ ■ ■

"So," Noel said over dinner that night, "the bottom line is, your boss wants you to hide who you are. Who *we* are."

Vividly Rae recalled — though it had been ten years ago — the scene on the quad at college, when furious protesters had carried signs reading *God Hates Dikes and Fagots* and chanted, "Fire the queers, fire the queers." She would never forget her last conversation with Dr. Gottlieb, who had been both mentor and father to her. The angry words they had exchanged still burned in her memory, the expression on his face when he told her "You do not understand the ways of the world."

Perhaps he was right. For a long time — five years before Noel, and five incredible years with her — Rae Dawn had lived in the insular bubble of the French Quarter, a universe unto itself where the unusual was commonplace. Even during the Civil Rights Movement, when people were being attacked by police dogs and set on with fire hoses, interracial couples in the Quarter barely merited the lift of an eyebrow. Gay Mardi Gras krewes had been taking part in the Carnival celebrations since the late fifties and early sixties. New Orleans was a progressive Mecca surrounded on all sides by the battlements of conservatism.

Now Rae Dawn's career was about to break out, but apparently that meant catering to a less liberal fan base. As Chase had put it, nobody wanted to be confronted with the truth that their favorite sexy torch singer was "belting out love songs to another woman."

Still, there were always compromises to be made. For anyone in the entertainment business, a larger public meant less privacy. It was part of the price you paid for success.

Rae just hoped the price wouldn't be too high.

Noel reached out and took her hand. "Is this what you want?" she asked. "Record deals, tours, national exposure?"

Exposure. The word sliced across Rae's nerves like a scalpel. The truth was, she was afraid of failure but equally terrified of success. What if she took the risk and couldn't make it in the big leagues? What if she did make it, and it changed her life forever?

"I don't know what I want," Rae said. "This is the chance I've worked for all my life, but —"

"Then let's just take it one step at a time," Noel said. "Meet the agents. Sing for the scout. We'll see what happens from there."

What happened from there Rae Dawn didn't like to think about.

An agent by the name of William Tyce. A contract from Arista Records. An album, entitled simply *Dawn,* with a corresponding name change to Dawn DuChante and a sultry close-up of Rae's "new look." Interminable months on the road in a tour bus, opening for Aretha Franklin and other stars of the Arista firmament.

The first year Rae thought she'd go crazy. She missed home, missed Noel. Static, furtive conversations on the telephone didn't begin to make up for long talks on a rainy afternoon or cuddling on the couch on Saturday morning.

And the worst of it, in Rae Dawn's mind, was the fact that she couldn't tell anyone. All the musicians on the tour complained openly about the difficulty of separation. They filled the empty hours with conversations about their husbands and wives and lovers. They all raced for the telephones whenever the bus stopped and never gave a second thought to being overheard saying "I love you."

Everyone had left someone behind to chase the dream; it was the common bond that held them together. All of them except Rae Dawn.

"You're lucky, girl," one of Aretha's backup singers once told her. "It's easier when you're single with nobody to worry 'bout but yourself." And always the assumption, always the assurance: "Focus on the music, baby. Time enough for love later on. You'll have your pick of men."

They all called her Dawn. They didn't even know her name.

The second year, two days before Christmas, Rae came home and fell exhausted and weeping into Noel's arms, ready to give it all up.

The third year, a call came from her agent, Will Tyce.

"The album's finally making its way up the charts," Tyce told her excitedly, as if presenting her with some magnificent gift. "Slowly, but it's getting enough attention that Arista wants another one as soon as you can get to New York to record it. We're going to book concerts all across the country to promote it. And we're sending down a photographer for some new publicity shots. This is it, Dawn. You're an overnight success."

An "overnight success" that took years to achieve.

And so it continued — another two years

of painful separation and silence. Concert audiences loved her. For a while the album sales held their peak, and money poured in like water. But money couldn't stop the drift. Money couldn't fill the awkward pauses during those late-night calls when both of them were too exhausted to talk. Money couldn't buy back what they seemed to be losing.

On the telephone from Boston, Rae negotiated a deal with Chase Coulter to buy out Maison Dauphine, which included the large apartment upstairs. On the telephone from Minneapolis, she and Noel decided what furniture to take to the new place and what they should buy. On the telephone from Seattle, she listened helplessly while Noel cried. On the telephone from Dallas, Rae cried while Noel listened.

And then the final straw: a Grammy nomination for Best Female R&B Vocal Performance. "Okay, here's the plan," Will Tyce said, taking charge as usual. "We'll get you a fabulous dress — black sequins, low cut in front. A great diamond necklace, the works. I'll take care of everything. February 26, in L.A. And you'll be going with —"

"Hold it," Rae Dawn said. "I'm taking Noel."

"No, you're not."

Rae's breath came in shallow gasps. "Will, this is what I've worked for, what Noel and I have both sacrificed for. She deserves to be there."

"Right. I'll get her a seat in the balcony. But you will not appear in public with her. Understood?"

Rae Dawn caved. Noel stayed home. And then, on the red carpet going in for the awards show, the unthinkable happened. Rae's escort — Arista's newest discovery, a handsome, arrogant jerk by the name of Brian Hearn — pulled her into a hip-crushing embrace, french-kissed her, and announced their engagement to the crowd. Brian, almost ten years younger than Rae, was a flaming queen who put on a macho act for the fans. Now he swaggered at her side, half-drunk already, and leered at her while one hand groped her butt.

Rae didn't win the Grammy, but the pictures, predictably, made the next day's papers. The tongue-thrust, the ass-fondling, all of it. National television. *Entertainment Tonight*. Front page of the tabloids.

The flight from Los Angeles to New Orleans was the longest of Rae Dawn's life. When she arrived, Noel was already packed.

"I can't take this anymore," she said, choking back tears. "The travel, the separation, the deception." She threw one of the tabloids down on the coffee table and pointed at the photo of Rae being groped by Brian Hearn. "You *kissed* him!"

"I didn't kiss him. He kissed me." Rae Dawn knew, even as she said it, that it sounded like a blatant rationalization. "Besides, we both know he's gay."

"It doesn't matter," Noel said. "All of this makes me feel —" She groped for words. "Cheap. Invalidated. Either I'm your partner, or I'm not. I didn't sign on for a part-time marriage. Or a secret one."

Noel let her gaze drift around the spacious apartment above the club, and Rae's eyes followed. The place was beautiful, but it didn't feel like home. Rae Dawn hadn't been here often enough to make it home.

They should have stood together on the balcony looking out toward the cathedral, watching the morning mist rise off the river. They should have eaten breakfast on the terrace overlooking the back garden. They should have built a fire and made popcorn and snuggled up to watch old movies on a rainy winter's night. They should have had a dog.

"I'll quit," Rae said as desperation and misery welled up in her. "I'll quit it all — the touring, the appearances, the record deals.

We've still got Maison Dauphine."

"*You've* got Maison Dauphine," Noel corrected. "I've got a job waiting back at the hospital in Picayune."

"Please," Rae said. "I love you."

"I love you too," Noel whispered. "I'll always love you."

Then she was gone. A week before Carnival. A week before their tenth anniversary.

New Orleans
September 1994

Rae got up from the piano and went to the front balcony. Through the windows of Mrs. B's apartment, she could see that the old woman had fallen asleep, her chair rocking a little and her head lolling to one side. Dreaming, no doubt, of her Robert, of the half-century of love they had shared together. Of the children she had borne and lost — one to a car wreck and one to breast cancer.

How sad it is, Rae thought, *to outlive everyone you've loved. . . .*

Her mind lurched from Mrs. B's life to her own, to the people she had loved and lost. Her mother, whom she'd never really had the chance to know before the heart attack

269

took her. Dr. Gottlieb, who had been both mentor and surrogate father until the issue of her sexual orientation had divided them. And Noel Ridley, not dead, but vanished from her life for nearly ten years.

She had friends, she supposed. Nate the bartender, Chuck Coulter the general manager of Maison Dauphine. Some of the younger musicians who took the stage and sang to the crowds downstairs, and then moved on as their careers shifted into high gear or fizzled out from lack of talent. But they all had families — or, in the case of the performers, an obsession for success that obscured everything else. They cared about Rae, they liked her, but with none of them did she really belong.

All she had now was the club. The insane schedule of tours and concerts and recording contracts was long since behind her. There had been no third album, no more tours or Grammy nominations. The few people who remembered Dawn DuChante thought of her as something of a legend, which in the music business translated to *has-been*.

But Rae Dawn didn't really care. Other artists now performed her songs, making her a quiet, behind-the-scenes success. Money would never be an issue — the profits from

Maison Dauphine and residuals from her own albums and copyrights would be sufficient to keep Rae and a small country afloat for decades to come. What mattered to her — what depressed her whenever she allowed herself to think about it — was that she was forty-seven years old and alone.

Even after all these years, precious few artists took the risk to come out. A handful of singers. A few actors here and there. Most, Rae Dawn suspected, got shoved into the mold, coerced into masquerading as straight or losing all hope of a career.

She wandered over to the stereo and picked out an album by a little known but magnificently talented young blues singer, Suede, then loaded the disc and sank down on the sofa.

Suede was singing "No Regrets," but Rae had plenty of them. She regretted not having the backbone to stand up to her agent, her studio, to the music industry itself. She regretted the pretense, the deception, the tidal wave of expectation that had swept her and Noel apart. But most of all, she regretted her own lapse of character. She should have been stronger, more determined, more honest.

She had started out that way, with Gottlieb, anyway. She had tried to explain to him that being gay was not a choice, any more than you choose to be blue-eyed or left-handed. You could learn to walk in heels; you could wear contacts; you could train yourself to be ambidextrous, but you couldn't alter what you were born with.

All you could do was accept it and live into it with integrity.

It was a commendable theory. But it had taken Rae Dawn a long time to get there.

And the turning point, oddly enough, had come through Gottlieb himself.

Rae Dawn walked back to the baby grand piano in the front window and touched its yellowed ivory keys. Dr. Gottlieb's piano, that familiar, battered old instrument with the glorious voice. He had willed it to her when he died. One sunny September afternoon in 1988 it had arrived in a truck, accompanied by two moving men and a sealed letter from the executor of his will.

With shaking hands she opened a small carved box to one side of the piano, smoothed out the letter, and read it for the hundredth time:

Dear Rae Dawn,
This letter comes too late, even though I have written it a thousand times already in my mind. I always hoped that, before I

died, I would have the opportunity to see you again and ask your forgiveness face to face. But that is not to be. I have waited too long.

Over the years I have followed your musical career with the pride of a father whose gifts have been handed down to his daughter. Still, I have let my stubbornness and arrogance get in the way of accepting you and loving you for who you are. Forgive me if you can. I wanted you to be different. I wanted you to be like me.

Now, too late I fear, I see that you are exactly like me. You refuse to give in, refuse to be broken. Refuse to give heed to the voices of prejudice and bigotry — even mine.

When I told you that I would fling myself before the Nazi rifles or go to the ovens to protect you, I imagined myself to be noble and self-sacrificing. I did not want to believe myself to be like my captors, those evil, arrogant men who sought to purge the world of diversity. But the end of one's life brings a terrible clarity of vision, a merciless mirror that forces us to see ourselves as we are, not as we wish to be.

I thought I had learned the lessons of captivity, the stripping away of all that is unimportant to bring us to the essential *truths of life. But one essential truth I never faced: Love comes to us as a gift and must be honored and received with grace.*

I trust that by now you have found some-one to share your life with. Love her, and keep on loving. Let nothing come between you. Honor her above all else. And be true to yourself, no matter the cost.

Your father, your friend —
Manfred Gottlieb

The irony pierced Rae's soul like a blade.

She had, finally, thrown off the disguises imposed upon her by others, had at last looked the music world in the eye and said "This is who I am — take it or leave it." A few gigs were canceled, a few fans wrote nasty letters expressing their outrage and disappointment. But for the most part the world kept spinning and the royalties kept coming and other singers kept asking to record her original songs.

The world kept spinning. But it was a world without the woman she loved.

PART 4
SHAME AND BLAME

Caught in the silver web,
we flail and thrash,
but struggle brings no liberty,
only a tighter cord around the heart,
a binding of the soul
that cuts off light and air,
hope, and the promise
of tomorrow.

Be still.
Let go.
Stop fighting.
For the way out
is not out
but through.

TWENTY-ONE: THE THINKING POOL

DURHAM, NORTH CAROLINA
JUNE 1969

There was no church wedding, no father walking her down the aisle. No flowers or reception or twin sister as her maid of honor. Just a hurried civil ceremony before Irving Neazle, Justice of the Peace.

"Do you take this woman to be your lawfully wedded wife?" the decrepit old judge yelled.

"I do," Trip murmured.

"Eh? What's that?" The old man put his hand to his ear.

"I *do*," Trip repeated, a little louder.

The judge narrowed his eyes at Trip. "Speak up, young man! Do you want to marry this girl, or don't you?"

"I DO!" Trip shouted.

Finally satisfied, Judge Neazle nodded beneficently and turned to Lauren. "Do you take this man to be your lawfully wedded husband?"

"I do."

The judge continued to stare at her, waiting.

"I DO!" she yelled at the top of her lungs.

"Well, that's better," the withered old justice said, patting Lauren on the arm. "I like to see a girl who's enthusiastic about getting married." He turned toward Trip. "You could take a lesson or two from her, young fella."

It would have been funny . . . if either of them had been happy about the wedding. But Lauren felt shame wash over her as she was forced to shout aloud what she had held in secret for so long.

As soon as the deed was accomplished, they fled the judge's office, ducking the barrage of good wishes and marital advice the old man flung after them at the top of his lungs. They dashed down the steps and hurled themselves into Trip's Corvair.

"Now what?" Lauren panted.

Trip shrugged. "I don't know. What do most couples do?"

Lauren leveled a glance at him. "The honeymoon."

"Oh yeah. Seems sort of . . . anticlimactic," Trip said.

In the end they drove around Durham for a while, picked up a bucket of chicken and a six-pack of beer, and found a cheap motel. After a few minutes of perfunctory sex, they lay in separate beds and stared at the television until they fell asleep. The next morning they bought coffee and doughnuts and a newspaper, and by noon they had rented a small furnished apartment in the basement of a widow's house a few blocks from Duke University.

The decor was horrible, and the stench was even worse. Cat urine and mouse droppings and mildew. The smattering of sunlight filtering in through high dirty windows did little to make the apartment less dingy. Still, it was affordable, and Lauren, who had never done any more housework than was absolutely necessary, found herself looking forward to making the place their home. The work would be her payback, penance for her betrayal of Lacy.

But as the weeks passed, she discovered that the immediate gratification of a clean toilet or a freshly scrubbed kitchen floor could do nothing to remove the taint of guilt and shame. She had thought it would go away, once she and Trip were honest about their relationship, once they were married. But the marriage was a sham, and she knew it. For the first time in years, she recalled her childhood Sunday school lessons and understood why Judas had gone out and hanged himself.

It wasn't that she regretted marrying Trip. They'd had no choice, really. But it was the *way* she had married him — the haste, the vain attempts at explanation, the expression on Lacy's face when they had finally told her.

At first it had been a game, a competition with her sister that Lauren won hands down. Experience had been on her side, after all. She knew what Trip Jenkins really wanted and how to give it to him. Poor Lacy was depending on charm and personality and emotional connection. All Lauren had to do was throw out the bait and reel him in. No contest.

After that bittersweet seduction during spring break, Trip continued to see Lacy — to let her down easy, he claimed. But he also met secretly with Lauren every chance he got. There was something intensely stimulating about the forbiddenness of their liaisons, and the sex was, frankly, incredible. The back seat of Trip's Corvair turned out to be horribly cramped and uncomfortable, and since neither of them could afford a motel room, they got very creative. A blanket in the woods behind the college maintenance building. The fourth-floor stacks in the library. Occasionally, on weekends when most of the fraternity brothers were out of town, they sneaked into Trip's frat house. Once they did it in the laundry room of Lauren and Lacy's dorm — an experience a bit too nerve-wracking for Lauren, although Trip seemed to find the danger arousing.

Gradually an unsettling realization formulated itself in Lauren's mind — the awareness that her relationship with Trip was turning out to be just like her relationship with Steve Treadwell and the others who had gone before him. Mostly about sex, with little else to attract them. All the things she had been so jealous of in Lacy's relationship with Trip — the emotional intimacy, the sense of knowing one another, the communication — seemed to be missing.

And something else was missing too. Her period. She couldn't recall when it was supposed to come in March. By April she was paying attention. By May, with graduation fast approaching, she was sure.

And so the confrontation with Lacy, the hurry-up wedding, the miserable apartment, the scrambling to make ends meet. And the boiling in her gut that never seemed to subside.

■ ■ ■ ■

All that first summer Trip worked on a construction site to support them. By the time law school started in September, with Lauren's last trimester drawing near, they moved to a better apartment, a place with south-facing windows and a second tiny bedroom for the baby.

But they weren't talking. They weren't having sex. Trip seemed morose and distant much of the time. Maybe he was just tired. Maybe he was being sensitive to her "condition." Maybe he didn't find her attractive, with her bulging abdomen and heavy breasts. Lauren tried to push the constant worry to the back of her mind. It was going to be all right. Somehow it would work out.

And then, in December, with Trip's constitutional law final looming the next morning, her water broke at three in the morning.

Trip had come to bed less than an hour ago, but he was sound asleep. She reached over to wake him, and a memory raked through her. For a moment she watched him just as she had watched him that spring day nine months ago, the first time they . . .

The first contraction hit her hard, and Trip, startled awake at the sound of her cry, sat bolt upright, dazed and confused.

"Is something wrong with the baby? Should I take you to the hospital?"

"No. Yes," she croaked between gasps. "It's time."

The next few minutes were utter chaos. Trip hopped around the apartment trying to pull on his jeans with one hand and brush his teeth with the other, while Lauren put back on the only clothes that still fit her. As she waddled toward the front door Trip found his lost keys by stepping on them with his bare foot. "Damn!" he yelled, and Lauren, despite herself, laughed.

It was like an episode of the *Dick Van Dyke Show*. Just as Trip helped her into the car, she remembered the suitcase sitting in the hall closet, the one she had packed diligently a month ago, just in case. He ran back in to get it and returned carrying his old bowling ball bag. She didn't bother to tell him.

As they pulled out of the parking lot, another contraction hit, and Trip slammed on the brakes in response.

"Just *go!*" she said through gritted teeth.

"Is the baby all right?" he demanded.

"The baby's fine. But *you* won't be unless you get me to the hospital now!"

Trip apparently knew better than to argue with a woman in labor. He ran seven stop lights and broke every speed limit getting her to the hospital.

They needn't have hurried. By the time they got her admitted into the hospital, the contractions had slowed down. At seven thirty, assured by the OB nurse that first babies take a long time coming, Trip left the hospital and went to take his exam.

Throughout the early hours of labor, Lauren lay alone in the hospital room crying, but not from the physical pain. She had never felt so alone in her life. She didn't blame Trip for leaving — law schools didn't reschedule exams for everyday events like babies being born. But her mother wasn't here to assure her that everything would be all right. Her father wasn't here to pace the waiting room. Her sister wasn't here to hold her hand.

And Trip had asked, "Is the baby all right?" Not "Are you all right?"

She wasn't all right. She had never been less all right in her life.

As the contractions quickened and strengthened, Lauren prayed with every breath that Trip would love this baby and that, in loving his child, he could find a way to love her too. But four hours later, when the doctor laid the infant in her arms, she gazed down at his innocent face and knew she was lost. He was not fair and blond like herself, like Trip, but olive-skinned with a thick mass of dark hair.

Like Steve Treadwell.

"His name?" the nurse asked, her pen poised over the birth certificate.

"Thomas," Lauren choked out. "Thomas Edward Jenkins IV."

"Why didn't you tell me?" Trip shouted. "You *lied* to me!"

At least he had waited to confront her. When Trip had arrived at the hospital, bleary-eyed and disheveled from his exam, she was still clutching the bundle and sobbing. He took the baby from her, kissed the red and wrinkled forehead, and uttered not a single word about the obvious truth that his infant namesake, whom they called Teddy, was not his biological son.

But now that they were home, the anger that had been building for days could no longer be contained.

"You intentionally deceived me, tricked me into marrying you, lying to me —"

"I didn't lie," Lauren repeated with an edge of desperation in her voice. "Not deliberately, anyway. I thought he was your baby, Trip, I really did. I had broken it off with Steve the week before spring break, but —"

"I should have guessed." Trip ran a shaking

hand through his hair. "Steve always bragged to everyone about his conquests. But when you got pregnant, it never even entered my mind that the child was his."

"Me neither," Lauren mumbled.

"I mean, if I'd known . . ." His voice trailed off.

"If you'd known, you'd have done what?" Lauren shouted. "You'd have dumped me and married my sister, after all? You'd have pretended this never happened? Or you'd have kept meeting me in secret, screwing me behind everyone's back?"

Her yelling woke the baby in the next room, and the child began to cry. "I didn't lie," Lauren repeated over the squalling. "I didn't know. Not until . . ."

She went to retrieve the baby and sank wearily into the rocking chair her mother had bought for them. Trip flung himself onto the sagging sofa. Lauren lifted her T-shirt, exposed a breast, and began feeding the infant. Little Teddy made soft sucking sounds as he nursed.

Lauren looked up at Trip, who appeared to deflate before her eyes. It seemed as if his anger had been the only thing keeping him upright and moving, and once it drained out of him, he was left looking empty and tired. He stared at the baby for a long time. Neither of them spoke.

When Teddy finished nursing, Trip took him from his mother's arms and cuddled him close. The baby stirred in his sleep and smacked his tiny lips.

"Are you going to tell Steve?" he asked quietly.

Lauren blinked at him. "And what? Ask him for child support? Divorce you and demand that he marry me? Not a chance." She bit her lip. "What are *you* going to do?"

Trip stared at the baby in his arms. "I'm going to do what I promised," he said at last. "I'm going to finish law school, get my degree, support my family. I'm going to be this little boy's daddy."

He had kept that promise, and then some.

Trip Jenkins turned out to be a wonderful man who adored his son. He taught the boy to throw a football, to ride a bike, to stand up to bullies, to be kind to the kids in school whom everyone else teased. He adored being a dad. But he was not Ted's father.

That knowledge, however, never stopped Trip from loving him — loving with fierce depth and frightening power. And now the boy was growing up to be smart and generous and handsome, even at the awkward, gangly age of fourteen. Ted might have inherited Steve Treadwell's looks, but his character was the result of nurture rather than nature.

Lauren looked out the window at her husband's back as he sat on the park bench at the edge of the koi pond. Rain was falling, pocking the surface of the dark waters, but he didn't seem to care.

Trip had built the pond himself. It was eight feet across, crafted of stone in an irregular kidney shape, with a small waterfall that rushed over the rocks and aerated the pool. A couple of water lilies floated on the surface, and beneath them, in the dim cold greenness, three lazy koi perpetually eased back and forth. Papa Bear, the largest of the three, was a Showa Sanke, red and black and white with a pattern just above his dorsal fin that looked like the state of Florida. The other two were dubbed, predictably, Mama Bear and Baby Bear.

Whenever Trip needed to work things out, he retreated to the waterfall pond, to the silent fish. Lauren watched him now, hunched over, oblivious to the rain.

What was he doing out there? What was he thinking?

She wondered. But she had learned not to ask questions.

Especially if she wasn't sure she'd like the answers.

Twenty-Two:
The Ties That Bind

The bus left Hillsborough at midnight, heading west. For an hour or more, Lacy sat next to the window staring into the darkness. Every now and then a car would pass, its headlights glaring into her eyes and making her squint. But for the most part, all she could see was her own reflection, the dim image of a pale, tear-streaked face, a shaken young woman fleeing for her life.

She had no idea where she was going, only that she had to get away. As far away from North Carolina as possible. As far away from *them*.

Mother and Daddy had tried to reason with her. It didn't make sense, just to take off for parts unknown when she had a job waiting for her at Hillsborough High. What would she do? How would she live? Why couldn't she just accept what had happened and go on with her life, find someone else? They weren't condoning what Lauren had done, certainly, but she *was* Lacy's sister. And family was family, no matter what.

But Lacy was adamant. She was determined to leave, and nothing they could say or do would stop her. In the end, Daddy had given her some money to tide her over and Mother had stood crying in the depot as the bus pulled out.

The thrumming of the tires against pavement lulled her, and for a while she slept with her head leaning against the glass. When she awoke, the seat next to her was occupied.

"Where are you going?" the woman asked when Lacy turned in her direction.

At first Lacy didn't answer. She didn't want a seatmate, didn't want to have to talk to anyone. And yet this woman, who looked to be a few years older than Lacy, had a kind face.

"I have no idea," Lacy answered candidly. "I'm not exactly going *to* anywhere; it's more like I'm going *from*." Tears welled up in her eyes and she turned her head back toward the window.

The woman laid a hand on her arm — the lightest of touches, a brief warmth — and then took it away. They sat in silence for a while as Lacy cried. When Lacy began rummaging in her bag for another tissue, the woman handed her one with a soft smile. "I'm Alison Rowe, by the way."

"Thanks," Lacy muttered. "Lacy Cantrell." She sighed and resigned herself to small talk. She looked down at the woman's hand, which bore a small diamond solitaire and a gold band. "What about you? Where are you headed?"

"Home to Kansas City."

"Is your husband there?" Alison glanced up with a startled expression, and Lacy pointed. "I noticed your rings."

"My husband is . . . dead." Alison bit her lip. "He was stationed at Fort Bragg before he was called up to Vietnam." She exhaled heavily. "There didn't seem to be any point in staying after. . . ."

"I'm — I'm really sorry," Lacy managed. "When did this happen?"

"A couple of months ago. I had to pack up the house and sell everything."

Something was bothering Lacy, and it took a minute or two to put her finger on what it was. "If you came from Fort Bragg, you were on the bus when I got on."

Alison nodded. "I was sitting a few rows back. I saw you crying. Looked like you might use some companionship." She appraised Lacy in the dim light. "You're very young to be setting off cross country by yourself with no destination in mind."

Lacy hadn't thought she wanted company, but clearly Alison Rowe was a woman who knew how to listen. And once the floodgates were opened a crack, everything came flowing out.

All through the night they talked. Alison told Lacy about her husband, Richard, who had, the army reluctantly told her, been killed by friendly fire. About growing up in Missouri. About her family — a mother, brother, and two sisters — in Kansas City. Lacy told Alison about Lauren and Trip, about her plans to marry Trip and teach at Hillsborough High School after graduation. About her sister's betrayal. About her anger and bitterness, and the need to get as far away as possible, to put the whole thing behind her forever.

To Lacy's surprise, it helped a little just to be able to talk about her pain. Alison understood suffering. And there was no risk in telling her the whole sordid mess. Once this bus ride was over, she'd never see the woman again.

But Alison had other ideas.

"Why don't you come to Kansas City with

me?" she said as they ate breakfast at a small depot somewhere in Tennessee. "My brother is on the school board; he can probably get you a job. You can stay with me at my mom's house until you can afford a place of your own."

It was an extravagantly generous offer, and before she realized quite what she was doing, Lacy said yes. What difference did it make, anyway, where she ended up — as long as it was far away from her sister and her ex-fiancé and the memory of their treachery and deception?

It took a long time for Lacy to emerge from the emotional wreckage of Lauren and Trip's betrayal. Like the victim of some natural disaster — earthquake, fire, flood — she wandered about in a fog, aimless, bracing herself for the aftershocks, for another explosion or a second rush of rising water.

She went on with life, certainly. She got her master's degree and established herself as a popular teacher at the high school where Alison taught literature. She dated a variety of eligible men, had even come close to being engaged once or twice. On the surface, anyway, she got along pretty well.

Years passed — two years. Five years. Ten. Twelve.

And in all that time she'd had no contact with her sister. She had kept in touch with her mother and father, of course, had written letters and talked to them on the telephone occasionally, but it was easier to keep things superficial when she didn't have to see them face to face.

Only once had she visited — in Christmas of 1982, when Mama had called to tell her that Lauren and Trip were spending the holidays in Dallas with Trip's parents. And the moment she set foot over the threshold of her childhood home, she knew coming back to Hillsborough had been a mistake.

A huge one.

On the mantel in the living room stood several framed photographs. Lauren holding an infant in her arms. Lauren and Trip with a dark-haired three-year-old at a birthday party. Trip with the same boy, a few years older, carrying fishing poles and holding up a large brook trout. School photos of the child as he grew, the metamorphosis of baby to toddler to disheveled boy to gangly preteen.

Lacy felt a numbness creep into her chest, and on wooden legs she made her way over to the photographs. "This is Ted, I assume," she managed to say. She peered at the picture of Lauren with the baby. Her own mirror image stared back at her. This should have been her photo. Her baby. Her life.

Somehow she forced herself through three days of torture. It was obvious her parents were attempting to be sensitive, but no matter how hard they tried, they couldn't keep from talking about their grandson — what a bright boy he was, how well mannered and considerate. What wonderful parents Lauren and Trip were.

By the time Lacy got on the plane back to Kansas City, her nerves were shredded raw. She tried to sleep on the flight, but every time she closed her eyes she saw that picture of Lauren holding the infant Ted in her arms.

Alison met her at the gate and followed her down to baggage claim. "So, how was it?"

"Don't ask." Lacy dragged her suitcase off the carousel. "Can we go get something to eat? I'm starving."

They drove through a light snow to the Fireside Grille, a restaurant that specialized in steaks and burgers. Lacy ordered a prime rib sandwich on crusty French bread, but once the order arrived she found herself unable to eat.

"Come on, tell me," Alison urged. "What happened?"

Lacy grimaced. "You know, I thought I was

done with it — the Lauren and Trip thing. But the minute I set foot in that house, it all came back. Mom had photographs of my nephew all over the house. There was one of Lauren and the baby — you know, the typical Madonna and child thing, with this ethereal light around the edges. I looked at it and thought —" She lifted her shoulders. "Well, I don't know what I thought."

"You thought it ought to be you," Alison said.

"Yeah, I guess I did." Lacy tried in vain to eat a bite of her sandwich, just to postpone this discussion.

Alison waved a french fry in Lacy's direction. "Jealous?"

"I don't know. Maybe." Lacy shrugged. "Alison, what the hell is wrong with me? I have a good life, don't I? I've got friends, I've got a great job. I thought I was over this."

"Of course you're not over it," Alison said. "How could you be over it when you've never dealt with it?"

Lacy felt her stomach lurch. "What do you mean, I've never dealt with it? I've spent the past thirteen years —"

"You haven't been *dealing* with it," Alison corrected. "You've been *suppressing* it. You were running away when we met, and you're still running." She leaned forward. "Lace,

I'm your best friend. We tell each other the truth. Why did you say no when Hank asked you to marry him?"

"Well," Lacy hedged, "it just didn't feel right."

"And Rob?"

"He wasn't the one."

"He wasn't Trip Jenkins, you mean."

"I didn't say that."

"You didn't have to. You've lived here for years, Lacy. How many of your friends even know you have a twin sister, much less how she betrayed you?"

"I don't know."

"Well, I do. None of them — except for me, and fortunately for you I know how to keep my mouth shut."

"What's your point?"

"My point is that you haven't dealt with your pain and anger over Trip and Lauren. You've just shoved it under the surface. And you can't risk letting anyone too close because they might find out what's down there."

The arrow found its mark, and Lacy winced. "When we met on that bus you were so tender and compassionate. What happened to that woman? How did you become so damned direct?"

"I became friends with you," Alison retorted with a grin. "And I got a lot of counseling. It's called tough love, Lace. Get used to it."

"So what do you suggest I do?" Lacy asked reluctantly.

Alison took a pen from her purse and wrote a telephone number on a paper napkin. "Call this number. It's my grief counselor. She can help."

"I don't need a grief counselor," Lacy protested. "Nobody's died."

Alison raised an eyebrow. "Just call her, will you?"

Dr. Mamie Witherspoon, a squat, maternal woman in her late fifties, looked more like someone's grandma than a therapist. But Lacy soon discovered how utterly deceiving looks could be.

Mamie took no bull from anyone, and she could spot a lie — or even a slanted half-truth — quicker than a robin could snap up a fat earthworm. She had a birdlike way of jerking her head and fixing Lacy with those bright, beady eyes.

"Thirteen years," she said when Lacy had finished the short version of her story. "And in all that time, you've never had contact with your sister or her husband or your nephew."

"No," Lacy mumbled. "Like I said, I've put all that behind me."

"Have you now?"

"Yes. I've made a new life for myself. I've become a self-actualized individual."

Mamie adjusted her wire-rimmed glasses and smiled. "Self-actualized?"

Lacy nodded. "When I was in undergraduate psych years ago, we studied Maslow's hierarchy. I remember it very clearly, because as a twin, I had never felt a sense of individuality. I wanted to discover myself, to be fully self-actualized, differentiated."

"And so you cut yourself off."

Lacy frowned at the counselor. "Haven't you been listening? I didn't cut *myself* off. I was the injured party here."

"The victim."

"Well, yes, if you put it that way. But I haven't let it control my life. I've moved on."

The bright bird-eyes fixed on her as if she were a particularly juicy worm. "It's hard to move on when you're dragging your baggage behind you."

Lacy tried to dismiss the image, but she felt the truth of it nevertheless — the weight of the past, holding her back, hindering each stumbling step toward the future.

"It's not that big a deal," she muttered.

"On the contrary," Mamie said. "It's an

enormous deal. Your fiancé was unfaithful to you. Your sister betrayed you. She stole the life you thought you deserved. That's enough to supply rage and bitterness for a lifetime."

"I'm not angry," Lacy protested, but even as she spoke the words, she knew it was a lie.

"Have you ever read *Lord of the Rings*?" Mamie asked.

The non sequitur jerked Lacy to attention. "A long time ago. But what does that have to do — ?"

"Remember Gollum? He finds the sacred ring and claims it, calling it 'my precious.' Even though it is destroying him, he clings to it, will do anything to get it back when it's taken from him."

"All right," Lacy said hesitantly.

Mamie tilted her head. "We all have a 'precious,' an obsession that well may destroy us, and yet we cherish it, hold onto it at any cost."

"And my obsession, my 'precious,' is — ?"

Mamie glanced at the clock. "Our time is up. Shall we make another appointment for you?"

Lacy stared at her. "You're just going to leave me like this, without an answer?"

"You have the answer within you," Mamie said. "You merely have to find it for yourself."

■ ■ ■ ■

Lacy spent eight months with Mamie Witherspoon, searching for the answers that lay within her own soul. It was hard work, emotionally grueling and mentally exhausting. But gradually she felt the baggage slip away a piece at a time, until there was only one issue left that bogged her down.

Forgiveness.

Mamie raised the subject. Lacy resisted.

Mamie raised the subject again. Lacy balked.

Alison raised the subject. Lacy told her to mind her own damned business.

Alison simply lifted her left eyebrow at Lacy in that annoying, I-know-you-better-than-you-know-yourself look. Lacy tossed her wadded-up napkin across the dinner table and grinned when it hit Alison directly on the forehead.

"Listen," Lacy said, "I've worked hard to face the truth about myself." She ticked off each item on her fingers. "I've dealt with the anger and the jealousy. I no longer feel like a victim. I've accepted the fact of Lauren and Trip's relationship, and I see that it might not have been the best thing in the long run if I had married him instead. I've become aware of my tendency to withdraw to avoid getting hurt again, and I've started letting people get closer. But forgive Lauren and Trip? Let bygones be bygones? Forget what they've done to me? There's no way."

Alison cocked her head and looked at Lacy. "Who said anything about bygones? Who said anything about forgetting?"

"Well, that's what forgiveness means, doesn't it? Letting stuff go, reconciling relationships, forgetting what someone else has done to you. Having everything go back to the way it used to be. Besides, Lauren and Trip haven't *asked* for forgiveness. They haven't said they were sorry for what they did."

"And the government hasn't apologized for causing the death of my husband," Alison replied softly. "That's irrelevant."

Lacy leaned forward in her chair. "Apologies are irrelevant? Taking responsibility is irrelevant?"

"Whether or not someone has apologized is irrelevant to our need to forgive." She took a deep breath and a large drink of tea before she continued. "Forgiveness is not absolution, Lacy. Forgiveness is the process of liberating ourselves from the web of pain others have imposed upon us. Forgiveness is about freedom, Lace. *Your* freedom. You forgive for your own sake, so that you no longer have to be controlled by what that person has done to you. You let it go, abandon any pretense of having power over the situation. You control your own life, because you certainly can't control anyone else's."

"I don't know how to do that."

"Ask Mamie" was all Alison would say in reply.

Lacy didn't like the feeling that her counselor and her best friend were tag-teaming her, but she also knew they were right. She was tired of the anger, the hate. It took her a couple of months, but she finally asked Mamie how she could begin to forgive.

"You've already begun," Mamie replied with a smile. "Think of a spider's web. You're all wrapped up in pain and heartbreak and self-imposed exile. Then you come to and realize you're caught. You have to do something, and thrashing around only makes the bondage worse. So one thread at a time, you cut yourself free. You face the truth. You give up being a victim. You accept reality. One thread at a time, until you can move and breathe again. The last thread that binds your freedom is unforgiveness. You need to understand that forgiveness is a process and doesn't always look like what it is."

Mamie smiled, and her beady eyes almost

disappeared. "If I might be permitted a personal anecdote —"

Lacy waved a hand. "By all means."

"I had a difficult relationship with my mother when I was growing up. She was very domineering and demanding, always had to have things perfect. And I wasn't perfect. I was plain and fat, and although I overcompensated by being intelligent and creative, that was never enough for her. I always felt put down, demanded. Then one day, pretty much out of the blue, I came to a decision. I was thirty-eight years old, had a Ph.D. and a growing counseling practice, and I still felt like that fat ugly child who couldn't please her mother. So I said — out loud, to myself, 'I don't give a damn what she thinks of me.' "

Lacy grinned. "If that's your example of forgiveness —"

"But it was, don't you see? I declared my independence from her opinion. And gradually, as that truth took hold in my life, I was able to forgive her, to realize that at her age she wasn't likely to change. I could either accept her as she was, or I could live under the cloud of her disapproval for the rest of my life. I couldn't choose my feelings, but I could choose whether or not I let her perceptions control me."

"And so with my sister —"

Mamie nodded encouragingly. "Go on."

"I can choose to forgive her not to set *her* free, but to free *myself* from the rage and bitterness that have controlled me."

"And what would that look like in practical terms?"

Lacy bit her lip. "I would be able to face Lauren and Trip and have some kind of relationship with them. I could be an aunt to the nephew I've never met. I could go home without feeling tense and self-protective." She paused. "And what happens then?"

"Then," Mamie said, "your time with me will come to an end."

The end came sooner than Lacy had expected. Just before Thanksgiving break, she received a frantic call from her mother.

Daddy had suffered a stroke. A bad one. Mama needed help and support.

The principal hired a substitute to finish out the semester and administer exams. Reluctantly Lacy tendered a midterm resignation.

It was time to go home.

TWENTY-THREE:
FAMILY CHRISTMAS

HILLSBOROUGH, NORTH CAROLINA
NOVEMBER 1983

When she pulled her fully loaded VW bug up in front of the house two days after Thanksgiving, Trip and Lacy were there to meet her, accompanied by a dark-haired intense young man who turned out to be her nephew.

Lauren stepped forward and gave her an awkward hug. "Welcome home, Lace," she said with a grave formality. "You, ah, remember Trip. This is our son, Ted. He's just about to turn fourteen."

He looked older than the pictures she had seen at her parents' house, but when he smiled, she could see the little boy in him. He hesitated, then gave her an awkward, one-armed hug. "I'm glad to meet you, Aunt Lacy. Finally."

Lacy regarded him. There was something

unusual about him, something she couldn't quite articulate. Then it dawned on her. Both Lauren and Trip were blond and fair. Her nephew had dark curly hair, olive-toned skin. And brown eyes.

This might be Lauren's son, but he definitely wasn't Trip's.

She glanced over at Trip, who was standing apart from them. He said nothing, but Lacy felt his eyes on her, as if he were trying to communicate without words. The awareness of his attention was unsettling.

"I sold everything I couldn't pack into the car," she said. "There's a big trunk in the back seat, a couple of suitcases, and up front there are six boxes of books." She moved to open the front hood, and her hand brushed Trip's as he reached out to grab the handle. Lacy pulled back as if she had touched a live wire, and after that she supervised the retrieval of the luggage from a safer distance.

Lauren looked . . . different. Lacy hadn't seen her since graduation, and although this woman standing next to her was readily recognizable as a sister, the twinness had succumbed to time in a way Lacy would have thought impossible. It was like gazing into a magic mirror and seeing ten years into the future.

She seemed tired. Weary. Worn out. She

was only thirty-six, but fine crow's feet already fanned out from the corners of her eyes. She had gained weight, about fifteen or twenty pounds, Lacy gauged. Enough to make her look saggy and bloated. Her hair had been bleached several shades lighter than her natural blonde. Its texture looked coarse and brittle, and the color did not complement her skin tone.

Trip, on the other hand, was every bit as handsome as he had been the day they met. Heavier, certainly, but he carried it well and in the right places. Once he smiled tentatively in her direction, flashing a dimple at the corner of his mouth. She remembered the eyes, lake-blue and liquid. How could she have forgotten the dimple?

"I hope you like the house," Lauren was saying, pointing to the little brick place sitting back a ways from the street. "It was the best we could find this close to Mom and Dad. We rounded up some furniture for you — just temporarily, of course, until you can get what you want."

"I'm sure it will be fine," Lacy muttered absently.

"Dad's still in the hospital. They say they're going to release him tomorrow. I told Mother I could manage things, but she insisted on calling you. I guess I should thank you for coming."

"It's okay," Lacy said. "I wanted to come."

It wasn't the whole truth, of course. She had returned out of duty, out of family responsibility, when the very last thing she wanted was to be thrust into an uncomfortable truce with Lauren. But it had been her choice. No one had pressured her.

"After we unload, we had planned to go to the hospital and see Dad, and then go to our house and have turkey sandwiches." She paused. "But we put some Thanksgiving leftovers in your fridge, just in case you were too tired."

Lacy pounced on this excuse like a terrier on a rat. "It *was* a very long drive," she said. "Two days on the road has left me exhausted. I think I'll unpack and rest up a little, then go to see Dad later this evening."

Lauren didn't protest. She, too, seemed relieved. "All right. I'll tell the folks you'll come by later."

And then, with perfunctory hugs all around, they were gone.

It didn't feel like home yet, this tiny rental house with its two small bedrooms and a pink tile bath that harked back to the fifties. But it was on a side street within walking distance of the house she had grown up in —

close enough to her parents to be helpful and, she hoped, far enough away to maintain a semblance of independence.

Lacy had a little money saved up, enough to make the move and keep her in groceries for a few months. The principal at Hillsborough High, thrilled to be getting such an experienced teacher, had promised her a position come September.

She missed Kansas City. Missed Alison. Missed the snow at Christmas. But coming home had been the right decision. Daddy was making progress, thanks to the exercises and speech therapy. On the days when the physical therapist didn't come, Lacy went over and made him do the painful stretches.

And she was doing some stretching of her own.

November burned itself out in a blaze of red and yellow leaves. The air grew cold, and the Carolina sky arched a brilliant blue above. Although still unable to walk on his own, Lacy's father seemed to be improving, and he insisted on having them all for Christmas.

This was what Lacy had been dreading. For a few weeks she had been able to negotiate a little two-step around Lauren and Trip, avoiding them whenever possible and being formally courteous when circumstances forced her into their presence. But there would be no escaping them at a family Christmas.

She arrived first on Christmas morning, resolutely determined to make the best of it. But the moment she stepped across the threshold, memories assaulted her on a wave of familiar scents. Turkey roasting in the oven, spiced pumpkin, yeast rolls. Her mind lurched and spun out a collage of old home movies with herself and Lauren in the starring roles. The twins in identical green velvet dresses, singing carols at the piano. The twins with their first bicycles. The twins in long white robes and halos, Mama's little angels.

She dumped the corn and broccoli casserole on the kitchen counter and took her packages to the tree. Arranging them gave her a moment to collect herself, to push back the tears.

She barely had time to paste on a smile, however, when the door opened and Trip came in on a blast of cold air. Lacy rocked back on her heels and looked up at him, pleasantly disheveled, his cheeks flushed pink from the wind.

"Merry Christmas," he said, his voice low and tentative.

Before she could respond, Lauren and Ted

pushed in after him, their arms full of brightly wrapped packages. "Gramma!" Ted called. "We're here!"

Lacy's mother came out of the kitchen wiping her hands on her apron. "Come on in," she said. "I was just taking out the last of the pies. Pumpkin, of course — Teddy's favorite." She glanced at Lacy. "Where'd you get off to?" she asked. "I was talking to you, and then I turned around and you were gone."

"Putting presents under the tree," Lacy muttered. As she moved to get up, Trip held out a hand to help her. Their fingers touched and their eyes met. The bottom dropped out of Lacy's stomach. "I'll — I'll come help," she said, pushing her mother back toward the kitchen.

"There's nothing to do right now," Mama said. "The turkey's got another hour to go, and the dressing has to bake. Let's all sit down."

Ted looked around. "Where's Grampa?"

"He's holed up in the bedroom, wrapping my gift." She laughed. "Always did put it off till the last minute. Why don't you go help him, Teddy? Don't know how he figured on doing it himself, with only one good hand."

Ted went off in search of his grandfather while the adults moved into the living room.

Lauren and Trip sat on the couch, and Lacy took the chair adjacent to them. Lauren reached out for Trip's hand. His head whipped toward her, and she smiled at him.

"So," Lauren said when they were settled. "We haven't had a chance to catch up since Dad got home from the hospital. Tell us about Kansas City, Lace."

The next hour or so they filled with small talk — Lacy's teaching, her friendship with Alison Rowe, the story of Alison's husband being killed in Vietnam. Lauren told family stories, mostly about Ted. And Trip, reluctantly dragged into the conversation, related a few tales about his law practice and odd clients he had represented. "One woman," he said, "wanted to sue her husband for having an affair. She didn't want to divorce him, just to get control of all their finances —" He broke off suddenly and flushed as Lauren pinched the soft flesh between his thumb and forefinger.

By the time dinner was ready, they had exhausted the supply of readily available superficialities. Conversation around the table centered mostly on the food — why fresh turkey tasted so much better than frozen, what recipe Lacy used for her corn casserole. Lacy watched as her mother cut her father's food into manageable bites. Although it pained her to see her father's helplessness with a knife and fork, she found herself warmed by the obvious love between the two of them. Her mother did not seem the least bit repulsed by the drooping muscles on one side of her husband's face or his inability to feed himself without dribbling. On the contrary, she gazed at him with conspicuous adoration, as if he were the handsomest, most vital man on the face of the earth.

She thought Lauren had noticed too, but she kept her eyes averted from her sister and Trip.

At last the uncomfortable meal was over. Lacy volunteered to do the dishes and for a blessed thirty minutes had the kitchen to herself. But when the call came to open presents, she had no choice but to rejoin the family in the living room.

"Teddy's going to play Santa Claus," her mother announced when Lacy had settled herself on the rug at her father's feet.

The tradition hadn't changed since childhood. Each present was delivered individually, and everyone watched while it was opened, uttering oohs and ahhs of approval. Lacy had bought generic gifts — a silk scarf for Lauren, a pair of gloves for Trip, a regulation NFL football for Ted. This last gift was a big hit, as was Ted's for her — a paperweight of bright red marble, in the shape of an apple with a bronze stem and leaf attached.

"Oh, Ted, it's beautiful," she said quite honestly as she held it up. "You couldn't have gotten me anything I'd like more."

Her nephew, rather pleased with himself, grinned and turned almost as red as the apple's shiny surface. "I picked it out myself."

"Well, thank you." She went to him and gave him a kiss on the cheek.

By midafternoon, after a second slice of pie, everyone was full and sleepy, and Lacy felt she could make her exit without offending anyone. She gathered up her gifts, said good-bye to the family, and headed for the door.

Ted caught up with her on the porch. "I'm glad you're back, Aunt Lacy," he murmured self-consciously as he hugged her. "I hope you'll stay."

Through the window over the sink Lauren could see out into the backyard all the way to the koi pond, where once again Trip sat motionless in a slant of winter sunshine with his head bowed and his hands clasped between his knees.

In this attitude of absolute stillness, he could have been praying, could have been a saint in meditation. He looked a bit like Rodin's sculpture of *The Thinker* — clothed, of course, and less muscular, but equally lost in the depths of his soul. Perhaps this was her husband's version of prayer, watching the fish gliding under the dark water, listening to his own breath and heartbeat.

She wondered what he heard inside himself in moments like this. Did he, like Lauren herself, question how they got to this point in their lives? Did he regret, as she did, the convolution of guilt and duty and good intentions that had left them, fifteen years down the road, stuck in an unhappy partnership and bound by promises that should never have been made?

Those years had changed Lauren more than she could have imagined. She felt old and wrung out, depleted. And now Lacy was back, still young and slim and looking like she had when they were in college.

Trip had noticed. Lauren could see it in his eyes, feel it in the tension that gripped him every time he came within a dozen yards of her sister. Well, if that was what he wanted — what Lacy wanted — she wouldn't fight this time.

The game was over. She was too tired to play again.

Besides, she had won once, and look where it had gotten her.

TWENTY-FOUR: EPIPHANY

JANUARY 1984

It didn't take long to clean a house as small as Lacy's. She had already vacuumed twice and now was dusting everything for the second time. She couldn't seem to sit still for more than a minute.

Nerves. It was just nerves.

She went to the pantry and stowed the dust rag. Wiped down the kitchen counter again. Paced around the tiny living room, fluffing up the sofa pillows.

A blustery January rain beat against the windows. In an attempt to dispel the chill and gloom, Lacy bent to turn on the gas logs in the small fireplace, and when she stood up again she found herself staring into the mirror over the mantel. The person who stared back at her was no woman at all, but an agitated schoolgirl anticipating a first date. She looked young and frightened and out of control.

318

"Get a grip," she muttered to herself.

But no grip was forthcoming. She glanced at the clock. In thirty minutes he would be here, assuming he was as punctual as he used to be. Half an hour, and Lacy would be sitting face to face — alone — with the only man she had ever loved, the man who fifteen years ago had jilted her in favor of her twin.

On the mantel in front of her stood the last of the Christmas decorations, a small crèche consisting of Mary and Joseph, the Baby Jesus in the manger, two sheep, a shepherd, and a single Wise Man riding on his camel. The set had belonged to their family. She and Lauren used to take turns — one reading from the Bible and the other walking the figurines into place as the familiar story was told. They had fought about it every year, Lauren always insisting that it was her turn to move the pieces. For several years the argument had escalated, resulting in the loss of one shepherd and two Wise Men, until their mother started putting a note into the box each year before stowing it away with the rest of the decorations.

In her haste to pack up the tree and ornaments, Lacy had forgotten the ceramic figures, and now she picked up the Wise Man and considered him.

Where, she wondered, did wisdom come

from? Was it written in the stars, or upon the human heart? Was it simply knowledge, an understanding that had its source in human experience? Or more than that, the gift of some higher power? Lacy didn't know, although at this moment she desperately wished she could find the wellspring and tap into it. With Trip arriving in thirty minutes, she could use all the help she could get.

A determined rapping on the front door startled her, and the figurine slipped from her fingers and crashed to the hearth below. It cracked cleanly in two, just at the saddle where the Wise Man joined his camel. Flustered, she bent down and scooped up the pieces.

He was early. *Very* early. Lacy took a deep breath and exhaled in a vain attempt to still the pounding of her heart, then went to the door and opened it.

Lacy's knees nearly gave way beneath her. It wasn't Trip.

For a moment she stared at her twin, uncomprehending. Again she marveled at the differences between them, at the haggard circles under Lauren's eyes, at her brittle, too-blonde hair.

Instinctively Lacy reached up to touch her own hair and realized she still held the Wise Man and his camel in her hands.

"May I come in?" Lauren said at last. Her voice sounded brittle as well, as if it too had been overbleached.

Lacy's eyes darted to the clock.

"I won't take much of your time."

Lacy nodded and stepped aside as her sister passed through the narrow foyer and went on into the living room.

"The house looks nice," she said. "Cozy."

"What are you doing here, Lauren?" The question came out more snappish than Lacy had intended, but she had neither the time nor the patience for games or small talk.

"I'm here to . . ." Lauren shrugged and sat down on the couch. "I don't know. To see you, I guess. To talk to you."

"Why now?"

"Trip's left me."

Lacy pretended this was news to her. "Really?"

"Really. He stuck it out fifteen years, so maybe I should be grateful. But losing him is . . . well, let's just say it's the first time I understand what I put you through. I didn't take the time to understand before. Too busy trying to hold things together, I guess. Now I know how awful it feels to be abandoned, to be alone."

"No kidding." Lacy crossed her arms.

Lauren raked her hands through her hair.

"Look, Lace, I'm not doing this very well. I've made so many mistakes and let them go on far too long. Trip's leaving woke me up a little. I can't change what's happened between us. Believe me, if I could, I would. But you're my sister. That should count for something."

"It should have."

"What do you want from me?" Lauren said with an edge of panic in her voice. "What can I do to make things better?"

Suddenly exhausted, Lacy sank into the armchair next to the sofa. Without realizing it, she had been gripping the two halves of the broken figurine, and the sharp edges had cut into her palms. She laid the pieces on the coffee table next to Ted's marble apple and surveyed the pinpricks of blood.

"The truth," she said. "I want the truth."

"All right." Lauren squeezed her eyes shut. "It happened that spring break, when Trip came home with you. We made love."

"You made love," Lacy repeated mechanically.

"I seduced him," Lauren amended. "I was jealous, and unaccustomed to coming in second. It was stupid. A moment of sheer madness."

"But you had what's-his-name. Why on earth would you be jealous?"

Lauren shook her head impatiently. "What I had with Steve Treadwell was nothing compared to what you had with Trip. Steve never loved me, and I never loved him. We hung out together, had fun, had sex. But as soon as I saw you and Trip together, I knew that I had settled for a whole lot less than I really wanted."

"So you decided to go after Trip."

"Not consciously. It just —"

"Don't say it," Lacy warned. "Don't say it just happened."

Lauren sighed. "You're right. I *made* it happen. I don't know why. I felt terrible about it afterward."

"And yet you got married."

"He did it out of guilt, out of some perverted sense of honor. There was the baby to consider —"

"Ah yes, the baby." Lacy didn't comment on her nephew's questionable parentage. She wanted to see if Lauren would come clean with that piece of the story as well.

"As it turned out, Ted wasn't Trip's child," Lauren admitted, much to her own credit. "But I didn't know that at the time. I thought he was Trip's; we both did. It only became obvious . . . afterward. And by that time it was too late." She picked at a loose thread on the arm of her sweater. "Trip thought he was doing the right thing."

"And now?"

"Now I think Trip is trying to get his life back. I don't blame him, really. He never loved me. It was always you, Lace."

Lacy felt a peculiar sort of trembling in her stomach. "He said that?"

"He didn't have to."

A strange metamorphosis had been taking place while Lacy listened to Lauren's confession. Time dropped away from her sister's face, a rewinding of the years. Lacy could see — almost — the mirror image of herself, as she had seen it since childhood. Their shared life, mangled by circumstance, certainly, and shadowed by pain, but still bound with cords that could not be broken. Her sister. Her twin.

Lauren got to her feet. "I need to go."

Lacy opened her mouth to speak and then shut it again. Forgiveness, Mamie Witherspoon had said, was both a decision and a process. A chasm created over fifteen years couldn't be bridged in a single moment, but the reconstruction could begin. Here. Now.

But the moment passed. Lauren did not ask forgiveness, and Lacy did not offer it. Instead, she stood and followed Lauren to the door. One final question churned within her, hovering there, demanding an answer. "Do you — do you love him?"

Lauren ducked her head, but not quickly enough. Lacy could see the tears that had sprung instantly to her eyes.

"Yes," she said after a moment. "I didn't realize how much until he left, until I was faced with the prospect of losing him forever. But yes, I do love him. More than I ever imagined."

Trip, when he arrived, looked soft and eager — the old Trip, her Trip, the one who had made her feel loved and special.

The sensation was intoxicating. Lacy's eyes drank him in, the first oasis in a long and lonely desert. She wanted to take his hand and run away with him, to make a mad dash toward a future she had long ago given up on. This time he would be completely hers, heart and soul. She wanted him to quit talking and simply hold her.

But he would not shut up.

Trip, like Lauren, obviously felt the need to unburden himself, to confess and seek absolution — or, at the very least, amnesty — for the sins of the past. The guilty never realize, she mused, what baggage they transfer to the innocent because of their own need for relief.

Still, she listened as he rambled on, circling

around his shame like a vulture homing in on its prey. His was much the same story as Lauren's — one mistake compounded by a lifetime of others. But his tale differed from his wife's by two notable exceptions. For one thing, Trip did not lay blame on Lauren for seducing him. Nor did he mention the fact that Ted was not his son.

These omissions caused Lacy's heart to swell with pride and love. Trip Jenkins was, despite all that had happened, an honorable and ethical man who did not shift responsibility or try to weasel out of his own guilt.

"I am sorry, Lacy," he concluded. "Sorry I let my hormones get out of control. Sorry I hurt you. Sorry for so many things."

Lacy regarded him, letting her eyes roam over his handsome features. He was more mature now, but still intensely attractive, and she found herself having difficulty focusing on what he was saying.

She could see it in his eyes, read it in his body language, the way he leaned toward her. All she had to do was say yes, and her dreams would come true.

Better late than never.

"I kept thinking that if I just tried hard enough, I could make it work," he went on. "I had made this mess, and I had to deal with it. And I wanted to be a good father to

Ted. But with each year, each month, each day that passes, I feel more and more trapped." He paused and looked at her intently. "Lacy, do you know anything about koi?"

She frowned. "The fish?"

Trip nodded. "We have three of them in a pond I built in the backyard. It's a beautiful pond, a shady glen with a rock waterfall and a couple of lily pads. I spend a lot of time there; it's my only place of solitude."

"It sounds nice."

"It is." He exhaled heavily. "Anyway, koi will only get as big as their surroundings will allow. They'll stop growing if their pond is too small. And that's me. For years I have been swimming in claustrophobic circles, trapped in silent misery, trying to atone for my sins. I want out. I want to be free."

Lacy's heart raced as she heard his confession. Her dreams would come true, after all. And what sweet revenge, for him to leave Lauren and come to her. She could almost taste it. . . .

But Trip wasn't finished. "I never stopped thinking about you, Lacy. Look at you — you're exactly the same. It's amazing. You haven't changed a bit since we were in college. It's like these years never happened."

The dream spinning out in her mind

snapped to an abrupt halt and fell to earth.

She hadn't changed since college, he said. In his mind, she had simply been waiting for him, caught in time and unable to move. Holding the torch aloft, keeping the flame alive. Praying someday he'd return.

And perhaps he was right. Maybe that's what she had done. The thought sickened her, but she tried to face it squarely, honestly. She recalled the angry years, and more recently, the empty ones.

"I'm not asking for an answer," he said. "Or any kind of commitment. I just want to know if we can go back to where we used to be. Start over, try again. Have a second chance."

The words echoed inside Lacy's skull. Her eyes drifted to the coffee table, where the broken pieces of the ceramic crèche figure lay side by side with Ted's marble apple.

Metaphors, Alison would say. The forbidden fruit. The camel. The Wise Man.

What was the proverb about the camel with its nose in the tent?

Already the beast had pushed its way in. The sweet flavor of revenge, the seductive idea of returning to the love that had captured her heart so many years ago.

The broken Wise Man, lying on his side, gazed into the distant beyond. Toward the stars. Toward an unknown future.

Go back, Trip had said. Start over. But there was no going back. She was not the same person she had been in college. She was older now and, she hoped, wiser. Wise enough to realize . . .

That he didn't love her. What he loved was the image of her, the memory of the girl she had once been.

There was no way to recapture the past. It was a beautiful illusion, but it wasn't real. He didn't love her. And she didn't love him.

The truth broke over her like a bright and liquid light. Lauren was real. Ted was real. The rest was smoke and mirrors, a mirage, a distorted reflection. At the end was a cliff and a deadly fall.

She looked at him again and saw him as he was. And once more she asked the question that demanded to be answered:

"Do you love my sister?"

Silence. He cleared his throat, pressed his hands against his knees, shrugged. "She doesn't love me. And how could we love each other when you were always there?"

Lacy smiled. Trip was a good man. A good father. He would be a good husband too, given the chance. "She does love you. So does Ted."

At the mention of his son's name, Trip's

countenance changed. She could see the agony there, the raw longing. He didn't want a divorce or a different life. He simply wanted to be free.

"Go home to your wife and son," she said quietly. "You made the right choice. You married the right twin."

He held her gaze for a moment, staring into her eyes as though wishing to see something that belied her words. Then, without uttering a sound, he made his exit, shutting the door behind him.

After he left she sat there for a long time, crying a little but not turning away from the pain.

Dusk was falling. She had not yet turned on the lamps, and in the flickering glow of the gas fire the shattered Wise Man still lay on his side on the table, gazing into the distant beyond.

Toward the stars.

Toward an unknown future.

TWENTY-FIVE: LABOR DAY

SEPTEMBER 1984

Lauren stood at the kitchen window and looked out into the backyard, where a slow gray drizzle soaked the lawn and ran in rivulets along the edges of the grass. What was Trip doing out there in the rain? For fifteen minutes he had been sitting on the bench next to the koi pond, getting drenched, just staring into the water.

After breakfast Ted had flung himself from the table and stomped upstairs to his room. Lauren could hear the steady *thump thump* as he tossed a tennis ball against the wall. Poor kid. He had been looking forward to the annual Labor Day baseball barbecue put on by Trip's office. Lauren suspected — although Ted would never confirm her suspicion — that he had a crush on the teenage daughter of one of Trip's colleagues, an adorable little redhead named Ainslee Long.

Ainslee attended a private school. Ted never got to see her except at office functions like the barbecue. Now the event had been canceled because of the rain, and Ted had lost his chance to impress his girl by knocking a home run out of the park.

She could, of course, invite the Longs over for dinner, but then Ted might feel as if he'd been set up, and the results could be disastrous.

Lauren sighed. Parents always thought the worst was over when their babies finally learned to sleep through the night, express their feelings in words, and use the potty on their own. They had no idea, when they lamented the sleep deprivation that came with infancy, that teenage romantic angst would try their patience to new limits.

She wondered what it would be like next year, or the next. Anxiety about drugs and alcohol and smoking, no doubt. Uncomfortable sessions about sex and condoms and deadly diseases and respect for the girls he dated. Late-night discussions with Trip about how to handle the most recent crisis. Constant worry every time Ted took the car.

But at least she wouldn't be in it alone.

Nine months ago Trip had left her, and then, like a miracle, he had come back.

Ted had assumed his dad was off on a

business trip, and Lauren had chosen not to tell him any different. Five days later, when Trip returned, it was no big deal. The boy never knew how close he had come to losing his father for good.

No one knew, except Trip and Lauren. And Lacy, of course.

Lauren hadn't spoken with Lacy since that day in January. Whenever the two of them were together with the family, they feigned politeness and avoided any genuine conversation. Lauren longed for a real reconciliation with her sister, yet she wasn't in a position to press the issue. She believed, though he had never admitted it, that Trip had visited Lacy too during his five-day absence from hearth and home. When he returned, he said not the first word about what he had been doing — he simply unpacked his suitcase and merged back into the family.

But since that moment, everything had changed. Whatever Lacy said to him had made a difference. And what Lacy had said to Lauren had changed everything.

Do you love him? she had asked.

For the first time in years, Lauren had been forced to consider the question, and her answer brought her face to face with reality. Up until that point she couldn't have articulated any realistic definition of love.

She had always thought love equaled heat, passion, sexual desire and fulfillment. But it had to be more than that. Commitment, focus, oneness. And yet not only oneness. Twoness was important as well, an identity both within and apart from the relationship.

Lauren's understanding of love still was not as clear as she'd like it to be. And yet she knew she loved Trip. Living without him seemed utterly unthinkable.

A week after his return, he had come to her with the news that he had scheduled an appointment with a family therapist and asked, politely and formally, if she would be willing to go with him.

She went. At first it was sheer hell, rehashing the past, dredging up old sins from the murky recesses of her soul and displaying them in the harsh light of objective scrutiny. Seduction and lies, betrayal and denial — all of it came out, including the truth about Ted's paternity. Everything seemed so much worse when you said it out loud. But admitting the truth resulted in a strange kind of catharsis too, a lifting of the weight that had pressed in upon her for all these years.

Trip's love for Ted, as it turned out, became the glue that held them together during the dark months of counseling. Just as Lauren couldn't imagine living without Trip,

Trip couldn't imagine abandoning Ted.

"I married her because it was the right thing to do," he had told the counselor one day. "And I don't regret it. I fell in love."

At the words, Lauren's heart leaped into her throat. And then he went on.

"I hadn't counted on falling in love with such a small, wailing, demanding little bundle of human potential," he said. "But the minute I took that baby in my arms, I fell in love with him."

The revelation shredded her ego, and in that moment any hope she had harbored crashed into shards at her feet. Trip was honest, at least. He didn't pretend to love his wife, but he did love his son.

"The problem is, love for my son isn't enough anymore," he continued. "I'm tired of feeling trapped."

Gradually, as the bitter truth emerged and they faced it head-on, therapy began to take an upward turn. The path through purgatory began to lead them toward the surface, away from the sulfurous hell that burned below. Silence gave way to a little laughter. They watched movies, played games, bonded, became a family as they had never been before.

Things were better. More normal. And yet a bittersweet longing swelled in her as her own love deepened. At night she wept silently in the darkness, soaking her pillow with remorse.

Nine months they had been in weekly therapy sessions, and in all that time he had never touched her. Not even the occasional dispassionate sex that had marked their marriage for years. Through it all Lauren had watched Trip, as she watched out the window now. Waiting. Searching for a sign.

What she saw, instead, was a flurry of activity. Trip suddenly stood up and strode to the shed. He returned with a net, a shovel, a length of black plastic liner, and a huge corrugated tub. He filled the tub with water, and then, after transferring the three koi to the tub, he began to dig.

Lauren sloshed through the puddles into the far corner of the backyard. "What are you doing?"

Trip looked up. He was drenched to the skin and covered with mud, but he had a look of utter delight on his face. "I'm enlarging the pond," he said, as if this should be perfectly obvious.

"I can see that. Why?"

"Because they don't have enough room to grow." He pointed at the tub, where the temporarily transplanted koi hovered as if in suspended animation.

The back door slammed and Ted came

loping across the waterlogged grass. "What'cha doing?"

"He's enlarging the pond," Lauren answered.

"Yeah, I know. But why?"

Lauren shrugged. "He says the fish don't have room to grow."

Ted dug the toe of his sneaker into the mud. "You're nuts, Dad, you know that?"

Trip leaned on his shovel and grinned. "Probably. So, do you two want to help, or do you want to just stand there and criticize?"

Ted grinned back. "I figured I'd just criticize."

Lauren wasn't quite certain who threw the first fistful, only that within five minutes all three of them were splattered with mud and laughing hysterically. She wiped the goo out of her face and chanced a glance at Trip. He was gazing at her as if he'd never laid eyes on her before, as if she were the most beautiful woman he had ever seen.

She walked to the shed and came back with two more shovels, one of which she pushed into Ted's hands. She raked her mud-caked hair back and placed one foot on the lip of her shovel.

"You want a bigger pond?" she said. "We'll give you a bigger pond. Let's dig."

■ ■ ■ ■

It was the lightest of touches, a tentative caress on her shoulder. Even before his fingers brushed her, she felt his warmth at her back, edging nearer. "Are you awake?" he whispered.

"No, I'm sound asleep," she responded, and he chuckled.

"That was fun today," he said. "Digging the pond and all."

She turned over, and his arms went around her. "It *was* fun. I'm still not certain I quite understand it, but —"

"I'm not sure I can explain it either," he said. "I just know it's time to put the past behind us and move forward."

Lauren shifted in his arms and peered at his face, illuminated faintly by the streetlamp outside their bedroom window. "What does that mean, put the past behind us?"

He let out a breath. "It means I've been holding out on you. Refusing to forgive. I want to let it go, all of it, and start fresh. Can we do that?"

"You're willing to forgive me?"

Trip tightened his hold on her. "I should have forgiven you a long time ago. Can you forgive *me,* for being such an ass?"

"What have you been an ass about?" she murmured

His muscles tensed, and his face went cold in the blue of the streetlight. "When I left in January, I went to see Lacy. I asked her to take me back."

Lauren exhaled sharply. "I know."

"You *know?* How —"

"I should say, I suspected as much."

"But you never said anything."

"I figured you'd tell me when it was the right time. I went to see her too. Tried to reconcile with her. It didn't work."

He was silent for a moment or two. Then: "What did she say?"

Lauren hesitated. "She asked me if I loved you."

"What answer did you give?"

"I said —" Lauren paused.

"I hope you said yes," he murmured. "Because she told *me* I had married the right twin."

"My sister," Lauren whispered, "is a very wise woman."

She nestled in his arms, and for the first time in years she felt safe. The last of the secrets had been told.

In the vague drowsiness that comes just before sleep, she thought she heard him whisper that he loved her. And then she surrendered to a dream of a wide lake fed by a waterfall, with enormous koi swimming in its clear green depths.

PART 5
MERCY

One voice
can lure us to our doom
or to our calling.

Let those who have
eyes to see
and ears to hear
watch
and listen,
perceive, interpret, understand —

For no one ever tells us
that doom can serve
as well as call
to lead us home.

TWENTY-SIX:
THE ROAD LESS TRAVELED

DECATUR, GEORGIA
SEPTEMBER 1994

For two weeks Delta had wandered around Cassie's house aimlessly, plagued by an empty churning in her gut. Rae Dawn had never returned her call, nor had she received any response from the answering machine messages she had left for Lauren and Lacy.

"Are you sad, Aunt Delt?" Mouse asked one night.

Delta looked up from the novel she had been pretending to read and surveyed her small niece, who lay facedown on the rug working word puzzles from a book Delta had bought her. The child reminded her so much of Cassie at that age — not her looks, but her intelligence, her quickness, her razor-sharp evaluations of her world and the people in it.

Delta hedged. "Why do you ask?"

Mouse shoved the puzzle book aside and sat up. "For one thing," she said, "you don't smile and laugh as much anymore."

"I'll try to do better."

Mouse frowned. "It's not about pretending. It's about really *getting* better on the inside."

Delta laid her own book aside. "Come here, honey."

The child scrambled up and settled herself on Delta's lap.

"You remember your uncle Rankin, don't you?"

Mouse nodded solemnly. "I'm losing my picture of what he looked like, but I remember him. *He* laughed a lot."

A knot twisted tight in Delta's throat. "Yes, he did. He was my husband, you know, and my best friend. I loved him very much. And I was very sad when he died."

"I know." The little girl gave Delta a worried look. "Mom and I talked about it before you came to live with us. She told me about dying, and how people react to it when someone they love a lot gets dead. But . . ." She hesitated. "I heard her tell Daddy that you have eight out of ten."

Delta peered down at the child. "Eight out of ten what?"

Mouse furrowed her brow in thought.

"Eight out of ten symptoms of chemical depression."

"Do you mean *clinical* depression?"

She bit her lip. "I think so. Is that like a tropical depression? I heard about that on the Weather Channel."

Delta stifled a laugh. "What's a six-year-old doing watching the weather channel?"

"I'm *seven,* Aunt Delt," Mouse said, looking offended. "And the Weather Channel is very interesting. You should try it sometime."

"I'll do that." Delta tightened her arms around the little girl's warm body. "Now, don't worry about the depression. I'll talk to your mom about it."

"Promise?"

Delta gazed down into the eager, trusting little face. "I promise."

Just as they were finishing their conversation, Cassie came in from the kitchen. "What are we promising? Or is it a secret?"

Delta gave Mouse a kiss on the top of the head and sent her back to her word puzzles. "We were talking about depression. About how I apparently have eight of the ten symptoms." She let out an exasperated sigh. "Look, Cass, I know you're a therapist, but —"

"But what?" Cassie sat down on the sofa

next to Delta. "I'm sorry my daughter overheard a conversation I had with her dad. But I can't just ignore this, Sis. I'm worried about you." She narrowed her eyes. "Did you ever call those friends of yours — the ones in the singing group?"

"I tried a couple of weeks ago. Left messages on the machine for Lauren and Lacy, and talked to some guy at Rae Dawn's club. I gave him the number, but she never called back." She shrugged. "End of story."

"You're not going to try again? This reunion would do you good, you know."

"Really?" Delta said, making no effort to keep the sarcasm out of her voice. "It would do me good to tell old friends about Rankin's death over and over like a gruesome video loop on the nightly news. To pretend I'm over it, that everything's back to normal. Whatever *normal* is."

"You could use a change of scenery, not to mention the support of those friends," Cassie insisted. "Besides, the telling makes it real."

"It's plenty real to me," Delta shot back. Having a therapist in the family wasn't all it was cracked up to be. She looked over at Mouse, who had abandoned her puzzles and was staring at both of them with wide, knowing eyes. "Let's not talk about this anymore," she said. "Trust me, I'm fine."

But the following morning, after another restless night interrupted by dark dreams, she knew she wasn't fine, even if she wasn't about to admit it to her little sister.

She had to do something. Had to pull herself out of this.

Maybe Cass was right — not about the reunion, but about getting out of the house, getting a change of perspective. Russell was at work, as was Cassie, and Mouse wouldn't be home from school until three. She could have the whole day to herself, outdoors in the sunshine, if she wanted.

Delta scrawled a note to Cassie and posted it on the fridge, then took her battered old journal and left the house.

The shaded sidewalks near Emory University were a perfect place to walk. The day was warm and bright, but not hot. The sky had cleared and the humidity had dropped. Leaves were beginning to change. Already she could feel a hint of fall in the air.

Autumn was her favorite season. The beginning of the academic year. A new start. A time of change and renewal. And although Delta herself didn't feel particularly renewed, she was at least able to appreciate the break from another stifling, sweltering Atlanta summer.

She wasn't paying much attention to where her footsteps were leading her until she looked up and found herself on campus, near Cannon Chapel. Bishops Hall, which housed Candler School of Theology, lay across an expanse of brick courtyard to the left, and to the right, Pitts Theological Library fronted on the grassy quadrangle.

She skirted the library and found an empty bench facing the quad. A few students loitered here and there, talking and laughing. Two young men in jeans threw a Frisbee back and forth across the sidewalk. A few yards away on the grass, four girls lounged together drinking Starbucks from tall cups.

College campuses always evoked nostalgia in her, but today more than usual. Delta dug in her bag searching for her journal and a pen, all the while trying to stifle the wave of longing that had washed over her.

After a moment's searching she found the journal, pulled it out of the bag, and ran her hands over it. The cover was a rich saddle-brown cowhide, worn smooth and soft by more than twenty years of use and rather dog-eared at the corners. It had been a gift from Cassie the Christmas of Delta's freshman year in college, when she was eighteen and her little sister was only five. Cassie had picked it out herself, she told Delta proudly.

And it was perfect — beautiful, durable, and infinitely practical, a standard five-by-eight cover that over the years had housed dozens of refillable notebooks.

Delta's fingers caressed the velvety surface. All she had to do was touch the journal, inhale its rich leathery scent, and her mind kicked into overdrive. She never knew what would come out of her when this Pavlovian response overtook her, but anything would be preferable to the inertia that had seized her of late.

She opened to a blank page and wrote the date in the upper left-hand corner. But before she could go any further, something arrested her attention. A stiff, yellowed page, folded and stuck between the notebook filler and the cover.

Delta pulled it out and unfolded it. It was a page torn from a sketch pad, a crayon drawing of a small-town main street, with a towering gray slab looming overhead. And in a careful, childish hand at the bottom: Cassandra Fox, Age 6.

In a split second all the pieces converged upon her: the campus. The quad. The journal. Cassie's picture. That first dinner with Bowen and Hart, and the discussions that followed.

Countless hours of conversation — about

politics, about God and religion (Dr. Bowen firmly denied that these two were necessarily connected), about civil rights and human rights and the state of the world. About the war in Vietnam, about literature and writing, about beauty and truth and Delta's future. Discussions in the back corner booth of the Goose, lubricated by gallons of black coffee. Arguments over egg foo yung at their house with the dogs lying at her heels, or slapdash suppers of a thrown-together rice and beef dish Dr. Hart called "hamburger mess." Even the occasional jaunt to the Bavarian Steak House out on the highway, for planning sessions over rare steak and cheap wine and fried crab claw appetizers.

So many discussions that Delta had long ago lost count.

But she never lost track of the *effect* of those conversations.

In ways she could only begin to articulate, Frankie Bowen and Suzanne Hart had helped Delta to discover herself. Because of them she had become an English major, and on an academic level, they had introduced her to the intricacies of great literary minds of the past: Shakespeare, Milton, Spenser, Herbert, Blake, Wordsworth. They had encouraged her to find her own voice in writing and to be meticulous about research.

They had even pulled some strings to get her a work study job as their office assistant.

But even more important, they had taught her how to *think*. How to exhume the universal truths in fiction and poetry and drama, and to make connections between those writings and her own twentieth-century soul.

In the same way that Dr. Gottlieb had taken Rae Dawn under his wing, guided her, and become a kind of surrogate father for her, Dr. Hart and Dr. Bowen had become Delta's mentors. They had given her a vision for the kind of difference she could make in her own students' lives when *she* became a professor.

She remembered it all: the challenge, the passion, the fire. The sense of coming home to herself.

It had simply been too long since flint had struck steel.

All around the Emory quad, doors flung open and students poured out, clustering in groups and heading toward the food court down the hill behind Cannon Chapel. Delta glanced at her watch. It was nearly noon, and her stomach rumbled.

She stowed her journal in her bag, walked down to the Park Bench Tavern, and ordered a Philly cheese steak sandwich, fries, and a

Diet Coke. The place thrummed with activity — a gaggle of undergraduate girls laughing and chattering, a table full of divinity students arguing theology. While she waited for her lunch, Delta sipped her drink and absorbed the atmosphere by osmosis.

This was where she belonged — on a college campus, teaching these eager, open young minds how to think for themselves, how to dig out their own truth from the great literature of their heritage. And yet, despite the influence of Frankie Bowen and Suzanne Hart, despite the love of learning that had carried her through her master's degree and beyond, despite the dreams she had once cherished, this wasn't where she had ended up.

She had ended up as a minister's wife.

A poem surfaced in her mind, one she had chosen so long ago for her final American lit paper: Robert Frost's "The Road Not Taken."

The poem had haunted her, day and night, as she was writing, as she was making decisions she never dreamed would change the course of her entire life. Subconsciously, she understood. This was her story — perhaps everyone's story. Two roads. A fork. A choice. No turning back.

Where would her path have led, Delta

wondered, if she had finished her doctorate? If she had become a college professor?

If she hadn't married Rankin Ballou?

MAY 1969

After spring break, graduation seemed to speed ever closer with the velocity of a steam locomotive on a downhill run. Delta could hardly believe that within a week, final exams would be over and the friends with whom she had spent the past four years would be scattering to the winds.

Although the day was warm and sunny, front campus was shaded from the afternoon heat, and a slight breeze stirred the damp hair on her forehead. Delta sat at the top of the steps leading to the Music Hall and settled herself to wait. A few more rehearsals, one last gig at the graduation banquet, and the Delta Belles would be history.

A current of memory swirled over her, catching her heart in the eddies. Delta herself would not be leaving the college, of course. Much to her relief, her major professors had not been dismissed. The tumult over Dr. Bowen and Dr. Hart had subsided, and her plans to stay on for her master's degree remained intact.

But everything else was changing — indeed, had already begun to change.

The chasm that separated Rae and Dr. Gottlieb persisted. They seemed to maintain a distant civility, but the warmth between them had cooled. Delta felt the loss too, for the music professor had been a great supporter of the Delta Belles. True to his word, however, Gottlieb had lobbied an old friend on Rae Dawn's behalf. She now had a part-time job lined up — as a backup pianist at a club in her beloved New Orleans — and had arranged to rent a small apartment owned by friends of Drs. Bowen and Hart.

Trip still had not popped the question, but Lacy had won the coveted teaching position at Hillsborough High School and would be living with her parents while he got settled in law school. Lauren, in typical Lauren fashion, was waiting until the eleventh hour to decide what to do after commencement. She blamed the procrastination on the fact that she'd had a stomach flu on and off for weeks, but everybody knew she was predisposed to be indecisive. Lauren would land on her feet, Delta was certain. She always did.

At home in Stone Mountain, Daddy had moved out and settled into an apartment in Atlanta with Caroline Lawler, leaving Mama and Cassie to rattle around the house like pinballs careening off the banks. Cassie phoned at least twice a week begging her to come home, and Ben Rutledge had called several times since spring break, wanting to get back together.

Delta felt sorry for Ben. She missed him, and a time or two was tempted to rekindle their relationship and see where it might lead. But every time she circled around the idea, her mind kept calling up images of her parents, divorced after more than twenty years of mind-numbing boredom, and she realized that pity was no basis for a lasting marriage. He would eventually realize that the breakup was as much to his benefit as to hers. They would be friends again. And in the meantime, as much as her heart ached for the impending finale to her college days and for the strange, awkward balancing act that her family represented, she had something else to occupy her attention.

A dinner date with Rankin Ballou.

Delta rummaged in her closet for something modest — preferably black. Her bed was already piled with rejects, and she still hadn't found anything appropriate to wear. "Rae, don't just stand there — help me. Get me out of this."

Rae Dawn laughed. "You don't want to get

out of it, and you know it."

"This date's already been postponed twice," Delta muttered. "I should have taken it as an omen. He's a minister, for God's sake."

"Well, you're not exactly a wild child," Rae countered.

"Yeah, but what if I slip and swear in his presence, or do something that offends him? What if he isn't interested in me at all? Maybe I'm some sort of project — a challenge. Maybe he only wants to lure me in and then corner me with the truth, get me saved or something."

The questions — particularly the ones about faith and God and religion — nagged at Delta. She believed in God in a vague, disjointed way — God in nature, in the universe, in beauty and creativity. But when pressed to accept a label, she called herself an agnostic. Years ago, as a young teen, she had abandoned the church and had never felt a need to return. And yet now here she was, dressing to go out to dinner with a *preacher!*

"So how come this date got postponed twice?" Rae asked. "Weren't you supposed to go out with him the week after spring break?"

Delta shrugged. "He had some kind of

emergency — somebody in the hospital, I think. That was the first time. The second was — well, I forget." She searched under the bed for her black shoes. "I've actually picked up the phone three times this week to cancel. But what reason could I possibly give?"

"You could tell him Satan called with a better offer."

Delta pulled her head out from under the bed and scowled at Rae Dawn. "Very funny." She slipped into her shoes and twirled in front of the mirror. "How do I look?"

"A little bit like the Salvation Army lady."

"Perfect." Delta grabbed her purse and headed for the door.

"I made reservations at the Boathouse," Rankin said as he held the passenger door open for her. "Steaks, seafood, that kind of thing. Hope it's all right."

He was wearing khakis, a pale blue denim shirt, and a burgundy tie. Very handsome, Delta thought. He had even trimmed his hair and beard.

She hoisted herself into the seat of the Volkswagen van, which turned out to be quite a challenge in three-inch heels. She could have used a stepstool — or a crane. "Sounds lovely," she panted when at last she was settled. "Is it on a lake?"

"Not exactly. It's a renovated warehouse, and to be perfectly honest, I don't think there's a lake — or a boat — within a hundred miles of the place." He laughed. "But I do believe there's a really big pothole in the parking lot."

"So, what's with the van?" Delta asked as they drove. "A holdover from your hippie days?"

He craned his neck and grinned at her. "What makes you think I was a hippie?"

"First impressions when I met you at the protest," she said. "You know, long hair, beard, jeans. Now the van. And —" She tilted her head. "Your ear is pierced. I can see the hole."

"Very observant. I did spend some time in San Francisco — in fact, I went to seminary in Berkeley — Pacific School of Religion. The van comes in handy for carting youth groups around. As for the pierced ear —" He shrugged and flushed pink. "The beard is enough of a stretch for my parishioners. I don't think I'll challenge them with an earring just yet."

They arrived at the restaurant and were ushered to a small table in a corner, away from the traffic flow. On the drive over in the van, Delta had felt relatively comfortable with him. But now that they were sitting face to face, all her misgivings came rushing back. She barricaded herself behind the menu and came out only after the waiter had taken their orders and pried the leather-bound folder from her grip. Suddenly she felt naked, exposed, vulnerable.

If Rankin was aware of her discomfort, he gave no indication. He smiled at her, his eyes warmed by the candlelight. "Nice restaurant," he said. "I've never been here before. I'll have to remember to thank Frankie."

Delta stared at him. "Frankie?" she repeated stupidly. "You mean Dr. Bowen?"

"Yes. She recommended this place."

"You *know* her?"

"Of course I do. I was at the protest when they wanted to fire her and Suze, remember?"

"Well, yes, I remember. I just thought that was — I don't know, part of the job."

Rankin grinned. "You haven't been to church in a while, have you?"

Delta felt her neck grow warm. "Not exactly. Why do you ask?"

"Because most pastors wouldn't consider advocating for gay rights as part of the job."

The waiter arrived with a bottle of Chardonnay and presented it to Rankin for his inspection.

"You ordered wine?" Delta asked. She had been so absorbed in hiding behind the menu that she hadn't noticed.

"Is there a problem? White with shrimp, isn't it?" He tasted the wine and nodded to the waiter, who poured a glass for each of them and disappeared. Rankin held up his glass, and the pale liquid sparkled in the candlelight. "To —" He paused, thinking, then smiled at her. "To the future." He lifted the glass to take a sip, but it sloshed onto his beard and dripped down his tie. "Damn!" he said, grabbing his napkin and blotting at the stain.

Delta snorted wine out her nose, and barely got her own napkin to her face in time to save herself from utter humiliation.

He finished mopping up and sat back in his chair. "I'm delighted to be such a source of amusement."

"It's not the wine," Delta said when she had regained her composure. "It's *you*."

"Oh, that makes me feel better."

She tried unsuccessfully to suppress another laugh. "I was really nervous to go out with you," she said at last. "I mean, you're a *minister*. I was afraid I'd do something stupid or say something offensive. But here you are, pouring wine down your tie and swearing."

He flushed an appealing shade of pink.

"And that's a good thing?"

"It's a *very* good thing," Delta said. "You're not like any minister I've ever met."

"I'll take that as a compliment," he said. "For the sake of my poor battered self-esteem."

"It *is* a compliment. I should have known you were different when you showed up to support Bowen and Hart. But you were — well, so *impressive* that day."

"And rather unimpressive tonight," he supplied with a self-deprecating laugh.

"More human," Delta said. "More approachable."

That first dinner lasted nearly four hours. They talked about music and literature, about the uproar over Bowen and Hart (who, as it turned out, were faithful and active members of Rankin's church). When they finally did get around to talking about religion, it was Delta who raised the question, and his answer wasn't at all what she expected.

"Why did you become a minister?" she asked over key lime pie and coffee.

He thought for a moment, toyed with his pie, sipped at his coffee. "I grew up in a home that was nominally Christian but functionally atheist," he began at last. "I was baptized, taken to Sunday school when I was little, forced to endure confirmation class. But my parents never attended church, never talked about spiritual things. Never lived as if God existed, or as if that divine existence made any difference."

"Sounds pretty familiar," Delta said.

"By the time I went to college, I had rejected the whole thing as a boatload of hypocrisy. I was proud of being an atheist — it made me feel morally and intellectually superior to all those mindless sheep still claiming to believe in an invisible god."

His eyes kindled with an inner fire as he warmed to the subject. Delta leaned forward, unable to break his gaze. "So what happened?"

"I wasn't very good at it — being an atheist, I mean." He grinned and ducked his head. "I kept seeing things all around me — the beauty of nature, the goodness of the human soul, the excitement of intellectual challenge — all of which pointed me to something beyond myself."

"You're talking pantheism. God in the natural world — like Wordsworth."

"Not pantheism. Pan*en*theism. God present in all things. Separate and differentiated from created life, and yet present. The experience is difficult to explain, but once I acknowledged the possibility, I realized I had often felt God's presence.

"It wasn't a Damascus Road conversion, by any means," he went on. "More like a slow and arduous journey toward the light. By the time I finished college, I was hooked on the search."

"The search for God, you mean? But you must have found what you were looking for, if you became a minister." Delta bit her lip, debating whether to be completely honest with him. Then she took a deep breath and said, "I'm an agnostic. I hope that doesn't offend you."

Rankin chuckled. "Agnostic. Interesting word. *Gnostic,* to know. Agnostic literally means 'not knowing.' By that definition, I too am an agnostic. A Christian agnostic."

Delta gaped at him. "But doesn't your religion tell you what you need to know? Doesn't the Bible specify what you need to believe?"

"The Bible gives me glimpses of God, hints of truth. But truth is not a treasure to be found and possessed. Perhaps the biggest heresy in the life of faith is the myth of certainty. Faith is not about knowing, about being sure. Faith is about seeking God, and continuing to seek. It's the doubts and questions and uncertainties that fuel my ongoing search for God."

He finished his pie and accepted a refill of coffee from the waiter. Slowly he stirred it, watching as the spoon created a tiny maelstrom in the center of his cup. "Tell me about this God you don't believe in," he said quietly.

Here it comes, Delta thought. *The sales pitch.*

But to her surprise it never came. He listened intently, respectfully, as she painted a picture of the God she had encountered as a child — an ancient gray-haired divinity who saw all and knew all and loomed overhead waiting to smite anyone who stepped out of line.

"Like Santa Claus without the presents," Rankin said. *"He knows if you've been bad or good —"*

"So be good, for goodness sake," Delta finished with a laugh. "I never thought about it quite like that."

"A God who lays down rules we can't possibly keep and then punishes us for violating them."

Delta nodded. "Right."

Rankin went on. "And then this demanding God further demands that we believe the incomprehensible without wavering, or we're slapped down for doubting as well."

"Yes."

He arched his eyebrows. "If that was my definition of God, I'd still be an atheist."

"But isn't that *everyone's* definition of God? And isn't your job as a preacher to get people to believe in him?"

"My job isn't to sell religion the way you sell a used car," Rankin replied. "My job — my *calling* — is to help people find their own paths. To do justice, to love mercy, to walk humbly with God. God is the ultimate mystery of life, the joyful darkness that lies beyond the edges of our sight. I hold to only one definition of God, and it can be summed up in a single word: love."

"So how did you know you had been . . . called?" Delta asked.

Rankin smiled. "I rejected the myth of certainty and embraced the mystery," he said. "It felt like driving on a country road with all the windows down. Like standing at the ocean at sunrise."

Delta gazed at him. "Like leaving home and coming home all at the same time?"

"Yes," he said. "Exactly like that."

Twenty-Seven: The Minister's Wife

Despite her initial misgivings, Delta felt drawn to Rankin Ballou. Magnetized. Theoretically, she didn't believe in love at first sight, yet she had never imagined so much as a glimmer of what she experienced when she looked into this man's eyes. A feeling of rightness, a sense of destiny. It both elated and terrified her.

On so many levels, they connected. She believed she could be with him forever and never be bored, never feel like she had settled for less.

This was exactly what she had dreamed of. Still, the specter of her parents' divorce hung over her like a shroud. How could you ever know, really know, what the future might hold? How could you be certain?

Rankin would say it was a matter of faith.

But faith, when Delta tried to grasp it, slipped through her fingers like oil.

They married on the summer solstice, outdoors in the sunshine, the year she finished her master's and turned twenty-three. Rankin was almost thirty-three, established in his life's purpose, certain about his call.

Delta didn't fully understand his sense of mission and hated the idea of moving around from church to church, but she thoroughly enjoyed the philosophical and spiritual discussions their relationship generated. He introduced her to theologians and mystics — Julian of Norwich and Teresa of Avila and the Desert Fathers and Mothers, whom he called the Abbas and Ammas. She gave him Donne and Herbert and Milton, Yeats and Auden and T. S. Eliot. He never talked down to her, never pretended to have all the answers. And yet . . .

And yet she always felt something lacking, a spiritual center he clearly possessed and she could never seem to find.

At first she tried to convince herself it didn't matter, that her identity lay in herself, not in her role as a pastor's wife. But she soon discovered a level of expectation she hadn't anticipated. Only a few members of the congregation openly criticized her for pursuing her education rather than staying home, and they kept silent once Rankin made clear his support of her. Yet the subterranean rumblings continued. Why wouldn't she organize a women's Bible study? Why hadn't she taken the lead in the Ladies' Aid? And why did she bring the same tuna casserole to every blessed potluck dinner?

The external disapproval hounded Delta, but even more the accusations of her own mind and heart.

Until she met Grandma Mitchell.

Three years into their marriage, Rankin received a call from a church in Asheville, North Carolina. Delta was halfway through her Ph.D. and had been offered an instructorship at the W. It was only an entry-level position, teaching grunt classes like freshman composition and survey of English lit, but it was her first job offer, and she loathed having to turn it down.

Intellectually, she knew that her relationship with Rankin was first priority, worth whatever rootlessness she had to endure. But emotionally, she left the college like Lot's wife abandoning Sodom, dragging her heels and looking over her shoulder, salting the way with tears of grief and resentment.

She hadn't reckoned on the grace of Gladys Elizabeth Mitchell.

They had been in Asheville less than a year

when old Mrs. Mitchell first came to live with her grandson Clay and his wife, Hannah. She had just turned ninety, and her declining health prevented her from coming to church. As soon as she was settled in, Rankin made a pastoral call, and Delta went along

She had expected a frail, elderly lady whose interests ran to crocheted doilies and scrapbook photos. Instead she walked into the room to find a beady-eyed crone sitting bolt upright in her wheelchair, pointing a bony, clawlike finger into Rankin's face.

"Sit down, Sonny Boy," she commanded, taking charge of the meeting without so much as an introduction. "And you too, girl. We need to talk."

They sat.

Gladys wheeled herself over until her knees nearly touched Rankin's. "So you're the preacher my grandson has been telling me about." She looked him up and down with a critical eye. "Tell me, what exactly do you believe?"

Delta watched Rankin's face. She didn't know quite what Mrs. Mitchell expected, but she was pretty certain a ninety-year-old woman would not cater to a liberal-thinking, justice-minded minister who stood in stark opposition to the conservative perspectives most people in the South clung to. How would he cushion the truth so that she wouldn't be offended?

The old lady saved him the trouble. "You stand up for the rights of Negroes, I hear."

"Ah, yes, ma'am."

"Ever been arrested?"

Rankin quailed visibly under her unflinching scrutiny. "Well, ah, yes, ma'am, I have, but it was —"

She interrupted him before he could finish. "My granddaughter-in-law Hannah is a member of your ministry council. I take that as an indication you don't agree with the biblical injunction against women speaking in the church."

Rattled by this inquisition, he hedged again. "Well, Mrs. Mitchell, there are various interpretations —"

"For God's sake, Sonny Boy!" she screeched. "Get a backbone! Whatever you stand up for, stand up for it, and don't let anyone push you around, least of all a mule-headed intractable old broad like me."

Delta suppressed a laugh and did her best imitation of a supportive wife. Never in his life had Rankin Ballou been called spineless. More times than she could count, he had been arrested at civil rights protests and antiwar rallies. He had always put himself on the line, had risked himself for the causes he espoused. It was part of his calling.

But this old woman had nailed him. Stunned into speechlessness, he stared at her. Then, after a moment or two, he said, "Forgive me, ma'am. I was trying to be considerate of your perspectives."

For the first time she smiled, and her face softened into a lattice of wrinkles. "Never judge perspectives by appearance," she said. "In 1917 I went to jail with Margaret Sanger over the issue of birth control. In 1920 I stood on the steps of the Capitol lobbying for the ratification of the Nineteenth Amendment. In 1923 I helped draft the equal rights amendment proposed by the National Woman's Party. In the sixties I campaigned for the passing of the Civil Rights Act. I was over eighty years old, and my children and grandchildren thought I was out of my mind." She gazed placidly at him. "I can assure you I was never more sane."

Delta looked at her, then slanted a glance at Rankin. She could almost see his internal battle. Caught in the web of his preconceived notions — his assumptions, his *prejudices* — he struggled to free himself, to find the words to make amends.

Again the old woman helped him. "All those years on the front lines," she said, "all those decades of fighting for justice, and rarely did the church step forward to help. Now the time has come to pass the torch, and I'm wondering — what do you intend to do about it? What's your plan, Sonny Boy, to make the world a different place?"

He considered her question carefully before answering. "We're going to affirm the essential worth of all people," he said at last. "We're going to shout at the top of our lungs until everyone has a voice. We're going to say 'No' to images of God that are violent and cruel and judgmental."

As he spoke, Delta could see a change coming over him. She could feel his conviction swelling in his words until renewed passion swept over him like high tide. "We're going to overturn the moneychangers in the temple and make sure the widows and orphans get more than the crumbs that fall underneath the table. We're going to redefine what it means to be a Christian."

"About damn time," she murmured. "Jesus would turn over in his grave if he could see what has been done in his name."

The image, so outrageously irreverent, hit Delta full in the gut, and she let out a bark of a laugh. The old woman winked at her and laughed too — not the harsh croaking laugh of an ancient crone, but a young, vibrant sound like chapel bells ringing on the night air. Then she turned and fixed Delta with her beady eye.

"And what about you, girl?"

Delta faltered. "What about me?"

"I hear tell you're not much of a preacher's wife."

Delta fought back the temptation to make excuses for herself. Instead, she looked Mrs. Mitchell square in the eye and responded, "That's probably right."

Rankin opened his mouth to defend her, but she waved him off. "I know a lot more about literature than I do about the Bible," Delta went on. "I don't play the piano or teach Sunday school. I'm not much of a cook. I'm not much of a Christian either, if you get right down to it. I guess you'd call me a seeker."

The old woman narrowed her eyes. "What is it exactly you're seeking?"

"My own path," Delta responded after a moment's thought. "My own experience of God's presence. I suppose you'd say I have a lot more questions than answers."

Mrs. Mitchell grinned broadly, showing a gold-capped tooth. "I'd be interested in hearing those questions someday, if you'd care to spend a little time with a crusty old hag like me."

Delta nodded. "I'd like that. I'd like that a lot."

The woman leaned forward and patted her hand, then turned toward Rankin again. "You got a cigarette?"

Rankin stared at her. "No, ma'am. I don't smoke. But, Mrs. Mitchell, do you really think you should —"

"Call me Grandma," she said. "Mrs. Mitchell was my mother-in-law, and I'd rather not go to my reward with *that* picture in my mind." She arched an eyebrow. "What, you think a cigarette or two is going to kill me? For God's sake, boy, I'm ninety years old. I'm living on borrowed time as it is."

"Yes, ma'am," he said meekly.

"Camels," she ordered. "Unfiltered. Bring 'em with you next time you come, along with those wafers and wine."

TWENTY-EIGHT: GOING OUT AND COMING IN

ASHEVILLE, NORTH CAROLINA
SPRING 1976

In Grandma Mitchell, Delta found both a willing ear and a compassionate heart. And more. Much more. For almost two years she had been going every week to visit, and every time she came away feeling as if she had knelt at the feet of the oracle. A visionary who helped her shape her own vision.

"I love Rankin," Delta confessed one afternoon. "And I love being married to him. But I still don't think I'm cut out for this pastor's wife thing."

The old woman had transferred herself to a porch chair and now sat there rocking and smoking her Camels. "Those old biddies still giving you hell?"

Delta shrugged. "A few. I've learned to turn a deaf ear, for the most part. But that's not the real issue. This is not about running

375

bake sales and chairing the Ladies' Aid. It's about me. My faith — or lack of it. People expect me to be some kind of expert." She sighed. "I used to say I didn't believe in God. Now the most I can say is that I don't understand God."

Grandma Mitchell leaned back in the rocker and puffed on her cigarette. "One of the great forbidden pleasures in life." She sighed. "How old are you, girl?"

"Twenty-eight. Almost twenty-nine."

"And how long have you and Rankin been married?"

"Six years in June."

Grandma Mitchell smoked some more and rocked some more. Delta waited in silence. Patience, she had learned, brought its own rewards. Despite the old woman's crusty exterior, she harbored a deep well of wisdom and a fiery spirit.

"I've lived ninety-three years on this earth," Grandma said at last. "And they've been full years too. I haven't wasted a lot of time on trivialities. And yet I can't shake the feeling that if I lived another ninety, I'd still go out with unanswered questions and an unfinished faith." She stopped rocking and fixed her watery blue eyes on Delta's. "Where do you find glimpses of this God you don't understand?"

Delta thought about this for a minute. "In nature. In poetry. In people. In Rankin's love for me." She averted her eyes. "In you."

She half expected this last declaration to draw a protest, but instead the old woman just laughed. "And where else?"

"Well, in some of the stories from the Bible, I suppose. Rankin and I always discuss the texts he's going to preach on each week. Some of them, frankly, baffle me, but I see images of the divine there too. Jacob wrestling with God, for example. That's a metaphor I can get my mind around — wrestling with an invisible foe and holding on for the light."

"That's one of my favorites too. Just remember that even after the dawn comes, the wrestling never ends." She smiled, and the web of wrinkles deepened. "You're young, my girl. Too young to realize that faith is the work of a lifetime."

"But some people seem so *sure!*" Delta protested.

"The problem with being sure," the old woman said, "is that you quit seeking. You quit growing. Life gives us two choices: change or die. My best advice is not to die until you're dead."

■ ■ ■ ■

Delta sat upright in the hospital bed and gazed down at the curve of the baby's cheek, the delicate lashes, the soft sucking motions as she nursed. A ripple of pleasure coursed through her as her newborn daughter's mouth worked the nipple, an unexpected arousal.

How could it be that all the mysteries of the universe were wrapped up in such a small package? Here, in this defenseless infant, lay the ultimate metaphor. Incarnation. Resurrection. Divine made human, and human become divine. The face of God, the Creator's touch and breath, a new world burst forth from the womb of the Holy.

Delta's own journey of faith might be a work in progress, a labyrinth of intellectual and emotional and spiritual questions, a seeker's way. But as she held the weight and warmth of her tiny daughter and fed her from her own body, she knew that one truth stood firm when everything else was shaken: God had a name, and that name was love.

The hospital room door opened slightly, and Rankin's grinning face poked through the crack. "Daddy's home."

Delta laughed and motioned him in. He looked handsome and formal in a black clerical shirt with black slacks and a gray tweed jacket. Just briefly, she wondered what the occasion was. He usually wore khakis to the office and rarely donned clerical garb except on special occasions. Now she found herself wishing he would wear a collar all the time. She found it oddly stimulating.

He moved closer to the bed. "How's my little Sugar?"

Delta rolled her eyes. What was it about men and their penchant for nicknames? Rankin Ballou would be thirty-nine this year, and to all appearances an intelligent, mature, sensible man. But the moment their daughter had emerged from the womb, he had taken that round, wide-eyed baby girl in his arms, stroked her fine fuzz of white-blonde hair, and dubbed her "my little sugar pot."

The child would no doubt be called Sugar until her dying day, but her given name was Mary Elizabeth. Delta knew the exact date and time of the conception — a rainy afternoon in December, the fourth Sunday of Advent, during halftime of the football game. The lectionary text for that Sunday was Mary's visit to her elderly cousin Elizabeth after the annunciation. Rankin had backed up and told the story of the old priest Zechariah, Elizabeth's husband, visited by the angel of God in the temple and told he was going to have a son. In the face of the impending miracle, the old man had been rendered speechless.

Perhaps men were always struck dumb by the mysteries of birth, Delta thought. Or maybe just struck stupid, so that they insisted on saddling their offspring with idiotic nicknames that stuck with them forever.

But she wasn't really annoyed with Rankin. How could she be, when he was the answer to every prayer she never dared to pray?

Faith, Grandma Mitchell insisted, was the journey of a lifetime. Certainty was a myth. The wrestling would go on forever. And yet as Delta glanced back over the past seven years, she could make out the faint outline of a serpentine path, drawing her on to where she was meant to be. She might not be able to see beyond the turns ahead, but she had become convinced that, in Dame Julian's words, "All shall be well, and all shall be well, all manner of thing shall be well." And if she'd ever needed evidence of the wellness of all things, she only had to look down, for she held the proof in her arms.

The baby had fallen asleep, and Rankin took her, cradling her against his chest. "I'm afraid I have some bad news," he said quietly. "Grandma Mitchell died."

A cold emptiness rushed into Delta, a winter blast through an unseen crevice. "No!"

"I'm afraid so."

"How? And when?"

He edged onto the bed next to her. "The night before last, while you were in labor. Her heart gave out, apparently. She died peacefully in her sleep. I'm on my way over to Clay and Hannah's now."

"When's the funeral? I want to go."

"A couple of days, maybe three. The family's coming in tonight and tomorrow."

"I'll be out of the hospital tomorrow."

Rankin stroked an errant lock of hair out of her eyes. "Sweetheart, it's too soon —"

"I feel fine. I'm going, Rankin, and I don't want to argue about it. I need to say goodbye."

He nodded. "All right. I know how much you loved her. Death was a release for her, I'm certain. But it will be a loss for the rest of us. I'll give your condolences to the family."

He kissed her — twice — and left her alone with the baby, and with her grief.

The gathering at the funeral home felt more like a church coffee hour than a visitation.

Delta recognized almost everyone except for five or six people gathered around Clay and Hannah Mitchell, whom she assumed to be their extended family.

Few of the church members knew the deceased, as she had been homebound. And yet half the congregation seemed to be there, not so much out of personal sorrow but out of loyalty. Clay and Hannah had been members of the church long before Rankin had come to be their pastor.

As if some invisible cue had been given, the hubbub died down and all eyes turned in their direction the moment Delta and Rankin walked through the door. Clay made his way through the milling crowd. "Delta! I didn't really expect you, but thanks for coming. Grandma would have wanted you here."

"I'm so sorry, Clay," she said. "I'll miss her so much."

Clay bent down over the blanket-wrapped bundle Delta held in her arms. Unshed tears glistened in his eyes. "So this is the new one. She's beautiful, Delta. I wish Grandma had lived to see her."

"Six pounds seven ounces," Rankin said, beaming over Clay's shoulder. "Her name's Mary Elizabeth — I call her Sugar."

Clay ran a hand through his hair. "The cycle of death and life," he mused. "I wonder

382

if it's true, that when one person dies as another is being born, part of the dying person's soul remains with the newborn."

Delta smiled. "I devoutly hope so," she said. "If a bit of your grandmother slips into our daughter, she will grow up to be a very fortunate woman indeed."

Clay turned to Rankin, drew him into a hug, and held him there for a minute. "Grandma was ready to go, but still we're going to miss her."

"So will we." Rankin nodded. "I'll come by the house later and we can finish up details for the funeral." He gripped Clay's forearm and looked into his eyes. "You guys doing all right? You know, food and all that?"

Clay barked out a laugh. "Lord, yes. Vinca Hollowell's inundated us with so many casseroles that we'll need to buy a second freezer. I suppose you'll be getting some of Vinca's lasagna too."

Clay moved back to his family, and Delta and Rankin began to thread their way across the room, greeting people with hugs and handshakes as they went. Everyone stopped them, wanting to *ooh* and *ahh* over the baby.

At last they got to Vinca Hollowell. Vinca was the chair of the social committee, a rotund little woman with bright darting eyes, a tireless worker. She squeezed Delta's hand

and congratulated her on the baby, promising that someone would come by the parsonage in the morning to bring food.

"We're fine, Vinca," Rankin assured her. "Delta and I can fend for ourselves. Don't kill yourself trying to get everything done all at once."

"Nonsense, Pastor," she said, fidgeting with his lapel and brushing an imaginary piece of lint off his shoulder. "I just — well, you know. I like for things to be done right."

"And you always do them beautifully, Vinca." Rankin smiled down at her. "Once we get the baby settled into a routine at home, I'd like to come visit you."

Vinca gave a quick glance at Delta, and she saw a shadow move behind the woman's eyes. "Well, I — that is — you know, my husband, Ham, he's not a churchgoing man, and he doesn't like to have —" She paused. "I'll come to the church instead, all right? I'll call you next week. See you at the funeral, Pastor." And she was gone, flitting with surprising speed back toward the refreshment table.

"Are you all right?" Rankin said when Vinca had disappeared into the crowd. "You look tired."

"I'm fine. You go do your pastor thing. I want to pay my respects to Grandma, and in a few minutes you can take me home."

He bent down and kissed her on the cheek. "Okay. But don't stay too long."

Near the open casket the scent of lilies nearly overwhelmed her. The smell reminded her of Easter, of resurrection, of hope and a new beginning. She gazed down at the face of Gladys Mitchell, serene in death as she had never been in life. No one — not Clay, not even Rankin — could ever comprehend what this woman had meant to Delta.

On the way in, Delta had overheard someone describe Grandma Mitchell as "that sweet old lady," but it was hardly an accurate portrayal. The woman was an institution, a matriarch — by her own admission a "mule-headed intractable old broad."

Delta stared at the emaciated body. How could such a frail shell contain that flaming spirit and not be burned to ash? She had given Delta so much — wisdom, enlightenment, a sense of direction. And now that bright soul was extinguished.

She heard the old woman's words echo in her mind:

Faith is the work of a lifetime. . . . Life gives us two choices: change or die. My best advice is not to die until you're dead.

Delta gazed down on the lifeless face in the coffin and cuddled the sleeping newborn close to her breast. "This woman," she whispered to her infant daughter, "is the wisest person I know. She gave me permission to seek, to grow, to wrestle, and to change. I'll do my best to pass those lessons on to you."

Then she reached with one hand and felt inside her purse to find half a pack of Camels still there.

No one was looking. She palmed the pack and slipped it under the satin pillow.

TWENTY-NINE:
THE GHOST OF CHRISTMAS YET TO COME

DECEMBER 1977

Delta sat cross-legged on the hardwood floor of the living room and considered the huge box in front of her — a dollhouse for Sugar, lovingly crafted by her doting grandfather. She had just enough of the Snoopy wrapping paper left, she thought, to go around three sides of the cardboard box. She could make it work.

From the hallway, she heard a commotion, a high-pitched shriek. Fifteen-month-old Sugar hurtled unsteadily into the room, fresh from her bath and stark naked. Hot on her heels was Nanny, the six-month-old golden retriever puppy.

Nanny had been Rankin's idea. Every child needed to grow up with a dog, he insisted. And the truth was, Nanny and Sugar adored each other. The dog was sweet-tempered and patient, if not the brightest

387

star in the firmament.

"Twee!" Sugar yelled with delight. She headed straight for the Christmas tree, grabbed a light string, and began to pull.

Delta lurched to her feet in time to save the Christmas tree, but just as she scooped her daughter up in her arms and turned, she caught a glimpse of Nanny, squatting her golden haunches directly over the Snoopy paper laid out on the floor.

"Nanny, no!" she yelled. "Rankin!"

Rankin appeared in the doorway with a towel thrown over his shoulder and a diaper dangling from one hand. But too late. Nanny had already left a wide puddle square in the middle of the wrapping paper.

He shrugged and grinned. "At least she went on the paper. That's progress."

Delta glared at him. "Very funny."

"I'll take her outside. Leave the mess. I'll clean it up in a minute."

Sugar was squirming to get down, flailing her pudgy arms. Delta set her on the floor and reconsidered the large cardboard box, wondering where on earth she would find enough paper to wrap it now.

Her back was turned only a second or two, but it was enough.

"Peeee!" Sugar squealed. "Nanny peeee!"

Delta wheeled around to see Sugar squatting on the paper, peeing in exactly the same spot Nanny had chosen, and puddling her hands in the mess.

"Shit," she groaned.

Sugar looked up. "Sit," she repeated with a wide smile.

Rankin chose that moment to return. With a single glance he took in the situation, then began to laugh.

"Yeah, it's hilarious," Delta said, shooting daggers at him. "You take her back to the bath, and I'll clean up the paper."

Rankin scooped up their daughter and, holding her dripping at arm's length, dashed for the bathroom.

Delta had finally learned to cook. The parsonage kitchen emanated the smells of Christmas — turkey roasting in the oven, apple and pumpkin pies cooling on the counter, cornbread dressing awaiting its turn in the oven. Cinnamon and sage and allspice. On the stereo Bing Crosby was singing "White Christmas."

Delta opened the oven door and inhaled the fragrance as she squeezed drippings from the baster over the sizzling bird. Perfect. Another hour, and it would be done, right on time. At two, the guests would start to arrive — members of the congregation who had no family, nowhere else to go. Millicent and Stella, widows whose grown children lived in California and Florida. Ron and Edie, newly married. Walter, whose divorce had just been finalized and whose two sons would be with their mother for Christmas. Libby and Sandra, whose parents had rejected them. James, the homeless man who sat in the back row at church every Sunday. Rankin referred to him as "James the Brother of Jesus." He always went away with a huge bag of leftovers to share with his friends on the streets.

It was a grand custom, Delta thought, this gathering of the outcasts. Since their first year in Asheville, she and Rankin had hosted this traditional Christmas dinner, and although the guest list changed from year to year, it always proved to be a time of great joy and gratitude. Exactly the kind of Christmas celebration, Rankin said, that God would have planned. Plenty of room in the inn.

In the breakfast nook Sugar napped in her playpen with Nanny dozing on the floor beside her. Delta watched her daughter for a moment, her cheeks flushed pink with sleep, a delicate line of silver drool at one corner of her mouth. Her pudgy baby hands closed and opened again, grasping at some bright plaything in her dreams.

A warmth filled Delta — a radiance that had nothing to do with Christmas. But then again, perhaps it had everything to do with Christmas. Maybe every birth was an incarnation.

She leaned down to slide the turkey back into the oven, and as she did so she bumped butts with Rankin, who stood opposite her in the narrow kitchen. She gave a little laugh and turned.

Her face was flushed from the heat of the oven, the front of her blouse dusted with flour. Yet the expression on his face told her he had never seen anyone as beautiful in his life. He gazed at her, and his eyes went soft and liquid.

"Care to dance?" Rankin held out his arms and she came to him, flour and all. They waltzed around the cramped kitchen in a rhythmic embrace and he kissed her while Bing sang softly in the background.

Just as the dance might have developed into something else — something neither of them had time for, given that Millie and Stella would probably get there half an hour early — the telephone rang.

"I'll get it." Delta lunged for the kitchen phone. Sugar stirred in her sleep but did not wake, and she breathed a sigh of relief. She picked up the receiver. "Merry Christmas."

"Delta?" a tentative voice said. "I'm sorry to bother you on Christmas day. This is Vinca Hollowell."

"It's no bother, Vinca." This wasn't the complete truth, of course — the dinner was half done and time was slipping away. But Delta didn't say so.

"I — ah, as I said, I'm sorry to bother you, but —" She hesitated. Delta heard something in her voice, an edge of desperation. "I didn't know who else to call."

"What's wrong, Vinca?"

"It's Ham. He's — he's been drinking. Again."

"Is he there?"

"Yes. It was all my fault. I burned the turkey roast, you see, and —"

Delta closed her eyes and prayed for wisdom, not to mention patience. Hamlin Hollowell was a nasty drunk, a cruel man who apparently delighted in making Vinca's life miserable. Through sheer repetition he had her convinced that she was worthless, even though she was as close to a saint as anyone Delta had ever met.

In the background behind Vinca's sniffling Delta heard a crash. "What's happening?"

"He's breaking up the kitchen," she admitted. "Throwing stuff, dishes and the like."

"Has he hurt you?"

"Oh, no, he would never —" Another crash, and Vinca broke into sobs.

"Vinca, go outside. Never mind Ham, just get out of the way. We'll be there in ten minutes."

Delta hung up the telephone and gave Rankin a thirty-second summary of what was going on.

"You stay here. I'll go get her."

This was the part of a pastor's life Delta hated most. Not the interruption of schedules — she was used to that by now. But the realization that Rankin could at any moment walk into a situation that could get nasty in a heartbeat.

She couldn't have stopped him from going even if she had wanted to. This was who Rankin was, what he was called to do. Being a minister — at least according to Rankin's definition — was not just about preaching on Sunday mornings, marrying and burying and visiting people in the hospital. It was about standing up for those who couldn't fend for themselves. About justice. About showing mercy, even in the midst of risk.

Delta might not be a pastor, but she understood that sense of call. How many times had she faced down racists and hostile policemen at voter registration rallies? How many times had the Delta Belles continued to sing in the midst of booing and jeers and shouting? Still, she couldn't help worrying when Rankin went off into what might turn into a volatile situation.

"Get Sugar's blanket," she said. "The turkey will keep. I'm going with you."

Rankin drove a little too fast, snaking around the mountain roads on his way to Vinca's house. Once he nearly missed a curve, sliding sideways onto the shoulder.

"You won't do anyone any good if you kill us all getting there," Delta muttered grimly.

He took his foot off the gas.

Grandma Mitchell had once warned Delta about Vinca. "Keep an eye on that girl," she had said bluntly. "Her husband's no good."

How Grandma knew this, Delta had no idea, but the old woman knew many things, and when she spoke, Delta listened.

Ham Hollowell was a big burly man, an unemployed construction worker with beefy arms and a protruding belly and red spider veins spreading across his cheeks from a lifetime love affair with liquor. Hollowell had been laid off, Delta knew, after sustaining an injury to his back, and had sued the company for worker's compensation but never collected. Vinca hadn't said why. Delta suspected the man might have been drinking on the job. For the past year Vinca had been supporting them with temp work, and Ham had been drinking up most of what she earned.

Delta had never been told how Vinca and Ham had gotten together, but her imagination had pieced together a story that seemed altogether logical. She could envision a young Ham, masculine and muscular, a man's man whose tastes ran to monster truck rallies and demolition derbies and guzzling a few brewskis with the guys after work. The kind of man who refers to his wife as "the little woman" and whistles at long legs in a short skirt. He might have been handsome in years gone by — a shadow of it still lingered in his strong jaw line and reddish blond hair.

Vinca, small and round and maternal, with bright optimistic eyes that saw the best in everyone, would have been a pushover for a man like Ham. She would have seen the need in him — the need for love, for a wife, for a home. She would have been convinced that faithfulness could change him, that if someone believed in him and loved him, he wouldn't need to drink and swagger so.

Unfortunately, Delta mused, love was not

always enough. Not even the most devoted wife could compete when her husband's mistress was alcohol.

They pulled into the gravel driveway of the shambling unpainted house and Delta wondered, just briefly, if the severity of Hollowell's injuries prevented him from keeping up his own place. *"The cobbler's children have no shoes,"* she heard Grandma Mitchell whisper inside her head.

Vinca sat on the lopsided porch steps, clutching a paper grocery sack. When she saw them pull up, she rose and came toward them, casting furtive glances back toward the house.

Delta stayed in the car with the sleeping child on her lap. Rankin got out. "Come on, Vinca," he said. "You'll spend the day with us. Have dinner. We've got plenty."

She thrust the paper bag in his direction. "It's mincemeat pie and corn casserole. For your dinner." She turned as if to go back into the house.

Rankin caught her arm. "No, Vinca. Leave him. Come with us."

Vinca hesitated. The screen door swung open and Ham lurched out onto the porch, reeling drunkenly. "Bitch!" he yelled. "Stupid worthless bitch!"

He lunged toward the edge of the porch,

and for just an instant Delta glimpsed a vision of a full-blown attack, with Ham Hollowell bearing down on Rankin intent on breaking bones. Then Hollowell took a step back, swayed, and collapsed into a rusted metal glider.

"He's out now," Vinca said. "He'll sleep it off. I'll be fine. He'll be sorry when he wakes up. He always is."

"Let's go, Vinca," Rankin said again.

She let out an enormous sigh, bit her lip, and followed him to the car. "Thank you, Pastor. I needn't have called, but thank you all the same." She slid into the backseat.

Delta turned and looked into her eyes. Unshed tears pooled there, and an expression of stolid resignation. "You have to leave him, Vinca. You have to keep yourself safe."

She looked up, and the tears fell, sliding down her cheeks in wide tracks. "He'd never hurt me, Delta."

"He hasn't hurt you *yet,* you mean," Delta said. "At least not physically. But what has he done to your spirit, Vinca? To your soul?"

She gulped back the tears. "He loves me — he does, in his own way," she insisted. "And I can't leave him, Delta."

"Why not? You've got plenty of reasons, plenty of justification."

Vinca smiled and patted Delta's shoulder

— a gesture that said Delta could never understand, not in a million years. "I'm his wife," she said simply, as if that explained everything. "And he needs me."

Somehow they managed to get through Christmas and New Year's without another incident. But the third week in January, Vinca Hollowell called again. This time Ham *had* hit her — beaten her so badly that she ended up in the emergency room with a broken wrist and three bruised ribs. They kept her overnight for observation, to make sure she showed no signs of internal injuries. At noon the next day he appeared, hung over, disheveled and sheepish, pleading with her to forgive him and swearing it would never happen again.

Rankin and Delta had been at the hospital when Ham arrived. Delta greeted him coldly, without a shred of Christian grace. Her concern was for Vinca's soul, not Hollowell's, for Vinca's battered mind and broken heart, her crippled spirit and pummeled body. Delta gazed at the livid plum-colored bruises across her face and arms, the plaster cast running from fingers to elbow, and could not find it within herself to show mercy to the beast who had inflicted those wounds.

Ham eyed the two of them with suspicion. "I wanta talk to my wife — alone," he said.

Rankin flicked his eyes from Hollowell's face to Vinca's. She looked at him, entreating, but said nothing. Delta could not tell if she was begging them to stay or go.

"We'll be right outside if you need us," Rankin said, and ushered Delta out of the hospital room.

He stood with his arms crossed and his back to the door. Delta leaned on the wall beside him. With the door ajar, they could hear every word. Vinca silent, sniffling a bit, uttering a little sob or two now and then; Ham by turns gruff and insisting or whiny and beseeching, vowing he'd quit drinking, get a job, straighten up and fly right, demanding that she come home where she belonged.

To her credit, Vinca made no such promise.

When Ham was gone, muttering curses to himself as he stumbled down the hallway toward the elevators, Delta and Rankin re-entered the room.

Vinca lay motionless with her eyes closed, the bruising vivid against the stark white pillowcase. Without looking up she said, "I guess you heard all that."

"We weren't trying to eavesdrop," Delta

said. It wasn't the whole truth, but she figured God would forgive her such a small prevarication.

"What am I going to do?"

Rankin stepped forward and took her hand. "I think you should press charges," he said. "But that's your decision, Vinca. I can't make it for you."

She sighed and reached for the tissue box on the table next to the bed. Delta saw her wince as her torso twisted. "You've been very patient with me, Pastor. Both of you. You warned me this would happen. I was just too stupid to listen."

Rankin gave a half-smile. "A good pastor never says 'I told you so.' "

"But you did tell me so." She blew her nose and wadded up the tissue. "I've always believed it was a wife's duty to stick by her husband for better or worse," she said quietly. "It's in the Bible."

"A lot of things are in the Bible, Vinca," Rankin replied. "Slavery, violence, incest, the subjugation of women and children as property. That doesn't mean God condones them."

"So you don't think I have an obligation to stay?"

"We've talked about this before," Rankin said. "No child of God needs to subject herself to such treatment."

Vinca nodded slowly. "But where will I go? What will I do?"

"You'll go to a shelter or a safe house; I'll arrange it. When you're feeling better we can talk about options."

JANUARY 1979

Delta sat in the courtroom behind Vinca, listening as Rankin testified against Ham Hollowell. As it turned out, Vinca didn't have to press charges against her husband. While she was still healing in the safe house, Ham had gone on another roaring drunk, attacked a guy in the bar, and left him beaten to a bloody pulp in the parking lot. By the time the police got there, the fellow had gone into a coma and died two days later.

It took a year to get to trial. The prosecutor told them that, given the dozen or so eyewitnesses to the bar fight, there would be no doubt about Ham's conviction. But the case would be infinitely stronger and the sentencing more stringent if they could demonstrate a pattern of violence from a hostile, volatile, unpredictable abuser.

Rankin testified. Ham got fifteen to twenty.

After the sentence was read, Vinca Hollowell sat dry-eyed and stony-faced as her husband was led away in handcuffs. Then she broke down and bawled.

"It's not your fault, Vinca," Delta said helplessly. "Ham did this to himself. You have nothing to feel guilty about."

"It's not guilt," Vinca said between sobs. "It's *relief*." She heaved a deep breath and got control of herself. "But I do feel a little guilty about feeling so relieved."

Delta laughed, and the tension inside her own chest released. She hadn't known, until that moment, how scared she had been. Scared for Vinca. Scared for Rankin too, and for herself and Sugar.

And now, thank God, it was over.

THIRTY:
BROKEN BREAD AND
POURED-OUT WINE

APRIL 1994

Early Sunday morning was Delta's favorite time. The sanctuary, not yet filled with milling, chatting parishioners and their energetic children, seemed a hushed and holy place. Morning sunlight filtered through the stained glass and arched across the empty pews in vibrant shapes and colors. Two pots of lilies left from last Sunday's Easter celebration emanated the fragrance of new life throughout the room.

Delta let her eyes take in the brilliant hues, the serenity of the space. She had quarreled with Rankin this morning, over something utterly insignificant, and as a result had come to church stressed and harried. Now the peace of this place worked into her, calming the storms of her inner sea. They would make it up, as they always did. Everything would be fine.

She went into the sacristy, a small room to the left of the altar, and turned on the light. She took down the rough crockery chalice and paten, laid out the bread, and poured the wine.

In the years they had been here, the church had grown, the faces had changed. But the spirit of the place had remained. Like bread from many grains and wine from crushed grapes, diverse individuals blended together into one. One community. One heart.

Including, much to her own amazement, Delta herself.

She still wasn't quite certain how it had happened. She had learned much from Rankin over the years, certainly. Through him, and in him, she had discovered and embraced an image of God far different from the vindictive and demanding deity of her childhood. But the real beginnings of the change, she believed, went back to Grandma Mitchell and her practical wisdom about faith and life. Somehow in Grandma's acceptance Delta had found permission to be a perpetual seeker. She didn't have to have answers, did not even have to know the right questions. All she needed to do was be open to the mystery, the miracle.

Perhaps it was just this openness that had made the difference. Shortly after Ham Hollowell's trial and conviction, Vinca had come to her and asked if the two of them could meet to talk about faith. Her own trust in God had suffered in the face of Ham's abuse, and Vinca felt that Delta was a person who could understand that struggle without condemning it.

Vinca came. Then Mary Beth, a single woman who desperately wanted to be married. Then Connie, angry with God over her miscarriage. Kathleen, who agonized over her son's problem with alcohol. And Deb, battling the enduring wounds of an emotionally absent mother.

Dozens of women cycled in and out of the group, all asking the same questions in different ways. Where is God? Who is God? How can I trust? What is faith all about?

Delta had no answers, but needed none. The important thing was to provide a safe place for the questions to be raised and the issues discussed. And if tears fell or voices were raised in anger, nobody got upset.

Gradually, almost without her noticing, Delta's own faith began to take shape. She became aware of a gracious presence that surrounded these women and the way their labyrinthine discussions always worked them back around to God. There was an invisible nucleus here, a force that held them all together. A center that could be trusted.

She mounted the two shallow steps to the altar and set out the elements for communion. The scent of the yeasty loaf and the tang of the grape reached her nostrils, and her heart leaped.

More than any other aspect of worship — more than the music, the scriptures, even more than Rankin's preaching, the sacrament of communion brought the Presence alive. For a long time she hadn't understood the ritual, but gradually the truth dawned on her. This was a palpable experience of connection with God and the community. The center was here. The nucleus. The still point of the ever-changing world.

On occasion Delta had stood with Rankin and served communion, and it was an experience she would never forget. One by one the people came forward, looked into her eyes, heard the words of hope and dipped the bread into the cup. They often sloshed wine onto the hand that held the chalice, and for hours afterward she could feel it, smell it, could touch it to her tongue and taste the grace that had dripped down her fingers. Broken bread and poured-out wine. The loaf of life, the cup of the covenant. The unmistakable flavor of love.

Behind her, she heard the door to the sanctuary creak on its hinges.

"Pastor?"

It was Vinca Hollowell. For years now Vinca had served as part-time secretary, and although she struggled with the computer and still didn't quite understand the intricacies of the voice mail system, Rankin liked having her around. Fleshier than she had been fifteen years ago, and grayer, she nevertheless exuded a buoyant energy, and she always made Delta smile.

"It's me, Vinca. Rankin's around somewhere."

Vinca nodded. "I just needed to make some last-minute photocopies for the adult Sunday school class. Tell him I'll be in the office if he needs me."

She turned and exited again. Delta heard the front door shut as Vinca headed over to the church offices, on the main floor of the parish house next door.

She finished the communion preparations and went back into the sacristy for the white cloths to cover the bread and chalice. The communion wine was running low; she'd need to remind Vinca to tell the chair of the Altar Guild.

The door between the narthex and sanctuary squeaked again. It was probably Rankin, coming in to get ready for service. She peered out the sacristy door and saw him behind the pulpit, going over his sermon notes.

She stood and watched him for a moment. An apology for her crabbiness this morning could come later. She wouldn't disturb him now.

Then at the edge of her peripheral vision she saw something else — a movement in the shadows, under the overhang of the balcony.

Rankin saw it too, and looked up. "Can I help you?" He glanced at his watch. "Worship isn't until ten thirty. There's Sunday school in the parish hall, starting in about half an hour —"

"Where is she?"

It was a man's voice, and something about it chilled Delta to the core. He stepped out of the shadows into the carpeted center aisle. He looked to be fifty, perhaps, but a very fit fifty, with close-cut gray hair, a broad chest, and muscular forearms. He wore blue jeans and a black T-shirt.

"Excuse me?" Rankin came down from the altar and stood at the base of the steps, where the carpet runner ended in a T with its arms stretching left and right in front of the first row of pews.

The man advanced. Something about him nagged at the back of Delta's mind, as if they had met before, but she couldn't place him.

"I said, where is she? My wife."

The voice. Delta knew that voice. Then the stench wafted toward her — the unmistakable, sickly sweet odor of whiskey — and the bottom dropped out of her stomach.

It was Ham Hollowell. And he had been drinking. In one hand he carried a half-empty bottle of Jack Daniel's. In the other, a tire iron.

"Ham," Rankin said.

"Ah, so you *do* remember," Ham slurred, his lip curling. "You cost me my life, Preacher. Fifteen years and four months of it, give or take a day or two."

"You don't want to do this, Ham," Rankin said, trying to keep his voice calm.

Delta looked about frantically. The sacristy was in the far corner of the sanctuary behind the organ console. There was no way to get out, and no telephone.

"What else have I got to lose?" Hollowell's voice rose and echoed off the vaulted ceiling. "I already lost everything. She divorced me, did you know that? Of course you did. You probably put her up to it. Soon as I got released, I went home. The place is empty and falling down. Now, answer my question. Where is she?"

"She's not here," Rankin said. "Put down

the tire iron, Ham, and let's talk about this like reasonable men."

The sanctuary door swung open, and Delta caught a glimpse of Vinca's round red face. She dropped the papers she was holding, and they scattered.

Hollowell turned his head, just slightly.

"Run!" Delta screamed. "Vinca, run! Call the police!"

But Vinca stood frozen, rooted to the spot.

Rankin's head snapped around, and his eyes fixed on Delta. At last Vinca fled.

For a man of his bulk, and in his condition, Ham Hollowell moved with surprising speed. "Goddamn interfering preacher!" he shouted. "I swore if I ever got out —" He lunged and swung the tire iron.

Rankin put up his hands to defend himself. The weapon connected. Blood ran like wine down his useless fingers and dripped onto the carpet. Delta felt the jolt as if in her own body.

The second blow caught Rankin in the side, just under his arm.

"No!" Delta lunged forward, crashed into the organ bench, and went down. As she fell she caught sight of Hollowell — red-eyed, crazed, full of rage and drink, closing in on Rankin. The tire iron rose and fell again as if in slow motion; Delta thought she could hear the crack as a shinbone broke.

"God!" Rankin cried. "God!"

Then the weapon found its mark and sank into his skull.

She scrambled to her feet and dashed toward him, but it was too late.

Sirens screamed. Ham ran for it, out the front doors onto the church porch. But Delta didn't follow.

The sanctuary had gone eerily silent. Across the front pews the stained glass windows split the sun into shards of green and blue and purple. The heavy odor of Easter lilies hovered on the morning air, mixed with the scents of bread and wine.

And all the while Rankin lay motionless at the foot of the altar with his arms outstretched, a pool of red-black blood gathering under his skull.

SEPTEMBER 1994

Delta stared down at the puddle of ketchup on her plate.

How long had she been sitting here, remembering? The Park Bench Tavern had cleared out; only a handful of students still clustered here and there around the dark wooden tables. The remains of her french

411

fries had congealed into a greasy mess.

She pushed the plate to one side.

"Anything else you need?"

Delta blinked and looked up. *Yeah,* she thought. *An angel from on high telling me what I should do with my life.*

The waiter rocked back on his heels and regarded her. The fellow who had served her had been short and dark. This was a skinny blond kid in his twenties with a name tag that read Gabe. Her mouth went dry.

"What happened to the other guy?" she asked.

"He had class at one," the waiter said. "I usually tend bar, but occasionally I pitch in and serve when they need me. I'll be sure he gets his tip." He picked up the plate. "Want some more Diet Coke?"

"That would be great. Thanks."

He disappeared, and a few minutes later set a fresh drink down in front of her. "Are you a student?"

Delta gave an involuntary chuckle. "Me? No. I'm a —" She swallowed down the rest of her answer. "Should I be?"

He shrugged and grinned. "Lots of old folks are coming back to college."

Delta cringed inwardly. *Old folks.* She was not yet fifty, but she supposed she seemed ancient to this twenty-something waiter. "I studied literature," she said. "Got my master's and did some work on my Ph.D. I was planning to be a professor, but —"

"You got married and had kids instead," Gabe supplied.

"Something like that."

"And now you've got an empty nest and don't quite know what to do with yourself."

Delta's mind flashed back to Bowen and Hart, to Rankin, to Grandma Mitchell, to Vinca Hollowell and the others who had gathered to talk about their questions and doubts. "I — I'd just like to be useful. To help people, you know?"

The young blond waiter nodded and laid her check on the table next to the Diet Coke. "You don't need a degree to help people," he said as he turned to go. "Even a bartender can listen."

THIRTY-ONE:
THE INVISIBLE HAND

NEW ORLEANS
SEPTEMBER 1994

Rae Dawn DuChamp sat on the empty stage of Maison Dauphine, fiddling with the piano keys. Delta's call — which she had never returned, even though it had been two weeks — had exhumed years of ancient memories, recollections she'd just as soon keep buried.

Why did she torture herself like this? At night, with the lights and the music and the raucous noise of the crowd, the club came alive, and she could almost make herself believe that going on was worth the effort. But in the harsh light of day she could not ignore the scars across the table tops, the stains in the rug. The place seemed vacant and sad, like an old chorus girl without her makeup. Across the silence of midafternoon, she could almost hear voices in the *whoosh* of the air conditioning, ghosts come back to haunt her. *Choices,* the eerie whispers chanted. *Choices, choices.* . . .

Fulfillment, Dr. Gottlieb had told her years ago, was in the choices. You couldn't determine what life handed you — that part of the equation was out of your control. But you could choose what you did with it.

And what, exactly, had she chosen? Two decades ago, in her twenties and full of righteous defiance, she would have said that she chose integrity above all else.

Then her career had rushed upon on her like a freight train on the downslope of a mountain, with all her dreams and aspirations on board. The confluence of work and talent finally paid off. It hadn't been so easy then to choose between success and love.

Nobody had told her that the real challenge in life was not the choice between good and evil, between right and wrong. The real challenge was the decision between good and good, between one dream and another. The real challenge was the fact that, unless you paid close attention, sometimes you made choices without even realizing you had made them until it was too late.

The telephone behind the bar rang, and Nate the bartender answered. "Maison Dauphine." A pause. "Hold on a minute and I'll see if she's here."

He covered the mouthpiece and held the receiver out in her direction. "Phone for you, Rae."

She shook her head. "Whoever it is, tell them I'm not available." She lowered her head over the piano keys and heard Nate murmuring to the caller.

Nate interrupted again. "Remember that call you got a few weeks ago, from a Delta Ballou?"

Rae Dawn sighed. She wasn't ready yet. "Take a number and tell her I'll call her back."

"I already gave you her number," he said. "Besides, it's not her. It's her sister."

A cold premonition slithered through Rae's veins. "It's Delta's *sister*? She wouldn't be calling me unless —"

She went to the bar and snatched up the receiver. Nate made himself discreetly busy washing glasses at the opposite end.

"Rae, this is Cassie," said the low female voice on the line. "I'm Delta's —"

"Her sister," Rae interrupted. "I remember. The little kid who wrote stories and drew pictures of a big rock when we were in college."

A chuckle. "I'd forgotten about that."

"What's wrong?" Rae said impatiently. "She called me several weeks ago and I haven't had a chance to return her call. Is she sick? Is she . . . ?"

"No, she's all right," Cassie assured her. "I mean, well, she is and she isn't."

Rae frowned into the telephone as if Cassie could see her. "You want to explain that?"

"Let me start at the beginning," Cassie said. "You remember Rankin, Delta's husband?"

"The minister. Sure, of course. I haven't seen either of them in years —"

"Rankin's dead, Rae. Murdered, actually. It happened back in April, the week after Easter."

The chill in Rae's veins turned to ice, and for a moment she couldn't speak.

"Are you there, Rae?"

"Yes, I'm here," she managed. "I had no idea, Cassie. She didn't call, didn't write. Nothing."

Rae listened while Cassie related a tale of unspeakable horror, about an abusive husband who took out his rage on the pastor who tried to help his wife. "Delta saw it all," she concluded, "and couldn't do anything to stop it."

"God help us," Rae murmured. "She must be devastated."

"She's putting on a good front," Cassie said, "but she's spinning her wheels. I wouldn't normally interfere —"

Rae ran a hand through her hair. "How can I help?"

"You were her best friend in college. As a pastor's wife, it's been hard for her to make close friends over the years. There are so many boundary issues — not getting too close to parishioners, conflicts of interest, that sort of thing. Rankin was her dearest friend as well as her husband."

"I understand," Rae said, willing her to get to the point. "What do you want me to do?" She paused, and then it hit her. "I get it. The reunion."

"Yes," Cassie said. "This idea of — what was her name?"

"Tabby? Tabitha Austin?"

"That's it. Tabby. She wants to get the Delta Belles together for one last concert. And although Delta's been resistant to the idea — to the entire reunion, actually — I think it could be a turning point for her. It would give her something to focus on besides her anger and grief. And it would be good for her to reconnect with old friends."

"But the reunion is less than a month away," Rae protested.

"I know," Cassie said. "The weekend of the reunion happens to be the six-month anniversary of Rankin's death."

Silence stretched between them — a deliberate silence, Rae felt sure, a silence designed to emphasize the importance of Cassie's request.

"If the three of you say yes," Cassie said at last, "I think you can convince Delta to join you."

Rae hesitated. If she agreed to do this, to go back to the reunion, to play the piano and sing, there was a good chance she would be recognized as Dawn DuChante, the Grammy-nominated torch singer. There would be questions: Why had she quit recording? What happened to her career? Why wasn't she . . . married?

And yet how could she refuse? Delta had been her best friend, had accepted her and believed in her and stood by her at one of the most crucial moments of her life.

"All right," Rae said at last. "I'll contact Lacy and Lauren and see what I can work out."

Lacy put down the phone and sank onto the sofa next to Hormel, who purred and rubbed his head against her thigh. Rae Dawn had sounded stressed and worried, and after hearing what Delta had gone through with Rankin's death, she understood why. Lacy didn't want to do this, but how could she possibly say no?

Still, a heavy lump formed in her stomach at the idea of getting the Delta Belles back together again. Since she had come home to Hillsborough — almost ten years — only once had she faced Lauren alone. Always she had the buffer of family around her, and as if by mutual consent, she and Lauren had kept things cordially superficial.

Besides, Lacy could tell that Lauren was uncomfortable in her presence. The two of them danced around each other like fire-walkers, forcing themselves across the hot coals and trying desperately not to get burned.

It wasn't an issue of forgiveness. Lacy had forgiven Lauren long ago and was glad to see that somehow Lauren and Trip had stayed together. But all of them put on such well-crafted fronts that she could never see behind the mask enough to know what her twin was really thinking.

Now Lacy had really stepped in it. She had agreed to join Rae Dawn in reuniting the Delta Belles for their twenty-fifth reunion. She would have to call Lauren and convince her to come, and then once the four of them were together, she would have to face Lauren without the rest of the family as a shield.

She blew out a breath and picked up the

phone. Putting it off wouldn't make it any easier. She just had to remember they were doing this for Delta.

Delta fumed and muttered to herself as she packed.

How had she let herself get talked into this? She had never intended to go to this reunion, never expected that any of the other Delta Belles would even consider getting back together. And now, suddenly, they were all gung-ho about it, and Rae Dawn had talked her into committing to the insane notion as well.

Rae had been extremely persuasive, Delta had to admit. But it wasn't the persuasion that had won her over. It was the shadow behind Rae Dawn's voice.

Rae hadn't wasted any time in small talk but got straight to the point. She and Lacy and Lauren wanted to do the reunion concert, she said, and thought it would be fun to get them all together. Rae had even called Tabitha Austin to make sure she could still get them on the program for the anniversary banquet. Tabby, of course, had been thrilled.

The reunion was Friday night through Sunday noon, on campus. The anniversary banquet for the class of '69 was scheduled for Saturday night. The plan was for the

Belles to meet on Friday evening at a bed and breakfast Rae Dawn had reserved. That would give them most of Saturday to catch up and practice.

Delta had hesitated, until at last Rae had said the words that convinced her. "We need you, Delta. *I* need you. I really want to see you again."

I need you.

"Is everything all right, Rae?" Delta had asked.

Rae hadn't answered right away. Then: "We'll talk when we see each other."

What was going on in Rae's life? Delta hadn't been in contact with her in a long time. Ten years or more with only a card at Christmas. She knew that Rae had been successful with her music — successful enough to own the club where she once played as a backup pianist. Her dreams had come true. And yet Delta had gotten the impression, largely unspoken, that Rae was in some kind of turmoil.

She wasn't quite sure what she could do to help. She was dead certain she didn't have Grandma Mitchell's wisdom. And yet, despite her misgivings and against her better judgment, she had finally agreed to join the Delta Belles for one last concert.

You don't need a degree to help people, the

waiter Gabe had said. *Even a bartender can listen.*

A fool's errand, a voice in the back of her mind nagged.

Maybe so. But she'd rather be a fool than let down a friend who needed her.

Once the suburbs of Atlanta had receded in her rearview mirror, Delta began to feel herself relax. She adored Cassie and Russell and Mouse, and appreciated their generosity in inviting her to stay with them until she got her feet under her. But only when she got away did she realize how deeply affected she was by the harried pace of the South's largest city.

Growing up next door in Stone Mountain hadn't prepared her for life in Atlanta. The city had mushroomed in the past twenty-five years, and the traffic — eight lanes on the perimeter loop going seventy-five miles an hour bumper to bumper — scared the life out of her. For all its talk of southern hospitality and casual elegance, Atlanta seemed to Delta to be a rushed, angry place where tempers seethed just below the surface.

The trip to Mississippi would take a little over five hours, not counting food and potty breaks. Delta had left early in an effort to beat rush hour, only to discover that rush hour started at six A.M. and lasted until ten. It had taken her more than an hour to get around the northern perimeter and out onto open road.

Now at last the traffic had begun to thin out. Exhaling tension on a sigh, Delta pointed the minivan west toward the Alabama line.

Here and there along the highway she could see hints of coming autumn. At home in Asheville, where the air was cooler and the altitude higher, the trees would be at their peak in mid-October, color creeping down the mountainsides like a spill of brilliant paints against a sky of clearest blue. A longing rose up in her, a palpable yearning for the Blue Ridge Mountains, for the beauty and serenity and protection those hills afforded.

Cassie had offered to cancel her appointments and come with her on the trip — an offer Delta quickly, and probably not graciously, refused. She had not wanted to be shut up in the car with her sister for six hours, but she hadn't counted on what it would be like to be locked in alone, with only her own thoughts for company. For the first twenty miles she had tried to listen to the radio, but no one played the kind of music she liked anymore, and by the time she got out of the city, she had become increasingly irritated with the puerile, asinine conversation on the morning shows. Even NPR couldn't hold her attention, and she hadn't yet figured out how to use the CD changer.

At last she turned the radio off and listened to the silence inside the car. Her mind drifted, predictably, to her college years with Rae Dawn and the others, to the early days with Rankin, to her life over a span of two and a half decades.

Through the years her contact — in Cassie's language, her *connection* — with her college circle had been sporadic at best. Lauren's marriage to Trip Jenkins had evidently caused an uncomfortable rift between her and Lacy. Somehow Lauren and Trip had managed to make it work; they had stayed together, anyway, and had a grown son. Lacy had gone away and come back still unmarried, and although Rae had said she seemed upbeat and enthusiastic about this reunion, Delta wondered whether the optimistic outlook was real or just a front, a posture assumed for an estranged friend. Theoretically she believed that a person could make a happy, fulfilled single life, but as she had never lived that kind of life, an experiential understanding of it was beyond her comprehension.

What would her own life have been without Rankin? The question disturbed her more than it should have. On one hand, she had been disgustingly happy with him — so happy, in fact, that Sugar as a teenager would feign retching every time she walked into a room and saw them kissing. The memory made Delta smile, and on the heels of the recollection came the palpable feeling of Rankin's arms around her, warm and inviting.

She had been so lucky. No, not lucky. *Blessed*.

It was a word Delta rarely used because of the sappy religious connotations it conjured up. People regularly talked about being blessed with a good parking space or a short line at the ATM. As if God rode around on a Mardi Gras float, throwing down trinkets from on high.

No. Being blessed was not about trivial answers to equally trivial prayers. It was about being graced with something so unexpected and undeserved that the only possible response was overwhelming gratitude.

Tears stung Delta's eyes as she recalled the years of unexpected grace with Rankin. The mountaintop experiences — their wedding day, the birth of their daughter, their recommitment ceremony after twenty years of marriage. The transfigurations, when truth pressed in upon her as they discussed theology and philosophy and poetry, those moments when she had, palpably, felt the presence of God. And the huge slices of ordinary time that make up a life together — such as that snowy night, so clear in her memory even after all these years, when they had held each other after making love and wept for the sheer joy of their oneness.

Yes, she had been blessed. And then the blessing had been snatched away.

Her mind began to veer in the direction of anger — the seething, simmering rage toward God that had burned inside her ever since her husband's death. Spiritual and theological dilemmas haunted her — questions of theodicy, of why terrible things happened to faithful people; questions of omnipotence and impotence, omniscience and ignorance; the reality of tragedy and the unquestioned assumption of divine love.

She had heard the question asked before, usually voiced by people in great pain: *If God loves me and has the power to intervene in my life, why did this happen? Why did my baby die? Why did my wife get cancer?* And now Delta herself was asking the unanswerable question: *Can God be at once omnipotent and loving?*

Rankin, in his wisdom, never let this surface question get in the way of real responses. This was the "presenting question," as he called it, this apparent dichotomy between power and love. People in crisis didn't want or need a theological treatise on natural law and the broken world. They didn't really want to know why. They wanted to know that God hadn't abandoned them.

She shook her head and forced her mind back to Rankin, back to the initial issue that had sent her down this path: What would life have been like without him?

The other side of the question nagged at her more than she wanted to admit. For all the joy and love and blessing of their years together, how much of her life had been sublimated to his? What had she missed of her own cognitive and spiritual development?

She remembered early discussions with Rankin, conversations that centered around her Ph.D. work and her sense of mission or calling as a college professor. He had agreed, quite vehemently, that she should have a life of her own, that his work in ministry should not dominate their lives or absorb her personality and gifts.

And yet it hadn't turned out quite that

way, had it? Gradually — especially after Sugar's birth, when all her attentions turned to being Mommy to this needy little bundle of warm energy — Delta had become Rankin's second. The woman behind the man. The pastor's wife. And most incredibly, neither of them realized it was happening. They just went along, ushered forward by the flow of life's stream, until the rapids took Rankin and Delta was left alone in the shallows with no idea how she got here.

And so, a thousand times since Rankin's funeral almost six months ago, she had asked the question. Another question with no answer, the cry of an anguished heart:

What the hell am I supposed to do now?

THIRTY-TWO:
HIGHGATE HOUSE

MISSISSIPPI COLLEGE FOR WOMEN
OCTOBER 1994

Delta had forgotten — or perhaps hadn't noticed when she was a student here — how many antebellum homes the town boasted. All along College Street and in a wide perimeter around the campus, enormous mansions kept watch over the old Southern way of life — lush gardens, broad porches, elegant columns rising toward the sky. Most were on the pilgrimage tour, she suspected. Several had been turned into B&Bs, with small tasteful signs out front, and a few were open to the public all year long.

Highgate House, a brick Greek Revival mansion two blocks from the college, sat back from Third Street on a shaded lot surrounded by magnolia trees. Somehow Rae Dawn had managed to get reservations there, booking its only three rooms with private baths.

Delta pulled into the driveway at Highgate and parked next to the carriage house. Her small rolling suitcase bumped noisily as she made her way around the brick sidewalk to the front door.

The door swung open and a small, birdlike woman with silver hair stepped out onto the porch. "Welcome to Highgate!" she said, opening her arms wide. "I'm Matilda Suttleby, the owner." She squinted at Delta. "Are you Dawn? You look . . . different."

"Do you mean Rae Dawn? No. I'm Delta Ballou."

"Of course, of course!" The woman beamed and swept Delta into an effusive hug which Delta, encumbered by the suitcase and a purse, endured but did not return. "Do come in."

Matilda led the way into a wide foyer dominated by a plush oriental rug and an enormous grandfather clock. To the right was a large parlor, decorated all in pink, with several uncomfortable-looking settees surrounding a marble fireplace. In a corner next to the window sat a very old and richly inlaid piano.

Delta abandoned her suitcase in the foyer and followed as Matilda turned to the left. Two steps down, the room opened into an enormous den with a low-beamed ceiling, another fireplace — fieldstone this time — and an assortment of deeply cushioned leather armchairs.

"You'll be in the Jefferson bedroom, up the stairs and to the right," Matilda was saying as she rummaged through a pile of paperwork spread out on a huge walnut desk in the corner. "I've put Dawn in Robert E. Lee, just opposite yours, and the other two, the sisters, in the large Stonewall room down the hall."

Jefferson Davis. Stonewall Jackson. Robert E. Lee. Delta's mind flashed to the Stone Mountain carving, and she suppressed a smile.

"I'm sure you girls will have a lot of catching up to do," Matilda was saying. "So you just make yourselves at home. Through there" — she pointed to a swinging door at the end of the den — "is the grand dining room, where breakfast is served at eight. Beyond that you'll find the kitchen. After hours feel free to forage for snacks. My room is the door to the right off the back porch. Call on me if you need anything." She got up and came toward Delta, who was still standing in the middle of the room, and pressed a large key into her hand. "This unlocks the front door, in case I'm in bed when you come home. There's a very nice enclosed garden out back — the weather is lovely in October, don't you think? Oh, and I serve tea from two thirty to three thirty," she finished breathlessly.

Delta struggled to take all this in. Finally she said, "Ah, thanks, Mrs. Suttleby."

"Matilda!" the woman corrected with a little bob of the head. "You must call me Matilda. I like to think of my guests as friends, you know."

She swooped out of the den and back into the foyer, hauling Delta behind her. "Now, up the stairs with you. Let's get you settled. I'm sure your friends will be here soon."

The Jefferson bedroom reminded Delta a little of rooms she had seen at the Biltmore House in Asheville — garish flocked wallpaper in shades of powder blue and green, dark mahogany furniture, and a bulbous blue floor lamp on a brass base. The carved rice bed was so high that she'd need a running start to get into it. From the wall above the fireplace a pen-and-ink portrait of Jefferson Davis, President of the Confederacy, scowled down upon her.

"All these bedrooms have private baths," Matilda was saying as she laid Delta's suitcase on the cedar chest at the foot of the bed and began to unzip it. "They weren't original to the house, of course. We converted the maids' sleeping chambers years ago."

Through a door to the right, Delta caught a glimpse of an expanse of white tile and a clawfoot tub large enough to swim in. When she turned back, Matilda had opened her suitcase and was beginning to transfer underwear to a dresser drawer.

"No, I can do that," she protested, returning to the woman's side and shutting the suitcase lid with a slap.

Matilda pulled back abruptly and gazed dolefully at Delta with the expression of a four-year-old who has just had her favorite doll snatched away. "As you wish," she murmured.

"I've had a long drive," Delta said apologetically, "and I'd like to freshen up before the others get here."

"Certainly." Matilda backed out of the room with a broad smile pasted on her face, a smile that did not quite meet her eyes. "I do hope you'll come down for tea."

"Of course," Delta said. "Two thirty, right?"

Matilda nodded and disappeared down the stairs.

Delta looked at the clock on the mantel under Jefferson Davis's picture. It was almost quarter to two. She'd have half an hour, at least, to rest before having to face the indomitable Matilda Suttleby again. She hung a few things in the narrow closet, climbed the wooden step stool, and collapsed on top of the enormous bed.

Only when a noise downstairs awoke her did Delta realize she had fallen asleep. As if from a great distance she heard the front door opening and shutting again, Matilda's piping voice, the sonorous chiming of the grandfather clock.

She struggled to wakefulness and peered at the mantel clock. It was two-fifteen. The half-hour nap had done nothing to refresh her; on the contrary, she felt groggy and drugged. She had drooled on the satin bedspread and tried in vain to wipe the stain off with her hand.

"Delta!" a voice called up the stairs, followed by the pounding of feet. "Delta! Are you here?"

Delta slid off the bed and willed herself awake. She was just running her fingers through her hair as a petite figure with short blond hair burst into the room.

"Lacy!" Delta grinned. "Damn woman, you look just the same."

Lacy launched herself across the room and hugged Delta hard. "So do you."

"Not really," Delta said. "But thanks for saying so."

"Is Rae here yet?"

Delta shook her head. "She called last night and said she'd be late getting in."

Matilda cleared her throat to get their attention. She was still standing in the doorway guarding a small bag, a bulky guitar case, and a large traveling crate that housed an enormous cinnamon-colored cat. "Your room is down the hall, Miss Cantrell," she said.

"Oh! Sure, all right." Lacy edged back to the doorway and retrieved her luggage She motioned to Delta with a snap of her head. "Come on. See my room."

Delta picked up the guitar and followed. Matilda ushered them into a huge square bedchamber that must have taken up one entire wing of the house. Dormer windows on three sides let in a golden afternoon light. The ceilings, painted in a pale heathery purple, slanted upward from side walls about seven or eight feet high. There were four double beds in the room, one in each corner, matching canopy beds covered with handmade quilts in shades of lavender, purple, and sage green. In the center of the room, on a floor of wide pine planks, a large floral rug flanked by two velvet love seats created a conversation area.

Lacy looked around. "Jeez. My whole house would fit in this room."

Matilda glared at the cat carrier. "I normally don't allow —"

"His name is Hormel. He's very sweet, really." Lacy opened the crate. Hormel streaked out, made one circuit around the room, and settled himself in a slant of sunlight at the foot of one of the canopied beds. "He won't be any trouble, I promise," Lacy said. "I've got a litter box down in the car, and he'll stay in the room with me."

"Well," Matilda said, "I'll make an exception this one time." She did not attempt to unpack Lacy's bag for her. Instead she placed it on a suitcase rack in the corner. "Tea in ten minutes," she said, and left the room.

"This is a great place," Lacy said when she was gone. "I feel like I'm in a time warp, gone back a hundred years." She turned a broad smile on Delta. "I'm so glad you're here."

"Me too." Delta sat on the edge of the bed and rubbed Hormel's upturned belly. He squeezed his eyes tight shut and purred loudly. "You're earlier than I expected."

"I left yesterday, spent the night along the way," Lacy said. "I'm too old for a twelve-hour road trip alone."

"Alone? Didn't Lauren drive down with you? You're sharing a room, right?"

A shadow passed behind Lacy's eyes, a brief cloud filtering the sun. "We didn't have a choice about the room," she said, "but we, ah, came separately. She'll be here by dinnertime, I think." The shadow retreated. "It looks like we get the luxury suite, anyway."

"Lace," Delta began, not knowing quite where to start, "is there something —"

Lacy held up a hand. "Later," she said. "After we have tea with Scarlett O'Hara."

It was three thirty by the time they were finally alone in Lacy's room. Hormel had discovered the window seat and was snoring loudly.

"All right," Delta said. "Tell me what's going on."

Lacy shook her head. "You first. When Rae Dawn called, she said Rankin had died. Delta, what happened? Why didn't you call us? We would have been there for you."

Delta fought for air against the heavy weight that settled on her chest. "There was this woman in our congregation — Vinca Hollowell. Her husband was a violent drunk and an abuser. Rankin was trying to help her. Anyway, Hollowell killed a man in a bar

438

fight, and at his trial Rankin testified. Hollowell got fifteen years, and when he got out —"

She shrugged helplessly, unable to go on. "It's been awful," she said at last. "I keep trying to get a handle on this for my daughter's sake, for my own sake. But I'm so *angry*, Lace. Angry and depressed. I can't seem to get past it."

"Angry at this Hollowell guy?"

"At him. At Rankin, for leaving me. At God, for letting it happen." Delta exhaled. "Ham Hollowell beat my husband to death with a crowbar in front of the altar. I saw it all and couldn't do anything to stop it."

"Shit," Lacy said.

Delta looked up and saw tears standing in Lacy's eyes. An unexpected warmth washed over her. Someone else — someone not directly related to Rankin's death — could weep with her. Someone else could say it was shit and never should have happened. The effect was instantaneous. The tension clenching at her gut released. Just a little, but it was enough.

Lacy sat there, stunned, as she tried to absorb the specifics of Delta's husband's death. Nothing in her realm of experience enabled her to understand such grief, and yet the tears came. Now she understood, though Rae Dawn had not told her the details, why it was so important for her to come to this reunion.

Delta began to cry too. For a long time they just held hands and wept together. When the tears at last subsided, Lacy spoke.

"I have a friend in Kansas City," she said. "My best friend. Her name is Alison Rowe. She was widowed at twenty-nine, her husband killed in Vietnam. Friendly fire, they called it." She paused, remembering. "He was halfway through medical school when his number came up, and he went as a medic. One day while his unit was on patrol, they got pinned down in the jungle by snipers. Somehow he managed to get out, to radio for help. Then, while the helicopters were on their way, he went back in. Pulled three wounded men to safety and was shot in the back by one of his buddies who panicked and thought he saw the sniper."

She looked up at Delta, who nodded for her to continue.

"At the funeral, Alison told me, people kept assuring her there was justification in her husband's death. The religious folks said it was God's will, God's time, that God had reasons beyond what we could understand. The military contingent said he was a hero who had given the ultimate sacrifice for freedom."

"Sounds familiar," Delta said in a choked voice. "Everyone told me that Rankin was in God's hands, that everything happens for a purpose. That Rankin died the way he lived, standing up for those who had no power, no voice."

"Not much comfort, is it?" Lacy said. "Alison told me she didn't want a hero. She didn't want God's will. She wanted her husband back."

Delta nodded. "She's more honest than most. Most of us can't deal with the paradox between an omniscient God and an omnipotent one. We believe — we *have* to believe — that God, or fate, or karma could have intervened, could have stopped the tragedy from happening. But when the miracle doesn't come, what kind of God does that leave us with? What kind of God stands idly by in the midst of pain and suffering? Not a loving God, but a monster, a tyrant. Or an impotent weakling."

"So what's the answer?" Lacy asked.

"That's the million-dollar question," Delta said slowly. "The question I've been asking myself for months — why a supposedly loving God would allow a man like Rankin to meet such a violent and undeserved death.

So far I've only come up with one answer."

Lacy leaned forward. "And that is?"

Delta shrugged. "Shit happens."

The moment the words left Delta's mouth, some tightly wound spring inside her let go. It was so simple, really. She didn't have to blame God for Rankin's death. She didn't have to blame anyone.

Not even herself.

"So," Delta said after a while, "tell me what's going on with you."

Lacy hesitated. "I'm all right. I've been teaching in Hillsborough, and —"

"I know what you *do,* Lace," Delta interrupted. "I want to know how you *are.*"

Lacy ducked her head and grinned. "All right. You want the real story, here it is."

Delta listened while Lacy told about her midnight run on the bus from Hillsborough, about the chance meeting with Alison, about her years in Kansas City. "She's a wonderful person, Delta. A great gift to my life. She helped me find purpose and direction. Alison drew me out of myself, helped me learn to live again."

"After Trip, you mean."

Lacy nodded. "When Lauren and Trip ran off to get married, I was pretty sure my life was over. It was hell. For years I had been competing with Lauren. When I met Trip and fell in love, I finally had something that was all my own. I was going to marry Trip, raise a family. When that didn't happen, I ran away. Resigned myself to being miserable."

"And Alison changed all that?"

"*I* changed," Lacy corrected. "Alison was a catalyst." She got up from the love seat and paced across the room. "On the surface, being a martyr or a victim seems very fulfilling, but it gets old after a while. Rage can be cleansing, but it only takes you so far. Sooner or later you have to let it go, get on with the business of finding purpose and meaning apart from the dreams that have died."

Lacy knew little of what Delta had been through the past few months, and yet Delta felt as if she had peered into her very soul. The effect was unnerving. "Go on," she said when Lacy sat down again. "You were talking about purpose and meaning."

"I found meaning — at least in part — in teaching. Ironic, isn't it? I took the job at the high school not because I felt called to teach, but because Trip was going to be in law school at Duke. Then I abandoned it and ran. Once I was in the classroom in Kansas City, however, I began to realize that my job wasn't to drill dates and facts into resistant young minds, but to challenge these kids to learn to *think*. To help them find the connection between their own experience and what has happened in the past." Her gaze drifted past Delta and fixed on the window that overlooked the garden. "The best days were the days when students came to me just to talk. I didn't need to have answers. I simply needed to hear them out, to be trustworthy. They got pretty honest about their lives when an adult they trusted would just shut up and listen."

"How long were you in Kansas City?"

"Almost fifteen years. When Dad had his stroke, Lauren had Ted to think about and couldn't spare enough time. I came home to help. But I had also hoped —" She shrugged and fell silent.

"Hoped things wouldn't work out with Lauren and Trip?" Delta ventured. "Hoped you might have a chance with him after all?"

Lacy's head snapped around, and she fixed Delta with an incredulous look. "Lord, no!" she burst out. "I don't want Trip. I want my *sister* back."

Delta frowned. "Wait. I'm confused. You came back to Hillsborough ten years ago. You and Lauren —"

"Lauren and I see each other," Lacy said.

"We do family things together. We're very polite and courteous to one another. But it's all surface, all a sham. We're not sisters anymore. We're simply . . . acquaintances."

"I don't understand," Delta said. "That one time Rankin and I came through Durham — when was it? Four years ago? — you and Lauren seemed okay. A little distant, maybe. But you acted like it was no big deal."

"We acted. Leave it at that." Lacy fell silent for a moment, and when she spoke again her voice sounded hoarse, cracked. "This isn't about forgiveness, Delta. I forgave them years ago. I've moved on. I just want things to be normal between us. But it's not normal. She never talks about Trip or their marriage. I know she's unhappy, and I'd be there for her, except that she avoids me whenever possible and keeps things superficial when we're forced to be together. She won't open up to me. And it seems like that's the way she wants to keep it."

"Sounds like a recipe for stress," Delta said.

Lacy nodded. "It's killing me," she said. "I'm sick of walking around on eggshells with her. It's worse than not having any contact at all. I can't do it anymore."

"What are you going to do?"

THIRTY-THREE:
THE ELEVENTH HOUR

Lauren did, indeed, arrive in time for dinner — in a limousine from the airport.

Delta and Lacy watched from rocking chairs on the covered porch as the long black limo pulled into the driveway. "One of Trip's business partners owns a private plane, I think," Lacy said.

Delta got up and went down the steps to greet her. When she turned back, Lacy was still sitting on the porch, waiting.

Lauren lingered in the back of the limo, peering into the gilt mirror from her purse, checking her hair and makeup. She looked all right, she guessed, but her face showed every single day of her forty-seven years. She looked closer. When her reflection caught in the beveled edges of the glass, the angles magnified her crow's feet and distorted the sagging skin around her jaw line.

Jowls. For God's sake, she was getting *jowls!*

She patted a little more powder on her nose and scowled at her reflection. Why she had agreed to this gig in the first place, she couldn't tell to save her soul. It was Rae Dawn's fault. Rae and her sense of nobility, her damned persuasiveness.

Lauren had no illusions about what Rae and Delta must think of her. The brazen hussy who seduced her twin sister's boyfriend and stole him away.

Brazen hussy? Where did that image come from? The Smithsonian, no doubt. Lauren would have laughed at herself if the language hadn't made her feel so abominably ancient. Might as well have called herself a tart or a strumpet.

At last she saw the front door of the limo open and the driver come around to her side. She plastered on a smile, wiped damp hands down the front of her skirt, and took the hand he offered her.

Delta was standing on the bottom step of the porch. The expression that flitted across her face was brief but unmistakable — the look of a visitor coming to a dying person's bedside for the first time. The oh-my-God glance that quickly rearranges itself into a false smile.

A lead weight dropped into Lauren's stomach and tears pricked at her eyes. To cover her distress, she reached out and drew Delta into a perfunctory hug. "I'm so happy to see you," she murmured into the air at Delta's ear. "It's been too long."

Delta was glad for the hug, not because it communicated any real warmth, but because it gave her a chance to collect her wits. Coming on the heels of her time with Lacy, the sight of Lauren Jenkins shocked her to the core.

Had she expected Lauren to look as young and vibrant as her sister? They were twins, after all. A shadow of Lacy's natural attractiveness still lingered about the edges of Lauren's appearance, but anyone who saw them together would more likely take them for mother and daughter than for sisters born from a single egg.

Delta could only hope Lauren hadn't noticed her reaction. She patted Lauren's back and extricated herself from the hug.

Lauren was dressed in a gray skirt and lavender cashmere sweater set, the cardigan arranged with careful indifference across her shoulders. A string of perfectly graduated pearls at her neck caught the fading afternoon light. Real pearls, Delta thought. Real cashmere.

"You look marvelous," Delta lied.

"Thank you." Lauren took her arm and steered her toward the porch. She waved at Lacy, still seated in the porch rocker, then quickly averted her gaze. "Where's Rae Dawn?"

"She probably won't get here until midnight," Delta said. "We're supposed to go on to dinner without her."

"Then let's take the car and go." Lauren pointed toward the limo. "I can settle in later."

The driver extracted two matching leather suitcases from the trunk and handed them to Matilda Suttleby, who fluttered nearby as if in the presence of royalty. "I'll just take these up," she said at last when no one was paying any attention to her. "You girls have a nice dinner."

The limo — apparently at Lauren's disposal for the weekend — took them to an upscale restaurant called Riverbend, on the edge of town where the river made a wide horseshoe curve to the north. The back of the restaurant, a wall of glass facing the river bend, opened onto a slate patio and a lighted garden sloping down to the water.

The evening was mild, so they opted for a table on the patio. Their driver, whose name

Delta had yet to hear, installed himself in the bar with a burger and an O'Doul's to watch clips from last year's Super Bowl.

Dinner, at Lauren's insistence, included a lobster appetizer, wine, and a decadent chocolate torte for dessert — all delicious and outrageously expensive. As a minister's wife, Delta wasn't accustomed to such extravagance, and she was certain Lacy couldn't afford it on a teacher's salary. But Lauren coerced them into letting her buy and encouraged them to get whatever they wanted. Delta chose a fresh trout amandine with brown rice pilaf and caesar salad. Lacy, much to her sister's displeasure, ordered the fried catfish special.

Delta had anticipated a quiet dinner and even hoped for some meaningful conversation. Shortly after the salads arrived, however, so did a gray-haired, round-faced man with a portable keyboard. He had been hired, no doubt, to provide live music for the entertainment of the diners, but his imitation of Frank Sinatra turned out to be so abominable that no one within earshot could talk of anything else.

Halfway through the meal, five ducks waddled up from the river to gorge themselves on bread hand-fed to them by indulgent patrons. When a waiter tried to shoo them back down the hill to the water, a large green-headed drake went on the attack and sent him scurrying back to the kitchens.

It proved to be an entertaining evening, certainly, but not a profitable one. The most Delta was able to accomplish was to ask Lauren about her family. She responded by passing around photographs of her son and his fiancée. Lacy barely glanced at them.

By the time they all climbed into the limo for the silent ride back to the B&B, Delta half wished she had joined the chauffeur for a burger and Super Bowl reruns.

Matilda Suttleby might be annoying, but she hadn't lied about the beauty of Highgate's small garden. Completely enclosed by a vine-covered stone wall, the place seemed miles away from the rest of the world. Stone walkways wound among the azalea bushes and dogwood trees. At the center, where Delta now sat on a carved wooden bench, a three-tiered fountain tinkled and shimmered in the moonlight.

Muffled footsteps sounded behind her, and she turned to see Lauren in navy satin pajamas, robe, and slippers.

"Have a seat," Delta offered, scooting over to make room.

Lauren edged onto the bench.

"What time is it?"

"Almost eleven. Lacy's asleep." Lauren fiddled with the sash of her robe. "It's very peaceful here."

"Yes it is," Delta agreed.

Unfortunately, the serenity hadn't seemed to rub off on Lauren. She shifted on the bench, crossed her legs, waggled one foot, agitated as a June bug battering itself against a window.

Suddenly a rush of compassion welled up in Delta, the desire to have a look into her friend's heart and find out what anxieties had aged her so. Was she still carrying around the shame and guilt of what she had done years ago? Was she afraid of what Delta might think of her? And did she know that her sister bore her no ill will?

She touched Lauren's arm. "How are you?" she asked. "We didn't get to talk much at dinner."

At the gentle touch, Lauren jerked back as if she had been stung by a scorpion. "I'm fine. Everything's fine." She stared up at the stars. "It's very peaceful here, isn't it?"

"You already said that."

Lauren got up and began picking fallen leaves out of the fountain. Delta followed.

"Stop," she said, taking hold of Lauren's hand. "I want you to talk to me."

Lauren relented, albeit reluctantly. She went back to the bench, sank down, and began to jiggle her foot again. But still she didn't speak.

"I don't mean to pressure you," Delta said, although she suspected that a little pressure wouldn't do any harm at the moment. "But clearly something's wrong."

"Am I ill, you mean?" Lauren finally said with a note of bitterness in her voice. "I caught the expression on your face when you first saw me. I look like crap, I know. Like an old woman."

"If you *are* sick, I want to know it," Delta responded. "But I'm not talking about your appearance. Hell, we're all getting older. I'm talking about your *soul*. Your heart." She looked into Lauren's shrouded eyes and opted for the direct approach. "You've been faking it since you stepped out of that limo. Like the last thing in the world you wanted was to see me again." She pressed her lips together. "Now, if you want me to shut up, say so. But at least be honest. We were friends once, Lauren, and might be again. But if all we do is make small talk —" Delta shrugged and lapsed into silence.

Lauren's countenance had taken on a fixed, stricken expression, the look of a small animal that wants to be comforted but is afraid of being hurt. She shook her head and shoved her hands into the pockets of her robe.

"No!" she said at last. "It's not you, Delta. It's me. You say I acted as if I didn't want to see you. But that's not the truth. I — I didn't want to see *myself*, reflected in your disapproval."

Delta sat back, floored by this unexpectedly profound insight. "Have I communicated disapproval?"

"No, not at all," Lauren admitted. "And that makes it even worse."

Delta shook her head. "I'm sorry, Lauren, I'm not quite following you. Talk to me, please. And start at the beginning."

Lauren fixed her eyes on the fountain. *Start at the beginning*. But where was the beginning, exactly? More than twenty-five years ago, when she seduced her twin sister's boyfriend on a secluded bank in the park? Or long before that, all the years of competition between herself and Lacy, the years of vacillating between jealousy and intimacy?

"Being a twin," she finally began, "is a strange life. In many ways it's wonderful, having someone so close, someone who understands you right down to your genes. But there are also stresses unlike those faced by normal siblings. Or maybe they are the same stresses, but infinitely magnified by the similarities between the two of you."

She paused, stared at the fountain, then took a deep breath. "I was always jealous of Lacy."

"Wait a minute," Delta interrupted. "I thought I remembered that Lacy was jealous of you. You were the one who was more outgoing, had all the boyfriends, the popularity."

Lauren waved a hand impatiently. Now that she had started, she didn't want her train of thought to be derailed. "Surface stuff. Superficialities. Lace and I shared the same DNA; we should have been just alike, right? But I knew better, even when I was very small. Lacy had something different, something I only later learned to name. She had character. Substance. Not that she was smarter than I was; our intelligence level was pretty comparable, I think. But she was . . . deeper."

This time Delta didn't interrupt. "I had loads of friends as we grew up — and later, boyfriends," Lauren said. "Adolescent boys don't usually value depth. But the few friendships Lacy formed were more significant, so still I felt jealous. I compensated by competing."

Delta listened intently, both surprised and impressed by Lauren's depth of insight.

"I've never been able to talk about this except to my therapist," Lauren said, slanting a glance at her.

"Therapist?" Delta repeated. "You've been in counseling?"

"Don't look so shocked. I'm forty-seven years old. I like to think I've grown up a *little* since the sixties."

Delta suppressed a smile. "Please continue. I'm riveted."

Lauren went on with her story. "What I did to Lacy was unforgivable."

Unforgivable. The melancholy word echoed inside Delta's head, desolate, hopeless, heartbreaking. If Lauren truly believed her actions to be unforgivable, it was no wonder a reconciliation had never taken place between the twins.

She opened her mouth to protest, but Lauren was speaking again.

"Trip and I almost divorced once, when Ted was fourteen. At the time I was, frankly, amazed he had hung on that long. He stayed with me out of guilt at first, and then out of a misguided sense of loyalty. I stayed with him out of shame, because I couldn't bear to face the enormity of the mistake I had made."

"That's why you didn't want to see me," Delta murmured. "And why all these years you've avoided any real relationship with Lacy. Shame."

A flash of the old Lauren-fire returned. "What do you mean, I've avoided a relationship with Lacy?"

"Lacy told me that you kept everything superficial at your family gatherings. That you never talked about your husband or your marriage. I assumed it was because you were still nurturing shame over the, ah, the situation with Trip."

"For God's sake, Delta, give me a little credit. It's been twenty-five years. I laid down the burden of shame years ago. I avoided talking about my family not because I was ashamed, but *because I didn't want to hurt my sister.*"

Delta had no idea how to respond. Lauren saved her the trouble. "When Trip and I separated — or, I should say, when he left me — I went to visit Lacy, to tell her face to face that Trip had left. To be perfectly honest, I expected her to jump at the chance to get back together with him, if for no other reason than revenge for what I'd done. Instead, she asked me if I loved him. That question

458

shocked me into admitting my true feelings for my husband, even if I didn't believe I deserved his love in return.

"When Trip returned, we agreed to go to counseling together, to try to sort things out. He didn't love me at the time, and I knew it. He had never really loved me. But gradually, as time went on and we got honest about ourselves, something changed. Love grew between us. Not just heat or physical passion, which I had once mistaken for love, but real love. Real intimacy. We let go of the guilt, the shame, the duty. And after more than fifteen years of marriage, we fell in love."

Delta hadn't expected this. She had anticipated a confession of blame and remorse, more than two decades of it. She had been prepared to talk to Lauren about putting the past behind her.

"My relationship with Trip," Lauren went on, "has been the saving grace of my life. Better than anything — except perhaps having Ted. Trip is an incredible father, a loving, attentive husband. We talk, we laugh, we love being together. All our friends are desperately envious of how well we communicate and how much we adore each other after twenty-five years."

Lauren turned to look into Delta's eyes.

"I'm aware that the years have not been kind to me. But Trip still thinks I'm beautiful."

Delta could understand. The facade was gone, the mask set aside. Despite the crow's feet and the sagging skin, Lauren *was* attractive, lit from within with the confidence only an older, more settled love can bring.

"Then why —" she began.

"Why have I kept at arm's length the one person more important to me than anyone except my husband and son?"

Delta nodded.

"Precisely for that reason. Because she *is* so important to me. You've seen her, Delta. She lives alone except for that cat of hers. She's never married. The only close friend she has lives halfway across the country. I didn't *want* her to see how happy my relationship with Trip has become, to be confronted with our love for each other. It would just make her life seem that much more miserable by comparison. Even if it means keeping an emotional distance, the last thing I want in this world is to hurt Lacy. To make her feel left out."

Lauren bit her lip and blinked back tears. "I love my sister, Delta. I will always love her. I miss the closeness we once had. The craziness. Even the fights. But I'll go on missing her, if that's what it takes to keep from hurting her."

Delta thought about Lacy, what she had said about forgiveness, about moving on. All this time Lauren had believed her sister to be living in perpetual grief, heartbroken and tormented over the loss of Trip's love. She had withdrawn herself so as not to pour acid into the wound.

" 'The Gift of the Magi,' " Delta said.

"Excuse me?"

"It's a short story by O. Henry, about a desperately poor couple who have only two prized possessions — Della's lustrous hair and Jim's gold watch."

Lauren frowned. "And your point is?"

"In the story, Della sells her hair to buy him a gold watch chain, and Jim sells his watch to buy her a pair of expensive hair combs. In the end, both have lost their treasures, but they've gained something even more important. The gift of the Magi, the wisest gift of all. The noble but ironic sacrifice of love."

"I don't get it," Lauren said.

Delta stood up and put a hand on her friend's shoulder. "Go talk to your sister," she said. "Really talk. Be honest with her. Tell her what you've told me tonight. Then you'll understand."

THIRTY-FOUR:
THE BLUES SINGER

Rae Dawn pulled up in front of Highgate House at ten minutes to midnight. The front porch light was on, and a sleepy, rumpled-looking Matilda Suttleby answered her quiet knock.

"Ah, Miss DuChante!" she said, coming instantly awake and pushing her hair back into place. "You finally made it."

"DuChamp," Rae corrected. "I'm sorry to arrive so late, but —"

"Not to worry," Matilda said. "I wasn't in bed yet."

Rae Dawn let the lie pass, although she couldn't have gotten a word in edgewise if she had been so inclined.

"I've reserved the best room for you," Matilda was saying. "The Robert E. Lee. Very spacious, and quite lovely. It's such an honor to have you here. I have all your albums —"

Rae arched an eyebrow. "All two of them."

"Yes, and I simply love your music," the woman went on without missing a beat. "All my friends will be absolutely green with envy when they find out I've hosted Dawn DuChante. You don't mind if I call you Dawn, do you?"

"Ah, it's Rae," she said.

"Of course, of course," Matilda gushed. Then, as if she had only now realized that she was still blocking the doorway, she gave a little jump. "Do come in. Are you hungry? I can whip up a snack, if you like. A sandwich, or some scrambled eggs —"

"No, thank you," Rae said wearily. "I'd just like to go to bed, please."

Matilda's face crumpled with disappointment. "Certainly. We can talk in the morning. I have a fine piano in the parlor if you —"

"Bed, please," Rae repeated.

"Yes, yes. Follow me." Matilda put a finger to her lips and dropped her voice to a whisper. "The other girls are already asleep, I believe. Up the stairs. This way."

Rae hefted her bag and dragged herself up the stairs, noticing as she went how flat Matilda Suttleby's feet were, her heels rough and red where they stuck out the back of her slippers.

"Here we go," the woman said when they

reached the landing. She opened the door to the right and flipped on the light with a flourish. "Ta da!"

"Thank you." Rae entered the room and slung her suitcase on an overstuffed armchair in the corner. "Thank you, Mrs. Suttleby," she repeated. "Good night."

Matilda Suttleby's eager eyes were still peering at her when she shut the door.

Rae stripped off her jeans and sweater, rummaged in her bag for a nightshirt, then went into the bathroom and brushed her teeth. She was exhausted, and expected to fall asleep as soon as she climbed into the big bed, but once she had turned out the light, she found herself staring wide-eyed at the ceiling.

If it hadn't been for Delta, she would never have made this trip. Would never have driven up Interstate 59 past the exit for Picayune, Mississippi. Would never have been inundated by memories of Noel Ridley and the love they once shared.

Illumination from a streetlamp outside the window cast a cold blue light into the room, cut into shifting shadows by the trees and the sheer lace curtains. She stared at the chandelier suspended from the center of the room. Traced the curlicues in the round plaster medallion that surrounded it. Tried to construct a pattern from the random flowers that dotted the wallpaper.

Who was she kidding, anyway? This pain — the sucking sensation in her gut when she passed by the Picayune exit, that sense of all the life being drained out of her in a single gurgling moment — was nothing new. Had there been a single day in the past ten years when she hadn't thought of Noel and cursed herself, cursed her career, cursed her own stupidity for letting the love of her life slip through her fingers? Had there been a night when she hadn't dreamed of Noel? A song she hadn't written with Noel in mind?

The music began to drift through her mind, songs of loss and longing, songs of joy and heartache and love gone wrong.

Did you ever sing the blues?
Did you ever wind up thinking
You're the only one who's sinking,
You're the only one to lose?
Does that melancholy music
Pull your heartstrings out of tune . . .

She hummed the tune in her head, fingered the piano riffs in her imagination, and finally, as the clock downstairs chimed two, fell into a restless sleep.

■ ■ ■ ■

Soft knocking awoke her from yet another dream of Noel Ridley — this time a nightmare in which the Airstream trailer was burning and Noel was trapped inside. Rae's mind swam to the surface of consciousness, and she pried open her eyes to see golden autumn sunlight streaming into the room. On the bedside table sat the framed photo she always carried with her when she traveled.

"Rae Dawn?" the whispered voice came again. "Are you awake?"

Rae sat up and looked around. "Delta? Is that you?"

The door opened a crack and Delta's face peered around the door jamb. It was an older Delta, a bit plumper, with a few streaks of gray hair at the temples. But the eyes were the same, and the smile. "Come in."

Delta, in blue flannel pajamas with fluffy little cloud-shaped sheep on them, tiptoed barefoot into the room and shut the door. She launched herself onto the bed and her arms went around Rae in an enthusiastic embrace.

Had it been so long since Rae had been touched? She savored the hug, not wanting to let go, feeling the warmth of Delta's arms through the flannel, through her own nightshirt. Tears stung at her eyes.

"Don't go anywhere," she said over Delta's shoulder. She slid out of bed. "I have to pee, and you really don't want to talk to me with morning breath."

In the bathroom, with the water running, Rae took a moment to compose herself. She doused her face and brushed her teeth, and by the time she was ready to go back into the room, she had gained control over the unexpected tears.

Delta was sitting upright, leaning against the headboard with a pillow behind her back.

"What time is it?" Rae Dawn asked, climbing back into bed.

As if in answer, the grandfather clock downstairs gave out a full sixteen-note Westminster chime, followed by seven sonorous bongs.

"Seven o'clock. I'm sorry if I woke you. Breakfast is at eight, and I wanted to see you before everybody else did."

"Seven A.M.?" Rae repeated. "I didn't know there *was* a seven A.M." She pointed to the window. "I'm to assume this is sunrise?"

Delta laughed. "That's right. You're the night person."

"Occupational hazard of being a lounge singer."

467

Although Delta was still smiling, her eyes were not focused on Rae Dawn but at a point just past her shoulder. She reached out for the photo on the nightstand. "You've been holding out on me."

"No, I haven't," Rae said. "I wrote to you —"

"Generalities, not details," Delta said. "Come on, give, who is she?"

Rae took the picture and looked at it. It was a candid shot of herself and Noel, taken by a stranger during a rare and brief vacation in the Bahamas. The two of them were perched on the windblown seawall with the brilliant blue waters of the Caribbean in the background, Noel seated behind with her arms around Rae Dawn. Rae was smiling at the camera, but Noel, with her head turned slightly, was looking at Rae. The expression captured in that split second of film never failed to take Rae's breath away, the utter adoration and commitment that shone in those tawny eyes, the contentment, the rightness of their love.

They had walked along the beach that evening, basked in the purple aura of sunset, held hands, eaten mountains of fresh shrimp and crab at a thatch-roofed beachfront restaurant. "It doesn't get any better than this," Noel had said.

Rae Dawn closed her eyes and inhaled a ragged breath as the memories flooded in. Bits and pieces of an ordinary life, like millions of other lives. Waffles and scrambled eggs on the balcony overlooking the courtyard fountain. Redfish fresh from the outdoor market. Wednesday movie matinees, Sunday afternoon football, Christmas carols at the piano. Arguments about time or money or who left the shower dripping. Long conversations, cuddling in bed while a white winter sun crept its way across the ceiling. And that one unimaginably beautiful afternoon, standing at a secluded river bend surrounded by a small group of friends, when they joined their hands and pledged to love each other for a lifetime.

It was all still here, so close — the sound of Noel's laughter, the warmth of her smile, her touch, her scent, her nearness. So painfully close that in the early hours of morning Rae could feel an arm wrapping around her, a breath on the back of her neck, a body curled around her in sleep.

And then some noise would wake her —

"Rae?" Delta's voice brought her back from the brink. "Are you all right?"

Rae Dawn blinked. "Yeah."

"Who is she, Rae?"

"Her name was Noel Ridley. She was a doctor." Rae avoided Delta's eyes but could not escape her voice. The voice urging her to spill all the emotion she had been hoarding these past ten years. A voice gentle and full of compassion.

"Tell me about her."

Rae Dawn had come here to support Delta, to help her through her grief over Rankin's death. She certainly hadn't intended to talk about Noel. But it was the first time in years anyone had asked what she was feeling. Besides, pressure was building behind the floodgates, and she wasn't at all sure she could stop it now.

"Noel was my mother's doctor," she began. "I'd been in New Orleans for five years, working to build my career, when the call came that Mama had suffered a heart attack. It was so strange — there I was, in the hospital, watching my mother die and falling in love all at the same time."

"So you knew from the beginning that Noel was the one?"

"I suppose I did — subconsciously, anyway. After they took Mama's body away, she drove me out to the trailer. It was the middle of the night, and at the sight of it, all those horrible memories came flooding back and I just went crazy. Raged, screamed, cried.

Noel accepted all of it in stride and didn't think I was crazy at all, even when I set a torch to the place and burned it to the ground."

Delta's eyes grew wide. "You burned it down?"

"Yes, I did." Rae smiled in spite of herself. "Did me more good than a year's worth of therapy too."

"That took a lot of courage."

Rae shook her head. "Not really. It was mostly instinct. But I did manage to get out some of what I was feeling, and I discovered that Noel could accept me at my worst. It was quite a revelation."

She went on talking, telling Delta about the development of their relationship, Noel's decision to move to New Orleans, the good years.

"She moved down, and we lived together for —" Rae paused. "Almost ten years. Our life together was wonderful."

Delta reached out a hand and squeezed Rae's arm. "I know how hard it is to lose someone you love so much."

Rae Dawn froze, and at that moment she realized her mistake. Past tense. She had been speaking of Noel in past tense. And now she had to backtrack, to correct Delta's misconception.

"She didn't *die,* Delta," she said, trying hard to keep her voice from shaking. "She left me."

Delta looked up at Rae and then back down at the photograph Rae still held in her hands. She had known enough gay and lesbian couples through the years to realize that their relationships were subject to pressures most heterosexual couples couldn't even imagine. There was no societal structure to support gay relationships. No marriage bonds, no civic connection, no protected rights. Virtually no public support, and often little acceptance from families and friends. And although Delta knew that paperwork did not a marriage make, the lack of legal status rendered same-sex relationships all too susceptible to easy dissolution when things got difficult.

Still, in this photograph, Noel's eyes were alight with love. It couldn't have been clearer if she had been wearing a sign. The woman was in love with Rae Dawn.

"Impossible," Delta breathed, half to herself.

"I'm afraid it's very possible," Rae shot back.

Delta leaned back against the headboard. "What happened?" she blurted out, and then, realizing what an impertinent question it was, tried to take it back. "Sorry, Rae. You don't have to —"

Rae picked at a knobby place on the coverlet. "No, it's all right. I might as well just get it all out."

Get it all out and be done with it, she was thinking. But if she wasn't done with it after ten years —

She pulled in a deep breath and set the photograph back on the bedside table. Noel's golden eyes, bright with love, shone back at her from the picture. Rae jerked her gaze away and faced Delta. "When I finished college, I went to New Orleans to play as a backup pianist."

"At Maison Dauphine. I remember. The year Rankin and I moved to Asheville, we came down to visit. That was, what, four years after graduation?"

"Something like that." Rae nodded. "It was before everything happened, at any rate. My mother died in 1974; that's when I met Noel. The following spring she moved to New Orleans and worked at the clinic while I played at the club. For a few years things were great. We didn't have much money, but we got by, and we had each other. Then —" She paused. "I don't know whether to say that my career took off or my life began to fall apart. Both, really."

She summarized those difficult years leading up to the separation — the launch of her first album, the long months on the road. "It would have been hard enough just being separated like that. But to have to hide our relationship —"

"Why did you have to hide it?" Delta asked. "I thought the music industry was pretty open-minded."

"It's not the industry," Rae said. "It's the fans. My agent, Arista Records, even Chase Coulter, who owned the club when I first went to work there — they all believed my career would crash and burn if people knew I was writing and singing all those love songs to a *woman*." She shook her head. "You have to remember, Delta, this was years ago. Things have changed —" She grimaced. "Well, a little."

"Not enough," Delta said. "Please, go on."

"Anyway," Rae continued, "the last straw came with the Grammys."

Delta's eyes widened. "You have a Grammy?"

"I was *nominated* for a Grammy," Rae corrected. "Best R&B female vocal album. I didn't win."

"Yes, but you were *nominated*," Delta said.

"That means more records, fame and fortune —" She stopped suddenly. "Why didn't I know any of this?"

"You'd have to be a big R&B fan, I guess." Rae Dawn shrugged and held up her fingers in a V. "Two albums. Two. I suppose you would say I was moderately well known in very small circles for a very short time." She gave a self-deprecating grin. "But success can be both a blessing and a curse. Noel and I had both sacrificed so much for my career, and when the Grammy nomination came, I fully intended to share that moment with her no matter what. But my agent set me up with a date and absolutely refused to let me be seen in public with Noel. She didn't even go to L.A. with me. When I got home, she was packed to leave."

"Just like that?"

"It wasn't *just like that,*" Rae said. "It had been coming on a long time. We had tried to work through the problems, but I was too shortsighted to see that I was choosing my career over the person I loved." Remembered pain stabbed at her, and she sighed. "It took several more years for me to see what I had done, not just to Noel and to our relationship, but to myself, allowing myself to be locked in that closet. A soul needs light and air and honesty, Delta. Living a lie isn't living at all, even when the money's good."

Delta watched Rae Dawn's face as she spoke, saw the agony and regret and raw longing that filled her eyes. She knew the pain of loss, certainly, but it was a pain tempered by the joy of more than twenty years with the man she loved. Good years, happy years. Years filled with a love unencumbered by discrimination and prejudice.

"And there was no one else," she said at last.

"I dated a little, now and then. Two or three of the women I met seemed interested in pursuing a relationship, but I didn't have the heart for it. It was hard to tell, by that time, whether they really cared about me or were simply in it for the money. Besides," she finished with a sigh. "Once you've known real love —"

"It's hard to settle for anything less," Delta supplied. "Rae, whatever happened to Noel?"

"She went back to Picayune, to her old practice. As far as I know she's still there."

"And you've never tried to reconcile with her?"

"At first, when I quit touring and came home, I thought about it. I wanted to. But I was ashamed that I had let my career get the better of my values. And then, as time went on, it just seemed like there was too much baggage between us."

"I'm sorry," Delta said. She wished she had more to offer. Silently she cursed her own helplessness. From the hallway downstairs she heard the clock chime seven thirty.

"Listen," Rae said, straightening up with a sigh, "that's enough of my sob story. I didn't come here for myself. I want to know how you're doing. I was so sorry to hear about Rankin's death."

Something clicked in the back of Delta's mind — something Lacy had said yesterday afternoon. Rae Dawn had told Lacy that Rankin had died. But how had Rae known?

She narrowed her eyes and glared at Rae. "What do you mean, you didn't come here for yourself?"

Rae blanched. "Well, I —"

"You came here for *me?* Because of Rankin?"

The color returned to Rae's face in a rush. "Yes."

"You put all this together — talked Lacy and Lauren into doing this reunion gig — and then convinced me to come? Why, Rae?"

"Because —" She hesitated. "Because you needed your friends."

477

Delta puzzled over this for a moment. Then the lights went on, and she understood.

Cassie.

"All right, I admit it," Rae Dawn said to Delta as they joined Lacy and Lauren around Matilda Suttleby's breakfast table. "Your sister did call me. She seemed to think you would agree to come if the rest of us did, and that it might be good for you."

Delta helped herself to a waffle. "Then you phoned Lacy and Lauren."

"She called *me*," Lacy interjected. "*I* called Lauren."

"And then Rae called me," Delta continued, "and convinced me that everybody else was enthusiastic about doing this reunion banquet, but couldn't do it without me."

"Yeah, something like that." Rae scooped scrambled eggs onto her plate and took a biscuit. "This breakfast is excellent, Mrs. Suttleby," she said as Matilda came in with a fresh pot of coffee.

The woman beamed and bobbed her head. "It's my pleasure, Dawn. It's such an honor — oh my, I forgot the apple butter. Homemade, you know, from apples off my own tree. I'll be right back." She skittered off into the kitchen.

"If she adds one more thing to this table, it'll collapse," Rae said. "Look at this — eggs, bacon, sausage, biscuits, waffles." She spooned a glob of blackstrap molasses over a biscuit and laughed. "I won't be able to sing a note, but it sure is good."

Lauren motioned for Lacy to pass the syrup. "Why does she keep calling you *Dawn?*"

"I was wondering the same thing," Lacy said, handing the pitcher to her twin. "She acts like you're some kind of big celebrity."

Rae Dawn rolled her eyes. "I'll explain later."

"Yes, don't get her off the subject," Delta said. "Right now she's explaining how she manipulated us all into being here." She shot a mock scowl in Rae's direction. "When you never returned my call — any of you — I assumed you didn't want to do this."

"I *didn't,*" Rae said.

"Me either," Lauren and Lacy said in unison.

"That makes four of us," Delta chuckled. "So, how come we're all here, sitting at Matilda's breakfast table on Saturday morning and scheduled to do a concert tonight?"

Rae Dawn shrugged. "God, fate, destiny —"

"Coercion?" Delta supplied. "Conspiracy?"

Lacy grinned at her. "I'd say it's poetic justice, given how we started with the Belles in the first place. If you recall, Delta, *you* were the one who signed us up for that first talent show without our permission —"

"That's right," Lauren added. "You're just getting what you deserve."

Delta was thankful she'd had a chance to talk privately with the twins last night and Rae Dawn this morning. All during breakfast Matilda Suttleby hovered nearby fawning over Rae, her ubiquitous presence offering little opportunity for any real conversation.

After breakfast and showers, they gathered in the parlor to rehearse. Lacy brought out her guitar, and as she tuned up and went through the music with Rae, Delta watched them. She sensed a change coming over her. Ever since her arrival here, she had found herself thinking less about the horrible details of Rankin's death and more about the rich years of love they had shared. A love that now spilled over onto these friends she hadn't seen in ages.

She wondered if Lauren had had time to talk to Lacy about the misunderstanding between them. They appeared to be all right — laughing together, poking fun at one another, just as they had in college. It might be an act, but it seemed real enough. At least they were on speaking terms.

Delta was more concerned about Rae Dawn. A shadow lurked around her, a phantom that haunted her, hovering behind her eyes in unguarded moments. This reunion concert was costing her. She had agreed to it for Delta's sake, because she wanted to help a friend, but Delta suspected she was paying a high price in disturbing and painful memories.

"All right, let's get started," Rae said. "It's been a long time, and I didn't know how much you'd remember, so —" She handed out photocopies of several songs, including "Blowin' in the Wind" and "Where Have All the Flowers Gone."

"What about 'If I Had a Hammer'?" Lauren asked. "That's one of my favorites."

"We'll do it, if you like," Rae said. "I don't think we need music on that one." She sat down at the keyboard and prepared to play.

Just then the front door opened and a noisy gabble blew into the parlor from the foyer. Matilda Suttleby swept into the room, followed by a gaggle of tittering gray-haired ladies decked out in their Sunday best.

"I didn't think you'd mind," Matilda said, reaching a hand in Rae's direction. "They're such great fans of yours." She cleared her throat and turned toward the knot of old women in the doorway. "Girls, *this* is Dawn DuChante."

Delta saw the roll of the eyes as Rae plastered on a smile. She left the piano and shook hands with each of the ladies in turn.

"Oh, would you mind autographing a few things?" one of the ladies said, holding out a couple of CD cases. "We brought our DCs with us, just in case."

"It's *CD,* Mildred," another woman corrected archly. "She is so technologically challenged that her grandson has to load the CD player for her."

"That's true," Mildred confessed. "But it doesn't matter, Miss DuChante, because I keep both your DCs in there all the time. You have such a *beautiful* voice."

"Thank you," Rae said graciously. Behind her back, Delta caught a glimpse of the twins' faces, which bore identical expressions of utter astonishment.

Rae perched on the edge of a pink velvet settee and accepted a pen from one of the ladies. "I'm Sarah, with an H," the woman said. "Sarah Thomas." Rae inscribed the CD case and autographed it. Sarah took it and peered at the signature. "Oh, honey, you've made a mistake. I want you to sign your *real* name."

"That *is* my real name. Rae Dawn DuChamp."

"Your name's not Dawn DuChante?"

"No, ma'am. That's a stage name."

"But if you sign it this way, nobody will believe it's really you."

Rae took the CD back and made the correction. The rest of the ladies lined up for their autographs. One exceedingly old woman who reminded Delta a little of Grandma Mitchell had a vinyl album of Rae Dawn's first recording. She leaned on her cane and held it out.

"I haven't seen one of these in a long time," Rae said as she scrawled her signature across the cardboard cover.

"Thank you, dearie," the old woman screeched. "An autographed copy will bring twice as much at the flea market."

Matilda brought up the rear, preening herself importantly. "I told the girls you might let them sit in on your rehearsal," she said to

Rae in a stage whisper. "We'll be quiet as mice."

Delta suppressed a laugh. The old women were clustered together, chattering about what an honor it was to have an autographed album and speculating loudly about the demise of Rae Dawn's recording career.

"She hasn't had a new album in years," one woman declared as she peered back over her shoulder. "Was it drugs, do you think? Or an unhappy love affair?"

Rae stood up. "Ladies, it's been a genuine pleasure meeting all of you," she said smoothly, "and I appreciate so much your taking the time to come. But if you'll excuse us now, we do need to rehearse for tonight's banquet. *Without* an audience."

Crestfallen, the old women slumped toward the foyer, casting venomous glances back at Matilda Suttleby as if she had deliberately plotted this turn of events to keep the star all to herself. When they had finally shut the door behind them, Matilda settled herself on one of the sofas and smiled. "Now that the groupies are gone," she said, "I suppose we can get on with the rehearsal."

Delta came over and sat down next to her. "Matilda," she whispered, "could I speak with you for just one moment?"

"Of course, dear." Matilda waved a hand.

"Ah, privately?"

Delta got to her feet and jerked her head toward the door. Matilda followed as she crossed the foyer and went through the den into the dining room.

"You know, Matilda," Delta said, putting an arm around the woman's narrow shoulders, "artists can be, well, a little eccentric. Rae — I mean *Dawn* — tends to get nervous before a concert, and she prefers not to have anyone present at her rehearsals. And even if it seems silly to us, we need to honor a star's requests in a matter like this."

"Oh," Matilda said. "Well, of course, she wouldn't want all those old biddies gaping at her."

"I knew you'd understand. I'll tell you what. If you sit in the den, you'll be able to hear her just fine, and she won't even know you're there. It'll be like — like a private concert, especially for you."

"Oh, the girls will be so *jealous*."

"Yes, they will," Delta agreed. "They'll be talking about nothing else for weeks."

Matilda nodded. "And how about if I make some coffee and cinnamon rolls for later? Say in an hour?"

Delta gaped at her. After that enormous breakfast, who could eat again? "That would be lovely," she said. "You'll join us, won't

you? I'll call you when we're ready to break."
She turned to go. "Oh, one more favor, if I
may."

"Certainly. Anything." Matilda gave her a
wide smile.

"Could I use your telephone for a moment? Someplace private?"

"Use the one in the kitchen." Matilda
pointed. "I'll be in the den if you need me."

THIRTY-FIVE:
THE FINAL GIG

It was a glorious October evening, cooler than Delta had anticipated, an early fall by Mississippi standards. At six, Lauren's limousine driver pulled to the curb and let them out. They walked through the iron gates, past the Kissing Rock, and around front campus, pausing for a moment to look up at the spreading ginkgo tree.

The leaves had already turned to yellow, waving like tiny fans in the autumn breeze. Through the amber curtain Delta could see dapples like gold coins from the last of the sunlight, and slivers of a deepening blue sky.

There, under the tree, was the spot where she had first met Tabitha Austin and signed up the Delta Belles for their initial gig at the Harvest Fest Talent show. Up above, the round tower on the third floor, had been Rae Dawn's old dorm room.

It had been a rainy summer throughout the southeast, and the grass underfoot was rich and lush as they walked across the lawn toward the banquet hall.

"Delta?"

The voice came from behind her, and she turned. It was a déjà vu two decades in the making — a voluptuous redhead running across the campus, waving to her.

"Delta!"

It was Tabby. Everything about her seemed to have enlarged and magnified over the years — her hair redder than it had once been, her figure rounder and pudgier.

"I saw you arrive," she said breathlessly. "Did you just get out of a *limo?*"

"Well, yes," Delta said. "We, ah —" She pointed in Lauren's direction.

But Tabby wasn't looking at Lauren. She was staring at Rae Dawn.

"I know you!" she squealed. "You're — you're —"

"Rae Dawn DuChamp," Rae said formally, extending a hand toward Tabby and giving Delta a sly wink.

"Well, yes, of course," Tabby said. "I know *that*. But you're also Dawn DuChante. I watched on television the night you were nominated for a Grammy — that was years ago, wasn't it? I have one of your albums too — one of the old ones. But on the cover you looked so — so *different*."

"Makeup artists," Rae said. "Between them and photographers, they can make anyone look good."

"I wish I'd realized," Tabby grumbled. "I would have advertised Dawn DuChante singing at our banquet."

"Oh, that would have drawn a crowd," Rae said. "Maybe two or three more people would have shown up."

Tabby ignored this, looked around, and finally realized that the twins were standing there. "Oh, hey, Lace. Lauren."

Lacy grinned. "Nice to see you too, Tabby." She turned toward her sister. "Speaking of makeup," she said, "your mascara is smeared right here —" She licked her thumb and rubbed at a smudge on Lauren's cheek.

"Will you quit spitting on me?" Lauren pulled away and slapped at her hand. "Jeez, you're worse than Mama ever was."

Everyone laughed. *Just like old times,* Delta thought. It felt good to be back again, good to be together.

She turned and gazed across the green expanse of front campus. In her mind's eye she could see them all — young and innocent, joyous, ready to take on the world. Nostalgia overwhelmed her, the bittersweet memories of those golden days. Laughter and heartbreak, love and longing, the passionate conviction that they could, indeed, make a difference.

The youth, of course, was long gone; their lives were mostly behind them now. And had they made a difference?

Delta didn't know. She thought about Rankin, about the causes he had stood for in his life. Equality. Justice. Inclusivity. She thought about Vinca Hollowell. About Grandma Mitchell. About Rae Dawn's story of love lost and Lacy and Lauren's tale of sisters separated.

Life was such a huge, complex puzzle. Perhaps all you could do was attend to your own small pieces and try to find the pattern in them.

"Come on," she said, pulling herself out of her reverie, "let's go make some music."

The banquet hall was packed. From backstage, Rae Dawn could hear the low roar of conversation filling the room. In a corner Lacy leaned over her guitar for a last-minute tuning.

Tabitha, looking frazzled and disjointed, rushed over clutching a clipboard to her chest.

"Are you ready?" She looked around.

"We're fine, Tabby," Lacy said. "Chill out."

490

"All right. Now, I'm going to give out some alumni awards first, and then I'll introduce you. Five minutes. Ten, tops." She muttered something inaudible and disappeared.

"This is going to be fun," Lacy said.

"Have you been to the bathroom?" Lauren asked with a wicked grin.

Lacy curled her lip in a mocking sneer. "I'll pee on *you* if you don't shut up."

Rae felt butterflies — or maybe it was caterpillars — moving around inside her stomach. She didn't know why she was nervous. She had done this a thousand times, in front of huge concert halls filled with fans, in the more intimate setting of Maison Dauphine. Besides, it didn't matter how good they sounded. It only mattered that they had done it for Delta.

Five minutes passed. Six. Seven.

"And now," Tabitha's amplified voice boomed into the hall, "the entertainment you've all been waiting for. From the class of 1969 — we know her as Rae Dawn DuChamp — but she is a Grammy-winning writer and recording star —"

"Nominee!" Rae hissed.

"Please welcome Dawn DuChante and the Delta Belles."

A wave of applause, hoots, and whistles greeted them as they came onstage from behind the curtain. Lauren and Lacy took one mike and Delta moved to the other one, beside the piano. Rae looked over the crowd but could make out only shadowy figures in the darkness.

Then, as her eyes grew accustomed to the stage lights, she saw movement. Someone threading among the tables, coming from the back of the room to the front table where Tabitha Austin sat. As the figure drew closer, Rae Dawn could see that it was a woman, small, petite. She crossed to the table, ducking down, and the spotlight caught in her auburn hair.

Then she slid into a chair, turned, and faced the stage.

It had to be an optical illusion, a trick of the light, a projection of a dream. All the air went out of Rae Dawn's lungs and tears stung at her eyes.

It couldn't be. But it was.

Noel Ridley.

And she was smiling.

The Delta Belles, like the audience, were waiting for the concert to begin. Delta followed the direction of Rae Dawn's gaze. She recognized Noel instantly, from the framed snapshot in Rae's room.

Rae turned to Delta and motioned her

over to the piano. "Did you do this?" she murmured.

"I didn't drag her here bodily, if that's what you mean," Delta whispered back. "But my sister Cassie isn't the only one who knows how to use a telephone."

Her eyes drifted to Noel again, who sat at the edge of the stage with her hands clasped in her lap and her eyes fixed on Rae Dawn's face. She was wearing the same expression as in the photo — the look of love, as if she might take off flying at any moment.

Rae reached out and squeezed Delta's hand. "Thank you," she said. And then, without taking her eyes off Noel, she launched into the introduction to the first number.

They played through all the old standards — "Blowin' in the Wind," "Where Have All the Flowers Gone," "If I Had a Hammer" — much to everyone's delight. Rae sang a couple of solos too, and as she wowed the audience with a smoky, steamy version of "Come Rain or Come Shine," only Delta knew she was singing for Noel.

The crowd loved it. Yet it wasn't so much the applause and cheering that moved Delta, but the music itself. The songs that years ago had molded a generation of activists and informed her own social conscience now gave her a fresh infusion of faith. Those who had paid the ultimate price for what they believed — famous people like Dr. King and the Kennedys, ordinary people like Rankin — weren't really gone. They were here, in the music, in the hearts of those who loved them and remembered them. Still inspiring, still empowering. Still hammering out justice and freedom and love.

Before she knew it, the concert was over. The audience was on its feet, demanding more.

Lacy stepped over to the piano. "We don't have an encore," she muttered to Rae and Delta. "We've sung everything we know."

Delta exchanged a glance with Rae, who nodded.

"I'd like to play one last song for you," she said into the microphone. The crowd hushed and resumed their seats. "It's a piece I wrote years ago, when I was a student here, and it reminds me of things my heart needs to remember. Of love and friendship, of hope when all seems hopeless, of healing that appears when we least expect it."

Delta knew what was coming. She stepped back from the microphone and closed her eyes as Rae Dawn launched into the opening measures of "Woman on the Wind."

She recalled, quite vividly, the night she

had first heard this music. That night so long ago when Rae Dawn had opened her heart and revealed the truth about herself. The night Rae had declared her independence from the past.

The music surged around Delta like a mighty wind, bearing her soul aloft. First the haunting, minor-key section, the song of a caged bird. And then the release, the letting go, the setting free. The climax she herself had once described as "making love with God and the universe."

She hadn't felt it for a very long time, that sense of Presence. She had held onto her anger, nursed it, unable to reconcile the unanswerable dilemmas that surrounded Rankin's death. But now, as the music soared, she began to rise above the questions and see things from a different perspective.

Inside her head, Delta could almost hear the tumblers of the lock falling into place, the door creaking open. She had blamed God for Rankin's death, as if God sat up there pulling the strings like some cosmic puppeteer, for good or ill. But now she understood: God wasn't *up there* at all, but down here, in the trenches, experiencing life's joys and agonies with us and within us.

The liberation came like a healing flood. Within the deep recesses of her soul, a cold, dark place suddenly illuminated and warmed as if a fire had been lit.

Shit happens, Delta thought. *Chaos impinges upon order. We live in a bent and broken world.* Whatever language you used, the reality was the same: Suffering was as much a part of life as joy. And for those who believed, or *tried* to believe — for seekers of truth and of holy love — there was only one conclusion. In our suffering, God suffers too, and when we weep, God's tears drip down like rain.

Now, on the other side of her anger, she saw her husband's death in a different light. And not only his death, but his life — their life together, with all its purpose and significance. At last Delta understood the wholeness of the gift they had been given, more than twenty years of joy and grace and love.

The music soared to its glorious crescendo, and Rae began to sing words Delta had never heard before. Instinctively she surmised that they were a recent addition — written, perhaps, during Rae Dawn's dark years alone. They blended flawlessly into the piece, rising upward on the final notes:

Reach and keep reaching,
Touch and keep touching,

Fear not the future, the pain, or the loss.
Sing and keep singing,
Hope and keep hoping,
Love and keep loving whatever the cost.

The music echoed into silence, and the house lights came up. No one applauded; no one even breathed. Stunned and astonished, the audience sat motionless. Some of the faces were streaked with tears.

The silence went on for a full two minutes, and then, as if on cue, the entire audience rose as one and began clapping.

Delta looked around the stage. Lacy and Lauren gripped each other's hands and gave a little bow. She moved closer.

"Have you talked with Lacy?" she said into Lauren's ear while the noise of the crowd roared around them. "About — you know. You and Trip."

"Not yet," Lauren said. "But I will." She turned away to take another bow.

Delta wanted to grab her, shake her, tell her that this time tomorrow might be too late. But she didn't. She had done all she could. She had been there. She had listened. The rest was up to them.

Rae Dawn was standing next to the piano with her arms around Noel. Rae motioned Delta over. "This is Noel!" she yelled over the chaos. "Honey, this is Delta."

"Thank you!" Noel shouted.

"My pleasure," Delta murmured. No one heard her, but it really didn't matter.

Just as they were about to leave the stage for the last time, the door to the banquet hall burst open and a flushed, fresh-faced young girl rushed in. She reminded Delta of the four of them more than twenty years ago — ardent and enthusiastic, full of the promise of an unknown future.

"The ginkgo tree is shedding!" the girl shouted. "If you catch a leaf by moonlight, you'll find your one true love!" And she dashed out again.

Delta looked at Rae Dawn and Noel, at Lauren, at Lacy. In unison, they shook their heads in disbelief and began to laugh.

And then, still laughing, the Delta Belles joined hands and took one final bow.

EPILOGUE

Delta booted up the computer and opened her e-mail files. In addition to the usual run of interdepartmental memos, she had three personal messages.

She clicked on the first, from Lace49KC:

Delta —

Just returned from my honeymoon and back to teaching first of next week. Hank sends his best, also Alison. So glad you could come for the wedding. Rae's song was beautiful, wasn't it? We're all so blessed.

Lacy

The message evoked both a smile and a pang of regret. Lacy had, as planned, re-

499

turned to Kansas City immediately after the twenty-fifth anniversary reunion. A bittersweet decision that had led to love for Lacy but no real reconciliation between her and Lauren. They had made up, Delta thought, but long-distance forgiveness was never quite the same.

The second e-mail, from Lauren, confirmed her suspicions:

Hi Delta —

Sorry I missed the wedding. Would love to have seen you. Lacy's invitation was very gracious, but Trip and I felt it might be uncomfortable for her. We've talked, sort of, although e-mail and phone isn't the same as face to face. I missed my chance, I guess. Less stress here now that she's moved, but I wish it could have been different. Call me sometime.

Love, Lauren

And the last, from CrescentCityBlues:

Delta —

Great to see you at Lacy's wedding. Wished there had been more time to talk. How about coming to visit us soon? We'll make waffles and scrambled eggs and have brunch on the patio.

Thanks for everything. Noel sends her love.

R & N

P.S. We adopted a dog, a sweet little shelter mutt. His name is Gottlieb.

Delta leaned back in her chair and grinned at the screen. Life didn't always work out the way you hoped, but sometimes, sometimes. . . .

A knock on the door arrested her thoughts. She turned and looked up.

It was Lily Quentin, a student from her English lit class. An exceptional student, for the most part, although she seemed distracted since returning from spring break.

"Dr. Ballou?"

Delta held up both hands. "This time next week you can call me *Doctor,* if all goes well. I still have to get through my dissertation defense."

Lily edged into the room and stood shifting from one foot to the other. "Did you know that T. S. Eliot never finished his doctorate? Wrote his thesis, but then wouldn't show up to defend it. Apparently he said that anything he wrote needed no defense."

Delta laughed. "If you're T. S. Eliot, maybe. I don't suppose he mentioned how many footnotes were necessary to make *The Wasteland* comprehensible."

Lily gave a weak smile and fidgeted with her backpack. "I don't mean to interrupt."

"What's up, Lily? Have a seat."

Lily sighed and sank into a chair. "I probably shouldn't be bothering you. This is not even about lit class. I just wanted to talk, if you have time."

Delta gazed at her desk. Two dozen ungraded term papers littered the surface. She had an exam to write, a composition class at two, a faculty meeting at four, and she still hadn't fully prepared for her dissertation defense.

But in the back of her mind she remembered Drs. Bowen and Hart, all those dinners and late-night coffees and conversations over brunch on the patio with the dogs at their heels. She saw the image of a skinny blond waiter named Gabe, remembered his smile, heard him say *Even a bartender can listen*. The echo of a feeling washed over her, like standing on the beach at sunrise. Like driving through the country with the top down. Like leaving home and coming home all at the same time.

And deep inside, she felt the spark as flint struck steel.

She clicked out of the e-mail program, stacked the term papers, and leaned forward to fix her gaze on her student's face.

"Talk to me, Lily," she said. "I've got all the time in the world."

ABOUT THE AUTHOR

Penelope J. Stokes is the author of numerous novels, including *Circle of Grace.* She holds a Ph.D. in Renaissance literature and has taught college-level writing and literature. She lives in Danbury, Connecticut.